"Having often been asked to commit to print these memories of my association with he late Sir John Fielding, the celebrated magistrate of the Bow Street Court, I now set pen to paper for the first time, determined not merely to illuminate the feats of detection for which he is so justly renowned, but also to set forth those prodigious qualities of character that enabled him to accomplish them. He was indeed a man of remarkable powers..."

BLIND JUSTICE

This edition includes a
special preview of Bruce Alexander's

Murder in Grub Street,

a new Sir John Fielding Mystery
available from Berkley Prime Crime.

MORE MYSTERIES FROM THE
BERKLEY PUBLISHING GROUP...

BLIND JUSTICE

JUSTICE

Bruce Alexander

BERKLEY PRIME CRIME, NEW YORK

BLIND JUSTICE

A Berkley Prime Crime Book / published by arrangement with the author

PRINTING HISTORY
G. P. Putnam's Sons hardcover edition / September 1994
Berkley Prime Crime mass-market edition / November 1995

ISBN: 0-425-15007-0

Berkley Prime Crime Books are published
by The Berkley Publishing Group,
200 Madison Avenue, New York, NY 10016.
The name BERKLEY PRIME CRIME and the BERKLEY PRIME CRIME
design are trademarks belonging to Berkley Publishing Corporation.

PRINTED IN THE UNITED STATES OF AMERICA

10 9 8 7 6 5 4 3 2

FOR JUDITH

BLIND JUSTICE

Chapter 1

*In which Sir John Fielding proves himself the most
just of magistrates*

HAVING OFTEN BEEN ASKED TO COMMIT TO PRINT THESE
memories of my association with the late Sir John Fielding,
the celebrated magistrate of the Bow Street Court, I now
set pen to paper for the first time, determined not merely
to illuminate the feats of detection for which he is so justly
renowned, but also to set forth those prodigious qualities
of character that enabled him to accomplish them. He was
indeed a man of remarkable powers. Although deprived of
his sight, what most would deem the cardinal of the senses,
Sir John nevertheless led an exemplary life. His professional achievements are, of course, well remembered.
With his half-brother Henry, the late, lamented romancer
and jurist, he organized and commissioned that band of
worthies known ever after as the Bow Street Runners.
These thief-takers have functioned as London's constabu-
lary and made safe even by night a city in which previously, as even one of their severest critics declared, "one
was forced to travel even at noon as if one was going to
battle."

As magistrate, Sir John sat daily, judging in all fairness the poor wretches who were paraded before him, giving unto each the full measure of his keen intellect, questioning witness and accused with like impartiality. Finding cause, he would of course bind over for trial. Yet such was his nature that the mere accusation of a felony was never sufficient in itself to doom a man to an ordeal before the bench at Old Bailey. Unlike many of his fellow magistrates, he demanded evidence. He required direct witness of the eyes, valuing above all else what he himself could not have given. Should one appear before him and have the temerity to offer as truth what had been merely heard or supposed, that unworthy would immediately feel the sharp, quick lash of Sir John's tongue and be sent on his way forthwith. In truth, he discharged more prisoners than he sent on for trial. Never lenient, he was albeit exact. And he was particularly watchful (if indeed one may use so fanciful a conceit with regard to one who lacked the power of sight) of those so-called *independent* thief-takers, masters of false witness and entrapment, who made it practice to deliver the innocent up as guilty. Of this sinister legacy from the days of the notorious Jonathan Wild I myself had direct experience, for I, reader, truth to tell, first laid eyes upon the good Sir John when I found myself brought before the bench of the Bow Street Court as one accused of thieving.

Pray, let not this confession shock you so that you be tempted to set aside this eulogy, for as it will soon be shown, accused though I may have been, my accusers themselves were the true thieves; though what they plundered from me and sought to destroy was my own good name. Indeed it may be said true that I, Jeremy Proctor, myself now a member of the bar, first saw the inside of a court of law as defendant. How I came to be there I shall briefly impart, though to recall those terrible circumstances now brings me pain some thirty years after the event. Nevertheless, now to my history:

* * *

I was born in the year 1755 in the town of Lichfield, also the birthplace of the great lexicographer Samuel Johnson. There, my father, a printer by trade, earned an honorable living for himself and his small family in the assistance of a master printer, one John Berkeley by name. Of us Proctors there were but four: my father, my mother, my brother, Matthew, who was two years my junior, and myself. When a plague of typhus settled upon Lichfield in the summer of 1765, it claimed my mother and my brother. Having then but two mouths to feed and being enterprising by nature, my father set forth the following year for the village of Stoke Poges with his savings and me, having determined to seek his fortune with a print shop of his own. He should have chosen a better site.

In the beginning he prospered, finding commissions aplenty from parishes in the area, a few merchants, and from the local squire. His stock-in-trade was handbills, programs and adverts of one nature or another. He also instructed me in the trade, and to this day my skill in setting type is cause for amazement among my colleagues, most of whom have no knowledge of trade of any sort. My father also tutored me in letters and sums, and by near my thirteenth year had undertaken to teach me some Latin and what he knew of the French language. What he knew was considerable. Though an autodidact himself, he took great interest in the language and literature of our near neighbors across the water. Yet it has ever been so that an interest in things French has carried with it a certain risk here in England, and so it was for him, for it ultimately proved his undoing and led to his death.

Being something of a freethinker himself, he had a great passion for the writings of the philosopher and romancer who signed himself Voltaire. He had arrived at a point where he wished to demonstrate that he was capable in his art of something more than the handbills he turned out daily, and so he resolved to print a pamphlet. Because he claimed no skill as a writer and no doubt also because he wished to propagate the views of M. Voltaire, my father set about to translate a pamphlet of the Frenchman, the name of which I have blotted from my mind. The resultant work, which he titled "A Call to Thought," he hoped to sell for the odd penny. But since he reckoned it primarily as a sample of his work as a printer, he freely distributed it gratis through the village, making sure in particular that copies were put in the hands of his regular customers. Among them were, as I earlier mentioned, certain members of the local clergy. They were generally displeased by the pamphlet; not my father's printing, of which they appreciated little; nor by his translation, which they appreciated less; but rather by the sentiments of M. Voltaire, whom they deemed an atheist and a troublemaker. One spoke sharply to him of the content of the essay, and my father was unwise enough to argue the matter with him.

That man, by name Mr. Pettigrew, who headed a congregation of Low Church brethren, felt most specially grieved by the pamphlet, and with him my father argued most vehemently and imprudently; for Pettigrew (I cannot bring myself to use the honorific further) preached a sermon of a Sunday against atheism in general, Voltaire in particular, and my father most specifically. I know not what was said, for I have not been from that time to this a communicant, but it was sufficient to stir the congregation to wrath and dispatch it forth as a mob of avenging angels to wreak havoc upon us. They marched straightaway to the print shop and beat upon the door demanding entry. My father, warning me to remain in our rooms above, descended bravely with the intention of calming and dispersing the mob. Yet no sooner had he appeared before them than they set upon him and abused him unmercifully. From above I watched, cowering shamefully, I allow, as the congregation knocked and kicked him senseless, then cast him aside and poured through the doors of our shop. Once inside, they smashed the press and scattered type. All this I heard and merely guessed at as I hid in our two rooms above. The destruction complete, the mob's fury somewhat dissipated. The good people of Stoke Poges retired, dragging after them the dazed and inert body of my father.

When next I set eyes upon him he had been clamped in the stocks. He had been brought before the local magistrate, charged with blasphemy, convicted as a matter of course, and sentenced to a week in the stocks. He was to be released the following Sunday, when he might then take himself to the church and beg God's pardon, the congregation's—and Pettigrew's, of course. Yet my father never lived past Tuesday. What know you, reader, of this cruel and humiliating punishment which is still practiced in some benighted corners of the realm? It is no joke, as some seem to hold it, for a man to be trapped head and hands between two blocks of wood, his face a target of all manner of filth which the brutes of the village may wish to pelt him with.

I visited him once and only once in that state. I carefully wiped his face clean of ordure and mud with the tail of my coat. He looked up at me gratefully and declared his sorrow at being seen in such condition. His face, revealed, was a mass of bruises from the beating given him by the mob. There were also fresh cuts and welts from the stones that had been cast at him. Although barely to his senses, he earnestly charged me to leave. ''There is nothing for you here, Jeremy,'' said he to me. ''Lock up the house. Board up the shop. Go to John Berkeley in Lichfield. I will meet you there.''

I nodded and whispered my promise to do as he bade, then departed, running away in tears as a pack of village lads approached. Some distance away, I stopped and looked back to see the jeering, noisome bunch pitching mud and stones at the poor figure bent double between the boards. This was my last glimpse of him alive. Word came ere I had finished with my preparations for the trip to Lichfield that my father was dead: pelted to death. The messenger was the fat deacon, one Kercheval by name. He informed me with a leer that I was now an orphan and that I was to be brought before the magistrate so that my future might be settled. I recall that the wild notion passed through my young head that I needs must take my father's place in the stocks. Yet on leaving I had the foresight to take up my little bundle of belongings with the coins from our cashbox rolled up inside. Kercheval grabbed me roughly and made to march me forth. In opening the door, he unwisely relaxed his grip, and I shook loose from him and took to my heels. I ran for the fields as though the devil himself were after me and not some lubbering, lumbering deacon going apoplectic in the chase. I distanced him in no time and made for a copse where I hoped I might hide. When I reached it, I had no thought of remaining, for from there I had a view of the crossroads at which stood the stocks, and I saw that what Kercheval had said was indeed true. My father's body had been removed from them and laid out beside the fiendish contraption, his shirt pulled up over his head to cover his face. A group of townsfolk stood around him, talking amongst themselves and shaking their heads. Whether he had been done in by a sharp stone or had suffocated beneath a weight of mud or manure I cannot say. It was, however, clear that he was dead. And so I continued on, running, walking, hiding from passersby. I slept in a field that night. It was not until the next day that I learned that the road I had taken led not to Lichfield but to London.

Of how I came to the great metropolis I shall not recount much here, reader. Let it be said only that the journey took the lesser part of a week and that sometime along the way I passed my thirteenth birthday. I arrived in London nearly exhausted in body and spirit, with only a few shillings between myself and penury. What was I to do? I had some vague plan of seeking employment from a printer yet had no notion of how and where to go about it. Even if I had, surely the sight of such a great city with its multitudes teeming through the streets would have expunged it from my mind. My first day in London I spent wandering about, dodging through the throng, my bundle clutched tight in both hands. I remember that I asked one man politely how I might find my way to a printer's and then was answered with such a torrent of abuse as I, in my young life, had never heard before. How had I offended the man, merely detaining him? Pondering that, I approached another and put the same question to him. He responded readily enough but in a manner of speech for which I had no understanding. The fellow was speaking plainest Whitechapel to me, yet my comprehension of it was so dim that he may as well have been speaking to me in another language—nay, French I would have indeed understood better! From him I got only the phrase "flight straight," and I wondered how he supposed I might manage any sort of flight, straight or crooked. But perhaps he meant I should continue straight ahead.

You can imagine my relief when, as I stood perplexed on a corner of the street, I myself was approached by a man. He was a rather rough-looking sort, but seemed friendly enough, with a smile fixed on his face. "You're a likely-looking lad," he said to me.

"I hope so," said I to him.

"How would you like to earn a shilling?"

Remembering that my supply of cash had dwindled to not much more than that, I answered enthusiastically, "Oh, indeed I would, sir."

He explained that there was an errand to be run for a man of his acquaintance, one that required a pair of swift feet. "Can you run, boy?"

"Oh yes, sir," said I, "like the wind."

He laughed heartily at that and led me a short way down the street. I could not help but note the stout staff he carried in one hand, using it to strike sharply on the stones of the street with each step. I thought it strange, for he was sure-footed and showed no signs of lameness. As we went, he explained that all I need do was carry a package at all speed to an address which I would be given. I informed him that

I was a stranger in the city and knew not London well, yet I was told I would be provided with directions to the location.

"Will it take me near a printer, sir?" I asked. "I seek employment as an apprentice."

"You've good fortune by you, boy, for there is one not two doors past." And then he halted me suddenly and indicated a way down a dark lane. "There," said he, "go to the end of this alley here, and you will find a man name of Slade awaiting outside the Cock and Bull. Just tell him you're the lad what Bledsoe sent."

I nodded. "You'll accompany me no farther?"

"No, I've my own matters to look after." And he turned and walked away in the direction we had come.

I stood, looking after him, thinking this a very queer business indeed. Yet I was new to London and eager to earn a shilling, so I turned down the lane and sought the Cock and Bull. It was as I had been told. Outside the grogshop a figure stood by the door, lounging indifferently. Was this the same Slade who was so keen for quick delivery he was willing to pay a shilling for foot post? His attitude did seem passing strange.

Yet as I approached him he roused himself and nodded with some show of interest as he listened to me repeat the formula given me by Bledsoe. From under his coat he produced a packet of goodly dimensions in a kind of woolen purse. This he offered me, saying, "Here, lad. You must make straightaway with this to one William of Threadneedle Street, a broker. 'Tis a mile from here, hard left at Shoreditch, whence you came. Can you run a mile?"

"I can, sir."

"Then show me your heels and do it."

I hesitated. "But the shilling, sir? Mr. Bledsoe said there would be a shilling for me."

Slade laughed at that—a bit testily, I thought. "You'll be paid at t'other end. Now, git hence with ye!"

Thinking myself stupid (for how else were they to ensure

delivery?), I turned about and set out at full speed with the packet clasped firmly under my arm. Coming to the end of the lane, I turned left, as I had been told, and began making my way through the crowded street as fast as I was able, dodging a fishwife at one step and a ballad-seller at another, proceeding as quickly as the mob would allow. Then, of a sudden, my feet flew from under me, and I sprawled flat upon the dirt of the street. Coming to myself, I heard someone shouting, "Stop, thief, stop!" and wondered for whom the hue and cry had been raised. Looking about, I was aware of a group gathering around me that looked none too friendly, and in the forefront was none other than Mr. Bledsoe, who looked least friendly of all. At me, still on the ground, he brandished his staff, and the thought came to me then that he had used it to trip me up. But why should he do that? As I raised up to protest, he cocked the thing above his head and heaved it down hard upon me.

And that, reader, is all that I recall of my gulling.

As I regained consciousness, I was aware, primarily, of a prodigious pain in my head, and secondarily of a great hub-bub around me. My eyes opened to a scene the like of which I had never before beheld: It brought fresh into mind the ideas of London roguery and wickedness which I conceived from my reading of *The Lives of Convicts* and other such pennybooks. There were whores and greasy blackguards assembled together. Had I been dumped into a convocation of drabs and cutpurses, or perhaps transported willy-nilly to Bedlam? The shrill babble and cackle from those about me set me to wonder.

I sought to raise me up for a better view of this curious assemblage and was thrust down instantly and rudely where I sat. Turning to my captor, I found him to be none other than that Bledsoe, who had involved me as victim of his malevolent charade. Beyond him sat Slade, his partner and conspirator. There was no chance for me to escape these two, for Bledsoe had his big hand wrapped around the back of my neck and with it held me in a tight grip. He bent toward me and, blowing his foul gin breath in my face, said, "There's a good lad. Cause us no trouble, and you'll not be knocked about."

"But I—"

"Quiet!" He interrupted me with a brutal squeeze of my neck. "We've not long to wait."

And indeed it was so. I sat miserably thus a few minutes more, aware at last that what little attention there was from the raucous crowd was focused toward the front of the large room upon two men who sat at graduated elevation, facing out above the rest. The man situated higher was then in earnest confabulation with a man who stood alone before him. Suddenly he broke off his parley and banged down hard with a mallet upon the high table at which he sat. The fellow with whom he had but a moment before been deep in talk was then led away by a burly pair who stepped forth from a side gathering of spectators. The other man, who was sitting below the first at a small desk, then rose and bellowed out: "Bledsoe, Thomas, independent thief-taker. Bring your prisoner forth."

With that, I was jerked to my feet and hurried down the aisle, pushed forward at all speed from behind by that same Thomas Bledsoe, until at last I stood before the two men. The lesser of the two, who had summoned us but a moment before, looked upon me gravely and asked my name.

"Jeremy Proctor, sir."

The man with the mallet leaned forward then with great interest in my direction. Perceived thus closely, he offered a rather fearsome visage. His corpulent face was set in a solemn expression. Yet it was not his features I found frightening but rather the fact that his eyes were completely hidden from me. As I gazed up at him, I saw that a band of black silk covered them. The customary tricorn which he wore had obscured this at the distance from which I first saw him. I realized that he was blind. At last he spoke: "How old are you, Proctor?"

"Just past thirteen, sir."

Bledsoe shook me roughly by the scruff of the neck. "You calls him m'lord—and don't forget it."

There came a great outburst of comment and snickering from the throng behind, so that the blind man was forced once again to beat with his mallet upon the table until order was restored. "Let the boy speak as he sees fit," said he. And then to me: "You are accused of larceny. How say you?"

"Sir?" Immediately I felt the grip tighten upon my neck. "I mean, m'lord?"

"Larceny—thieving. How say you? Guilty or not guilty?"

"Oh . . ." Suddenly realizing the magnitude of my predicament, I hesitated a moment, which I immediately feared might be taken as indecision on my part. And so I then nearly shouted my plea: "Not guilty!"

The blind man's stern face then softened into a smile of amusement. "Very good," said he. "Clerk, enter that Jeremy Proctor pleads not guilty to the charge." Then, with a sigh: "And now, Bledsoe, tell your tale."

A tale it was—and a tale of lies. According to his perjured testimony, Bledsoe merely happened to be strolling along Shoreditch when, of a sudden, he heard a great hue and cry of stop-thief and immediately noted a figure—"this lad here"—running at top speed out of Chick Lane with a man in pursuit. He then had no choice—or so said he—but to apprehend the malefactor by whatever means was available. He tripped him with his staff and then, when the lad made to resist and continue his flight, smote him sharply, knocking him senseless, and brought him direct here to Bow Street.

"You stand by that?"

"I do, m'lord."

Though all that was in me cried out against what I had heard, I had the good sense to hold my peace. I waited, hopeful that this blind man would see through it all. He then called out loudly, "Are there any witnesses?"

"There is one, m'lord," Bledsoe piped up. "And the very one he stole from, William Slade by name."

"Let him speak."

The man who had sent me from the Cock and Bull on that bootless mission now came forward and bore false witness against me. He alleged that he had just stepped forth from that establishment, purse in hand, when he was suddenly set upon "by this young rogue," who wrenched the purse from his grasp and started away at great speed. He set out in pursuit, crying after him as he went, and turned onto Shoreditch just in time to see the young thief tripped up "by this heroic gentleman here"—Bledsoe—who recovered the purse and invited his company to the Bow Street Court in order to prosecute the miscreant before that paragon of the judiciary, Sir John Fielding.

That last bit clearly annoyed the blind man, whom I now knew to be Sir John. He scowled, sniffed, and said, "Spare us, please."

"But, m'lord, I only—"

"You say the purse was recovered?"

"It was, and ain't I glad, for it contained a goodly sum."

"Hand it over to the clerk."

Slade looked dubiously at Bledsoe, who answered with a sharp nod. Reluctantly, he did as he was bade. The clerk immediately set about ransacking its contents.

"And now, Master Proctor," said Sir John, "you have heard the testimony offered against you. What can you say in your own behalf?"

"Only the truth, sir," said I. And I then gave a simple and direct account of the events already described to you, my reader, only in somewhat abbreviated form.

When I finished, Sir John seemed well pleased by my recital. He nodded, said nothing for a moment, then leaned forward as though to see me better. "You are well spoken, boy, though not from these parts. Am I correct?"

"Yes, sir—m'lord."

" 'Sir' is an acceptable form of address. Where are you from then?''

"I was born in Lichfield.'' I wished to make no mention of the town I had left.

"Lichfield? Close, close, but I would have put you somewhat nearer to us. Penkridge, say, or Stoke Poges?''

I was amazed. Could he fix me so precisely by my manner of speech? Yet fix me he had, and I saw nothing for it but to admit my dissimulation. Hanging my head, I said, "I was the last years in Stoke Poges.''

"Ah-hah!'' he crowed loudly in delight, "done it again, have I not? There's not a man in London can place a body by his speech as I can!'' He roared out a great booming laugh of triumph. But he calmed suddenly and grew serious again. "Mark you,'' said he, speaking in the direction of the clerk yet to the court at large, "the boy told no falsehood. I asked him where he was from, and he said he was born in Lichfield, which I'm sure is true. He thinks as a lawyer thinks, which is both a blessing and a curse. But it strikes me, Master Proctor, that you wished to conceal from the court that you had come to London from Stoke Poges. Why is that?''

"Well, I—''

"Have you run away from home? Do you fear your father's retribution?''

"My father is dead, sir. There was only him and me.''

"How came he to die?''

"He . . .'' I hesitated, unable to speak of it. Yet fearing not to, I pressed on almost in a whisper: "He was pelted to death.''

A murmur came from the crowded court behind me. Yet Sir John sat silent a long moment before he spoke: "Pelted, you say? In the stocks?''

"Yes, sir.'' I knew that tears at this moment would be quite inappropriate, and so I struggled to hold them back.

"And that was when you ran away?'' he asked quietly.

"Yes.''

Suddenly I felt Bledsoe's furious grip once more at the back of my neck. He squeezed yet harder upon it than heretofore, and I was unable to suppress a cry of pain, as he whispered loudly in my ear, "*M'lord!* I *told* you to say m'lord."

"*Bledsoe!*" shouted Sir John from the bench. "Do not harm that— Clerk? Mr. Marsden?"

"Aye, Sir John?"

"Is he touching the boy?"

"He got his hand about the boy's neck."

I felt it drop away.

"Remove it," said Sir John to Bledsoe. "Distance yourself from him." I watched my captor take an uncertain step away and had to endure his angry, threatening gaze until the blind magistrate resumed: "Mr. . . . Mr. Slade? Is that how you call yourself?"

"Oh, yes sir, m'lord."

"I'm interested in that purse you said was stole from you. There was in it, you said, a goodly sum of money."

"Well . . ." he temporized, "to a poor man like me . . ."

"Clerk, what was the amount?"

The small man seated at the desk nearby dipped into the woolen bag and brought up a few coins. After taking a moment to count them, he called out loudly, "Two shillings thrupence and a farthing."

"Is *that* your goodly sum?" asked Sir John, miming his amazement broadly. "Nay, sir, I call that paltry. And for two shillings thrupence and a farthing you ask me to bind this thirteen-year-old boy for trial on a serious offense?"

Screwing his courage to the sticking point, Slade puffed up visibly and took a bold step toward the bench. "But, m'lord, it's the principle of it, ain't it? I mean to say, if this boy's not made to pay, then where will it end? He'll pursue his life of crime and set an evil example to his fellows."

"And so you hold for the principle of justice? You insist on pressing charges?"

"I do indeed, m'lord."

"Then let justice be applied evenhandedly. Clerk, what more does this man's purse contain?"

Once again the small man dove into it, this time emptying its contents on the table. He picked through the mess before him for a moment, then called out, "A most fouled kerchief." The crowd behind me exploded into raucous laughter. Even I had to smile, though it was perhaps unsuitable, considering my situation. The clerk waited until the outburst had subsided, then continued: "He also got a letter and some receipts for goods and an account book."

"Excellent!" said Sir John. "Now, give us the name to which the letter is addressed and to which the receipts are made out—but no, wait! Let me guess. Could that name perchance be Will Sayer?"

"It could, and it is."

The features beneath the black band of silk contracted for a moment in concentration. "Now, how do we explain the discrepancy between the name this man has given in court and the one borne on the documents he carries?"

"I was keeping them for a friend!" cried the man who had presented himself to me as Slade. His face betrayed his fear.

Sir John nodded agreeably. "That could certainly account for it. Yet we are left with another question. How came I to guess the name? Could it be that I have had previous acquaintance with this Will Sayer? Could it be that he appeared before this court not nine months past as a receiver of stolen goods? He was bound over, convicted, and sentenced, yet word has lately reached me that he bought his way from Newgate. Now comes William Slade bearing the documents of Will Sayer—*and speaking with the selfsame voice as Sayer.* Is this coincidence or *deceit?*" he thundered.

With that, there was a sudden hubbub in the court. Slade—or Sayer, as he was now revealed—looked about him wildly, as though thinking to escape. As if to answer that thought, a large man emerged from the crowd to one side and took a place beside the false complainant, where he displayed to him a club of intimidating size. Sir John hammered the court back to order, and leaning forward, he addressed the man before him: "Think you, sir, that because I lack the power of sight I also lack the power of memory? To one such as myself the human voice is as sure and distinctive a means of identification as the human face is to the rest. Perchance surer. Mr. Marsden?"

"Aye, Sir John?"

"Do you recognize the man before us?"

The clerk studied Sayer and finally shook his head. "All I can say is he looks familiar. We gets so many here."

"Indeed we do. But I put it to you, Mr. Slade-Sayer, you have perjured yourself as to your proper name, which to my mind impeaches your entire testimony. At the very least you have displayed your contempt for this court. Do you still wish to press charges against this boy?"

All eyes were upon the man, yet he had eyes for none. With his head hung low, he said quietly, "No, m'lord."

"There remains the matter of Mr. Bledsoe, our independent thief-taker. Good sense suggests to me that Master Proctor's account of the events leading to his appearance here is the true one. He might wish to press charges himself. Yet for want of a corroborating witness his case would be a weak one. Would you wish, Mr. Slade-Sayer, to serve as witness against Mr. Bledsoe?"

My attention went, as did Sayer's, to Bledsoe. The gaze he returned to his partner in perjury was the fiercest I have seen any man give another. In it was the threat of murder. The import of it was not lost on Sayer. He simply said, "No, m'lord."

"I thought not. Considering Mr. Bledsoe's reputation, you have probably made a prudent decision. However, under the circumstances, I have no choice but to sentence you to sixty days for contempt of court." Sir John banged down with great finality, making it official, and Sayer was led away by the big man with the club. This left only Bledsoe and myself before him.

"Mr. Bledsoe, take this as a warning. If ever you appear before me again seeking a bounty on the head of some poor unfortunate you have gulled, as in my heart I am sure you did this boy, then I shall find you out, sir, and I shall have you publicly thrashed by our Mr. Bailey, who is a bigger man than you and a far better one. And I shall throw you into Newgate for more years than either you or I can count. One thing I shall not do, however"—and this, oddly, he directed at me—"is have you clapped in the stocks and pelted, for that is not fit punishment for any man, not even such a sorry one as you. The case against Master Proctor is, of course, dismissed. . . ."

As he banged out his judgment, the room once again went into such turmoil that I believe I was the only one who heard as Sir John Fielding added the words that changed my life: "And he is remanded to the custody of the court."

Chapter 2

In which I am taken in search of employment

WHAT HAD HE IN MIND? THE WORD JUST SPOKEN, "RE-manded," quite unfamiliar to me, had to my young ears the sound of "command" and "demand," both terms of coercion. Though I understood it little, I liked it not.

Not knowing what more to do nor where else to go, I simply held my place before the bench and waited. I stood gazing up at the blind man who had but moments before exposed my false accuser and saved me from gaol. What manner of man was this Sir John Fielding? By the set of his features, no less than by his actions, he appeared to be of a kindly nature. As he waited for the next case to be called from the docket, his face had an air of amused expectancy. One would have guessed by the tilt of his head that he was staring off at some distant point above the crowd.

His attitude altered not in the least as the clerk rose to read off the last matter of the day. Yet the small man—Mr. Marsden by name, as I was soon to learn—caught sight of me as he set to bellow forth, and so leaned over to remind

Sir John of my presence before him. There was the pause
of a moment as the magistrate considered; then he leaned
down and spoke into Marsden's ear. The clerk nodded and
gestured grandly to the bank of seats behind me where he
wished me to take a place. Room was made for me between
two drabs. And so between them I sat, vaguely aware of
their veiled glances of assessment, as I fixed my attention
on Sir John and his court.

Marsden summoned to the bench one Moll Caulfield,
street vendor, and her accuser, a Covent Garden greengrocer, one Isaiah Horton by name. It was a simple matter of
money between them. The facts were not in dispute. The
widow Caulfield had been extended credit by her supplier,
Horton, and through misfortune or mismanagement, had
fallen somewhat in arrears in the discharge of her debt.
Horton was now not only unwilling to extend her further
credit, or to do business with her in cash, he was also demanding full payment of the debt or that she be sent off to
debtors prison.

"And what is the size of the debt, sir?" Sir John asked
Horton.

"Three shillings sixpence."

"So little? And what is the advantage to you if she go
to prison for it? She is not likely to find the opportunity to
pay you there."

"As an example, m'lord. I've carried her long enough.
The rest who owe me must be made to know I am not to
be trifled with."

"Ah, an *example!* Our Mr. Slade-Sayer was also very
keen on examples, as I recall. Tell me, Mr. Marsden, has
the court still in its possession the purse of that Mr. Sayer
who called himself Slade?"

"It has, m'lord."

"And what was the amount left in it?"

The clerk hauled up the woolen bag from the floor and
once more dipped in and counted. "Two shillings thrupence and a farthing."

"Yes. That would come close to satisfying the debt, and since Mr. Sayer will have no immediate use for the amount, I rule that it be handed over to Moll Caulfield as an act of charity on Mr. Sayer's part. We take this into consideration and reduce his sentence to thirty days. But this leaves her short by a bit. The court acknowledges this and . . ." He plunged his hand down into the voluminous pocket of his coat and came up with two coins which he handed over to the clerk, Marsden. "The court donates one and three to her cause. The farthing she may keep for her trouble."

"May God bless you for this, Sir John," Moll Caulfield wailed.

A smile wrinkled his sober mien. "I hope so, Moll. Truly I do."

"And love apples for you as you like them from this day forth," she promised.

He nodded. "And now, Mr. Marsden, divide the money. The debt is satisfied. The case is closed. This session is ended." He slammed down the mallet once only but with great finality. Then he stood and descended from his perch with sure steps and disappeared through a door at the rear of the large room.

Satisfied, the spectators also stood and began milling toward the doors. Still I held my place. The drabs departed, bidding me farewell and good fortune. I watched the clerk hand over the three-and-six to Isaiah Horton, greengrocer, and award Moll Caulfield, street vendor, her farthing; then he beckoned me over.

"Sir John wishes to see you in his chambers," said he to me, then turned and pointed. "Through that door, young sir, and across the hall."

I thanked him and made straightaway for it. Knocking, I was bade to enter and did so. Truth to tell, it was quite a plain room. A few law books were crammed into a case. The walls were bare of pictures or further ornamentation. Sir John I found much altered in appearance. He had doffed both tricorn and periwig and sat fuzzy-headed close by a table, his stockinged feet propped up on a chair before him. On the table stood no more than a bottle of strong, dark beer. The first sound he emitted in greeting was a considerable belch. Yet it was immediately followed by this salutation: "Ah, Master Proctor, is it? Come, come, sit down here."

He gave the chair a gentle kick and dropped his feet to the floor. I took the place he had made for me and sought to express my gratitude for his generous disposition of my case. But he halted me halfway through my little speech with a wave of his hand.

"Quite unnecessary, quite unnecessary," said he. "Our man Bledsoe was the prime mover in this affair. I'm put on my guard whenever he appears before me. Mark my words, I'll have him in gaol soon."

"Yes, Sir John."

"But he is no longer your worry. You must give some thought to your future." He paused a moment to consider, and as an aid to his cogitation, availed himself of a mouthful of beer from the bottle. "What are we to do with you, young man?"

"Sir?"

"With your father dead, you've no kin, I take it."

"None that I know of."

"I'm sure you've no wish to return to Stoke Poges."

"Oh, none, sir," said I, earnestly. "Why, the very thought that I might—"

Again, he silenced me. "You've no worry there, believe me, boy. But you simply cannot remain alone and on your own here in London. It is a dangerous city, Master Proctor. You have appeared before me today in all innocence accused of thievery. Left on your own here, you might appear here again in six months time, yet not so innocent as before."

In my ignorance, I was shocked at what I judged to be his low opinion of me. Thus I sought to convince him: "Sir

John, I should never stoop to thievery. I'd indeed rather starve first!''

"Ah, Jeremy Proctor, let me offer to you some advice. If you remember it well and carefully examine its implications, you may find yourself well on the way to wisdom. My advice is simply this: Never say never. You cannot possibly know the circumstances in which fortune may thrust you, nor can you be certain of how you will react to any given set of circumstances.'' In the course of this peroration, he leaned forward earnestly so that his face was only inches from mine. In spite of the band of black silk covering his face from the bridge of his nose to his eyebrows, I had the distinct feeling, as I often did on occasions afterward, that he was staring directly into my eyes. But then he pushed back suddenly and grabbed up the bottle, treating himself to yet another deep draught. Having drunk his fill, he raised the bottle in my direction and admonished me once more with it: "Mark my words," said he. "Never say never.''

I liked not the notion that my fate was so much in another's hands, yet had it to be so, there was none I could imagine whose hands I would trust better than Sir John's.

By and by, his considerable head, which had sunk slightly with the weight of thought, elevated itself, and he spoke to me as though inspired by a fancy: "Have you ever wished to go to sea?''

"Why . . . why, no,'' I stammered out my reply.

He sighed audibly. "I thought not. When I was your age I thought and dreamed of nothing more. And indeed I went to sea in time, and . . . Ah, but that is another story—and a very old one at that.''

I thought that passing strange. He seemed so complete in what he was—a magistrate, a blind man—that I could not conceive of him being otherwise.

"I have sent boys in your predicament to sea,'' he continued. "Though some, I allow, were older than you and were keen for the life. I have no wish to send a boy where he has no wish to go.''

"Perhaps I would custom myself to it," I offered.

"Perhaps."

I hesitated then, not knowing the propriety of what I wished to suggest. But finally: "Is there some way I could be of use to you? I'm good with sums. I can read, sir, and write a good hand. And I even know some French."

"Ho! French, is it?"

"And I can set type."

That gave him pause. "There we may be on to something. Of course, your father, the unfortunate printer, would have taught you, would he not?"

"He did, sir."

"Well, Jeremy, in all truth, I pride myself that I need no special help from anyone—man or boy—to get me through my daily round. In short, I must decline the generous offer of your personal service—though not, I confess, without some hesitation. No, I sincerely believe work as apprentice to a printer would fit your talents and background better."

I felt it only right to inform Sir John that even as I had my unfortunate meeting with Bledsoe, I was seeking a print shop in order to inquire after employment. "My father told me I was as fast with a stick as some journeymen. He . . . he taught me well."

Sir John reached out toward me and, groping slightly, found my arm, to which he gave a gentle touch. "I've no doubt of it, boy." Then, abruptly, he was all business: "There is a man I know. He is less than a friend and more than an acquaintance. But he has great influence in the printing trade. A word from him would establish you with any one of several printers. I dislike asking a favor of him, but pride must be put aside on such occasions. So, Jeremy Proctor, there will be time enough for such matters on the morrow. It will be Tuesday, and Mr. Saunders Welch sits in his court. The chief magistrate of the Bow Street Court has an entire day to himself, part of which he shall devote to your cause. You have his word on that. In the meantime I have a spare bed in my garret, and you will be most welcome as my guest.''

Thus it was settled. Sir John summoned Benjamin Bailey and sent me off for a tour in his care. I found, when we two emerged in the street, that the day had all but passed. Nevertheless I looked with interest at all around me and gave particular attention to Covent Garden as we passed it on our way. I had no notion to find such country greenery displayed here in this great city. And I asked Mr. Bailey if there were many such places about.

''None but this,'' said he, ''and a good thing, too.''

''Why is that, sir?'' I asked.

''Well, m'lad, the truth of it is this. Full many a black-guard can hide himself among the stalls and stands come nightfall. And the lanes what lead into the square are many so narrow that it makes this a most difficult precinct to maintain.''

''Maintain?''

''Patrol. Keep clear of the lower element. And the fact that there's gentlefolk lives here and the court so near, well, it's sometimes an embarrassment is what it is.''

I had no doubt of Mr. Bailey's ability to handle what he called the lower element. Obviously a man of intelligence, he was most notable, however, for his size and strength. He stood well over six feet and must have weighed twelve stone or better, and in his best days (which were then not long past), he could have given the great Daniel Mendoza himself a considerable tussle. Yet with me he was then, as ever afterward, extremely gentle.

As night fell, the flow of people in the streets seemed much diminished. I noted that some passersby gave us a wide berth, though others who knew Bailey by sight and name were quick to give him a cheerful greeting. They seemed to take heart in his presence—as, I confess, I did myself.

"Is his house nearby?" I asked after we had covered some distance.

"Whose house would that be, m'lad?" Mr. Bailey seemed preoccupied with all on the street about him. He glanced watchfully to the right and left as we moved on.

"I meant Sir John's."

"Oh, well, yes, Sir John. He lives back where we started from, above the court. I thought to give you some notion of the surroundings. Seen enough, have you?"

We circled back to Bow Street, I marveling at the vast structures fixing the limits of the Garden, wondering what they housed. "Has he always lived here? Sir John, I mean."

I caught Mr. Bailey's quick smile down at me. "Well, now," he said, "that I can't rightly say. Perhaps previous on the Strand for a time. Here in the city, before he married, he lived with his brother, who was the previous magistrate of the Bow Street Court until he took ill and died. It was they who put together the Runners."

"The Runners?"

"Aye, the Bow Street Runners, constables, as fine a band of thief-takers as ever sent a ruffian to heel. We rule the streets of London, m'lad. Or rather, Sir John rules them through us. It's our pride we've made them safe to walk after dark—most of them, anyway."

Mr. Bailey stopped beneath a street lamp and grinned down at me. "I can see we wasn't well met, we two. Allow me to introduce meself to you proper, Master . . . Master Proctor, is it?"

I nodded, somewhat abashed.

"Then I present meself to you, Master Proctor. I am Benjamin Bailey and am no less than captain of the Bow Street Runners, and I am at your service, *sir!*" With that, he snapped a smart salute that bespoke his military background. Then he ended his performance with a great, grand wink.

I was much delighted—so much indeed, that I attempted

to return his salute in my own unpracticed way. But there and then Mr. Bailey set about to correct it, raising my elbow, flattening my hand, until he was satisfied. ''There,'' said he, ''we'll make a Runner of ye yet.''

Wishing to believe it might be so, my heart leapt. ''How old must I be?''

He perceived the eagerness in my eyes, for he immediately set about to put me to rights. ''Oh, well, a bit older, I fear, and a bit bigger. But ye'll be there quick enough. Take it from Benjamin Bailey.''

My arm drooped down as did my spirits. But Mr. Bailey would have none of that. He clapped me firmly on the shoulder and set us walking again. ''Ah, young Master Proctor, I was young as you meself once. And I well remember that like yourself I couldn't wait to get on with things. Now I know I was wrong.''

''Wrong? How so, Mr. Bailey?''

''I could have waited.''

We were well back on Bow Street. We walked along in silence for a short space until Mr. Bailey offered, ''I hear tell he was in the Navy for a time.''

My mind was elsewhere. ''Who is that?''

''Why, Sir John, m'lad. It was him we was speaking of, was it not?'' He winked down at me, but then he continued in a more serious manner: ''It was there he lost his sight. There are many stories told of it, but I know not the true one.''

He led me back through Number 4 Bow Street. I noted upon our reentry a gathering of men down the hall, some as stout and imposing as Mr. Bailey himself. They spoke together in low tones with an air of preparation. Mr. Bailey led the way up two flights of back stairs. ''Does Sir John's wife await him?'' I asked.

''Lady Fielding is ill. You'll not see much of her,'' said Mr. Bailey rather strangely. ''But there is Mrs. Gredge. You'll see a good deal of her—more than you wish, I vow.''

I knew not what to expect from this as we presented ourselves at the door at the head of the stairs. Mr. Bailey knocked stoutly upon it. A moment passed, and of a sudden there was a sound of screeching inside of such volume and duration that I wondered that there might be a pet corbie inside. But the noise grew louder and was at last heard in words and phrases of alarm from a spot just beyond the door: "Who is there? Who, I say? I'll not open this door to a stranger! Make yourself known or wait for morning!"

" 'Tis I, Benjamin Bailey," he shouted loudly, "and I have a young charge for you sent by Sir John."

A stout lock was thrown, and the door came open slowly no more than a foot. A grizzled female head appeared, regarding first Mr. Bailey and then myself in a most skeptical manner. Then to him: "Oh, it's you, is it? The night watchman." Truly she did screech. Her voice, even as I recall it today, was something between a corbie's and a parrot's. Good woman that she was in many ways, her style of speech and desire to command would have put off the best of men, of whom I would certainly number my companion there on the doorstep.

"*Not* the night watchman," he corrected her, "but Bailey of the Bow Street Runners." I could tell from the glint of anger in his eye that he wished to say more.

"As you wish, as you wish," she said in a manner of dismissal. And then, directing a finger at me, "Who is he?"

"His name is Jeremy Proctor, and a fine lad he is," said Bailey directly. "Sir John directs you to prepare a bed for him, for he will be your guest this night."

She opened the door a bit wider, though not in welcome. Her purpose was to get a better look at me. It was evident she liked not what she saw. Her lips pursed and her nose wrinkled as she regarded me. "He's dirty," she said at last.

"Be it as it might, madam," said Mr. Bailey with great finality, "he is your guest for the night." With one last clasp to my shoulder, he smiled down at me, turned, and briskly descended the stairs.

She watched him for a moment, then finally turned her eyes back to me. "Well . . ." she said at last, "come in." Never, it seemed, was entry granted more reluctantly.

Once inside, she slammed the door after me and marched me down the short hall to a point where a candelabrum burned brightly. There she made a closer inspection. She removed my hat and rubbed through my hair. Twisting my head this way and that, she looked sharply at my ears and neck, then tugged at my collar to view what lay beneath. At last the ordeal of buffeting and pulling was ended. She stepped back, frowning, and said, "You've slept in those clothes."

It was true. I had. "Yes, Mrs. . . ."

"The name is Mrs. Gredge. You may call me ma'am." Then she added sharply, "And only that."

"Yes, ma'am."

"Take them off."

"Take them off, ma'am? My clothes?"

"Yes, Jeremy. I'll warm water for a bath. I'll not have you crawling between clean sheets as filthy as you are. Now do as I say."

"But—"

"No but's. Get on with it. I'll not see anything I've not seen before. I raised three boys of my own." She looked at me crossly and then at last relented. "Oh, all right, I'll hang a blanket out for you in the kitchen if it is of such moment. Though mark you, I'll be in to see you get yourself clean. Your ears and neck are filthy. Indeed I shudder to think what the rest of you looks like." Indeed I had no wish to show her.

There was no choice but to do as she directed. After eating some cold mutton and a few crusts of bread, I undressed in the pantry while she filled the tub. I handed out my clothes, which she accepted, making no effort to hide her distaste. Then, waiting until she had vacated the kitchen, I plunged into the tub.

My father had not been overly concerned with cleanliness. His shop he kept neat as a pin, and our living quarters were tolerably well swept, yet he did not bathe often and saw no need for me to. And so, though not as well practiced as I might have been, I gave myself to the job at hand with great zeal. I must have made good work of it, too, for when I presented myself to Mrs. Gredge, the blanket clutched about my middle, she passed me with reluctance.

"Well," she said, "you'll do. Sir John does not often send home stray cats such as yourself, and when I set eyes upon you, I wondered at his wisdom this time. Yet now I see you clean, I suppose you'll do. Come along."

She led the way up two more flights of stairs, a candle in her hand and a finger to her lips. We went to the very top of the house, past the fourth floor and then up a narrow way that led to a small eyrie that was barely visible from the street below. The height of the room was such that it permitted both myself and Mrs. Gredge, who was nearly my size then, to stand erect. Yet a man the stature of Mr. Bailey would have been forced to bend double. It held a bed and a table, a few odds and ends of broken-backed furniture pushed into a corner, an old chest, and against one wall a great pile of books. The presence of these last seemed curious to me. "Are they Sir John's?" I asked, and wondered that a blind man would have so many books about.

"They belonged to his late brother. He had more books than Dictionary Johnson himself—more than was good for him, you may be certain. For if the man had not spent all his time away from the law in reading and writing and had attended to healthier pursuits, he might be alive today."

"Yes, ma'am."

She lit a candle on the table by the bed. "I doubt you'll need another blanket tonight," she said, "but if you do, take the one you're wearing." Speaking not another word, she turned and left me standing alone there. I heard her steps descending.

Without a moment's hesitation I went to the books. Although a bit dusty, they were in good condition with no trace of mildew or rot. I ran my hands over their spines, twisting my head to and fro to read their titles. They were of all sorts—histories, geographies, personal narratives of distant voyages, romances, books of verse and all manner of science. It might have suggested to me then, had I but known the identity and fame of Sir John's late brother, the extent and interest of his wide-ranging intelligence. A man can be known by his library better than by his house or dress.

Choosing one at random, an account of life in the American colonies, I took it with me to the bed and settled in between the muslin sheets, a luxury I had all but forgotten since my mother's demise; and warm beneath the blanket, I began to read. I was interested in what the book had to offer, yet nearly a week of hard traveling and a day so full I could scarce contain it in my mind, had left me wearier than I knew. I had gone but a few pages in the text when I fell fast asleep.

I came awake with a start. Although the morning light streaming in through the narrow windows half-blinded me, it was rather the racket in my ears that brought me abruptly to my senses. "Just look at you, boy, look what you've done! Fallen asleep reading, have you? And let the candle burn down to nothing at all! For shame! Tallow candles as Sir John buys are ever so dear—and you've wasted one. Just look!"

And look I did—from Mrs. Gredge, who was of course the source of these accusations, to the table by the bed. And indeed it was so. There stood what was left of the candle, guttered down to the merest stub, the holder now a crusted cone of white rivulets.

"Has no one taught you that—"

"Mrs. Gredge!" There thundered a voice from below that was recognizably Sir John's.

She turned from me, this scolding corbie of a woman,

now suddenly meek as a wren. "Yes . . . Sir John?"

"Leave the boy in peace. You have wakened me and my poor wife with your wrath. Desist at once."

"As you wish, Sir John." She turned back to me then, just as cross as before but now much quieter: "Well, you've done wrong, and I've told you. Here. I've brought you your things." She hefted an armful of clothes which she then dumped on the bed. I had failed even to notice them before, so overwhelmed was I by her vehement indictment. "Get yourself dressed, and you may have breakfast." With that, she left just as quickly as she had the night before.

I crawled out of bed and examined my clothes. All that could have been washed had been washed. The rest—coat and pants—had been so well brushed that most would have judged them clean. I dressed quickly and with the promise of breakfast hurried downstairs.

Afterwards, having eaten my fill of bread and butter, Mrs. Gredge put me to various tasks about the house, sweeping and scrubbing up, at which I satisfied her. But soon she exhausted her fund of work, and I was left free to resettle myself in my garret room and return to my book. Mrs. Gredge shuffled quietly about downstairs. Indeed there was a stillness in the house through most of the morning that evidenced illness within its walls. I recalled such quiet from my mother's last days in Lichfield and wondered at the gravity of Lady Fielding's malady.

But well toward midday I heard a great symphony of sounds from the floor below—hawking, wheezing, spitting, groaning, followed by a loud, long splashing in the chamber pot. At last he had risen to meet the world. I found such noises reassuring with regard to Lady Fielding's condition. More time passed during which I heard the voices of Mrs. Gredge from the first floor, then later, from the floor below me, the muffled, gentler tones of a woman in quiet discussion with Sir John. Visitors came and went, one of them unmistakably Benjamin Bailey. At last toward the end of the day, I was summoned to the study.

The magistrate of the Bow Street Court sat comfortably at a desk which was quite clear of paper. As I entered the open door, he turned to me, immediately aware of my presence. "Ah, Jeremy," said he, "well rested and well fed, I trust."

"Yes, Sir John. Thank you."

"No need. Mrs. Gredge informs me of your willingness to work about the house. For that I thank you. Let us say that you earned your keep. Her only objection, which I recall being voiced loudly early this morning, was that you had fallen asleep and allowed the candle to burn down. I count that not at all objectionable. The price of a candle is nothing to the education of a mind. You discovered what little is left of my brother's store of books above, I take it."

I started at that. Had I done wrong to help myself? "Why, yes, I hope that—"

"In all truth, Jeremy, I'm pleased to have you put them to use. I know my brother, were he with us, would be delighted. My own library, as you see, is much more modest and has to do with the practice of law. Some of these were also his. He was a remarkable man—an excellent barrister, a superb magistrate, and a marvelous and entertaining creator of romances and plays."

"What was his name, Sir John?"

"Henry. Henry Fielding. In point of fact, he was my half-brother. His mother was not my own. Had you heard of him?"

"My father had a book of his, which he read with great delight but forbade me to open."

Sir John laughed heartily at that. "That would have been *Tom Jones,* I venture."

"It was, sir. The story of a foundling."

"More or less, Jeremy, more or less."

"He . . . he must have been a man of great wit and learning."

"Henry? Oh, indeed he was. But he was something more—something altogether rarer. He was a good man. He was a fine husband to two wives—not simultaneously, let me assure you—a good father, and the best brother a man could want. I read law with him." With that, Sir John hesitated, then added, "He gave me my life."

He had turned from me, and I had the feeling that his last words were addressed not to me but to himself. He was silent for a moment, as though lost in thought, but then he roused himself from his musings and said to me, "Well, enough of that. We've a dinner to eat, we two, and a man to seek out in your behalf. And I had thought to show you a bit of London before the sun goes down."

And so, after Sir John had taken time to say his goodbye upstairs and warned Mrs. Gredge that we might be late, we set out on our excursion. He started us off on Bow Street in the direction opposite the one from which I had come the night before in the company of Mr. Bailey. There was more to London than I had dreamed, and my guide to it all was to be a blind man. Although in retrospect this may strike me strange, as indeed it may you, there seemed nothing odd about it as I set out with him, for he went not as a blind man but as one alive to all the sights of the great city. He carried a walking stick but for the most part used it as any man would, moving along at a swift pace with sure step. He did, however, slow somewhat at street crossings, reaching out and testing the way before him, tapping at the cobblestones and listening at the curb for horse traffic, of which there was plenty even then.

At the first crossing to which we came, I touched Sir John's elbow to indicate that the way was clear, thinking merely to be helpful. Yet he shook his head firmly at me and said, "No, Jeremy, please. I should prefer to make my way alone. Short of saving me from certain death before a team of horses, or great embarrassment from a patch of dung, you must resist the temptation to help. Now, are we ready?'' With that, he stepped boldly onto the cobblestones and led *me* across the street.

People who passed seemed to take no special notice of him, not out of callous indifference, though some simply hurried by intent on their own affairs, but rather because most seemed to be accustomed to seeing him moving about in their midst. In the streets nearby he received many respectful greetings from passersby and shopkeepers which he returned in friendly fashion, almost invariably by name.

''. . . And a good day to you, as well, dame Margaret.''

''Ah, Joseph! Business going well, I hope.''

Et cetera.

We continued on our way, then turned onto the Haymarket, which surprised me by its great size and what I judged to be the modishness of its strollers. The women who walked there were powdered and painted and, to my young eye, quite pretty; they were decked out in the gaudiest raiment that ever I beheld. They offered smiles quite readily.

Sir John must somehow have perceived my interest. ''You have observed the plenitude of unaccompanied females hereabouts?''

''I have, Sir John. Who are they?''

''Unfortunates,'' said he, and hurried me on.

Although that seemed not a suitable description of their state, I offered no word of contradiction. However, I noted that he seemed quite well acquainted with several. In fact, one, whom I detected to be a bit senior to the rest, halted him with a hand to his arm and after exchanging a few pleasantries and being introduced to me, lowered her voice and said in an earnest tone, ''I would only say to you, Sir John, that I received a letter from Tom—all the way from India. He asked to be remembered to you.''

''Ah, Kate! How good to hear it. And how is the boy?''

''Quite well, I think. He claims to have grown three inches in the year he's been gone—though I can hardly credit it.''

"Oh, quite possible. At his age they sprout just so."

She inclined her head in my direction. "Is he for the Navy, too?"

"Jeremy? No, I think not. The lad has a trade, and I should like to see him pursue it."

She addressed me directly: "And what might that be, Jeremy?"

"Printing, ma'am."

"Well, you've a fine man to look after your interests in Sir John. None better."

"I know that, ma'am."

"You're too kind, Kate," said he to her.

"Don't talk to me about kindness, John Fielding. Why, the way you dealt with Tom was more than I could . . ." Her voice trembled. Through all her paint I saw her on the verge of tears.

He seemed slightly abashed at the display of emotion he sensed. His feet shuffled, and he beat the walk with his stick. Clearly, he wished to be on. "He'll make you proud of him, Kate."

"I believe it. I do. Well . . . oh, just one more thing."

"And what is that, Kate?"

"I've moved to a more respectable location at Number Three Berry Lane. There is a side entrance that is quite discreet. I should be pleased—honored—to have you come for tea some weekday afternoon. Only as a friend," she added, "to show my gratitude."

"Very kind of you. By all means I shall try to accept your invitation."

And then with a goodbye and a God-bless-you she hurried away. Without a word to me, he started off suddenly, and I ran to catch him up. He said not a word for quite some space, and I wondered that he even knew I was by his side. But at last he addressed me: "You may have wondered, Jeremy, that I characterized these women of the Haymarket as unfortunates. I offer Katherine Durham as an example—a widow of intelligence and breeding forced to pursue this life on the street. It is a sad matter indeed.''

''Her son was one you sent off to sea?''

''He was—and it was not easy arranging it. He and his two fellows were guilty of a theft in which severe bodily injury was inflicted upon the victim. They truly wanted to hang those boys, Jeremy, and not a one of them older than you.''

The thought made me most uncomfortable. ''But you sent them to sea?''

''Two of them.''

I dared not ask what became of the third.

He remained silent until we emerged from the Haymarket and turned onto Pall Mall. I exclaimed at the sight, and he brightened considerably: ''Ah yes, I wanted you to see this. Isn't it beautiful? It certainly *smells* beautiful. So much of London could be like this, and so little of it is.''

I looked about me. There were trees and flowers—gardens as I had never seen them—and gentry as I had never imagined them. They were dressed finely but not so gaudily as the courtesans and their gallants whom I had seen in the Haymarket. Ladies and gentlemen ambled carelessly along as we passed them by, and there were groupings of a few posed most decorously here and there, all of them conversing in modulated tones. Even the horse traffic differed notably from what I had seen elsewhere. Only carriages and single mounts seemed to be allowed here. I saw no wagons or drays.

We walked Pall Mall up one side and down the other, which gave me a glimpse of Green Park and St. James and of many fine houses along the way. It was all so much more than I had expected that I felt quite the bumpkin there. Even Sir John, whom I had judged to be well dressed, seemed plain by comparison to the gentry around us. And here he did seem to be treated with a certain cold indifference. Little notice was taken of him, and he received no salutations. When attention was given, it came in the form of rude stares. And thus, much as I was impressed by what

I saw there, I was relieved when at last we turned down Charing Cross and found our way to the Strand.

There was a swarm of people before us, the great ocean of humanity in full tide. Sir John halted there at the head of the great street, listening, smelling, taking it all in. "Is it not wondrous?" he asked. "This great gang of people before us, all of them so different and yet all human and therefore much the same. Is it not glorious? A man who has written many foolish things and a few wise ones once said that when a man is tired of London, he is tired of life, for there is in London all that life can afford."

"That must have been one of the wise things he said."

"Indeed it was. He, by the by, is the man whom we shall now seek on your behalf."

"Who is that, Sir John?"

"Samuel Johnson."

"*Dictionary* Johnson?"

"The same, my boy, a man of many admirable qualities, though overvalued in certain respects."

"Which respects are they?" For I had only heard good spoken of him by my father, both natives of Lichfield, after all.

"For his wit, chiefly. He feels qualified to speak to every subject, including the law, in which he has no foundation, and when he speaks he wishes to be *listened to* by all and sundry. The man is a bore, and he has the way of all bores: that practice of talking at you, not with you. Even in literature, where he is held to be a great judge, his opinions are quite fallible. Mr. Johnson—or *Dr.* Johnson, as he styles himself—had the audacity and bad sense to write ill of my brother and his work."

Reader, you will recognize this last as the true cause of Sir John Fielding's restrained animosity toward Dr. Johnson, though I did not for many years. One should rather have spoken ill of the King in Sir John's presence than criticize his late brother.

"But let us be off, Jeremy," said he. "It is dusk, and

we must try to find him at the place he often takes his supper, an inferior eating place frequented by scribblers and their masters that is known as the Cheshire Cheese.''

And so we plunged into the throng there on the Strand, swimming along with the tide, he calling my attention to shops for the gentry along the way. I was then quite surprised when, somewhat past these, my nose was assaulted by a stench as foul as any I had known in the country. Involuntarily, I exclaimed at it.

''At last you smell it, do you?''

''Would that I did not, sir!''

''That is the Fleet River, so called, yet hardly more than a stream flowing into the Thames. Actually, it is little better than a sewer running beneath Fleet Street, open at some points, one of them nearby. The odor will lessen somewhat as we leave here, so let us do that with haste.''

At last he halted me at a small alleyway hardly noticeable from the street itself. ''Just here, I believe, is it not?''

I looked down the alley and in the gathering dark I saw a sign giving announcement to the Cheshire Cheese. I conveyed this to him. Yet how could he have known his location so well?

''Johnson lives just around the corner in an alley square, and he takes his meals here. His housekeeper is, by all reports and unlike Mrs. Gredge, a foul cook. I have no wish to knock upon the man's door in search of a favor, but I had thought, were we to meet and talk with him at his eating house, it might be easy to present you and your predicament to him. He is not without good qualities. I'm sure he would be moved to help.''

With that we proceeded to the Cheshire Cheese, yet just at the door he halted once again. ''One more thing, my boy. When we meet Johnson he may be in the company of one James Boswell, a popinjay and a libertine who calls himself a lawyer. He is visiting and has attached himself to Johnson as a veritable lamprey. My point in mentioning this to you is that Boswell is a Scotsman from Edinburgh and has that manner of speech common to his countrymen. You must in no wise laugh at him, nor even show notice, for he is *very* vain.'' I promised, and we entered.

Although outside darkness had nearly fallen, inside it was darker still. Sir John found a waiter and inquired after Dr. Johnson. He was informed that although the lexicographer had not yet arrived, he was expected and that Mr. Boswell awaited him in the Chop Room. Thence we were conducted. The man whom I rightly took to be James Boswell jumped to his feet and welcomed us—or rather, the magistrate—with great ostentation. In truth, his accent was not much pronounced. It could be detected, certainly, in his rolling of the letter ''r'' and in the flat nasal inflection he put on nearly all his vowels. However, I found him not in the least amusing.

If Dr. Johnson was a bore, what was I to make of this man who claimed loudly and at length to be his friend? A popinjay? No doubt, and a gossip and a wiseacre, as well. I am aware of the tradition that charges us to speak well of the recently dead, and in the main I hold to it, yet I saw this James Boswell exhaust the time and patience of Sir John on so many subsequent occasions that I find little good in my heart to say of him. Worse still, later, as a young man, I myself heard him deride the chief magistrate of Bow Street, and I hesitated not to take him to task for it directly. Yet I anticipate somewhat. I cannot pretend that my first estimate was as fully formed as this nor as prejudiced. He seemed to me then only a tedious and long-winded man, one so keen to make a good impression on Sir John that he would continually solicit the opinion of the magistrate, and before it was half-stated rush in with his own.

It was thus they discussed a range of topics, chiefly the then notorious John Wilkes, the Parliamentarian who had previously been jailed for fomenting riot. When Boswell noted to Sir John that Wilkes had recently been returned to Parliament in absentia, he then swore the fellow should be clapped in the stocks forthwith, but it soon turned out his objection to the riotous Wilkes was due chiefly to the latter's abusive pronouncements against the Scots.

"Is it true that he went to you to recover the blasphemous papers His Majesty's Government had seized?"

"Why, yes," said Sir John, "he—"

"He had the gall, had he? Why, if you were to ask me, I . . ."

Et cetera.

They went from Wilkes to the French and on to Boswell's book on Corsica, which he advertised shamelessly to the magistrate; they spent over an hour on the voyage. I was by this time quite famished. Sir John must have perceived this, for he managed to silence Boswell long enough to order a steak and kidney pie for me and a joint of beef for himself. By that time the place was quite packed, but there was no sign of Dr. Johnson.

Sir John, in fact, remarked on that to Boswell, mentioning only that he had expected to encounter the lexicographer. Was he expected?

"Aye, indeed he was and *is* expected," said Boswell. "He'll not be long."

At last our dinner arrived. And shortly behind it, to my great surprise, came none other than Benjamin Bailey. I was barely three bites into my pie when his tall figure filled the doorway of the Chop Room. He ducked through and proceeded directly to our table.

"Mr. Bailey," I exclaimed, "why—"

He touched me on the shoulder, perhaps with the intention of silencing me: In any case it had that effect. He then leaned over and spoke at some length in Sir John's ear. I watched the magistrate's expression change from one of shock to stern resolution. At the end of the whispered speech, he nodded and rose.

"Forgive me, Mr. Boswell, but we must take leave of a sudden."

"What is it, Sir John?" Boswell's interest had been whetted. "Riot? Wilkes?"

"Nothing so grave. This errand is all in a night's work for a poor magistrate."

With that we left, Mr. Bailey leading the way and Sir John close behind. I mumbled my goodbye to Boswell, who had given me no notice whatever, then grabbed up a few slices of bread from the table and ran to catch up with the others. I found them at the door. Sir John was just pushing past a stout, red-faced man with a large nose who greeted him by name and made attempt to open conversation with him.

"No time now. Sorry," blurted Sir John. "Something I wish to discuss with you later, though."

As we hurried into Fleet Street, I asked the identity of the man at the door.

"Oh, that one," said he. "That was Johnson."

"I've a hackney carriage waiting," Mr. Bailey called from ahead.

Waiting and open. He held the door at an attitude of attention. All that was lacking was the salute. As I, too, stepped up and in, I turned curiously and asked, "What is it, Mr. Bailey? What's happened?"

"Never you mind, lad. In with you now."

With a word to the driver, Bailey himself jumped inside, and we were under way.

"I think we may as well tell Jeremy since he must accompany us," said Sir John. And then to me: "There has been a shooting at Lord Goodhope's residence. He himself is apparently the victim."

Chapter 3

In which clean hands prove a man of quality

WE ALIGHTED FROM THE CARRIAGE: I FIRST, THEN MR. Bailey, and Sir John last of all. Although no word had passed between them, I soon enough learned that the house at which we had stopped was situated on St. James Street, inside the precincts of Westminster, which was then the jurisdiction of Sir John.

It was indeed a grand house from the last century and can be judged so today, for still it stands on that street, though now dwarfed by others even grander. Lately, while investigating the details of this matter to write its account, I ascertained what was then common knowledge: to wit, that although the Goodhope family had great holdings and a manor house in Lancashire, Lord Goodhope was known to spend most of his time in London, sometimes in the company of Lady Goodhope, though more often without it.

For all our haste in getting to the place, Sir John showed no immediate hurry in proceeding to the door. As Mr. Bailey took a moment to instruct the carriage driver to wait, the magistrate simply stood on the walk before the house, his head tilted slightly upwards. As I observed this, it occurred to me that were it not for his affliction, I should have thought him to be staring at the Goodhope residence by the dim light of the street lamp.

"Mr. Bailey!" he called out.

The thief-taker hastened to his side. "At your service, Sir John," said he.

"Would you describe for me this house we are about to enter?"

"Well, it's a big 'un. 'S' truth, it is."

"*How* big, man?"

"Three floors up," said Bailey. "That's counting the ground floor as one of the three. But wide, sir, wide."

Rather than ask *how* wide, Sir John called me to witness: "Perhaps you can contribute something to this, Jeremy."

"I'll try, sir." And I did so, noting its brick construction, and the fact that its upper floors were five windows across, with the space of a yard between each, and a yard to each corner. The place of a window in the center of the ground floor was taken by a large double doorway to which three steps led.

"Very good," said Sir John. "And which of the windows is lit?"

"None, sir, that I can see. All the windows seem to be shuttered."

"Ah, well! They're keeping old customs then." With that, he plunged toward the house, his walking stick ahead of him slightly, seeking contact with the lowest step. "Mr. Bailey, give that double door a sound rap, and let them know we have arrived."

It was oak-upon-oak as Bailey beat thrice upon the door with his club. As we waited for admittance, he gave me a wink and a smile, as if to assure me that he bore no grudge that I had bettered his performance in description. He was a small man in neither size nor spirit.

In less than a minute, the door opened a crack, and the face of a man was partially revealed.

"John Fielding has come," announced the magistrate, "to inquire into the calamity that has befallen this house."

Both doors were thrown wide, and we entered. The black-clad butler, dressed as a gentleman to my eyes, showed us immediately into a sitting room just off the spacious hall. There Lady Goodhope awaited us. She rose and walked directly to Sir John. Although the light from the single lit candle within the room was quite dim, I saw that she was well, though discreetly, dressed in the style of the day, a rather thin woman with a countenance not so much of great beauty, but rather one that displayed a certain purity. I also noted that her eyes were dry.

"It was very kind of you to come, Sir John, and so promptly. I trust my call did not greatly interrupt you."

"Nothing that cannot keep." He groped forward with his hand, found hers, squeezed it sympathetically, and brought it to his lips. "I am deeply shocked at what I've heard. I offer my condolences."

Lady Goodhope had given neither Mr. Bailey nor I so much as a glance. She did not inquire into our presence but stared at Sir John, waiting.

Having waited a space himself, Sir John resumed: "We must view the remains, of course. Mr. Bailey here will assist me in that, due to my obvious deficiency. And, if it is not too much to ask, Lady Goodhope, I should also like you to give me a statement as to how you became aware of the deed. That, however, can be put off until such time in the future as you may feel more capable."

"I am quite capable, thank you."

"Then you wish to speak?"

"Yes," said she bluntly. "Let's be done with it."

Benjamin Bailey fetched a chair for Sir John, and after Lady Goodhope had taken her seat again, settled him down into it. They were not five feet apart, each facing the other.

"When I heard the shot—"

"I do sincerely beg your pardon," said Sir John, "but it will be necessary for me to interrupt you from time to time to ascertain certain facts. I must do so now. At what time did you hear the shot? Where were you? How were you engaged at that moment? Be as detailed in your account as you can be.''

"Yes, of course," she said, "I understand."

"Then proceed."

"It is difficult to be exact as to the hour," she began once more. "There was no clock at hand, and I have not viewed one since. In all truth, I have no idea of the time at this moment."

"Mr. Bailey, you have your timepiece with you?"

"I do, Sir John." Mr. Bailey stepped forward to the candlelight, squeezed the egg-sized orb from a small pocket in his breeches, and announced, "It is just on eight o'clock, three minutes to the hour."

"Thank you, Mr. Bailey. Now, Lady Goodhope, reckoning backward, how much time would you say has elapsed since the fateful moment?"

She was silent for a moment. "About an hour, I should judge. There were minutes of confusion, which I shall describe, but once I was sure what had happened, I sent a footman with the news to Bow Street."

"You did well. So let us fix the event at seven, past dark, in any case."

"Yes."

It was just about that time, I reflected, that the coxcomb Boswell had begun his recital at the Cheshire Cheese. Such a waste of time!

"Very good. And where were you?"

"I was above in my chambers, reading."

"You and Lord Goodhope maintained separate apartments?"

She hesitated. "We do, yes. Or we did."

"Continue, pray."

"I heard a sharp report, though somewhat muffled. I was not immediately aware of its nature, for I have no familiarity with firearms. I thought perhaps something had fallen below, and so I laid aside my book and went to investigate. Halfway down the stairs, I was met by Potter.''

"Potter?" queried Sir John.

"The butler. He met you at the door." Then she continued: "Potter was in a greatly agitated state. He had quite rightly recognized the sound I had heard as a gunshot and wished my permission to enter the library.''

"From which the sound had emanated?"

"Yes.''

"Why should it have been necessary to seek your permission? I should think in such a state of alarm, he would have entered immediately.''

"He asked my permission because it was necessary to break down the door. I of course gave it, and—''

"Lord Goodhope had locked it from the inside?" Sir John seemed a bit perplexed by this.

"He had, yes.''

"Was this his custom?"

"Perhaps not his custom, but he did so frequently." She stopped and sighed. "Lord Goodhope was . . . somewhat secretive in his habits.''

"I see. And so you gave permission, and the butler sought to force the door.''

"It was not an easy task," said she. "This was the period of confusion I mentioned earlier. I stood by, waiting, quite beside myself with fear, as first Potter, then Ebenezer, the footman, attempted it with no success. At last, they thought to use a log of wood from the hall hearth. With that, they at last broke the lock, and the door swung open.''

"That was when you viewed your husband's corpus.''

"That was when I . . . had a glimpse of it.''

"You did not enter the room?"

"I stepped just inside, saw what I saw, then leapt back.''

"And what was it you saw?"

"I saw the figure of a man. There was a great deal of blood, and I had an impression of terrible disfigurement. The posture of the body was such that he could only have been dead. That was when I sent Ebenezer to Bow Street.''

"Then you, yourself, have not looked upon the corpus in such a way as to be certain it is your husband?''

"I could not,'' she said. "I cannot. In any case, Potter made certain identification, and Ebenezer has confirmed it.''

"I see,'' said Sir John. "And having sent the footman off, what did you then do?''

"Then I came to this room and waited for you. Here I have been since.''

"You sent word to no one else?''

She seemed quite puzzled at that. At last she asked, "To whom?''

"Oh, to friends, those as might give you bolster in such an hour.''

"I have no friends in London,'' she said simply. "Richard's friends—Lord Goodhope's—were not mine.''

With that, Sir John nodded and rose to his feet. "Naturally,'' he said to her, "I'll not ask that you reenter the library.''

"Potter will show you inside.''

"That will be most suitable. I do ask, though, that you remain here until we have finished our inspection. There may be further questions. We take our leave then temporarily with thanks to you for your assistance in this painful matter.''

He turned then and made straight for the door, we trailing behind. Behind us, Lady Goodhope called out the butler's name in a voice that seemed almost unseemly loud. Yet there was little need to summon him. Potter was there at the door to the sitting room, his appearance so silent and swift that it seemed likely he had been eavesdropping.

"At your command, Sir John.''

"Potter?''

"The same, sir.''

He was a stout man of a little more than average height.

Bowing, clasping his hands, he was the very picture of servility.

"You will take us to the scene, please."

"Gladly, Sir John. This way."

The butler then cupped his hand at his elbow, thinking to conduct him thus down the long hall. But Sir John shook off his hand, just as he had mine earlier while walking in the street. He pointed forward with his walking stick and said, "You lead. We'll follow."

Potter looked questioningly at Mr. Bailey, who answered with a firm nod, then he set off, looking back solicitously and often until he himself bumped into a chair along the way.

"Careful," said Sir John.

"Uh, yes, quite."

A few steps beyond his mishap, the butler stopped at the last door off the hall. It gaped open, leaning slightly, half off its upper hinge.

"Just here, Sir John, to your left."

Hesitating just slightly, the butler stepped inside and waited. But the magistrate delayed, examining the splintered wood at the doorpost and then the broken lock on the door.

"Ha!" said Sir John. "You did well to get it open at all, Mr. Potter. This is a very stout bolt. You were aided in this . . . ?"

"By one of the footmen, Ebenezer Tepper."

"Is he about?"

"He should be, certainly. Shall I summon him?"

"Not now. Perhaps later."

The butler, just inside the room, looked uneasily to his left. Something like a shudder passed through him. He turned quickly away, a look of pained distaste on his face. There had to be the body of Lord Goodhope, just out of our view.

"At what time did you hear the shot fired?"

"Just at seven," said he with great certainty.

"How can you be so sure?"

"I have a timepiece."

"And you consulted it immediately? That seems passing strange. I should have thought your first concern would have been to get this door open to see what might be done to help your master."

"Oh, it was!"

"But you delayed to check the time?"

"Now I remember!" The man was quite flustered by now. "When Ebenezer and I went to fetch the log from the fireplace near the front door, I noticed the time on the clock on the mantel."

"And it said seven?"

"Uh, no, just after. It indicated just after the hour."

"So you merely calculate that the shot was fired at seven."

"Just so, sir," said he, deflated.

"And with Ebenezer Tepper's help, how long would you say it took you to break through the door, using the log as a battering ram?"

"A very short time, sir."

"And where is the log you used?"

"Just here, on the floor. We threw it aside as we rushed into the room."

"And the corpus is exactly as you found it?"

"Exactly, sir."

"Very good, Potter. That will be all."

"Sir?"

"We have concluded," said Sir John. "Thank you. Be gone from here."

"I thought . . . ." He hesitated. "Yes, sir. As you wish, sir."

With a look of embarrassment at Sir John and then at Mr. Bailey and myself, he slipped past us and walked swiftly down the hall.

"I shall no doubt have questions for you later," Sir John called after him.

The butler merely half-turned and nodded as he continued on his way.

"All right, Mr. Bailey, let's inside and be on with it. Jeremy, you may wait, if you choose, or enter. You'll no doubt see worse sights if you remain in London." He then stepped through the door and into the room.

Mr. Bailey followed him inside. "Watch the log, sir. It's just ahead."

Sir John touched it with his walking stick and nodded. "As he said."

"Very harsh you were on that Potter, sir."

"Oh, I suppose so, but the man had obviously been listening at the door earlier and had decided to give precise witness to what his mistress merely reckoned. He had no better idea than she what time the event occurred, timepiece or no. Put a bit of a scare into him because I didn't want him about, neither with us nor just outside the door."

"He'll not come back."

"No. Well, come along, Mr. Bailey. Describe the room for me."

And the two of them left the doorway and my sight as I held back, still standing in the hall. I was strangely filled with trepidation. As I look back on my state of mind at the time, I believe it was my father's recent death that restrained me. That, and perhaps also the look on the butler's face when he glanced into the depths of the room. In any case, I soon mastered my unease, squared my shoulders, and marched into the library.

In all, we three must have been there on that visit to the room for nearly half an hour. Sir John, early on, took a chair put for him by Mr. Bailey in the exact center of the place and began ordering us about and throwing out questions as to the dimensions of the room. (It was large: nearly a rod square.) Sir John wished to know if it were a proper library. Were there bookshelves? Of what dimensions? Were they filled with books? A few or many? Was there a fireplace? Of what size? What about the room's furnishings? What were they and where were they placed?

He demanded exactitude and detail from us of the same sort he would have asked of any witness: or more perhaps. Deploring Mr. Bailey's tendency to generalize, he chided him on a pair of occasions, and asked him to reckon in hands and fingers if he was not sure of feet and inches. I, too, was put to work, climbing about the room to examine the windows. All of them, I found, were shut and locked.

There was, of course, a fourth member to our party. He was seated quietly behind the desk, his head thrown back, a quantity of his blood spilled out over his chin and throat and splattered down upon his shirt and waistcoat. I had managed not to look directly upon him as I ran about, doing Sir John's bidding. But there came a time at last when all that could be noted about the room had been noted, and there was no place to put our attention but upon the dead man at the desk.

Reader, I make no joke to tell you that he was the deadest dead man that ever I set eyes on. The position of his head had before disguised from me the nature of his wound. But as I approached timorously behind Mr. Bailey and viewed the disfigured face of the corpus, I found myself astonished, then fascinated by the destruction wrought by that single shot. Once I had forced myself to gaze upon the sight, I found I could barely take my eyes away.

What made it particularly irresistible was Mr. Bailey's precise description of the wound. He had, I was to learn, spent half his life in a Guards Regiment: I shall not name it since there was some slight irregularity about his departure. He had been in battle against the French in North America. He knew wounds: It would not be overstating to say he was something of a connoisseur. Sir John had no reason to complain of his descriptive powers on this occasion. No surgeon could have done a better job of it.

If I may attempt to duplicate from memory, and with the aid of childish notes I took shortly afterward, his commentary went something as follows:

"Ooh, Gawd, it's a nasty 'un, Sir John. I'd say the muzzle of the pistol was close but not directly onto the face when the shot was fired. There's black powder burns all over the skin. The ball entered at a thumb's width from the bridge of the nose, two thumbs down from the right eye. It went upwards and across, making porridge of the nose and cutting the nerve to the left eye as it went into the brain. The wad slapped him sharp between the eyes. Not too much blood, though. I've seen more from like wounds."

"The optic nerve of the left eye?" put in Sir John. "Not the right?"

"Aye, sir, it went across, so to speak."

"Diagonally?"

"As you say, Sir John."

"How can you tell the optic nerve was severed?"

"The left eye is popped a bit. It ain't hanging, but it's pushed out in a way that ain't proper, if you follow me."

"Yes, Mr. Bailey, I do." Sir John was silent for a moment. "Is there a wound proving the exit of the ball?"

"Aye, indeed there is, sir. It's blown his wig akilter. If I may remove it altogether, I'd have a better look."

"Yes, of course, Mr. Bailey. Proceed."

That he did, pulling off the periwig in one swift movement and tossing it upon the desk. The head of the dead man bobbed in a grotesque manner.

"Now here," began Mr. Bailey, "we've a spot about half a palm's width above the left ear and just behind it where a bit of skull about two thumbs wide has been blown away. There's some nasty matter leaking out there. It wasn't no dueling pistol did this but a proper piece of military weaponry."

"Where *is* the weapon, Mr. Bailey?"

"Ah, let's see now. It ain't on the desk, so it must be . . ." He bent down, and I with him. The pistol lay at the feet of what once was Lord Richard Goodhope, butt on the floor, barrel across his left foot. I marveled at how the dead man's hands simply rested in his lap, the unsullied hands of a gentleman. He seemed quite at peace.

Mr. Bailey picked the pistol up carefully and inspected it as he rose to his feet. "Yes, it was here, sir, on the floor beneath him. It's as I said, a military sort of weapon, calibered for a ball a good thumb's width, nearly an inch, so to speak."

"Well and good. Now, could you possibly trace the path of the ball and find where it entered the wall? If, indeed, it did. Perhaps you could help there, Jeremy."

I did help, though not materially. It was Mr. Bailey who located it by the gouge it had left. He pulled his knife out of the sheath on his belt and dug out the battered chunk of lead from the wall.

"Got it, Sir John."

"I take it, since you have not mentioned it, Mr. Bailey, that no note of explanation has been left."

"The desk is empty, sir."

"Then I think our business here is complete. Take the pistol with you."

He rose from his chair then and led us from the library, touching the log of wood with his stick, turning to his left at that point, and walking out into the hall. I left last of all, and at the door could not resist one last look at the grotesque figure at the desk. And for the first time I considered Lord Goodhope in some sense as a person and not simply as a dead man. What, I wondered, could lead one in such fortunate circumstances to do such positive and final harm to his person? Thus puzzling, I joined the others.

"Mind the chair on your right," said Sir John, chuckling to himself as we set off down the hall. "It seems to cause difficulty to some."

We arrived at the door to the sitting room. The butler, Potter, was nowhere to be seen, and so Sir John directed Mr. Bailey to knock. "But softly, man," he added, "softly, please."

Lady Goodhope appeared in response. "You have finished?" she asked.

"We have, m'lady. The room was given a thorough inspection, as was the fatal wound to Lord Goodhope. He died, as you yourself must have surmised, by pistol shot. It went directly into the brain. Death would have been instantaneous, and as nearly as can be judged in such matters, without pain."

"I see."

"No note of explanation was immediately seen, though one may turn up. I thought it improper under the circumstances to go rummaging through his desk. If one should be found, I must ask that you communicate its contents to me. Barring that, I would sincerely advise you to look to Lord Goodhope's accounts. Have them examined by someone you can trust. I can provide a name, if you wish."

"Yes, thank you, but what are you saying, Sir John?" She seemed honestly not to understand.

"Why, that Lord Goodhope's wound was self-inflicted, that he died a suicide. And I assure you that in most such cases the root cause for such drastic action is some financial problem."

"May I assure you of one thing?" She seemed absolutely calm, completely in control of herself.

"Of course. What is it?"

"My husband—my late husband, that is—would *never* have committed suicide, no matter what his problems." Her words were pronounced with intimidating certainty.

"But," objected Sir John, "the door was bolted. You saw what effort your men had to put in breaking it down. There is no other door. All the windows were locked. The weapon with which he dispatched himself was there at his feet. How could it be anything but suicide?"

"I don't dispute your findings, but I reject your conclusion."

"Then you theorize murder?"

"I have no theories," she said simply. "As I told you,

I was in that room only briefly. I doubt that I shall enter it again. But I simply *know* that he would *not* have destroyed himself.''

For the first time since I had met him, Sir John Fielding was speechless. He sputtered a bit. There was a ''Why . . .'' and a ''Well . . . ,'' neither of which led to any proper end. His hands made uncertain movements.

Lady Goodhope, who had conducted their interview in the doorway of the sitting room, then inclined her head slightly and took a step back. ''Thank you for coming, Sir John. I'm grateful for your efforts. Now, if you'll forgive me, I wish to be alone. Goodbye.'' Saying that, she turned and shut the door.

Sir John continued to sputter. He fumed. One could very nearly see steam rising from beneath his periwig.

As if by magic, Potter then appeared, handed Sir John his tricorn, and opened the double door wide for us. There was the hint of a smile on his face. Mr. Bailey and I exchanged looks, something between apprehension and confusion passed between us.

It was not until we were out on the walk before the waiting carriage that Sir John finally found words; and when they came, they came in a torrent. Without cursing them, he called down God's judgment on all womankind. He remarked in particular upon their baseless certainty, their refusal to face cold facts, the indifference of educated women to simple logic, et cetera. And he ended with a verbal flourish that I myself have since had occasion to quote: ''If God had truly meant women to be our helpmates, as scripture informs us, then He should have provided them with brains sufficient to the task.''

Then he fell silent.

We were all quiet for a moment, then Mr. Bailey cleared his throat and said, ''I'll leave you now, Sir John. I'm past due making my rounds. All the watchmen are likely to be asleep in their boxes. Time to rouse them.''

Distracted, Sir John failed for a moment to respond. Perhaps he was giving further pious thought to the Creator's intentions as regards women. But at last he came to himself: "Yes . . . yes, of course, Mr. Bailey. You'd best be on your way. And thank you for your help."

"Don't mention it. Goodbye, Sir John, and goodbye to you, young Jeremy."

I mumbled my own goodbye, then watched him disappear down the darkening street.

"His is the harder job," said Sir John to me. "If we could but keep the streets safe, it would be worth three Lord Goodhopes." Then, about to haul himself up into the hackney, he added, "Or ten."

And so he, after calling out the address on Bow Street to the driver, settled back for the drive home. He ruminated still. At last, he said, "A strange woman."

"Did she speak strangely?" I had noted it but felt, perhaps, that she spoke as every noblewoman did. I was then in no position to judge such matters.

Sir John considered this. The horse ahead clip-clopped along. Then: "Perhaps slightly in some foreign mode—though in very good English, of course."

"Oh, yes sir, very good." I thought back, remembering a visitor we had once had to our place in Lichfield. "Would you say . . . French?"

He thought about that. "Yes," he said, "something Frenchy, not so much in her pronunciation as in the rhythm of her speech." He paused at that. "Very good, Jeremy. I must look into that." We lapsed into silence again, until he said, "But a lady, certainly, by any measure. Great dignity there."

"She had no tears, Sir John."

"Yes, I sensed as much."

Again I listened to the plodding regularity of the horse's hooves on the cobblestones. Somehow, his tribute to Lady Goodhope and the dignity she had shown led me to think back to her husband in death there at the desk in the library. What was there to think about him? Not the ruined face, certainly. That was nothing to remember him by. But then, quite unbidden, the picture of his hands came to me: at peace, resting in his lap. I thought of those. "It's true, isn't it," I asked rather sententiously, "that you can always tell a man of quality by his hands?"

"It may be. What are you getting at, boy?"

"Well, Lord Goodhope, sir. He had very clean hands, polished nails, not a smudge."

Sir John seemed suddenly much taken by this. "Lord Goodhope had clean hands, you say?"

"Oh, yes sir. Very clean."

"*Both* of them?"

"Both of them, sir, as I remember. And I'm sure I remember correctly."

He suddenly pounded the floor of the hackney with his stick. "Damn me for a fool!" he exploded. Then said he, "And damn Mr. Bailey, too, for not noticing." And making an awful racket on the ceiling of our compartment with his stick, he called out loudly to the driver to turn the hackney around and take us back to the house from whence we had come.

Our second entry into the Goodhope residence was not managed so easily. Potter was at first reluctant to admit us at all, saying that Lady Goodhope had retired for the night. Sir John said he had no need to see her but had returned to give further examination to Lord Goodhope's body. Potter then informed him that the body had just now been removed from the library to be prepared for the casket which would arrive in the morning.

As if suddenly propelled by that bit of news, Sir John burst past the butler and into the house, and I at his coattails. "*We* must see the body at once!" he bellowed.

"I must ask her ladyship's permission," whined Potter.

"You need ask no such thing," retorted the magistrate. "May I remind you that we stand here in the City of Westminster, where I am the law. Now take us there."

Complaining all the way, the butler led us down the hall

and through a door under the main staircase. This, in turn, opened to another set of stairs leading downward. Having once been rebuked for offering aid, the butler plunged ahead and within a moment had disappeared. Sir John put down a tentative foot, then muttered a request for my assistance. The steps were narrow and steep and dimly lit from below. With his hand on my shoulder, we made it down in good order and successfully navigated the bend midway, where we had lost our guide.

At the bottom of the stairs we found ourselves in the kitchen. I marveled at this, never before having considered where such a necessary room might be placed in these great houses. Besides us three newly arrived, there were four there: two men who had recently conveyed the body downstairs to the kitchen; and two women, kitchen slaveys, who were making ready to wash the body. Water was heating in a kettle on the cookstove. Between them, in the middle of the room, lay the body of Lord Goodhope stretched out on a long table: not quite long enough: feet and ankles, now seen only in white hose, dangled over the edge at midcalf. The corpus was thus in a state of preparation: shoes off, waistcoat open, shirt unbuttoned.

"Have they begun washing the body?" Sir John whispered to me.

"No sir," I whispered back, "I think they have not."

"Good, and thank you, boy." Then, banging down his walking stick and speaking in a voice of great authority, he addressed all and sundry: "I, as the magistrate of the Bow Street Court in the City of Westminster, forbid this process to continue. There will be no washing of the body, according to custom, until a qualified surgeon has viewed it and made his report. Is this understood?"

There seemed a general unwillingness to speak in response. Finally, Potter coughed and spoke up: "Understood, Sir John."

"Very good," said Sir John, and continued: "My advice is to store the body in a cool place and wait for word from either me or the surgeon. Whichever comes first. Is this also understood?''

''Completely,'' said Potter, gaining strength. ''It will be done as you say. I promise it.''

''All right, Mr. Potter. I shall hold you responsible.''

The young men and women who were there in the kitchen seemed to breathe easier. There was a general relaxation. The women (girls they were, truly, about my own age), especially, seemed to welcome the postponement. One of them giggled.

''Master Proctor!'' A shock ran through me as I heard myself addressed so formally.

''Yes, Sir John,'' said I, with all the gravity I possessed.

''I wish you now to inspect the body of Lord Goodhope, as it was brought down from the library.''

''I will do so,'' said I, hoping to impress him with the formality of my reply, and perhaps also the kitchen slaveys: the one who had *not* giggled was quite comely.

And so, thus empowered, I strutted round the table, giving my full attention to the body of the deceased. It no longer gave me pause to look upon him, the porridged nose, the bulging eye: They were all the same to me. I concluded my tour next to Sir John.

''Is the body as you first viewed it?''

''It is, sir.''

''With particular reference to our earlier discussion, Master Proctor, are the hands clean and unsmudged?''

''They are, sir.''

He addressed the room: ''Have they been cleaned? Have the hands of the corpus been washed?''

The answers came back variously, but they came back from all four who had been there in the kitchen. All were in the negative.

''Very good,'' said Sir John. ''Please remember my orders with regard to the remains. A surgeon will come sometime tomorrow.'' He half-turned then, but remembering a detail, came back to ask, "Is Ebenezer Tepper, the footman, in this company?"

There was a pause, but then the younger of the two men, a lad fit and strong of about eighteen years of age, stepped forward. "Aye: Ebenezer Tepper." He seemed a stalwart sort.

"Thank you for identifying yourself. We shall return tomorrow morning. Please be available to answer questions." Then Sir John added, "You too, Mr. Potter."

He then clapped me on the shoulder and let his hand remain there as I led him up the stairs as we had come. Potter trailed behind in a manner less certain.

As we arrived in the hall, Sir John dropped his hand but stayed close as we made our way swiftly to the street door. But ere we arrived a figure on the grand staircase above detained us. It was Lady Goodhope dressed in a robe of such finery it would have done for a ball gown.

"Sir John," she called out.

He stopped and turned to the voice.

Potter puffed up behind us. "Your ladyship, I regret the intrusion. I had no choice but to admit them. He—"

She cut him off: "Never mind, Potter. They are rightly here." Then: "What have you found, Sir John, on your return visit?"

"I have two matters to communicate and a question to ask."

"What is the question?"

"Was your husband right- or left-handed?"

"Why, left-handed, always the exception."

"So. Yes, thank you."

"And what have you to communicate?"

"First, that I shall return tomorrow to question members of your household staff. There will also be a surgeon who will come to examine the body of your late husband."

"Are those the two matters?"

"No, I count them as one. The second matter is that

indeed you were right, Lady Goodhope: He was not a suicide.''

What struck me then was how little she altered in either posture or expression. She removed her hand from the rail of the stairs and clasped her robe a bit tighter at her throat. If what Sir John had told her caused any change in her face, I could not detect it. ''Thank you. You will, of course, be welcome here, and your surgeon, too. Please keep me informed of your findings. Good night.'' And with that she turned and marched up the stairs.

It was not until we two were settled in his Bow Street kitchen, gnawing on two-day-old cold leg of mutton and fresh bread and butter, that Sir John deemed it proper to tell me what it was that had persuaded him to change his mind so completely. By then, of course, I had my own suspicions, so that what I heard from him did not come as a complete surprise.

''You'll recall, Jeremy,'' he said to me, ''that Lord Goodhope's face bore powder burns.''

''One side of his face was dark as any blackamoor's.''

''So it must be with a pistol of such power fired at such close range,'' he explained. ''It takes considerable black powder to propel a ball the size of the one Mr. Bailey dug out of the wall. With the ball comes also a great quantity of black powder: enough to be-soot his face complete.'' He paused. ''You see where this leads, perhaps?''

''I think so,'' said I.

''Then tell me.''

''Well, if powder comes out the front of the pistol along with the . . . ball, then some of it must also leak out the back: I mean to say, it's an explosion inside that makes the ball go. Isn't that how guns work?''

Sir John smiled indulgently and nodded. ''It is. Yes.''

''The explosion at the back of the gun would be enough to dirty the hand that held it. Lord Goodhope's hands were clean, so he did not hold the pistol when it was fired.''

"Exactly." He pulled a morsel of rare mutton away from the bone, dropped it on a chunk of Mrs. Gredge's bread, and popped the two together into his mouth. Taking time to chew thoughtfully and silently, he washed the generous mouthful down with a gulp of beer: enough, in any case, to encourage a manly belch from him.

"I take it," he said to me then, "you've had no experience of firearms."

"Oh, no sir."

"Your father: Did he shoot?"

"Him neither. He had a great dislike of guns."

"He sounds a good man from what you say of him."

"Oh, he was, sir. He was."

"Well, I credit him for fathering a bright boy: and educating him well, too."

It took me a moment to catch his drift. When I did, I blushed and thanked him. Then, remembering, I brought up a matter that had given me pause earlier. "Before we left on our second visit, you asked Lady Goodhope if her lord was left-handed or right-handed. What was the importance of that?"

"Consider it. If he had been right-handed, the wound just to the right of the bridge of the nose, and the path of the ball diagonally to the left into the brain, would have come quite naturally. But for a left-handed man to achieve the same wound with the same result, it would have been necessary to hold the pistol at a most unnatural angle, perhaps even to pull the trigger with the thumb. You see? Possible, but unlikely."

I did consider it, even to the extent of moving my left hand to my face to try what he had described. He was indeed correct: The angle was possible but unlikely. "But, Sir John, when you asked her that," said I, "you knew already that Lord Goodhope had not pulled the trigger in respect to his clean hands."

"You're right, boy: just a detail. But in matters of murder, it is good to collect as many details as we can. It's the weight of evidence that proves guilt, seldom one fact alone.'' He took another swig of beer before he continued: ''And tomorrow, we'll go again to St. James Street in search of more details. God grant that we may discover the most important of them all.''

''And what is that, Sir John?''

''How the perpetrator of this deed could have committed it and then have vanished from the room.''

Chapter 4

In which further puzzling details come to light

READER, AS I WRITE THIS FOR YOUR ENLIGHTENMENT IN the last decade of our century, you cannot but imagine the lawlessness of the London streets, even in the year 1768. I put it thus, for if it were bad then, it was very much worse when Sir John Fielding received his appointment as magistrate of the Bow Street Court. That was in 1754, a year before my birth. His brother Henry had drawn up a plan for permanent, paid constables to be on call day and night from Bow Street. But, having seen its passage through Parliament and being fatally ill with the dropsy, Henry Fielding left the implementation of the plan in his brother's hands and went off to Portugal to die.

The streets could be made safer, said Sir John, by "quick notice and sudden pursuit"—and so they were. Yet whoso may believe that crime may ever be eradicated completely from the world's largest city is either childish or foolish. The battle is constant. The sudden victories that were achieved by the Bow Street Runners (as the constables came to be known) were followed from time to time by losses. Robbery gangs were broken only to be reformed by surviving members. Petty thievery continued. Idle apprentices were led to lives of crime to pay for their dissolute pursuits, gambling and whoring. Thus it was that while, in the year of which I write, the streets were much safer than before, they were not near as safe as they are today.

All this above is preamble by way of explanation to the shocking news I received from Sir John himself next morning just past breakfast. I had heard him thumping about very early. In fact, he had departed briefly to return as I was down on my knees, scrubbing the stairs, as Mrs. Gredge had bade me do. I heard his steps rise from below. I turned and found him just a few stairs down.

"Jeremy?" queried he.

"Aye, Sir John," said I, jumping to my feet.

"I must ask you to leave off what you are doing and accompany me." He seemed no little concerned, and I was made to wonder.

Jumping to my feet, I said, "As you wish, Sir John." In truth, I was glad to be called away from stair scrubbing. "I'll be but a minute."

And it hardly took more than that for me to empty my scrub bucket out the window, put it aside, and seek my coat. Mrs. Gredge was not on hand to hear my excuse nor Sir John's explanation, and so she would have to think ill of me when she discovered me gone.

As I followed him, I made bold to ask, "What is the matter?"

"A sad one, I fear," said he. "Mr. Bailey was struck last night by one wielding a cutlass."

"Does he live?" I asked. "Is it serious?"

"Yes, indeed he lives. As to whether it is serious or no, we must go to his lodging house together to ascertain."

And that we did, making our way through Covent Garden and its horde of vegetable hawkers to the streets behind it. I noted that once past Covent Garden Sir John held back somewhat. At last he confessed to me, "I am not so well acquainted here, Jeremy. Perhaps it would be best for me to give you the address of Mr. Bailey's lodging place. It is Number Ten Berry Lane: nearby, I have been told, a bit north and a bit west of the Garden. Perhaps you might ask our way: And I should have no objection if you took me by the arm when you deem it necessary in this terra incognita.''

When we arrived at Number 10, I informed Sir John and positioned him before the door. He beat upon it stoutly with his walking stick. There then appeared a dame of perhaps forty years, plump and red-haired.

She was quite overcome when she espied the visitor on her doorstep. ''Ooh, b'Gawd, it's his lordship himself, it is,'' said she. ''Welcome to my house, Lord John.''

He smiled in amusement at that: ''Madam, you elevate my rank unnecessarily, but I thank you for your ready recognition. You will have guessed I have come to see your boarder, Mr. Bailey, to make sure of his recovery.''

She ushered us in and danced ahead of us, leading the way, bugling our arrival loudly. Over her shoulder, as it were, she informed us that she had installed Mr. Bailey in her bedchamber so as to make him more comfortable. ''The couch is good enough for me, sure.''

''Very kind of you, madam, indeed.''

''The surgeon's with him now, Sir John.''

She stopped then before an open door at the end of the hall and gestured us inside.

There was Mr. Bailey, sitting up comfortably in the large bed, bare-chested down to his middle where the coverlet maintained his decency. Upon his left forearm was a large bandage. On that side of the bed sat the surgeon: a rather young man, not yet thirty, I judged. Both were smiling as if some joke or pleasantry had just passed between them.

''Come in, come in, Sir John, and make acquaintance with my surgeon, Mr. Donnelly. He's cousin to the lady who met you at the door, Mrs. Plunkett.'' Then Mr. Bailey added, as if to make certain we knew that all was in order, "Widow."

Mr. Donnelly jumped from the bed and pumped Sir John's hand vigorously, declaring it an honor to meet him. In this instance, Sir John took care to introduce me to Mr. Donnelly and Mrs. Plunkett, who had joined us in the room, as "my young charge, Jeremy Proctor." I took heart in that.

Thereafter followed a report by Mr. Donnelly on Mr. Bailey's wound, not superficial for he had stitched it last night, but not deep either. "What saved him was his musculature, you see," said Donnelly, "which is considerable. There is so much meat on those arms of his that the bone was well protected."

"And the nerves?"

"It's a bit early to tell. His left hand is somewhat incapacitated, but that's to be expected. I shouldn't think the cut was deep enough to do much damage of that sort."

"Oh, I'm fine, Sir John," declared Mr. Bailey. "I'll be back on the job in a day's time."

"Could be a bit longer than that," said Donnelly with a wry smile. "We must watch for fever, infection of the wound. I'll come by daily."

He then began gathering up the tools of his trade and dropping them in his bag.

"If you have time, Mr. Donnelly," said Sir John, "I wonder if you might wait a moment while I talk to Mr. Bailey. Our meeting here may be quite fortuitous for me. There is quite another matter I should like to put before you."

"Why, certainly, sir." He turned to Mrs. Plunkett. "Perhaps I might beg a cup of tea from you, dear cuz."

And so the two cousins made off to the kitchen as I found a chair for Sir John. The one I put my hands on was littered with male and female garments, mixed, which I set at one corner of the bed. The thought was planted in my mind that this was perhaps not Mr. Bailey's first visit to Mrs. Plunkett's bedchamber, nor perhaps was it solely for *his* comfort that she made him a guest.

Be that as it may, Sir John settled into the chair close by his chief constable and asked for the story of his wounding. "The villain who did this will appear before me this afternoon. The robbery victim will be present, of course, but I must depose you as the arresting officer. Give me the story, the who, when, and where of it, and it will count as testimony in my court."

Thus, with frequent interruptions from Sir John calling for details, Mr. Bailey gave his account of robbery, pursuit, and apprehension.

He had been on St. Martin's Lane up in the vicinity of the notorious Seven Dials not long after midnight. The street was not empty but neither was it full. There were dark, empty places aplenty for a thief to hide and a robbery to take place. From one of those, an alley off the lane, he heard a commotion, the sound of running footsteps, and then the hue and cry was raised: "Robbery! Stop, thief, stop!"

When the villain rounded out the alley, Mr. Bailey was but twenty yards distant. He added his "Stop in the name of the law" to the victim's cry and had no difficulty running him down. "The fool thought he could scare me off with the cutlass he carried," said Mr. Bailey. "He heaved it about over his head, making circles in the air in a threatening way. Then, when I continued to come at him, he made some sort of speech about knowing how to use the thing, which proved to be a lie. He was remarkable awkward with it."

"But what of the pistol?" interrupted Sir John. "You took it with you from the Goodhope library, did you not? Surely you could have tamed the fellow with that, empty though it be."

"Might have done, sir, but I'd stopped in at Bow Street and left it off there. I had by me naught to rely on but my usual."

Mr. Bailey had his oak club out, and while ordinarily no

match for a cutlass, in this instance it proved sufficient. "He came at me, feinting," he continued, "and I jumped to one side, giving him a sound clout on his left shoulder. That angered him so that he overstepped himself, hacking at my neck. I dropped back, but not quite far enough, for the hack ended as a slash across my forearm. He was off balance with that so that I had only to step forward and deliver another sound clout to his head. One more laid him out in the street."

The robbery victim, grateful to Mr. Bailey and concerned for his wound, managed to bring a hackney down from Seven Dials. All three, the victim, the arresting officer, and the perpetrator of the crime, went in style to Bow Street. The villain came to himself in the hackney with the point of his own cutlass against his belly.

"What is his name?" asked Sir John.

"Dick Dillon, or some such, perhaps Davey: It's in my report. A big sort but clumsy on his feet."

"And the amount stolen?"

"Twenty guineas and a bit. The victim, Hawkins by name, won it from Dillon and others, and was daft enough to think he'd be allowed to stroll home with it. Now he wants his purse back, of course."

"Of course." With that, Sir John rose to his feet and thanked him. "What you've given me will do very well. I'll be in to see you again, perhaps even tomorrow. Now, if you'll excuse me, Mr. Bailey, I've a matter to take up with your surgeon."

"A good one he is, Sir John. He sews a good stitch. Five years he was a ship's surgeon."

"A Navy man?"

"So he was and just left His Majesty's Service."

Gabriel Donnelly was Dublin-born, the son of a successful shopkeeper with great ambitions for his son. The medical profession, for which the father intended him, was then, as now, virtually closed to the Catholic Irish, except by means of apprenticeship to an established Catholic physician. Since no place could be found for him and their hope was for no less than a university education, the shopkeeper scraped together his savings and made liquid his investments; thus he put together sufficient to send his son abroad for his education. France was out of the question, due to the war: so he was sent to Vienna. It was a long and difficult time for Gabriel away from home and language so long, but he did well in his studies. When he completed them he found the only place open to him was as a ship's surgeon. The Royal Navy was willing to overlook the matter of his religion, so great was its need for qualified surgeons during the last two years of the French war. Now, the term of his agreement completed, he had come here and used what money he had saved to open a surgery in the area of Covent Garden.

"But why to London?" Sir John had asked him as we rode together to St. James Street.

Mr. Donnelly replied: "It is such a great city, sir. I thought, surely, it would be less provincial in such matters than my native town. A man of my confession should have a better chance here."

"Vain hope, I fear."

"There are many Irish here in London."

"Oh, indeed there are. A few come before me every week at Bow Street Court."

Mr. Donnelly had no reply to that. He sat back in the seat of the hackney and simply shrugged as expressively as any Frenchman or Italian.

He had given Sir John his history as we three proceeded to St. James Street and the residence of the late Lord Goodhope. Hearing of Sir John's need for a surgeon to examine the corpus and something of his suspicions, he had willingly agreed to accompany us.

"Perhaps you should have remained in the Navy," suggested Sir John.

"There was no future for me there."

Sir John considered this. "Probably not," he allowed. "And in truth, a man with your diploma deserves a better post than ship's surgeon. In any case, Mr. Donnelly, you'll be paid for your ministrations to Mr. Bailey."

"But I was called by my cousin. It seems she and Mr. Bailey are great friends." There was no hint of a smile there. He accepted the situation, whatever it might have been.

"Be assured," said Sir John, "that the court has funds to pay for the repair of its constables. Also, by the by, to recompense you for the time you spend in this examination to which we hasten."

"Well, Sir John, I'll not pretend that the fees, no matter how little, will not be welcome. My surgery, so far, has not attracted many."

"I count myself lucky to have run into you, as I did."

The hackney drew up in front of the Goodhope residence.

"Ah, but here we are at the house on St. James Street," said Sir John. "You are about to prove yourself."

"To your satisfaction, I trust."

We entered without difficulty. Potter said nothing, simply threw open the doors to us. I, entering last, noted a look of hostility in the eyes of the butler. Yet it disappeared as Lady Goodhope stepped forward to greet us. She was dressed, already, suitably in black. Sir John introduced Mr. Donnelly to her and stated the need for him, as a surgeon, to examine her husband's body. Hesitating a moment, she consented and directed Potter to take the surgeon to the cellar. Mr. Donnelly bowed and gave his thanks, then left to do his job, leaving us alone with Lady Goodhope.

"I hope this will be the end of it," said she. There was the hint of pique in her voice.

"Your ladyship?" Sir John turned to her. His attitude was one of confusion.

"My expectation is that once this examination is concluded I may be permitted to advertise Lord Goodhope's death and prepare his funeral. Is that correct?''

"You may do so whenever you like," said he. "But tell me, what do you plan to announce as the cause of death? Foul murder? Homicide?''

"Do you dare to make light of this? Why need I make anything of how he died?''

"It is customary, and it will soon out. The servants will talk, if they have not already.''

"Oh!" she exclaimed, making fists of her hands and stamping her foot in frustration. Then: "I want only to be done with this and back at Grandhill.''

"Grandhill, Lady Goodhope?''

"Our residence in Lancashire. That is *my* home. I have a son to raise. He is but eight years of age and will be the next Lord Goodhope when he reaches his majority.''

"I understand the need you feel," said Sir John, "but thinking of the boy, there is much to be done here.''

"What do you mean?''

"Have you taken my advice and had Lord Goodhope's accounts examined?''

"No, but you urged that when you were convinced he was a suicide.''

"It would be a necessary step in any case. Who was your husband's banker? His solicitor?''

"I have no idea. I'm sure it's among the papers in his desk.''

"But you have not yet looked?''

"No.'' There was both anger and resignation in her voice.

Sir John sighed, took a step toward her, and spoke in a quieter tone, hardly more than a whisper: "If he was not a suicide, then he was murdered. We agree on that?''

"I suppose so. Yes.''

"Who would wish to kill your husband, Lady Goodhope?''

"My husband had political enemies, I suppose. He was active in Parliament and known at court.''

"Quite. I can make inquiries."

"And no doubt there were many who would have been happy to see him dead for other reasons, as well."

"Who would they be?"

She said nothing for a moment. But then, casting her eyes about, she looked for the first time directly at me. At last she had noticed me. "Who *is* this boy who is always at your side, Sir John?"

"Jeremy Proctor, mum," said I with a bow, before Sir John could answer.

"That is *who* he is," said Sir John. "As to *what* he is, we may call him my helper."

I liked that even better than "my charge."

"Well," she said, "be rid of him for a bit, and we'll discuss the matter of who in my sitting room."

He nodded his agreement, perhaps a little reluctantly. He then said to me, "Jeremy, go into the library and prepare things for me. I shall be questioning the servants there shortly."

I sulked a bit for having been sent away as a child (which of course I then was), though I could not fault Sir John for his handling of the matter. Furthermore, to be named by him as his "helper": *that* was very heaven. If he had called me such, then that I determined to be. I would do all I was told to do, of course, as now I set about to arrange the room as he had asked: set two chairs facing in the middle of the room, the more comfortable intended for him. But more, I would help him to see. If my unknowing observation on the condition of the victim's hands had proved to Sir John such an important matter, then I would be ever watchful for such discrepancies and those details he judged to be of great importance.

He was not occupied long with Lady Goodhope, and when he entered the library, he had Ebenezer Tepper in tow. Bidding the young footman sit down, he took me aside and said in a voice so quiet the intended subject of his interrogation could not hear, "Jeremy, I should like you to go over every bit of this room and look for places that a full-sized man might hide: an alcove, a closet, even a chest. For at the present, the best interpretation I can give to this odd sequence of events is that whoever it was fired the pistol into Lord Goodhope's face did then hide himself until the single door was opened by force; waited further until at last the room had cleared out, as eventually it did; and then clandestinely made his exit through the only door available to him."

I nodded and whispered eagerly, "Yes, it could have been exactly so!"

"But then," said he, more to himself than to me, "we are left with another problem."

"And what is that, Sir John?"

"How did our man get into the room in the first place?"

He turned from me then, shaking his head, puzzling, and I guided him into the chair I had set out for him.

Then said he to the young man directly opposite him, "Your name, as I recall, is Ebenezer Tepper."

"Aye, sor, 'tis," said Ebenezer with a sober nod of his head.

Sir John leaned forward with sudden, keen interest. "You'd be from Lancashire, would you not?" asked he.

"Aye, sor, 'am."

"Tibble Valley?"

Ebenezer smiled broadly, pleased to be recognized. "Aye, sor."

"Well," said Sir John, "this should be interesting. Tell me, Ebenezer, what do you remember of last night's events?"

"Aye. T'lady, oo called me in t'hus hard seven . . ."

I shall not press this attempt at mimicry further. I have neither the skill nor the memory for it, and you, reader, doubtless lack the taste. You may gather that I understood little of what Ebenezer conveyed to Sir John. I could scarce believe the fellow was speaking English, yet he was understood. The magistrate nodded wisely and put questions to him in decent English at appropriate intervals. He seemed to have no more difficulty with the footman than he had had earlier with Mr. Bailey, though he seemed to enjoy himself far more.

Perhaps, indeed, it was just as well that I was discouraged from eavesdropping on their conversation, for it put me to the task Sir John had assigned me. I did as he directed, covering each foot of the library, searching for hiding places of any sort. To give the late Lord Goodhope credit, his was indeed a true library. There were books of all sorts in shelves against the walls, some of which detained me on my tour. And while there were indeed alcoves of a sort, where the bookshelves left off and the windows intruded, none seemed sufficient to hide a man. The thick curtains, which may have been shut, were close against the windows. What was not visible of these alcoves from the door was visible from the desk where Lord Goodhope's corpus had been found. It seemed unlikely that these supposed alcoves would have hidden the murderer.

Yet so careful was my search (and, I admit, so frequent were the interruptions to browse the more tempting books on the shelves) that I was but half done when Sir John dismissed Ebenezer Tepper and asked him to send in Potter.

Then he called to me, "How goes your inspection, Jeremy?"

"I've found nothing so far."

"Well, carry on with your search. You may turn up something."

"Sir John, if I might have a word with you!"

The last speaker was not Potter but rather Mr. Donnelly. He came striding into the room and made directly for the magistrate.

"You may have as many words as you like, Mr. Donnelly," said Sir John, rising from his chair.

I could not resist sidling close to them to hear what those words might be.

The surgeon spoke urgently to the magistrate: "I have a request that may seem a bit out of the ordinary."

"And what is that, pray?"

"I should like to remove the corpus of Lord Goodhope to my surgery for further examination."

"Oh?" said Sir John, who seemed to be caught off guard a bit by the request. "Is the wound so difficult to read?"

"No, the wound presents no problems. It is remarkably as you described it at my cousin's. The conclusions you drew are, I think, correct. It was not self-inflicted."

"What then?"

"There is another matter," said the surgeon, "a discoloration of the tongue that I find most curious."

"What would it mean?"

"I hesitate to say, Sir John, until I have examined the corpus further."

"And why can you not attend to that here?"

"It would be, well, awkward, I'm afraid." The surgeon sighed. "What I propose is what in my Vienna studies was called an *obduktion.*"

"You must speak plain, Mr. Donnelly," said Sir John, somewhat in exasperation. "I have a little Latin, less French, and no German at all."

"I wish to perform an autopsy."

"You mean that in the medical sense? You wish, in other words, to cut open Lord Goodhope's body and examine his inwards and organs?" He thumped his walking stick on the rug, not as I thought at first in anger, but rather to give sharp emphasis to what he next said: "That is *not* something to which I can give a yea or nay. To be honest, if it were the corpus of some poor soul picked up off the pavement at Seven Dials, I would have no objection to you cutting at will. But damn, sir! Lord Goodhope is *Lord* Goodhope, after all. It's not entirely up to me, it may not be up to me at all, to give permission. This must be Lady Goodhope's decision, and I doubt, frankly, that she will look favorably on your proposal."

Again, Mr. Donnelly sighed prettily, like some unhappy lover. "Well, Sir John, let me at least try her on the matter."

"I've nothing against it, and good luck to you. You'll find her in the sitting room just off the street door. That, at least, was where I last encountered her."

Gabriel Donnelly turned and started from the room. I spied Potter at the door, intent upon all that transpired. He would have heard as easily as I.

But then Sir John called after the surgeon: "Mr. Donnelly, two things I would make clear to her, if I were you."

"What are they, sir?"

"First of all, that you are not some sawbones sort of barber-surgeon, but a doctor of physic with a diploma from Vienna. And second, that if she gives permission, your autopsy will be conducted for purposes of this investigation only and not before students or apprentices for their education."

Mr. Donnelly considered that for a moment, then said he, "Agreed. Thank you, Sir John, for your advice." And then he walked through the still gaping and splintered doorway to the library, barely brushing the butler, Potter, as he walked out.

The magistrate settled back into his chair facing opposite and called out, "You may enter now, Mr. Potter."

"Thank you, m'lord."

"A simple 'sir' will do. Now, if you will take this seat across from me, I have a few questions."

"Certainly, sir."

"But only a few. First of all, is there a plan to this house?"

"A plan, sir?"

"Yes, of course, an . . . architect's map, a design, so to speak."

"Oh, I understand, sir. No, sir, none: none that I know of."

"Well, one must have existed."

"Oh, yes sir."

"It may still exist."

Potter thought on that for a moment. "Yes, sir."

"Find it."

"Sir?"

"Find it, I say. Ask Lady Goodhope, though I daresay you'll not get much from her. But you are the butler, are you not?"

He pulled himself to his full height. "Indeed I am, sir."

"Then you know all the likely places such papers are likely to be kept. Go to them, look through the documents. Find the plan to the house."

"Uh, all right, sir."

"My next question," said Sir John, "concerns the age of the house. When was it built?"

"In the last century, sir, as I understand."

"Very good, but *when* in the last century."

Potter seemed troubled, almost vexed, by these questions of Sir John's. Yet he answered meekly, in due respect to the magistrate's position: "Well, it is difficult to be exact without the architect's plan in hand, yet my understanding is that it was put up early in the reign of the first Charles."

"As you suggest, Potter, all this will be made clear when you find the plan."

"Uh, yes sir."

"Now, one last question. Has this house a garden?"

"Oh, indeed, sir, and a lovely one it is, sir. Lady Goodhope takes a special interest in it."

"I'm sure," said Sir John, "I'm sure it is. Now, Potter, if you will now conduct Master Proctor into the garden, so that he may view it, and be kind enough to answer any questions he might have."

"*Master* Proctor?" The butler looked around the room as if I were not there.

"Indeed. *Master* Proctor. Now, if you will be so good as to wait by the door, I would have a word with him."

I then left off my survey of the library, which in truth

had not advanced far since Ebenezer Tepper's departure, and went straight to Sir John's side. Potter, as ordered, went to the door. There he pouted.

Sir John groped forward and grasped me by the arm, pulling me close. "Jeremy," he said in a whisper, "what you must do is observe this room from the *outside*. Look for any suspicious thickness in its walls at any point. Ask him anything you like, but try not to give out precisely what you are looking for. And be reasonably quick about it. I must be back to prepare for today's court session. Understood?"

"Understood, Sir John."

"Very well, I shall be waiting for you: probably in the hall, near the street door."

"I'll not be long."

He released me then, and I went off to follow Potter through a door beneath the stairs just beyond the one we had passed through the night before to reach the kitchen in the cellar. There were three steps down, leading to a door to the outside. Potter made a great show of producing a key from his pocket, not a ring of keys but a single key, and unlocking the door.

"Was this door locked last night?" I asked, making my youthful voice as deep as possible.

"Of course it was, *boy!*" said Potter to me rudely. Clearly, he did not fancy being guide to a thirteen-year-old.

However, he told no less than the truth when he called the garden lovely. Indeed it was lovely. There were blooms of every sort in abundance in every corner. They mocked the rich disorder of nature, laid out not in sections but rather in a gay, scattered profusion in which colors and varieties mixed in a way I had not seen before. A path led through this array. Potter stood aside and allowed me to look as I liked. I took the path and walked to where it ended at a high privet hedge as Potter trailed behind. There was a gate, which I tried. It was locked.

"And where does this gate lead?" I asked, maintaining my serious demeanor.

"To a narrow mews between the houses," said he, snappish as any snapping turtle.

"And was it locked last night?"

"Of course!"

"Do you now have the key?"

"No, I do *not!*"

"Will you fetch it, please, Mr. Potter?" Even I was amazed at my coolness in these circumstances. For his part, Potter was quite shocked at my request. I read his face as he fought back the impulse to strike me for my presumption, or at least to refuse me. Yet in the end he thought better of it, doubtless remembering that I was there in the garden as the agent of Sir John Fielding, no less.

And so he had no choice but to turn around and stalk off to the house, calling over his shoulder that he would be back in a moment.

That moment was all it took for me to make the inspection I'd been charged to make. I darted to the house and looked around it to the right, looking for any extension or protrusion from the walls, anything at all that seemed amiss.

But no, there was nothing.

Then I walked along the library windows at the rear of the house, looking up, checking below. There were two, separated by the chimney which accommodated the fireplace in the library that stood directly behind the desk where I first saw the corpus of Lord Goodhope seated. All was just as I supposed it should have been from having looked over the room so carefully from the inside.

Or was it?

I backed up the garden path away from the house, continuing to study the rear of the library, feeling there was something there to be seen: if I could but see it.

* * *

We were together in the hackney, Sir John and I, before he at last spoke to me of what I had seen, or not seen, from the outside of the house. He seemed still a bit disturbed by what he had learned from Mr. Donnelly.

As I had approached him in the hall, he had been occupied in animated conversation with the surgeon. They were discussing details pertaining to the transport of Lord Goodhope's corpus. Mr. Donnelly was assuring Sir John that he need not concern himself with the details of the removal: The surgeon would attend to them himself.

"You alone, sir?" Sir John had asked.

"I and members of the household staff," replied the other. "A simple coffin arrived this morning. A dray wagon will be made available."

"Then, you have got what you wanted, and I congratulate you, though I confess I am surprised."

"She was very gracious."

"And you, evidently, very persuasive." He had then cocked his head in my direction. "Jeremy? Was that you who just arrived?"

"Yes, Sir John."

"Then let's be off to Bow Street."

Thus it was that we began our short journey in silence. Had not the black ribbon covering his eyes and the tricorn hat he wore virtually obscured his brow, I would have been sure he was frowning. As it was, I could only guess that to be so.

We were many streets beyond St. James when he spoke at last: "So, Jeremy, tell me, did you discover anything from the garden?"

"I'm not sure, Sir John," said I in all truth.

"Not sure? Come, boy, you've a keen eye. You've proved that already."

"But I saw nothing to make me certain."

"At this point," said Sir John, "you need not be certain, you need only be suspicious. Now what, exactly, has made you suspicious?"

"The chimney," said I. "It's an odd shape."

"The chimney? Hmm, well, that's a possibility, isn't it? As I recall, from your own and Mr. Bailey's careful description of the room last night, the fireplace it serves lies just behind the desk where Lord Goodhope was found. Is that correct?"

"Yes sir, correct."

"How did it look from outside the house? Built out to surprising depth? A bit too capacious?"

"Not exactly. It was built out, yes, but to both sides. It was shaped in such a way that it spread out under the two windows."

"Interesting. That should bear further investigation tomorrow." I thought that might be all he had to say, but then he roused himself and asked about the garden.

"Oh, quite beautiful, sir."

"Come now, Jeremy, you can do better than that. Describe it to me."

He was quite right to object, of course. I had done no better with it than Mr. Bailey had the night before when asked to describe the house. And so I thought for a moment, bringing a picture of the garden to mind, then simply telling him what I saw.

"It is," I told him, "about half the size of the house in depth, though wider on both sides, of course, which are bounded by wood fences."

He nodded at that but indicated with a gesture of his hand that I was to go on.

"Flowers and small trees are planted on either side of a path that leads down the middle. There are two benches."

"The path leads where?"

"To a gate in a privet hedge. The hedge is about six feet tall."

"And beyond the gate?"

"A mews. Potter seemed a bit reluctant to open the gate, or perhaps that was only because he hadn't the key with him. I made him fetch it."

"You did, did you?" Sir John laughed heartily at that. "It must have put him in a black mood, eh?"

Remembering how Potter's keen wish to deny me was written plainly on his face, I, too, joined in the laughter. "It did, it truly did!" I cried.

"Good boy. But tell me, what sort of mews was it?"

"Well, it went the length of the street and was probably wide enough for a wagon and horses, though perhaps not. Potter said that dust and garbages of all sorts are collected there. It is a dirt way and has a bad smell."

"There are no smaller structures behind the house?"

"None, sir, no."

"Then the entire household staff must be housed below the stairs. None too comfortable, I daresay. But—" He broke off at that point and turned toward the street. "Yes, here we are at Covent Garden. It is time for me now to adopt my official mien."

I looked out the window of the hackney and, marveling, saw that indeed he was right. I had not realized we were so close.

As the hackney driver slowed and halted his horse at the Bow Street Court, I could not help but ask, "Sir John, how were you able to tell our location?"

"Jeremy," he declared, "as I go about, I simply make use of my other four senses. You who have sight are so wasteful of the rest. Here, I simply put my nose and ear to work. I smelled the green and earthy smell of the green-grocers' stalls and heard the greengrocers calling their wares. You may take my word for it, boy, there is no place in London that smells and sounds like Covent Garden."

As he indeed had demonstrated.

The hackney driver paid, we went our separate ways, he to his court and I, alas, to Mrs. Gredge. But his last words to me were in the form of an invitation: "Should you complete your tasks to her satisfaction, you may feel free, if you like, to come into my court and observe the proceedings." I accepted gladly.

But there were stairs to be scrubbed, two great pots to be washed, and a bit of sweeping to be attended to. When I finished with all I'd been given to do, I was of course tempted simply to run off to Sir John's courtroom. Yet I knew that would be unwise, and so I held my place there in the kitchen, not even daring to sit down at the table, but rather puttering about, bringing some arrangement out of the chaos of knives, forks, and spoons I found in a keep in the sideboard. I knew the result of my labors must be approved by Mrs. Gredge before I was properly dismissed.

She was not immediately present. And if I were to judge from the murmurings from above, she was in Sir John's bedchamber attending Lady Fielding. At last I heard a door open and close, then steps on the stairs, and Mrs. Gredge entered the kitchen. She seemed much troubled.

She sank down in a chair at the table, her hand propped to her cheek, taking little notice of my presence. After waiting more than a minute, I shuffled my feet a bit and coughed discreetly.

Of a sudden, she looked up at me and said, "Ah, Jeremy, a swift end is the best any of us can hope for."

"Is Lady Fielding very ill then?" Her state had not yet been made clear to me. "When will she be better?"

"Indeed she is very ill," said Mrs. Gredge. "And as for her growing better, it's not likely, I fear."

I waited an awkward moment, curious, yet hesitant to inquire. Then I screwed my courage up and asked: "What sort of sickness has she?"

"A wasting disease of some sort. The poor, good woman simply dwindles." Then, as if coming to herself, Mrs. Gredge sat up straight in her chair and looked at me critically. "And have you completed the tasks I assigned you, Jeremy?"

"I have," said I. "The stairs, the pots, the brooming. I have even arranged the hardware in the sideboard."

"Well and good," she said with a sigh. "You've no doubt done a fair job." Then she added, with a little of her earlier fierce spirit, "If not, you'll hear from me later. Rest assured."

"Yes, mum."

"You're free to go upstairs and read. Better to do it in the daytime than waste candles at night."

"Yes, mum. But, well, Sir John said I might sit in his court and look on."

She shook her head once or twice. Her face reflected her dismay. "Go if you like, then," said she, "though why you should want to stand witness to that parade of human misery and iniquity, I can't guess."

"Well," I blurted out, "because Sir John offered."

"I understand. On your way then." But as I made for the stairs, she called after me: "Jeremy!"

"Yes, mum," said I, stopping and turning.

"He thinks highly of you. See that you don't disappoint him."

Thus making my promise to her, I then headed down the back stairs.

A good deal of the afternoon had passed by the time I made my entry into the Bow Street Court. There were not so many defendants or witnesses left, and what I later came to recognize as Sir John's usual audience had reduced to just a few. I had a wide selection of places, but made my choice of one close enough that I might hear the proceedings, yet might do so without attracting attention to myself.

Sir John seemed to be moving ahead quickly through the court's business. A prisoner had been led out as I walked in. What his offense was, I knew not. It was evident, though, that he would be bound over for trial at Old Bailey. I looked upon him sympathetically, a young man not much older than myself, knowing that it was only due to Sir John's interest in justice that I had not also gone before him to Newgate two days before. I wondered then if this one could be the notorious Dillon who had delivered the slash to Mr. Bailey's forearm. If so, I assured myself, I need not be quite so sympathetic.

There were then two matters of little consequence that passed before the magistrate: a dispute over a deed of property which Sir John settled in favor of the deed holder; and that was followed by an accusation of pickpocketry. The outcome of the latter case was of some interest, so let me describe it to you here. To summarize briefly: Peg Button, of no profession (in reality, a woman of pleasure), had detained one John Turley, factor, in Black Boy Alley at about eleven o'clock that morning and made certain proposals to him. As he considered her proposals, he felt a certain slight movement in the pocket of his coat, and realized she had filched from him a silk kerchief worth a guinea or more. By the time he had missed it, however, she was in the act of passing the kerchief to her confederate, a young boy of ten or so. Turley grabbed at the boy, but managed to do no more than wrest the item from him before the latter disappeared quickly around a corner and into the street. The woman, however, impeded by her skirts, was easily caught. And once caught, was brought straightforward to the Bow Street Court, where the charge of theft was thus lodged against her. This account came from Turley. There were no supporting witnesses.

Sir John listened patiently to the story, then he asked, "What have you to say to the charge, Peg Button?"

" 'Twasn't me what took it, yr lordship, 'twas the boy."

"Do you know him?"

"I seen him abouts."

"It's been sworn to that it was you who took the silk kerchief, that the boy accepted it from you. What say you to that?"

"I say that the gent'man was mistook, sir. I seen the boy with his hand in the gent'man's pocket, and I sought to grab it from the boy to return to the gent'man."

"Logical, I grant you, logical. Then why did you run?"

"Because he was yellin' I was the thief of his foul kerchief, which I in no way was, but his mind seemed made up, it did."

"Is the item in question in possession of the court?"

"I have it here, Sir John," said Mr. Marsden, the court clerk.

"Is it, in fact, foul?"

"Well, it's a bit stiff with dried snot and spittle." There was general laughter from the remaining members of the regular audience. "It once was white but now is mostly yellow."

"Have you a cold, Mr. Turley?"

"I have, Sir John." He hacked once or twice in demonstration.

"Well, at least we have established ownership." There was further laughter. Then pondered the magistrate: "Or have we? Mr. Marsden, will you examine this once-white item and tell us if there are any distinguishing marks on it?"

John Marsden opened it gingerly and looked it over carefully. "Two initials, Sir John, an *F* and an *A*," he called out.

"Well, how do you explain this, Mr. Turley? How came it into your possession?"

"It was a gift, Sir John, a gift from one who didn't know me well."

"No indeed, not very well, not by name, in any case." Sir John was silent for a long moment. "Frankly," he said at last, "I'm dubious. First of all, even the accusant has given it in testimony that he retrieved the kerchief from the boy, who then escaped. How the boy got it has been reasonably contested by the accused. And then there is the question of the item itself. Mr. Turley claims it, but there is reason to doubt his claim. And so the court discharges Mistress Peg Button and charges Mr. Turley to go his own way without his kerchief. The court claims it. If it is boiled for a day it may again be fit to use."

The gallery, which usually stood on the side of the accused, broke into applause as Turley turned and angrily marched away. Mistress Button called her thanks, but then

Sir John summoned her to return.

"Yes, sir, yr lordship," said she, all smiles.

He leaned down toward her and said in a voice only we in front could hear: "Go and sin no more, Peg."

She left with a sober nod to the magistrate.

There was then what seemed a long conference between Sir John and Mr. Marsden, at the end of which the clerk got up and left the courtroom briefly. Returning, he left the door open and returned to his place near Sir John with just a further word between them. Then Marsden, a smallish man, stood to his full height and bellowed out in a large voice, "Bring the prisoner forward."

Through that same door to the rear of the courtroom a man was brought forth in chains by two constables. It was, unmistakably, Mr. Bailey's attacker, Dick Dillon. He was, as had been described, a big man. Whether he was clumsy on his feet, it was impossible to tell, for he was in leg irons which would make even a dancing master heavy-footed. He flashed an angry look around the court, thus making an ill impression upon the gallery. Ushered by his guards to a place before the bench, he stared defiantly at the magistrate: a gesture lost on blind Sir John.

Francis Hawkins was called forth and gave his account of the robbery by force of arms which was perpetrated upon him by Dillon. At the point in the narrative when Benjamin Bailey appeared upon the scene, Sir John took over. He announced that he had taken the deposition from Mr. Bailey that morning and proceeded to repeat it from memory word for word, except for a few corrections in grammar and diction. At the end, he declared, "Let the court record read that this was the testimony of the arresting officer."

There was a long, impressive silence then. At last, Sir John called out, making his voice both louder and deeper than seemed normal: "Dick Dillon, what have you to say?"

"What have I to say?" echoed Dillon, as if mocking Sir John's solemn inquiry. "What I have to say is I wants transportation."

"In other words," said Sir John, "you prefer not to hang."

"Dick Dillon'll not hang," yelled Dillon. "He's something to trade."

"And what might that be?" asked Sir John.

"Can you promise me transportation to the colonies?"

"As one indentured for life? A slave?"

"I'll take my chances with that."

"I can promise you nothing, Dick Dillon. But if you have information to give on criminal matters that lead to impeachment or conviction, it will be taken into consideration at your trial and in sentencing."

"I wants transportation!" reiterated Dillon.

"And I cannot promise it."

"Then I'm talkin' to the wrong one, ain't it?"

"No doubt you are," said Sir John. Then, waiting a bit so that the words he was about to speak would be heard by the entire court in all their gravity, Sir John began again: "To all here, I call attention to this man before me. There is clear and sufficient evidence to hold him for trial on the charge of theft. The testimony of the victim and the deposed testimony of the arresting officer make that clear. As we all know, however, there is theft and theft. On the one hand, we may have a ten-year-old boy attempting to filch a dirty kerchief: reprehensible, of course, but such sneak-thievery pales to nothing when compared to the crime of Dick Dillon. His was theft with a deadly weapon, a cutlass. The victim, Mr. Hawkins, was lucky to escape with his life. In that, I do not exaggerate, for according to Chief Constable Bailey's deposition, when confronted, Dillon made clear his intention to murder Mr. Bailey, and in the affray did succeed in wounding him before he was subdued. This I consider far more serious, for in striking an officer of the law, Dillon struck at the law itself. This cannot, should not, be tolerated. And so he is bound for trial, not only for theft but also for the attempted murder of an officer of the law while in the rightful performance of his duties. I do not

believe that any judge or jury at Bailey Court will treat
these charges lightly, nor with clemency.

"Take the prisoner, Dillon, away to Newgate, where he
will await trial at the convenience of the Crown."

Whether it was for the sense of his statement or the
power of his extemporaneous rhetoric, the gallery (no more
than twenty souls present) applauded Sir John Fielding
roundly. He, thinking such display unseemly, banged with
the flat of his hand on the bench and called for order.

Yet Dick Dillon would have the last word. As he left the
courtroom, he shouted back, loud as he could, "I'll not
hang. You'll see!" And then he was pushed through the
door.

"This court is dismissed," said Sir John. He stood then
and, without faltering, without a misstep, made his way
quickly out of the courtroom, leaving by the same exit
through which Dillon had been propelled only moments
before.

As I myself was leaving, I was detained by Mr. Marsden,
who informed me that Sir John had requested that should
I make an appearance, I was to visit him after court in his
chambers. Thus invited, I made my way through that same
door, caught one last glimpse of the notorious Dillon and,
after announcing myself with a knock, was admitted into
his presence.

He sat as informally as before, feet elevated, shoes off,
his periwig tossed aside. Bidding me sit down, he asked
my opinion of Dick Dillon.

"He seemed a true villain," said I.

"And to me, as well," said he, then more to himself
than to me: "I wonder what he knows that makes him so
confident."

Since I had no notion, I made no answer.

"Did you," he asked, "catch the distinction I made in
my oration, sending him off to Newgate?"

"Between his theft and his attack upon Mr. Bailey?"

"No, Jeremy, I meant that between sneak-thievery and

armed robbery. You see, the law looks upon both as the same. You heard the case that preceded it?''

"I did, Sir John.''

"Well, in all probability Peg Button did pick the fellow's pocket and was caught by him passing it to the boy. It was simply her word against his. Had he seized the boy and brought him in as well, then in theory, at least, Mistress Button and the boy could both have been tried, condemned, and hanged.''

"All for a silk kerchief?''

"Yes, worth a guinea, or so the owner claimed: that amount being sufficient in the eyes of the law to warrant capital punishment.'' He shook his head solemnly, as though in bewilderment. "I call that fellow, Turley, the owner; more like, he was merely the possessor. He probably bought it from another like Peg or her young confederate for a few pence when he felt his cold coming on.''

I was quite overcome by what I had heard. I saw mirrored in their theoretical fate my own predicament of two days past. At last I asked him, "Would they truly be hanged for so little?''

"In all likelihood, no. Children under fourteen are not to be executed, though a number have been sentenced to death. I understand that in certain rare cases in the counties the sentence has been carried out. Would Mistress Button, or one like her, have been hanged? Also unlikely. While our laws are the most severe in the Christian world, our trial procedures favor the defendant. Turley, or one like him, would have to do far better at Bailey Court: produce witnesses to the act, establish ownership of the item stolen, prove its worth, and so on. But had she been tried, convicted, and sentenced to death, she would also likely have had her sentence reduced to flogging, a term in prison, or the transportation to one of the colonies that Dillon seeks: not, by the by, a happy fate. In actual practice, only about half of the condemned—''

A knock at the door of his chambers interrupted him.

He turned in annoyance. "Jeremy," said he, "would you see who that is? Unless it is Mr. Marsden, or one of the constables, send him away."

I bounded out of my chair and to the door. Opening it a bit, I saw the eager, excited face of Mr. Gabriel Donnelly. It would be difficult to shut the door on him. And in the event, it proved impossible.

"I *must* talk to Sir John," said he, pushing against the door, forcing it back.

"Who is that?" bellowed the magistrate.

Having thus made his entry in spite of me, Mr. Donnelly rushed forward to him, leaned across the table in an urgent posture, and declared, "It is I, Gabriel Donnelly, and I've come—"

"Why could you not wait to be properly announced?" demanded Sir John. His feet were down from the table now, and he was groping about for his periwig.

"Because, don't you see, my news is too important to wait, even for that. Let me tell you of what I am sure. I have conducted the *obduktion;* have examined most, though not all the organs of the corpus. I found the texture of the kidneys quite destroyed; I found the liver in a bad state with lesions of a most remarkable sort. The lining of the stomach was badly inflamed and had also lesions and ulcer-like sores. The alimentary canal—"

"Enough, enough! What are you saying, Mr. Donnelly?"

"I am saying, Sir John, that Lord Goodhope was poisoned by a strong caustic, a sample of which I have taken from his stomach. That, and not the gunshot wound, was the cause of his death. I am sure of it."

Chapter 5

*In which I hear a shocking story and once more
meet Mr. Boswell*

THIS INDEED PUT ANOTHER COMPLEXION ON MATTERS.
Even I immediately saw the awful discrepancy that followed from Mr. Donnelly's startling revelation. If Lord
Goodhope had been poisoned, then why had he been shot?
Why should it have been necessary to kill a man twice? Or
could it be that he himself took poison, and then in his
death throes had a pistol exploded in his face? This last
seemed to make no sense at all. But then, what in this
contradictory set of circumstances did make sense?

If such thoughts as these passed through my childish
mind, what more grave considerations occupied Sir John at
that moment after the surgeon announced his news? He sat
silent as a stone for a great space of time, withdrawing into
himself as only a blind man can. The expression on his face
did not alter. It showed not so much surprise as some slight
vexation at this added complication.

Growing impatient at the prolonged silence, Mr. Donnelly spoke out rather impetuously: "Did you hear, Sir
John? I said it was poison that killed him."

"I am not also deaf," said he, grasping his periwig firmly at last and placing it casually upon his head. "In point of fact, I hear better than most." (Indeed, I knew that to be an understatement.)

"Forgive me. That was both unnecessary and unkind."

"It's of no matter. What does matter, of course, is that this tells me I had been asking the wrong questions entirely. For instance, I had placed some weight on the time the shot was fired. That would hardly matter so much now since you inform me he was then already dead." He paused then put it to the surgeon quite directly: "You would swear to that in court."

"I would," said he without hesitation.

"Could you venture to say how long he had been dead before the shot was fired?"

"No, there was virtually no food in his stomach. By your description of the body at the time your Mr. Bailey viewed it, the rigor of death had not yet begun." For the first time since he had pushed past me at the door, Mr. Donnelly turned to me and said, "Jeremy, at the time you looked at the corpus the limbs were still pliable, were they not?"

"The neck, too?"

"Yes, I suppose so."

I described how Lord Goodhope's head had flopped most hideously when Mr. Bailey had pulled off his wig to examine the wound behind the ear. Then I recalled something more: "The footmen had carried the body down to the cellar. He was there, laid out flat, when next we viewed him. So . . ."

"Just so," said Mr. Donnelly. "No rigor. He could not have been dead more than four hours, six at the most."

"A long period of time," said Sir John, then sat silently musing for a moment. "Damn me for a fool," he exclaimed of a sudden. "So taken was I with the matter of the pistol shot I haven't even established *when* he went into the library, his condition at the time, none of it. I've made a hopeless botch of this inquiry so far."

"Och," said the surgeon, "don't scold yourself so. It was cleverly done, with the pistol and all. Who would have guessed it?"

"*I* should have guessed it," said the magistrate with conviction. Then, with a sigh, he began in a more constructive manner: "What little do we know? If there was not food in his stomach, then it is not likely the poison was administered in that way?"

"Quite right you are."

"Perhaps disguised in liquid: Jeremy, was there a decanter or a bottle on the desk? In the room? Do you recall any such thing?"

I tried to call up a picture of the place, or rather some several pictures since Mr. Bailey and I had roamed the room so thoroughly. "No," said I at last, "I can't recall any. But I can only be certain about the desk. The desk was empty, quite bare of bottles."

"Hmm. That in itself is unusual." Then to Mr. Donnelly: "Do we know what *kind* of poison it was that killed him?"

"No," said the surgeon hesitantly. "As I said earlier, I took a sample of liquid from the stomach. I shall deliver it to a chemist, but in all truth, it was so mixed with blood and bile that it may be impossible to identify. It did such damage, though, so that it must have been a caustic, some sort of acid: a very painful death."

"What will you now do with the corpus?"

"Why, return it, sir. My promise to Lady Goodhope was that I should bring her husband's corpus back in a few hours' time, so that it might finally be prepared for funeral. Putrefaction has already begun: not yet far advanced, of course."

"Well, I must ask you," said Sir John, "to write a report addressed to me on this. Include all those details I was too impatient to hear. Give all the details of any kind you can, for this document, I pray, will go beyond me to the Crown prosecutor."

"I'll do that, certainly."

"What do you intend to tell Lady Goodhope?"

"The truth. Any sort of fabrication would be not just wrong but difficult to support. She'll know eventually, anyway."

Sir John sighed. "You're right, of course. But ask her to keep it to herself. And when you *do* tell her, make sure there are no servants listening in. The butler is particularly bad in that regard. There's no need for this to get out just now."

"I understand, but won't *you* tell her that *yourself*? Aren't you coming along, sir?"

"No, I had planned to spend time with my wife."

"With your wife, Sir John?" It was, I fear, quite obvious from his tone and expression that Mr. Donnelly had supposed that the information he had brought would be of such moment that Sir John would be drawn immediately back into the inquiry.

Yet it was just as obvious from Sir John's set expression that he had no intention of altering his domestic plans for the evening.

Then he addressed the surgeon with brutal directness: "Mr. Donnelly, no blame falls upon you in this, for you are ignorant of my private matters. But I intend to spend time with my wife, for it is certain there is not much more time to be spent with her. Simply put, sir, she is dying."

Mr. Donnelly was instantly overcome with remorse. The French say *désolé,* in their bombastic way, as a simple expression of sorrow or regret. But he did then truly appear desolated. His face crumpled so that I thought for a moment he might weep, but he did not.

He nodded and took a step back from the desk. "Sir, I cannot tell you how—"

Sir John waved his hand as if chasing away a fly. "No need to, Mr. Donnelly, no need to discuss it further. You had no way of knowing."

"Could I help? Perhaps if I visited her . . ."

"And bring along your diploma from Vienna?" He

sighed. "Forgive me. That was uncalled for. No, sir, a whole troop of medicos have looked at her. Medicines have been tried: all without help."

"What is her sickness, Sir John?"

"A tumor, the doctors agree on that, but all seem to disagree as to its location. All believe the end is near, however, and I feel it myself. I was away from her last night and this morning. I must be with her tonight."

"Of course. I understand. But do let me pay a visit in the morning."

"She's beyond diagnosis, beyond help. My poor, dear Kitty must weigh no more than five stone. She who was once a corpulent woman."

"But I'm sure she's not beyond pain. I may be able to give her something to ease that a bit."

Sir John remained silent for a moment. "Then by all means do come," said he.

"You do well to carry on in the courtroom," said Mr. Donnelly. "And this inquiry . . ."

"Which could not have come at a more inopportune time, believe me. No wonder I make such a botch of it. But hold, sir, although I have no intention of coming along tonight, let me send Jeremy with you. He might be of more help to us than you might suppose."

My young heart leapt at this new opportunity. "How, Sir John?" I asked. "How may I help?"

"Why, by talking to those below the stairs. Don't mimic me by questioning them formally. Converse with them. They will have questions of their own, be sure of it. Answer them all, except any to do with this latest matter of the poison. There is no need for them to know that. But give information so that you may get it in return. Be my spy."

"I'll try, Sir John."

"Does that satisfy you, Mr. Donnelly?"

"I shall be happy to have Jeremy with me."

* * *

Thus came I to be seated astride a discreetly draped coffin in the back of a dray wagon driven by the incomprehensible Ebenezer Tepper. Mr. Donnelly rode beside him and seemed to have no better understanding of him than I. He had made a few attempts at conversation with the Lancashire man: a question about the route and a comment on the crowded thoroughfare. These were put to him in his usual speech, which was good King's English softened and sung a bit in the Irish manner. Ebenezer had no trouble understanding him, but his responses, fairly long and windy they were, clearly bewildered the surgeon. With the second of these Mr. Donnelly cast me back an inquisitive look. All I could give him in answer was a shrug. Nothing passed between them after that.

And so, for the most part in silence, we made our way slowly through the streets of the city, until at last, quite near St. James Street, we turned down a narrow, dirt way which seemed quite familiar to me. It took me but a moment to realize that we were making passage to the rear of the house on St. James along the bleak, tight way I had viewed briefly with Potter. Ebenezer had proved what I had a little doubted. I had judged it perhaps too narrow for a wagon as wide as this. I told myself that I must amend the description I had given to Sir John.

Ebenezer reined the horses in before the privet hedge and just beyond the gate. Mr. Donnelly called to me to get down from the wagon and hold the team. This I did somewhat reluctantly as the two men hauled down the coffin and struggled with it through the gate. Although by the standard of London I was a country boy, I had little experience of animals and next to none of horses. On the few occasions my father had found it necessary to rent a team and a wagon, he had handled matters without my questionable aid. We were pedestrians, the two of us, as are most of the folk in England's towns and villages.

And so I could but hold on to the traces of these two huge beasts and hope for Ebenezer's early return. One was gentle and one was not. The gray grew restive, shuffling his feet in an impatient manner, making the wheels of the wagon behind them creak. I tried talking to him in a gentle and reasonable manner, but he would have none of it. He turned his head sharply and made to bite me on the arm.

Quite by instinct, I left my feet and leapt back, dropping the traces and landing against the hedge: the way was just so narrow. There was a dull thud where my feet landed. It was one of those details not at first noted. Indeed I had no mind just then but to grab hold of the traces once again and master that fractious gray. Fright made me bold. I cursed him in my childish way, calling him a devil and making threats I could not hope to carry out. Harsh words worked better than sweet. I took a grip lower down and pushed against his head. When the wheels of the wagon ceased to creak I knew I had triumphed.

It was not until then that the sound my flying feet had made when they hit ground echoed in my mind's ear. I had no certainty about it: simply the feeling that it was not quite as it should have been. Twisting about, managing to keep my hold on the horses, I searched out the place where my heels had dug in the dirt. It looked no different from the place I now stood. It had been firm under my feet: yes, perhaps a bit *too* firm. Testing, I made a jump in place, found the ground softer, and got no answering thud. This peculiar exercise disturbed both horses, however, and so I determined to do no more until Ebenezer arrived, which was soon after. In the end, however, all I did was estimate the distance from that spot to the hedge gate and thus mark it for further investigation.

Relieved of my onerous task, I made through the gate and the garden, and entered the Goodhope residence through the rear door. Then to the cellar and the kitchen. There I found the staff not engaged, as I had expected, in the preparation of dinner; but rather, dawdling about their own evening meal, all seated at the long table whereon Lord Goodhope's body had laid the night before. In addition to the two young females I had met upon then, there was Ebenezer's companion footman, whose name I would learn was Henry, and a woman unknown to me and senior to them all, whom I judged rightly to be the cook. Where Potter was I could not guess. I was, however, glad to note his absence.

As I entered, all conversation ceased. I should not have been surprised at that, for when last I visited them, I had performed in an official capacity quite officiously. But I wisely approached them on this occasion all meek and humble.

"I was wondering," said I to the assemblage, "if I might beg a little something to eat; a crust of bread would do me well."

"And who might you be?" asked the older woman. "In off the street, are y'?"

"By no means, mum," said I to her. "I arrived with Mr. Donnelly, the surgeon."

One of the kitchen girls, the one who had giggled the night before at Potter's discomfiture, whispered earnestly in the cook's ear, and the expression on the latter's face softened considerably.

"Well," said the cook, "you talks like a gent'man. P'rhaps I ought feed you as one. You may eat as we're eatin', if you like: dining as ladies and gents ourselves, we are. Must eat it up. Meat don't keep forever." She paused, assessing me. "What about a chop?"

"A chop of what?" I asked rather boldly.

"A chop of good English mutton," said she.

"Done!" said I, as if engaged in commerce.

This brought a lightening of mood at the table, a place set for me, and in no time at all, a thick chop, a bit of dripping, and a chunk of bread to sop it up with. This was indeed sumptuous dining.

In no time at all, those at the table with me were laughing and talking as before, but this time, as predicted by Sir John, most of the talk was directed at me in the form of

questions to do with the swift and unexpected demise of
Lord Goodhope.

"Was it not by his own hand then?" asked Henry, the
footman. He had recognized what his master's two clean
hands might mean and communicated it to the others.

"Sir John does not think so," said I. But there I was,
acting officiously again, speaking for the magistrate. "What
would you say?" I added.

"Well," said he, "if a man fires a pistol, it's sure his
hand will show it."

I simply nodded in agreement as I cut into the chop.

"Who're you to him?" asked the giggler, who introduced herself as Annie. "Y'seem a bit young to be a constable."

I sought the proper title and then remembered the one
Sir John had given me. "I am his helper," said I. "You
may have noted he has a bit of trouble with his sight."

"Indeed," she said, "wi' that black band over his eyes,
I sh'd think he would."

There was a general murmur of disapprobation at her
saucy comment. I moved in swiftly to show that no offense
had been taken.

"I help him in observing details," said I, "reporting
them to him. He then puts his wit to work on them. He's
a powerful thinker."

"Aye," put in the cook, "he's known for that."

"Was it you noticed Lord Dickie's clean hands?" asked
Henry.

"It was," said I immodestly, failing to add that I had no
sense of the significance of what I had seen.

"That was quick of you," said he.

And so it went around the table, I chewing away on what
the cook had rightly called good English mutton, answering
questions as they were put to me by the company. The only
one at the table who remained silent was Annie's much
comelier companion, she whom I had noted the night before. That one kept her silence, speaking only with her eyes.

There was something of fright in them. Could it be awe? I quite swelled with her admiration.

The only questions I failed to answer were those Sir John had foreseen: Why had Lord Goodhope's body been removed by the surgeon? What had the surgeon discovered? The first was put to me by Henry; the second by the cook. I wondered at her. Had she some notion of poison? In the ordinary course of things, suspicion might fall upon her in the case of poisoning. Yet Mr. Donnelly had made it clear that the murderous agent had not been introduced by means of food. She seemed uneasy. I wished to allay her unease but was unable to do so without divulging information I had been strictly charged to keep secret. And so I shrugged away the cook's question much as I had the footman's, declaring that the ways of doctors and surgeons were beyond me, that I put little store by them, as indeed Sir John did not. That last, perhaps not entirely a lie, seemed to relieve her.

Whereupon, the talkative Annie then tripped me up with a question for which I was quite unprepared. She wanted to know why, if I was so little taken with medicos, I had arrived with Mr. Donnelly.

I hemmed and hawed a bit, then said quite truthfully, "Sir John sent me."

"To what purpose?"

I hesitated.

"Come on," said she, "give out!" She giggled again.

"To go through the library once again," said I, blessed at last with inspiration.

"You ain't in the library."

Then I looked around me, as if observing my surroundings for the first time. "Oh," said I, all innocent, "so I am not!"

This won laughter from my audience, as I hoped it would, and to my relief the subject was dropped. But here I had nearly consumed my mutton chop and had gained no

information from them whatever. All the questioning had
been of me.

Yet the course of my visit took a new turn when four
more of the staff arrived, smelling of the stable. Ebenezer
was among them; I later sorted the other three out as coachman, postilion, and ostler. Ebenezer nodded and gave me
what I took to be a greeting, not in the least surprised to
see me dining there. The cook called for the two kitchen
maids to give up their chairs, adding that it would probably
be an hour before she'd need them for washing up. The
silent, comely one disappeared immediately through an
open door with just a solemn glance back in my direction.
I was quite taken by her. Then saucy Annie hung back
before the door and beckoned me to follow.

I looked about. None seemed to mind or even take notice. And so, wiping my plate clean with the last bit of
bread I had, I put it with others in a pile and trailed out of
the kitchen behind Annie. The next was a common room
nearly as large as the kitchen; off it and down a hall were
small individual chambers wherein the members of the
household staff were separately situated.

Annie, buxom and bold, grabbed hold my hand and
pulled me to a sofa which was slightly the worse for wear,
whereon her kitchen colleague had already taken a place.
The hall was furnished with just such pieces of grand odds
and ends cast down from the rooms of the great house
above. It was ill lit: A few candles tucked away in the
corners served the entire room. Alas, in spite of touches
made here and there to brighten it (there were pictures on
the pale yellow walls), the place had a rather dreary aspect.
Big though it may have been, it was nevertheless a cellar
room.

I was placed at one end of the sofa with Annie between
me and her companion. I asked to be introduced. When
Annie did not immediately respond, I leaned forward,
stretching my hand across, and said my name to the girl

with a friendly smile. She touched my hand timidly and nodded.

"But what is your name?" I asked.

There was no direct response. The girl looked away.

"Her name is Meg," said Annie.

"Can't she speak?" I whispered.

"Sometimes." Then, clearly wishing to change the subject, she said, "You get it from Lady Goodhope she means to close up the house in London?"

"She hasn't told me, certainly," said I.

"No, but you bein' Sir John Fielding's helper and all, I thought you heard her, like, discussin' her plans."

I thought a moment. "Well," said I, "she did declare that her home is in that place in Lancashire. And she said it in such a way that meant she wished to return."

"That's what we're afraid of, all of us. This was Lord Dickie's house. She wasn't here but a few weeks a year. And God be my witness, what a difference it were the rest of the time."

"What do you mean?" I asked, glad at last to be learning a little.

"Well, the upstairs staff liked it then because there was parties sometimes three, four times a week with Lord Dickie, dinner parties and other parties. The footmen and Potter would line up in the hall to collect their vails. They'd make as much in a week at such affairs as us downstairs would get in a year." She gave the girl next to her a powerful nudge. "But we had our ways, eh, Meggie?"

With that sally directed at her, the girl known as Meg jumped up from the sofa and ran from the room. Whether she was weeping or not I could not say, for she was away and gone down the hall too swiftly. I was quite dumbfounded. All I could do was stare at the point where I had last seen her.

"That was wicked of me," said Annie. "In all truth I wanted to be rid of her, but my means was bad."

"Is she mute? Can she speak, truly?" I reflected that she

seemed bright enough, but terribly timid, frightened.

"Meg's half-daft, maybe more."

"Has she always been this way?"

"No," said Annie with a sigh. "These other parties of Lord Dickie's, they wasn't no proper dinners where he'd have all the lords and ladies. There's even been a few of those with Lady Goodhope about. Then didn't we slave down in the kitchen! No, most of Dickie's evenings was what he called his 'impromptus,' like. Fancy word that, ain't it? Must mean something bawdy, for that's what went on those nights. Dickie might go out to a theatre, or some such place, and come back with a great crowd of bucks and their bawds. He'd rout Cookie out and demand supper for the lot. Late work for us.

"On'y sometimes they might be a bawd or two short for the night. Sometimes he'd send Potter out to pimp one off the street. But they come to the habit of pulling Meg and me up from the kitchen. It was our young years they preferred, y'see. Usually we got off laughin' and dancin' and carryin' on, actin' in their theatricals, but sometimes not. We was well paid, in any case. Wasn't the footmen and the servers jealous of *our* vails!

"Now, all this hugger-mugger between bucks and bawds, I can take it or I can leave it alone, y'see. But it begun to prey on Meg something fierce, the sin of it and all. So one night there comes a special rowdy crowd. Lord Dickie had his new one, that actress Lucy Kilbourne, with him, and after supper, sure enough, he sends down for me and Meg. On'y this time she refuses to go. I have to go up and tell the master. Now I should've said she was ill, but I didn't; I said she wouldn't. This put him in a right fury. He went down after her himself, dragged her up he did. And then a group of them took her to the bedchambers above and used her most shameful. I wasn't witness to it myself, thank God, but I could hear her screamin' and yellin', and then all of a sudden she quit, and I thought for fair they'd taken her life. I don't mind tellin' you it put a damper on the party in the dining room.''

Annie stopped talking then as if she'd ended her tale. I drew the likely conclusion: ''And this has affected her speech?''

''Oh, ain't it, though! This happened near a month ago, and she ain't talked yet. Except I caught her babblin' on to herself once or twice. So it ain't like she can't talk; she just won't.''

I was thrown into profound confusion by the story. Remember, reader, I had but just turned thirteen. My upbringing by my father had sheltered me a good deal from such mysteries as were involved here. I had no specific notion of what went on between men and women, though I strongly suspected that this area of my ignorance was a large and important one. I had begun to look upon women as women and girls as girls. I sometimes stared. I sometimes spied. And in a general way, I had become most curious. But Annie's account of Meg's ordeal had put a dark shadow over matters that I had previously regarded as sly fun. I had no idea what could have been so hurtful to her. And though I was profoundly confused, I did not wish Annie to explain things to me in great detail. That would have been far too painfully embarrassing to me.

''I think she fancies you,'' said Annie. ''That's why she's in such a dither.''

How could I respond to that? Particularly in light of what I had just heard?

''But then,'' said she, ''I fancy you, too—and that's why I drove her away!''

That said, she fell to tickling me most fiercely.

I begged away from such sport as quickly as possible, giving as my excuse that I must do what I was sent to do and continue my inspection of the library. Annie feigned hurt but grabbed me and kissed me on the cheek as I bade her goodbye: my first since the death of my mother. I colored red and near ran from the room.

Moving through the kitchen, remembering at last to say a tardy thank-you to the cook, I noted new faces there and wondered how many could be employed at that single residence. (A dozen, it turned out, was the total number.) Then up to the library where at last my breathing slowed to a comfortable rate.

I surveyed the place. It seemed little changed since my last visit. The door still stood open and askew. The log with which it had been beaten open, however, had at last been removed. I walked idly about, first noting that the desk was, as I had remembered, quite bare: specifically, there were no bottles, decanters, or flasks atop it, and I was sure that was as it had been. Then I went roaming, looking for places where strong drink might be stored. There were cabinets, two of them, to the left of the desk. One contained writing materials and a disordered pile of papers. The second cabinet contained liquor. There were three bottles and a decanter, and an assortment of glasses.

"Ah, there you are, young Jeremy!"

I turned and found Mr. Donnelly at the door to the library. He seemed in remarkably good fettle for one who had just delivered a corpus to a widow.

"I've found where the spirits are stored," said I, making more of the discovery than need be.

"Ah, well," said he, ambling indifferently toward my end of the room, "let's have a look."

He knelt down beside me, laying down his stick upon the floor, and reached into the cabinet; he pulled the bottles out one by one.

"What have we here? A bottle of port, a bottle of usquebaugh, and one of Spanish brandy. A good haul, eh?"

Then he uncorked them and smelled each, with a careful shake of his head.

"No," said he, "none of these did him in, I fear."

"But," said I, "how can you tell: unless they be submitted to a chemist, or actually tasted?"

"You wish me to taste them? I shall be happy to oblige."

He then, as if on a dare, took a swig from each bottle, corking them, each one again, as he went.

"There," said he, "are you satisfied?" This came with a bit of a laugh. He was indeed in an exuberant, reckless mood.

"Indeed I am," said I, "but had you been wrong, you might be dead or dying this very moment."

"But, you see, Jeremy, I couldn't be wrong. Two things militated against the possibility of poison in these bottles. First of all, the strength and nature of the *gift* would be such that it would give a strong and distinctive odor, even mixed with spirits: It makes me wonder how he managed to get it down without first becoming suspicious. But then there is the second matter, related to the first. The dosage was so powerful, so caustic, and would have worked so swiftly, that the victim would hardly have had time to replace the bottle in the cabinet. You see?"

"I do, yes, but all the same it seems a risky trial."

"Ah, well," said he again, "we must take such chances in life from time to time, don't you think?"

I could not suppose what had altered his mood so. He rose swiftly and indicated with his stick that I should return the bottles to their proper place, which I did and closed the door to the cabinet.

"Well," said he to me, "perhaps we've presumed too long on the hospitality of Lady Goodhope. Let's be off, shall we?"

And so he led the way out of the room and down the hall to the street door, twirling his stick as he went, the very picture of the happiest man in all of London. Potter was at the door to hand him his tricorn, give him a bow, and see us on our way.

Once outside on St. James Street, Mr. Donnelly paused and turned to me. A broad smile animated his face.

"I have only one complaint against the widow," said he,

"and that is that I was offered nothing to eat: nor dinner, nor supper. It seems she is fasting, good woman that she is, in penance for *his* sins. So I must confess to you, Jeremy, that I have now upon me a most prodigious hunger. Have you any idea where we might eat that might not cost too dear?"

I gave it hardly a moment's thought, for I knew only one place nearby.

"Perhaps," I suggested, "the Cheshire Cheese would do."

"The very place! It is off Fleet Street, is it not?"

"I believe so, Mr. Donnelly."

"Then I know the way."

We set off at a swift pace. His legs, being longer than mine, demanded that I stretch to match his stride. Yet I managed to keep up as he regaled me with some of what he had found out during his time with Lady Goodhope. He was quite pleased with himself to have learned what Sir John had omitted: *when* Lord Goodhope had entered the library and his condition at the time.

"It was about half an hour before the shot was heard," said he. "Lady Goodhope did not witness this herself but had it from two sources: that fellow Potter, whom Sir John is no doubt right not to trust; but also from the housekeeper, who happened to see him from above as she descended the stairs. Both agree that he seemed to be in good spirits, not in the least as one who had just taken poison certainly."

"But isn't that strange?" I responded. "Was he then poisoned and shot within the space of half an hour?"

"It is most perplexing," he agreed. Then, after we had walked a bit, he put to me a question to do with my conversations below the stairs.

"Well," said I, "they seem greatly fearful that the house here in London will be closed up and they be turned out to look for work where it may be found."

"And well they might fear," said Donnelly. "Between us, Jeremy, Lady Goodhope has confided in me her extreme dislike of this city and her wish to return permanently to Lancashire.''

''They will be much disappointed,'' said I.

''No doubt,'' said he rather absently. Then, reflecting his true thoughts, he added, ''She confided much to me this visit.''

Yet he said no more of that. He grew silent, pondering matters; though what he pondered, it seemed, was of a cheering nature. Picking up his pace a bit, he moved along in such sprightly fashion that I found it necessary to break into a trot to keep up. Then he, noticing my difficulty, begged pardon in good gentlemanly style and slowed to accommodate me. Not long afterward he began humming to himself. It was some Irish ditty, a jig or reel of a distinctly happy sound. Remembering his earlier urgency with Sir John, I found his change of mood most perplexing.

I offer this in explanation for the fact that I withheld from him the weightier matters I had learned in my conversation with Annie. How could I repeat the awful story of Meg struck dumb to one so lighthearted? Would he even give it his full attention? I kept my silence.

It was now well past dark. Hackneys, carriages, and coaches plied the streets. The street lamps winked off in the distance ahead like so many stars. As we proceeded down the broad Strand, making our way through the crowd which had seemed to swell in spite of the hour, a cold wind blew up at our back, giving me reason to wish I had brought my heavy coat when I left Bow Street that very afternoon. Perhaps the mild days of spring that had sustained me on my hike to London were now ended for a bit. Strange to think that all that had taken place was so near in time. Much in my life had changed since then and might soon change greatly more.

When we reached the Cheshire Cheese and entered inside, we found it filled quite to the walls with drinkers and diners. As we wandered about the room heavy with tobacco smoke looking in vain for an empty table, I felt a sudden

tug at my sleeve. I looked about and found to my consternation that it had been grasped by none other than the
windy Mr. James Boswell. He had recognized me from last
night's visit and insisted we sit down at the table which he
held alone. There was method to his kindness, as there always is with such men, for it soon developed that he was
bursting to know on what mission Sir John had been called
away the night before.

"I recall," said he to me, "that Sir John had hoped to
see Dr. Johnson. A great pity: the eminent lexicographer arrived immediately you left. And you left in a great
hurry . . . ?"

Mr. Boswell was already at dinner. He paused, a good-
sized bit of beef at the end of his fork, as he shifted his
inquiring gaze from me to Mr. Donnelly.

"It was a grave matter," said Mr. Donnelly.

"Oh, I've no doubt, Mr. . . . ? Mr. . . . ?"

Alas, my social graces were those of a child. I had failed
to introduce the two men when we sat down. Yet they managed this without me. Mr. Boswell took particular pride in
presenting himself, going so far as to say, "You've probably heard of me of late, Mr. Donnelly . . . ?"

My older companion seemed to shift uncomfortably in
his seat. He glanced at me for aid I could not provide. At
last, he managed to blurt, "I've not, no sir, but I'm only
lately settled in this city."

"And I've only lately published my first book! Surely
you've heard of it! *An Account of Corsica*? It is much discussed."

"Well, yes, now that I hear the title," said Mr. Donnelly,
"I do, of course, recall your name, Mr. . . . Boswell. I'm
honored, sir."

"Tish-tosh," said Boswell, playing falsely at modesty.
"But you would do well to look at it, if I may say so. I
can tell you are a man of affairs. Mine is the first account
of the Corsican struggle for independence. I gathered my
intelligence at firsthand in an extended visit to that troubled

island where I became a friend and confidant to the leader of that struggle, General Pasquale Paoli.''

"I had no idea," said Mr. Donnelly. "Then of course you are a true literary man.''

"An amateur only," said Mr. Boswell, at last popping that bite of beef into his mouth (after having waved it about for more than a minute).

Just then a server appeared and Mr. Donnelly ordered a chunk of beef like Boswell's and insisted, over my objections, that I have one, as well. Inwardly, I sighed, unsure that I could do it justice, having already dined well on a chop of mutton.

But then, with the server departed, the Scotsman returned to his true subject: "As I say, Mr. Donnelly, I am but an amateur author. I am by profession a man of the law, a member of the bar in Edinburgh. That is why I have a keen and healthy interest in this grave matter of the night before. You termed it so yourself." He glanced searchingly in my direction and, getting no response, focused himself on Mr. Donnelly.

Perhaps worn down by Boswell's insistence, or perhaps (it is possible) wishing to claim some importance for himself, Mr. Donnelly gave out a sigh worthy of an actor, leaned across the table (for the room was very noisy), and said in the loudest possible whisper: "You may as well hear it somewhat in advance, sir, for there will be a notice in the *Public Advertiser* tomorrow."

Boswell joined in the mood of secrecy, thrusting his face across his plate so that only a foot of space separated their noses. "Tell me, sir," said he. "Please do."

"Lord Goodhope died last night."

"But this is remarkable news. He was a man in his prime, less than ten years older than myself, I should judge. What was the cause?"

Mr. Donnelly's eyes, which just then moved in my direction, may have caught the look of alarm on my face. Surely he would not tell this gossip all he knew! But when his answer came, it sorely disappointed Boswell.

The surgeon leaned still closer and said: "Misadventure."

"*Misadventure?* But that is not a cause of death, sir. It is a . . . a euphemism. For what?"

Mr. Donnelly pulled back then and gave me a look I took to be reassuring. Then to Boswell: "Why, I quote from the notice, merely. More I am not at liberty to say."

Attempting to disguise his disappointment at Mr. Donnelly's show of discretion, Boswell nodded and went back to his dinner just as ours appeared. I dug in manfully and, may I say, hopefully at the considerable slice of beef roast placed before me.

"I understand, of course," said Boswell. "Sir John Fielding would not want it otherwise. I assume the matter is indeed grave, as you say, and is presently under inquiry."

"You are free to draw that assumption. Many shall do so tomorrow when the notice appears."

And then Boswell picked up the bottle before him and splashed wine in the empty glasses around the table. He began a discourse which, had it come from any other source, should have won my respect. He was not, after all, a stupid man: merely one, as I later came to judge, who was vain, sometimes to the point of foolishness.

"Let us consider this," said he. "If we take 'misadventure' to mean, as it so often does, an *accident*—that is, an unplanned and disastrous occurrence—then there would be no need to use the word. Unless, of course, the facts of the 'misadventure'—that is, the accident—were of such an embarrassing nature that they could not be disclosed. There are such occasions. Yet they are not such as to rout the magistrate of the Bow Street Court from an eating place before he has eaten—and *before* the arrival of Dr. Johnson, the meeting of whom seemed to be the reason for his visit to this establishment. And in *such* a *rush,* I might add. It would have been handled in more leisurely fashion. No, I believe we may put aside 'misadventure' in its more common meaning, in this case. It was surely not an accident.

"What other possibilities are there? Suicide? Had Lord Goodhope reason for such an extreme act? He was known at court, was until recently said to be a favorite of the King as a defender of the King's less defensible policies. A gifted speaker, I'm told: part actor and part controversialist. I myself never heard him and saw him but twice and then only at a distance. But I did say he was *until recently* a favorite of the King, did I not? Word reached me even in my distant northern eyrie that he had fallen somewhat from grace. My informant pleaded ignorance as to the reason. He knew only with some certainty that the Royal door had been shut to Lord Goodhope. Would that be enough to move a man to take his life? Hardly.

"Financial problems? More likely. He was a gambler, a reckless frequenter of the Bilbo establishment, as you may or may not know. Yet he drew good rents from his holdings in Lancashire. And if not inexhaustible, his resources would certainly be difficult to exhaust. He was not a poor man, nor would he ever be likely to become one.

"There is another matter that dissuades us from considering suicide. Perhaps you are aware of it, Mr. Donnelly?"

"Perhaps I am."

I did not like Boswell luring my companion into his conjectures. I did not like it because I was sure Sir John would not.

"You are Irish, are you not?"

"I take pride in it, sir."

"And Roman Catholic, as well? Donnelly, I'm told, is a Catholic name."

"That is my faith, yes."

"So, I've heard it whispered, was it also Lord Goodhope's."

Whatever effect Boswell hoped to achieve by this, he failed to achieve it, for the surgeon simply sat and looked the other man in the eye for many long seconds, gave an abrupt nod, and returned to his meat. The effect of this was to rattle Boswell somewhat. Whereas up to this point he had spoken in measured fashion, using a somewhat insinuating tone, he now fairly exploded forth.

"Well . . . well . . . you see my implication, of course!" He got no response from Mr. Donnelly, and so he blundered on: "His family is a very old one in Lancashire, which as *you* must know, is a very hotbed of Papist loyalty. They rose under the Stuarts. They got their title from the second Charles and rose in favor under the former George."

"You are very well studied, sir."

"Then murder! It must be murder! Suicide is out of the question! In law, misadventure may signal accidental homicide without blame. Why not *with* blame? Misadventure by murder!"

Boswell was fairly shouting it out. Talk had stopped at a number of tables around our own. Patrons leaned over on their benches to catch what would be said next.

Mr. Donnelly kept chewing solemnly, swallowed his bite, and then said: "When I told you in advance the contents of tomorrow's notice, which I now understand to have been a mistake, I unwittingly left serious matters open for discussion. I did not, however, give you leave to publicize them, sir."

Boswell then looked around him and noted the expectant faces. He dropped his voice to a whisper: "Forgive me, do. I became a bit carried away, I fear. But I should think you as a lawyer would understand that I—"

"I am *not* a lawyer, Mr. Boswell."

"But I assumed you were somehow associated with the Bow Street Court . . . the boy . . . Sir John . . . last night . . ." He trailed off quite pitifully, seeking words to take him out of his predicament. At last he came to a full stop and forced a smile. "What is your profession, if I may ask?"

"I am a surgeon, until recently of the King's Navy."

A certain glint came into Boswell's eye. Without asking

leave, he took the bottle before him and emptied it into Mr. Donnelly's glass. Then he waved the empty bottle at the server, calling for another.

If Boswell had previously impressed me, in spite of myself, with his lawyer's logic, he now came forward seemingly as a conspirator, looking this way and that before he spoke. Would that he had been so circumspect when speaking of Lord Goodhope's "misadventure"!

"I had not realized, of course, that you were a surgeon," said he. "Had I but known, I would not, of course, have troubled you with such matters as I did earlier. Please accept my apology."

"I accept it," said Mr. Donnelly, taking a good gulp of Boswell's wine. He belched manfully and pushed his empty plate away. I was still struggling with mine.

"I would, however, have taken up another matter with you. It is a medical matter that has troubled me greatly over the past years. I take it that you possess a diploma. You are not . . . a barber?"

"My diploma is from the University of Vienna," said Mr. Donnelly, puffing a bit. He may have seen in Boswell the possibility of a patient. "What is the nature of your difficulty?"

"Venereal."

Mr. Donnelly looked suddenly so uncomfortable that I ransacked my English, Latin, and French vocabularies for some meaning to this new word. I could only suppose, having done so, that it had something to do with the goddess Venus. Was Mr. Boswell then lovesick? He didn't seem the sort, somehow.

"Please," said Boswell, "let me explain. You, as a ship's surgeon, must have treated complaints such as mine scores, even hundreds, of times."

"Well, I . . . I . . ." Now Mr. Donnelly seemed at a loss for words.

"Let me explain. I have had eight attacks since the age of nineteen, or perhaps not quite so many. It's difficult to say. Oh, trust me, I know a full-fledged case of it: the gleet, the sore on the member, the painful pissing, the nasty discharge. Oh, believe me, I know!''

''You're talking . . . you're talking . . .'' Mr. Donnelly seemed quite at a loss for words.

''Of the clap, simply put. Yes, sir, the clap. Now, there are two things that trouble me. First of all, there is my difficulty at putting a number to my attacks. For instance, does a clear discharge without the other symptoms constitute a full attack? The doctors in Edinburgh differ on this.''

''Please, sir, the boy!'' He gestured toward me, though I had no idea how I figured in this.

''Ah, well,'' said Boswell with a shrug, dismissing me as a consideration in this matter. ''Secondly,'' he continued, ''and again I address you in particular as a ship's surgeon, I must ask, how may I prevent this in the future? I've tried armour, and it may work, but it prevents pleasure. What do you suggest?''

''Have you considered . . .'' And at this point Mr. Donnelly jumped to his feet. ''Have you considered *abstinence, sir?*''

''Ah yes,'' said Boswell, ''abstinence. It never seems to work so well with me.''

''Jeremy, are you done with dinner?''

''Oh, quite,'' said I, glad at last to be released from my task.

''Then let's be off.''

''Oh, don't go,'' said Boswell. ''Dr. Johnson promised to come by. He's at dinner with that dreary Mrs. Thrale, who didn't invite me. When he comes, I'll introduce you.''

''Tempted as I am by that prospect, I must, with Jeremy, take leave of you. This has been, let me assure you, a most interesting meeting.''

Boswell stood, and the two men then shook hands. As he did so, Boswell assured him that it had, for him, been a great pleasure. With that, Mr. Donnelly took me by the sleeve and dragged me out of the Cheshire Cheese, pausing only long enough to settle up the bill on his way out.

Finally, we were out on the street again, and if the air that we then breathed may not have been as pure as what Mr. Donnelly had breathed on occasions in the Austrian Alps, it was at least immeasurably purer than what we had inhaled for the past hour or so inside the Cheshire Cheese.

My companion drew in great draughts of it. I, too, took it in, feeling the healthier for it.

Then we set off walking exactly in the direction we had earlier come. For a few minutes we moved along together in silence. Then Mr. Donnelly turned to me and asked: ''Jeremy, who *was* that terrible man?''

Chapter 6

*In which Mr. Clairmont is heard from and
a discovery made*

THE NEXT MORNING, A VERY BUSY ONE, BEGAN WITH MR. Donnelly's promised visit to Lady Fielding. The knock came early. Mrs. Gredge led the surgeon to the kitchen where I sat at breakfast. I jumped from my chair, thinking it the polite thing to do, but he waved me back to my place.

"Would you like something, sir?" asked Mrs. Gredge. "All I can offer immediate is bread and butter. But if you like, I'll cut a pair of rashers off the flitch and cook them up."

"Nothing, thank you," said he. "If you will but notify Sir John of my arrival. He's up, I take it?"

"Up and about. In truth, I think he barely slept at all last night. She passed a terrible time, she did."

"Well, I may be able to help that."

"It would be a blessing."

That said, she disappeared up the stairs. The surgeon had with him his black bag. He placed it on the table and opened it up. With a nod to me, most professional, he busied himself with its contents, taking from it a mortar and pestle and a large corked bottle.

"Sir John will see you up here," called Mrs. Gredge from above.

Mr. Donnelly started off, then turned to me as with an afterthought. "Jeremy, would you be a good lad and put some water in the pot and put it on the fire?"

"For tea, sir?"

"A kind of tea: a potion. You needn't fill the pot full. A little water will do."

And then he, too, marched up the stairs while I busied myself doing his bidding. A few minutes later, I heard the two men talking in hushed voices on the stairs—not so quietly, however, that I could not hear them plainly.

"What is the nature of the potion?" inquired Sir John most somberly.

"A tea of opium. I have a considerable supply of seeds from India."

"I asked after it to one of the doctors who preceded you. He advised against it: He cautioned there was great potential for an addiction which might be difficult to satisfy."

"Addiction? Yes, but it hardly matters now, does it?"

Sir John took pause at that. "Hardly," he agreed after a moment. Then of a sudden, he asked, "It will not shorten her life, will it?"

"Believe me, I could never in conscience—"

"Forgive me for asking."

The pot was boiling when they arrived in the kitchen. Mr. Donnelly took it off the fire, allowing it to cool a bit as he made his preparations. Then he turned to me and asked, "Jeremy, would you go up and fetch the woman? What is her name?"

Sir John looked up from the place he had taken across from me at the table. "Mrs. Gredge," said we both together.

"I want her to know how this is done."

Without another word, I raced up the stairs but held myself back from knocking loudly on the door: tapped, rather, and gave a quiet call to Mrs. Gredge inside.

When she appeared, I instructed her that the surgeon wished her below in the kitchen.

And then, from inside, a faint voice: "Is that the boy? Is that Jeremy?"

"Yes, mum, it is," said Mrs. Gredge.

"I should like to meet him."

As she passed by me, opening wide the door, Mrs. Gredge whispered fiercely in my ear, "Don't dare upset her, now!"

I advanced timorously into the room. There in the bed, near hidden by the bedclothes, a tiny figure rested, propped slightly on two pillows. It was as if her head itself, the only part of her visible to me, had shrunk inside her nightcap.

"Come ahead," said she in that same faint voice, which was like unto a sick child's. "I want to see you close."

I went to her bedside. Her face, once quite comely, for I have seen an earlier likeness Sir John kept ever after, was then so wizened by her disease that she seemed an old woman. I learned later that she was not yet forty. Her lips were pursed against her suffering.

I stood there awkwardly for I know not how long and then attempted a bow.

"Well done," said she. "Are you a good boy, Jeremy?"

"I try to be, mum . . . Lady Fielding."

"Jack thinks you are."

Who could Jack be? And then, of course, I knew. What was I to reply? Since I had no notion, I did what is best in such a situation and kept my silence.

"He is usually good in matters of character, and so I shall trust him in this. Jeremy, if he chooses you for a son, I want you to be a good son to him. Help him as much as he will allow." She stopped of a sudden, her words occluded by a new and fiercer flash of pain. Her lips quite disappeared into her mouth. It frightened me to look upon her.

Then the spasm passed, and at last, her eyes bright, she

resumed: "He needs a son. I was never able to give him one. Be not forward, but help him, and do all he asks of you."

Together we heard the trio ascending the stairs.

"I'll do as you say, Lady Fielding." I choked it forth somehow.

"I know you will. I'm glad . . . for the chance to meet you."

They entered, Sir John, Mr. Donnelly, and Mrs. Gredge. I fell back from the bedside, leaving them room to do whatever they had come to do. Mr. Donnelly had in his hand a small, steaming cup which he bore with great care.

Mrs. Gredge grasped me by the wrist, and in that same sharp whisper I had heard from her last, she said, "You may go now, Jeremy." Then she released me, sending me on my way.

Truth to tell, reader, I was glad to be gone from that room. Quite overwhelmed was I by the meeting and by my brief conversation with Lady Fielding. Only to be there beside her brought back to me woeful memories of my mother's last hours. She had no last words to give me: delirious or unconscious she was through it all, ignorant even of my brother's death. My father nursed her to the end. Strange to say, neither he nor I were infected by the fever.

But the import of Lady Fielding's words filled me with awe, even something akin to terror. In the truest sense, I had not grasped their meaning. The idea that one might trade a dead father for a live one seemed near monstrous to me. Though in spite of her pain, she seemed in full possession of her faculties; still, what she had said seemed perhaps the product of delirium. In short, I was confused and greatly burdened.

This should explain my state when Sir John entered the kitchen. I had been weeping at the table, but upon seeing him I wiped my tears and set about to hide it from him. I might have succeeded, but my nose betrayed me. I sniffed quietly twice.

He went straight to where I sat, felt for my shoulder, found it, and gave it a squeeze.

"Aye, Jeremy Proctor," said he, "it is a sad thing, is it not? Sad beyond telling."

By the time we had settled once again in the library of the Goodhopes' residence, carpenters had arrived to repair the broken door. They were a noisy pair, making plain with whistling and joking their indifference to us and our concerns.

It had taken the better part of two hours for us to arrive thus far. Although Mr. Donnelly had left immediately after he had ministered his potion to Lady Fielding, such faith had he in its working, Sir John sat by her bedside until she succumbed to a deep sleep. Mrs. Gredge found diverse chores for me until Sir John appeared, his tricorn on his head and his stick in his hand, ready to depart.

As we had walked together to St. James Street, I gave him a summary of my findings of the evening before. I was disappointed that he set little store by my hope that I had found the secret exit from the house out beyond the privet hedge through my experience with a fractious team of horses. "I do believe there is something there," said I to him, "perhaps a plate of some kind covering a tunnel to the house." He replied: "I think it more likely that what you stumbled upon was the coal hole, or perhaps some entry to the cesspool. You might look into that sometime today." Of my report on Lord Goodhope's "impromptus," he had only this to say: "Although I am grieved at what you tell me, I am not surprised. It confirms Lady Goodhope's suspicions, which were told me in your absence. I shall want to talk to both of those young girls when we arrive at our destination." And finally when I sought to repeat James Boswell's clever discourse on the likely meanings of "misadventure," and found myself floundering somewhat, he waved me to silence. "Enough," said Sir John. "Though the man is a popinjay, he is no fool. And as he reasons his way to murder, so will the multitude by means more crude. They seek sensation, and murder provides the greatest. I would that she had not placed that notice, but I suppose it had to be done. In truth, what Boswell said of Goodhope was quite correct. I had occasion to hear his lordship speak against a bill I had helped write, and he was most eloquent: pernicious in his reasoning, but eloquent nonetheless. What he had not for arguments, he supplied in histrionics. The man had a voice, though, I vow, quite unforgettable."

And so we came to St. James Street, all lathered from our brisk walk on that raw spring morning. Once set on his course, Sir John traveled as well by shank as young Mr. Donnelly. His demanding knock at the Goodhope residence was answered late by none other than Ebenezer Tepper, who pulled on his forelock country-fashion and threw wide the door.

When Sir John inquired after Lady Goodhope, the footman said quite respectfully, "Oo's getten a gast, sor." Then he gestured grandly toward the sitting room nearby.

At that moment she appeared at the open door to that room, appearing quite distressed; in her hand she held what appeared to be a letter with a broken seal. Behind her, to my surprise, stood Gabriel Donnelly. I wished to notify Sir John of this last, yet saw no opportunity. He was immediately aware of her presence, however, and turned to her with a bow.

"Your ladyship," said he.

"Sir John," said she, "you are most welcome this particular morning, for I have received a most worrying communication."

"Of what nature?"

"Of . . . well, of a financial nature. Would you not say so, Mr. Donnelly?"

"Mr. Donnelly?" said Sir John, showing some surprise. "*You* are the guest?"

"I summoned him," said she, "the moment I received this crude, presumptuous letter. I needed his counsel. Yours, of course, is also welcome."

"That is gratifying," he allowed; and then he observed a bit slyly: "Mr. Donnelly has had a busy morning."

"That I have," said the surgeon, "and each of my calls has been made in friendship and with due respect."

"Indeed," said Sir John, mollified and near apologetic, "I am sure that is true. My poor wife sleeps now in spite of her illness, thanks only to you. But now I understand your wish to get on quickly to your next appointment."

"Enough of this," said Lady Goodhope in a manner most willful. "Will you or will you not listen to this letter?"

"Of course! Of course!"

"Then come in, and shut the door. I do not wish this to get past Potter. I shall explain his role in a moment."

She led the way into the room. All seated themselves save for me. I remained standing by the chair Sir John occupied, thinking it the proper attitude for a magistrate's helper.

I noted that Mr. Donnelly regarded her with the utmost seriousness and sympathy. Lady Goodhope, holding the letter close and thus betraying her myopia, cleared her throat and began to read: " 'My dear Lady Goodhope,' it begins. Can you imagine such impudence in that salutation? Especially from one such as this?"

"Such as what, Lady Goodhope?" asked Sir John.

"Well, just listen!"

"Please continue."

Again, she cleared her throat: " 'Please have my condolences as is due you at a time such as this, for I saw early today that Lord Goodhope died in the *Public Advertiser*. It grieves me sore, for he was known to me well since he was often in my establishment as gentlemen do for games of hazard which is what I offer. And it grieves me special for I must inform you that Lord Richard, now deceased, piled up such a pile of unpaid debts and promises of payment that I was forced two weeks past to ask of him some earnest of payment. So we two settled on an agreement which was drawn up by my lawyer. The nature of it is such that I would call it a mortgage, but my lawyer says it is a lien. The amount of this lien, giving the benefit of the doubt to the lawyer because I knew he must have the right name for what he himself wrote, is twenty thousand pounds, and the property in question is the house to which I have directed my man to deliver this. To make it plain, unless you or someone in his name can pay this debt by the end of the month, you must move out and give the house to me. I could show you or anybody the debts I hold on Lord Goodhope, whilst he was alive, and you would see that his debts amount to far more than twenty thousand pounds. Yet it is a handsome house, and I would like to live in it. So I will settle for that. Send anyone you want to look at the lien and the promises of payment.' ''

She looked up. Her eyes flashed. She beat a well-shod foot down upon the floor. ''There!'' said she, ''would you not say he has tested my limit?''

''How is it signed?'' asked Sir John.

''With great effrontery, of course!'' She brought the letter up close again and read the last two lines: '' 'I remain your humble and obedient servant, John Francis Bilbo.' '' She sniffed nobly. ''Servant *indeed!*''

''Hmmm,'' said Sir John, ''Black Jack Bilbo.'' He mused a moment. ''And how does Potter figure in this?''

''That was my suggestion,'' said Mr. Donnelly.

''To wit?''

''That we send someone to examine the document in question, at least insofar as to say if the signature on it is truly Lord Goodhope's.''

''Is there any reason to doubt that it is?''

''Well, I . . . I . . .'' Lady Goodhope seemed quite at a

loss for words. "Certainly Lord Goodhope gambled. Yet to such an extent as this? Surely not!"

"Some," said Sir John, "have lost far more. You'll recall, Lady Goodhope, that my first advice to you was to look into Lord Goodhope's finances. Have you done that yet?"

"No," she admitted, her ill temper still somewhat in evidence.

"But we intend to do it now, certainly," put in Mr. Donnelly.

"In any case," said Lady Goodhope, "that was when you supposed his death to be a suicide. I taught you your error in that."

"Ah," said Sir John, with a bow of his head, "indeed you did, indeed you did."

"But could it be," asked Mr. Donnelly, "that Lady Goodhope is liable for such debts as this one?"

"Not she," said Sir John, "but rather Lord Goodhope's estate. If she wishes to keep it somewhat intact for her own comfort and the prospects of her son, then she must see that her late husband's debts are paid: even those to which she may have some moral objections, *such as this one.*"

"Surely, Sir John—"

"That is the law, Lady Goodhope," Sir John interrupted her sternly. "We cannot pick and choose among debts. We must pay them all. Again, I can only advise you to look into your late husband's finances. Find his solicitor. It may well be that this lien held by Mr. Bilbo can be paid from other funds. You have, after all, until the end of the month: better than a week. Use that time."

She also put a stern face to him. "To be frank," said she, "I had been considering quite seriously the thought of selling this house. As I believe I told you previously, this has never been my home. That has always been in Lancashire. This was the place that my husband maintained his city life and, if you will pardon me, held his revels. To it he required me to come a few weeks out of the year, spring and autumn, and the rest of the time it was his. And so, you see, I have no sentiment attached to it. I would gladly sell it, but I'll not see it *given* away to some gambler to whom my husband may have owed a few quid.''

''You count twenty thousand as a few?'' asked Sir John, rather severely.

''That debt has yet to be verified,'' said she.

With that, Sir John rose, dropped his head in a casual salute, and said to her: ''Well, Lady Goodhope, I wish you good fortune. I sincerely hope that the matter of verification goes in your favor. But now I must get on with the criminal aspects of this matter. You have on your staff of servants two kitchen helpers by the names of Annie and Meg, family names unknown.''

''Do we?'' She seemed quite ignorant of them. ''I was unaware.''

''I wish to talk to them in that order: Annie first, and then Meg.''

She fluttered her hand from where she sat. ''Let that be known to Potter, or perhaps better, since he is away, to Ebenezer.''

''Ah yes, Ebenezer Tepper. I wished to ask you about him. He is quite the stranger here, is he not?''

''Indeed he is.''

''How came he here, and when?''

''When? Oh, quite recently, only in the last few days.''

''And how did that come to pass?''

''Shortly after I arrived, but ten days past, one of the regular footmen turned up missing.''

''Missing?''

''Yes, he simply vanished. To fill the place, I suggested we send to Lancashire for Ebenezer. I make no secret that I am somewhat partial to him. He is a good lad generally, and a year ago he saved my son from bodily harm. My late husband had no objection, in fact seemed quite indifferent in the matter, and so it was done.''

Sir John stood silent for a long moment. ''And why was

I not apprised of the disappearance of the footman? What was his name?'' he asked at last.

"I've no idea. Servants,'' said she with a grand shrug, ''they come and go. Do you think it may have some bearing on Lord Goodhope's death?''

"It may.''

"Then it is good that it came out now, though I don't see how it could matter.''

"That is my job, Lady Goodhope: to see how things matter.''

"As you say, Sir John.''

"I take my leave, then, and thank you.''

We started for the door accompanied by Mr. Donnelly, who had risen with Sir John and waited patiently for the leave-taking. We paused there as Mr. Donnelly stood, one hand on the knob of the door, and spoke earnestly to Sir John in a low voice.

"I thank you, sir,'' said he, "for speaking reason to her. She has not the slightest notion of how her husband's accounts stood. I understand from her that you offered names of reliable men who might make a survey of the late Lord Goodhope's situation. If I could have them now, perhaps I could . . .''

"One name only can I supply here and now, that of Moses Martinez. He is a Jew and an honest man. He has a place of business just down from Cheshire Cheese on Fleet Street. I do not recall the number, but he is well known thereabouts.''

"I shall find it.''

"Just one question, Mr. Donnelly. Where is the corpus in question?''

"Lord Goodhope's? Why, at the embalmer's. Lady Goodhope has decided to bury him at a cemetery near Grandhill—that is, near the estate in Lancashire. It seeemd appropriate to have him embalmed for the journey.''

"I see. Well, if she intends to follow soon after for the funeral, I may have to detain her.''

"I had suspected as much, Sir John. Mr. Martinez may well require her presence, as well."

"Indeed."

Then, just as Mr. Donnelly made to open the door to ease us into the hall, a knock came upon it. The surgeon swung it wide and revealed Potter standing rigid and erect but somewhat out of breath, as if he had just run a great distance.

"I have a report for Lady Goodhope," he announced loudly in a manner most important.

It seemed to be me who was blocking his way. He frowned me out of his path, and strode to the center of the sitting room.

"You may deliver your report, Potter," said she. "There is nothing to hide from these gentlemen."

"As you wish, your ladyship. But I fear I bear bad news. I have viewed the document in question, and I must vouch for the signature. It is indeed Lord Goodhope's. Mr. Bilbo was most cooperative. He also showed me the individual promissory bills. They also bore m'lord's signature, often not legible and merely scrawled, but indeed they seemed to bear *his* scrawl."

"We shall see," said she, making of her face a mask without expression.

"Indeed, your ladyship. There is one more thing, however."

"And what is that?"

"While at the establishment of Mr. Bilbo I chanced to meet Mr. Charles Clairmont, who is known to you. He was distressed at having just heard of his brother's death and wishes permission to call on you."

"That he may not have," said she with great certainty. "That Mr. Clairmont may *never* have."

Having heard what I have quoted, Sir John turned from the room and stalked down the hall with me in hot pursuit. Catching him up, I found him in a sudden dark temper. He stopped suddenly, growling to himself in a tone I had not heard from him before. I could but wonder at his sudden change. I hesitated, torn between my fear of disturbing him in such a state and my wish to help.

At last I made bold to offer: "May I do something for you, sir?"

He turned to me, seething with anger, though not (I was relieved to note) at me. "Jeremy," said he, "do you recall those intemperate remarks I made but two nights past on the defects of womankind?"

"Yes sir, I do," said I.

"I may have later given the impression that I repented them. *I do not!* They all obtain!" He slammed his stick down upon the carpet. "What now do we find as addenda to Lady Goodhope's reluctant account? A missing servant and a materialized brother! Not one but two surprises! Well, I tell you, my boy, I've had my fill of surprises. Do you see that pompous ass of a majordomo about?"

"You mean Potter, sir?"

"I do indeed. *Bring him here.*"

In fact, I did see Potter, for at just that moment he was showing Mr. Donnelly out. I hurried to him and, just as he shut the door, informed him that Sir John wished to talk with him at once. He greeted this with a rather pained expression, but accompanied me halfway down the hall to the point where Sir John had taken his position.

For the most part, I think you will agree from the samples offered thus far that Sir John Fielding tended to be a rather gentle interrogator. He was not gentle with Potter. He demanded to know the history of Charles Clairmont. Potter exhibited reluctance, pleading discretion in a family matter, but Sir John would have none of that; shaking his stick at him, he threatened him with a charge of impeding a criminal investigation. The butler quailed at that and gave in summary a history of the man in question.

Charles Clairmont was indeed the brother of the late Lord Goodhope, though a half-brother only. There was no question of him inheriting the title, for a bar sinister separated him from succession. Clairmont, approximately the same age as the late lord, was the son of their father's London mistress, acknowledged, brought up in good circumstances, with a comfortable fortune settled upon him at the time of his majority. An ambitious man, he subsequently took that fortune with him to the West Indies where he engaged in commerce with great success. He had returned to London many times since, on each visit exhibiting evidence of his growing riches in the purchases that he made of costly goods for transport back to the Caribbean.

"And why such hostility between Lady Goodhope and Mr. Clairmont?" demanded Sir John.

A look passed over Potter's face which indicated he was about to tell Sir John to ask her ladyship herself about that. But then he thought better of it: "It stems, I believe, from the fact that he attended their wedding uninvited. And because uninvited, he took the occasion to make a drunken commotion that was in no wise seemly. Rather ugly, really. Nevertheless, he and Lord Goodhope had continued to maintain relations over the years of a more or less cordial nature. Mr. Clairmont never failed to call on him during his visits to England, though always in London and never when Lady Goodhope was in residence."

"And you chanced to see him at the Bilbo establishment this very morning?"

"I did, sir, yes."

"And what was his business there?"

"I cannot rightly say. He was not there for gaming. The tables had not opened yet. His business was with the proprietor. It was from him he had learned of Lord Goodhope's death. He said he had just arrived from the islands."

"Where?"

"He did not say, sir."

"Ah, well." Sir John took but a moment to ruminate over the matter. "If he sought permission to call on Lady Goodhope, he must have given you an address where he might be reached."

"Uh, yes, he did, sir: a lodging house of good repute on the Strand. I have it here."

The butler began fumbling through his coat.

"Keep it," said Sir John. "Send one of the footmen, or go yourself, and convey Lady Goodhope's harsh message. Tell him, too, that his presence is required in my chambers at Bow Street Court promptly at five o'clock. Mind you, Potter, the word is *required*. Is that understood?"

"Understood, yes, sir." He began shuffling his feet, as if making ready to go.

But Sir John had not yet finished with him. "Now," said he, "we come to the matter of the vanished footman. When did he disappear?"

"Ten days past—or eleven now, I suppose."

"Which is it, man," said Sir John harshly, "ten or eleven?"

Shaken somewhat, Potter spoke quickly, his words came all in a rush: "A bit difficult to say, sir. The man vanished overnight with his clothes and possessions. He had wages coming, too!"

"You count this as passing strange?"

"Oh, I do, sir, yes! Yes, I do!"

"And what was his name? What was his appearance? How long had he been in employ?"

Now was Potter truly rattled. He looked right and left, as if he were seeking the answers elsewhere. Not finding them, he faced up to Sir John at last: "He had been on the house staff about a year, no more. He was a large man, strongly built, whose strength made him useful moving heavy loads about the house."

"Good, good. And his name?"

"Richard, sir, same as the master's."

"Is that how he was called about the house?"

"Uh, no, sir. That might have caused some confusion. About the house he was called Dick."

"I take it, " said Sir John, "that he had a family name. Even the least of us is granted one."

"I'm sure he had one, sir, but it slips my mind at the moment."

Then, to my surprise, Sir John, who had been most severe in his tone up to that point, chose to soften it. Yet in his words there was lodged a dark threat.

"Well, think upon it," said he to Potter. "It must surely be listed in the household records for the past year. Search it out as you continue to hunt for the house plan I directed you to bring me. But think upon that footman's family name, and whilst you do, think also upon that charge of impeding a criminal investigation with which I threatened you. It was not an idle threat, nor is it a charge to be taken lightly. Conviction could lead to months, even years in prison, depending upon the circumstances. But though serious, it is not half so grave as complicity in a capital crime. That, as you may know, is punishable by hanging. Now with all this in mind, would you like to make one last effort at recollection?"

Sweat stood forth on Potter's face. The proposition put to him by Sir John could not have inspired the fear there, were he as innocently ignorant as he pretended to be. Perhaps he feared his interrogator less than some other not then present.

He struggled apoplectically to speak, and finally, after taking a deep breath, managed to form the words he sought.

"It has just come to me, sir—I mean, the footman's surname. It was . . . Dillon."

"His name then is Dick Dillon?"

Quite deflated, he managed a nod, then added quietly, "Yes, sir."

"Well, perhaps I have good news for you then, Potter. You have exhibited signs of mortal dread that, if I may say so, even a blind man could read. If Dick Dillon has frighted you so, and he is doubtless to be feared, then you may rest easy. He is now in custody at Newgate, awaiting trial on a capital crime."

Far from resting easy, Potter then exhibited the greatest

confusion. Yet he managed to present this to Sir John: "I am relieved somewhat. He left a note, threatening any who sought to follow."

"Ah, you neglected to mention that."

"So I did."

"Do you have the note here in the house?"

"No, sir. I showed it to the master, and he destroyed it."

"A pity. Now, if you will be so good, please send word to the kitchen that I wish to speak to the cook's helpers, Annie and Meg, in the library. And do look into notifying Mr. Charles Clairmont of my demand to see him at five in Bow Street."

Sir John nodded pleasantly then, and added, "Thank you, Potter. That will be all."

Thus came we finally to the library where the carpenters whistled and joked and sometimes did a bit of work; and where I interrogated the interrogator on his knowledge of his subject.

"Sir John," said I, "his fear was written on his face. How came you to know that? He spoke well enough."

"My boy, fear has a smell. You may not credit it, but it is true. It was very rank upon our man Potter during those last few minutes."

"Was it you he feared? The law?"

"I should like to think so," said he, "but probably only partly. He seemed to be caught betwixt and between. There is something, or more exactly someone, he also fears. And it is not Dick Dillon."

"I felt that, too," said I, agreeing eagerly.

"Did you? Truly? Good lad." He proceeded through the room with his stick and found the desk, and then the chair where the dead man had sat. There he took his place, and having mused a moment, he added: "Perhaps I should have turned the screws on him a bit tighter. The man obviously has more to tell us. But it should be interesting to see which way he runs now that he has had a scare put in him. We may learn more that way.''

It was at that moment that Annie-of-the-kitchen appeared, causing comment and stir immediately among the carpenters. She was indeed a buxom lass, the kind to whom men make remarks on the street: or did in those times. Remarks were made to her at the door by the youngest of the carpenters, probably an apprentice, down on his knees before the door. She giggled and slapped him playfully on the shoulder as she pranced past him and made her way into the library. As she passed me close by, she reached out and pinched my arm in a way I found quite painful. And she whispered a sharp accusation: *''Tattler!''* Then, quite ladylike, she settled into the chair opposite Sir John and smoothed her apron.

''At your service, m'lord,'' said she to him.

Yet he spoke not to her but to me: ''Jeremy, I wonder if you might remove yourself a bit from us? Perhaps to that far corner of the room? I remember you taking a particular interest in books. Why not pick among them a bit there? We must do all we can to make Mistress Annie comfortable talking here, don't you think?''

''As you say, Sir John.''

And so, disappointed, I left, looking back just in time to see Annie sticking out her tongue at me quite impudently. The carpenters laughed at that, and I slunk into my corner. All I lacked, it seemed to me, was a dunce cap and a stool. I pulled down a book almost at random and began riffling the pages, as I strained my ears to hear what passed between the two seated at the desk.

Alas, without much success, I fear. Their conversation passed between them in low tones, and at the distance to which I had been exiled, not quite distinct. From time to time, a word, a phrase, or more likely a name would emerge. There seemed to be, at one point, a good many names passed from Annie to Sir John. He would, of course, be interested in those who were present at Lord Goodhope's "impromptus." Were these the names she gave him? I do recall Lucy Kilbourne's and Black Jack Bilbo's were bandied between them.

What struck me as most odd then, though less so now, was the frivolous fashion in which the two conversed. Though they continued to speak throughout in hushed tones, not to say whispers, their talk was frequently punctuated by laughter: deep rumbles on the part of Sir John and giggles from Annie. It was as if the two were old chums gossiping together. Such a contrast was it with the severe, even threatening manner which he showed, only a few minutes before, to the butler! Could Annie's winning way have caused him to soften? Or was it perhaps some stratagem, by me then misunderstood? The latter, surely, for I never knew him to question two witnesses in exactly the same manner.

Unendurably long as the time seemed to me there in my corner, Annie's interrogation, if such it could be called, lasted no more than a quarter of an hour, and quite probably less. When it was finished, he rose, dipping his head to her most politely, and gave her his thanks. She, in turn, curtsied to him prettily and said goodbye.

As we passed, I making my way to Sir John and she heading for the door, she gave me a saucy wink of her eye and said, "He ain't half bad, is he now?"

"Oh, Annie, my dear!" called Sir John, thus detaining her on the spot.

"Yes, m'lord?"

"Would you be so good as to send in Mistress Meg?"

"I will, m'lord," said she, "though you'll not get much out of her."

"Well, we must try," said he. "We must try."

"He'll see," whispered Annie to me. And squeezing my hand, she said: "I forgive you for tattling."

Then she left in a great, flouncing rush, and I saw no more of her.

I went to Sir John, who had remained standing at the

desk. "A lively child," said he to me of Annie, "though I fear for her future. Perhaps I can find a place for her on some other household staff. Otherwise, I warrant that she is for the streets."

Not quite grasping the import of this, I said: "As you say, sir."

"But Jeremy, listen. I intend to vacate this room to talk to the other young maid. I should like you to remain and begin a serious search for the hidden exit from this room. I'm sure one exists, house plan or no. You indicated that your inspection from the outside led you to question the design and construction of the chimney. I urge you then to give special attention to the fireplace. It is here behind the desk, is it not? Look for protrusions to push, knobs to pull, anything that might set to motion a machine of weights and pulleys to move a section of the wall. That is how—"

At that Sir John turned from me and toward the door. There stood Meg, appearing even more fearful than when last I had seen her. Her eyes were wide. Her hands fluttered over her apron. The carpenters regarded her with indifference.

"Is it she?" asked Sir John of me.

"Yes," said I, "it is Meg."

She came forward in a most uncertain manner.

A transformation came then over Sir John. Of a sudden, he became physically inept and clumsy. He bumped into the corner of the desk, which he had danced around earlier, and cried out mournfully: "Oh, damn!"

I reached to help him, and he growled at me in a whisper: "Away, Jeremy. Leave me be."

And then he advanced with halting steps into the middle of the room, swinging his stick before him with his right hand as with his left he made palsied circles in the air. I had never seen him in this state. He seemed older, weaker, much less able. I followed him quite uncertain.

"Mistress Meg, is that you? Are you there?"

"She nods, Sir John," said I.

"Thank you, Jeremy," said he in a voice most pitiable. Then to her: "I wonder, my girl, would you show a poor blind man out into the garden and sit with him there for a while? Jeremy tells me that the flowers there have begun to bloom and are quite beautiful. If I cannot see them, I should like to smell them. Will you take me there?"

Without a word, of course, though less fearful than moments before, Meg stepped forward with an air of solicitude and took Sir John by the arm.

"Oh, thank you," said he, "you are most kind. And, Jeremy? Carry on."

And together the two left the library. The carpenters paid them not the slightest heed.

Thus left alone, I went to the fireplace and surveyed my task. It was large, as corresponded to the size of the room, about three feet across. The mantelpiece and side masonry were of solid, dark stone, well blackened from long use. It had been fixed for the burning of coal, whereas the fireplace in the hall had not; the latter had no doubt been kept for show, a country touch in a city house. Though I'm sure no cooking was done, a swinging crane, sufficient to suspend a teapot, hung to one side.

In every particular, it seemed most solid. The rear wall was bricked and sturdy. The fire surround was unusually imposing. I stood there and heaved a sigh, wondering where I ought best to start.

Truth to tell, it mattered not. I busied myself for better than a quarter of an hour tugging and pushing. I swung the teapot crane this way and that, even tried hoisting it up and pushing it down. Separately, I tried each of the iron bars of the hob gate, twisting them, pulling them, pounding them. Trying the bricks along the back wall and the side, I managed only to blacken my hands. It was all, in fine, to no avail.

I stood up, stepped well back from the fireplace, and having reached the limit of my patience, gave it a fierce look. Could I have supposed I might frighten it into submission? "Damn!" said I aloud in callow mimicry of Sir John.

Then, in my perplexity, I began to pace. I was attempting to picture the chimney as I had seen it from the garden. What were those details that had stirred my interest? It was the wide, sloping shape of it, was it not?

Perhaps better to remember, I went to the window that overlooked the garden at the rear of the house. My attention was immediately taken by the pair who occupied the stone bench just off the garden path. Sir John sat, his head bowed in silent concentration. He was listening! For Meg, who sat just next to him, her face full exposed to my view with a most earnest look, was speaking into his ear.

For a moment, I stared in amaze. Then I shrank back from the window for fear I might be seen by her. So completely was I taken up with the problem of the fireplace that I had given no thought to them in the garden. Had I done so, I should have been curious that Sir John had spent so long with one so mute as Meg. How he had induced her to speak I could only ponder. What she told him I could only guess.

Unaccountably, this vexed me. Not only had I failed to discover the secret of the fireplace, I had also been forbidden the details divulged first by Annie and now by Meg. It is possible, reader, that it was lustful curiosity thwarted that sent me into a sulk, for I had had time to wonder at those things hinted at so broadly the previous evening by Annie. However that may be, I was vexed and wished to show it. I marched across the room and demanded a hammer from the carpenters. They regarded me with surprise. The younger of the two seemed about to deny me, when the master made a shrug, reached into his box, and handed one over. At least I had the grace to thank him.

Thus armed, I returned to the fireplace and began tapping with the hammer against the back wall and the sides. I must have hoped to touch some hollow place where before my hands had met only solid brick. But hearing no answer to my tap, I tapped even harder, until Sir John came and saved me from doing damage to the bricks.

"What *are* you up to, Jeremy?" said he quite loud behind me.

So taken was I with the task that I had not noted his entrance. In a start, I let the hammer fall from my hand as I jumped to my feet and faced him. "Tapping," I blurted. "I've been searching a hollow behind the bricks."

"Tapping, is it? Nay, Master Jeremy, *banging* is what it was—banging in a most loud and unseemly fashion! Leave off this minute. We cannot further disturb this house."

Quite humiliated by his displeasure, I could only mutter, "Yes, Sir John," as I bent to retrieve the hammer.

"Come along now."

And I trotted to keep up as he led the way from the room. He paused only a brief moment at the door to test the open space with his stick, which gave me a chance to return the hammer to its owner. Then back up the hall we went again. Sir John seemed driven by some urgency which I did not understand. But then, having reached the door to the street, he stopped, turned to his right, and took a few steps forward. He reached out with his stick.

"Is this the door to her sitting room?" he asked. He had it exact.

"It is, yes sir."

With his stick, he made three light touches on the door. "Now those," he said to me, "are taps. Do you detect the difference?"

Before I could answer, the door swung open, and Lady Goodhope stood, curious at the interruption. I noticed that from her closed fist dangled a few beads and a crucifix. "Come in, Sir John," said she. Though she regarded me skeptically, I followed behind him.

He stood in the middle of the small room and delivered his message with dispatch: "M'lady," said he, "I must be to my court session. I ask your permission, however, to allow my young companion to remain. There is more looking to be done in the library."

"Has he not seen it all three times over?"

"The fourth may prove the charm."

"Oh, as you will then."

"Just one more thing," said Sir John. "Have you a likeness of Lord Goodhope about?"

"A very good likeness," said she. "This portrait was painted but a year ago." She gestured to the picture hanging over the fireplace. It was just barely possible to discern in the shape and general outline of the handsome face in the portrait that blackened and bloodied visage I had studied with Mr. Bailey but two nights before. "Do you think there is something accusing in the eyes?" continued Lady Goodhope. "Somehow they persuade me to feel guilty. Why I have no— Ah, but of course you can't see what I mean. Your affliction."

"Indeed," he said, "my affliction. Take a good look at it, Jeremy."

"One thing I must insist on," said she. "If that boy remains, he must take himself down to the kitchen for a good washing. His hands and face are filthy. I'll not have him besmirching the silks and linens about this house. He makes me uneasy merely standing in this room."

"Oh? Is this true, Jeremy?"

I looked at my hands. They were soot covered from the bricks. In the course of my exertions I had wiped perspiraton from my face and no doubt smeared it, as well.

"It would seem so, Sir John. The fireplace . . ."

"Ah yes, of course. Well, I assure you, Lady Goodhope, that he will remedy that directly. You needn't see us out the room. Let's be off, Jeremy."

He found the door without difficulty and in the hall instructed me to close it. "Mind you besmirch nothing, lad," he whispered. "Besmirching is a powerful sin. You have only to consult Mrs. Gredge on that."

We were met at the door by the footman—Henry, not

Ebenezer. He presented Sir John with his tricorn and
opened the door to the street.

"You can find your way back to Bow Street?" Sir John
inquired of me.

I assured him I knew the way.

"If you become disorientated, you have but to inquire.
All know the Bow Street Court. But by no means stay to
nightfall."

I promised, we said our goodbyes, and he left. I then
made direct for the back stairs and the kitchen. While I
well knew my duty was to wash myself, I hoped also to
find young Mistress Meg there. Perhaps, I thought, since
Sir John had persuaded her to speak, she would now talk
generally. I wanted no more than to acquaint myself better
with her. I liked her delicate way and pitied her the mys-
terious ordeal she had suffered.

But alas, when I came to the bottom of the stairs and
into the kitchen, Meg was nowhere to be seen. It was
empty, indeed, except for Ebenezer, who was taking his
ease at the table with a cup of strong tea before him. We
greeted one another politely in our two tongues, and I went
straight to the sink. Filling a basin from the storage tank, I
found soap, took off my coat, rolled up my sleeves, and
got to work.

As I washed, I thought. And as I thought, it seemed to
me that perhaps I had gone about my search in the wrong
manner. Sir John had told me to look in the library for the
concealed exit. I had done his bidding, and it had not
proved fruitful. Perhaps to explore from another direction
might work better. I would need help for that. Would Ebenezer do? Well, thought I, perhaps, for even if I could not
understand his speech, he could understand mine. Could I
persuade him? But surely persuasion was not the answer.
A bold and authoritative tone would suit my cause better.
After all, I was the helper of Sir John Fielding, magistrate
of the Bow Street Court—was I not?

I grabbed a greasy towel and wiped myself fair to dry,

face and hands. Then I turned to Ebenezer and said in my deepest voice: "I shall be needing your help just now. Find a shovel or a flat spade, and get a candle and matches, for we shall be needing them, too."

Ebenezer jumped to his feet immediately and went off in search of the necessities.

No more than an inch of good London dirt concealed the cover to the hole. It had not been hard to find. I had marked its location well by my eye in relation to the hedge gate. Taking the flat spade in hand, I had begun banging down into the soil, moving steadily to the left some distance from the gate. Each downward blow I placed about a foot distant from the last. When, on my seventh or eighth effort, the blade hit a hard surface and the spade danced out of my hand, I recovered it, knowing I had found the spot where my feet had landed in fearful flight from the monstrous horses.

Ebenezer, beside me, had widened his eyes in surprise at my discovery. He grabbbed the spade from my hand and began clearing away the dirt. That did not take long, for the dirt was loose, indicating to me that it had been recently shifted. Had it not been so loose, I might never have detected the place.

What Ebenezer uncovered was a stone cover a little less than a yard square with a pull-hole in the center for lifting. He stuck three fingers of his right hand therein and gave a considerable tug. Yet he, for all his strength, could not pull it completely off. I jammed in the spade and held it, not without difficulty, as he shifted his hold and with both hands eased it back. He rested it against the hedge, a safe distance from the hole that it uncovered.

Together we regarded it. There was a ladder in reasonable repair leading down. From his pocket, Ebenezer produced a thick candle of about eight inches. He then said something to me that I quite failed to understand. After another dip into his pocket, he produced matches and bade me light the candle. That much I understood. I lit the candle, and in a moment he had begun his descent down the ladder, candle in hand. I followed him down.

We descended to a point about ten feet below the level of the ground. There, ducking our heads, bending nearly double, we proceeded in the direction of the house. No mephitic effluvium greeted us, so I could be sure, at least, we were not headed toward the cesspit. It seemed unlikely, too, that we had entered through the coal hole, for it was too far from the house. The passage was wide enough for a man, but it had been buttressed along the way with old timbers, which made it seem dangerous as an old mineshaft and narrowed the way at regular intervals.

In any case, we came to the end, which terminated in another ladder like the one we had descended. Ebenezer, holding the candle, looked to me for instruction.

"Climb to the top," said I, "and tell me what you see."

He went up with a firm step to a point well above me. Ebenezer's feet on the ladder were all I saw of him. All I could make out, peering upward, was an imposing system of gears just to Ebenezer's left, against a wall of bricks.

"Do you see a lever? Something to make the machine turn?"

He moved the candle about, pushed one thing, pulled another, but all without result.

"Nay," said he at last. " 'See nought t'here."

"All right," said I, "stay where you are a bit longer. Give me time to return to the library, and then begin knocking at regular intervals on the wall before you. Do you understand?"

"Aye!"

I then left him, returning the way we had come through the passage, now pitch dark except for the dim shaft of light which marked our entrance to the tunnel. When I arrived at that point and glimpsed the afternoon sky above, I clambered up the ladder as swift as a monkey might. In this way, I reached the level of the privet hedge in just a moment. And in but a moment more, I was through the gate, across the garden, and back into the house.

My first glimpse of the library door gave me pause. It was closed—shut for the first time since Ebenezer and Potter had battered it down. I concluded, rightly, that the carpenters had successfully completed their work in my absence. Had the room then been locked?

Ah, but no. The door gave at the first push of the handle. I pushed it wide and ran straight for the fireplace. Already Ebenezer's knocks had begun. Yet to my surprise and confusion, they were not directly there at the fireplace, but rather a few feet to the left, among the books and behind the bookcase. I took a moment, and with my ear close to the shelves, ascertained their exact location.

Thinking to return his signal, I hastily began pulling books helter-skelter from the shelves. Indeed I was not careful. Some flew left, and some flew right, and some flew open on the floor. Yet I broke none, and therefore felt I had not earned the fury which I was, in the next moment, given.

"You wretched boy!" cried Potter. "How dare you treat the master's books so!"

This, spoken, was my only warning, for when I turned to explain the matter to him, I found him lunging toward me, both hands outstretched as though to throttle me. I ducked and shifted to one side, yet I could not escape one of his vengeful hands. It caught me at the shoulder and slammed me hard against the bookshelves at the spot where Ebenezer had been rapping.

I feared I was in for a thrashing, and indeed I might have been, except as I cowered there, I was surprised by a slow, steady movement against my back. The entire shelf of books was shifting with me upon it.

I stepped clear and sought to read Potter's face. I saw at once surprise, dismay, and anger written in it. He said nothing, but stood quite fixed and staring as the moving bookcase revealed the smiling face of Ebenezer Tepper. In triumph, Ebenezer waved the lighted candle in his hand and let forth a great hoot.

Chapter 7

*In which Charles Clairmont presents himself to
Sir John and we visit the theatre*

IT HAS OFT BEEN SAID THAT IT IS ON THOSE OCCASIONS
when we endeavor to make great haste that we are most
wasteful of time. And so it was proven that afternoon when
I left the Goodhope residence determined to give swift notice to Sir John of my discovery.

Potter, having gawked only a moment in consternation,
had said not a word but stormed from the library in a great
huff. Though I was then sore tempted to follow him out
and make immediate for Bow Street, I remained long
enough to ascertain with Ebenezer the nature of the trigger
device that set the machinery of the secret door in motion.
It operated from both sides of the false wall, though it was
so cleverly recessed on the outside that it had escaped Ebenezer's notice. Then, instructing him to return through the
tunnel and replace the stone cover at its entrance, I pressed
the trigger and sent the bookcase and false wall back on
their slow journey to their rightful place next to the fireplace. I replaced the books I had torn from the shelves, alas
with no greater care than I had given to their removal. That

done, I ran from the room, down the long hall, and out the door. Potter was nowhere to be seen.

In truth, I was certain of the way back from St. James Street when I made my hasty departure. Nevertheless, dodging through the crowded streets, I took a wrong turning and then another, and found myself down an alley much like that one in which I had been so perniciously gulled by Messrs. Bledsoe and Slade-Sayer. Quite at a loss, I returned to the thoroughfare and sought directions. I thought it wise to consult with a woman, believing there was less to fear from the gentler sex.

Thus it was that I approached one of indeterminate age who stood leaning against a wall, smiling at all and sundry who passed her by. She seemed friendly enough.

"With your pardon, ma'am," said I to her, "I should like to ask of you the way to Bow Street."

The smile swiftly faded. She thrust her face close into mine and, quite overwhelming me with a cloud of gin breath, demanded to know what such intelligence as she might provide would be worth to me.

"Why," said I, "I should be grateful to you for it."

"There's grateful and grateful," said she. "How much will you pay, young sir?"

I looked round me a bit in a quandary. On the one hand, it seemed right to leave her where she stood and ask the way of another. Yet my earlier experience with strangers in the city had made me fearful of contact with strangers. Fear won out. We negotiated. She asked a guinea. I laughed at that, and offered her tuppence. And so by degrees we drew closer until we agreed on a shilling. I drew from my pocket one of the four I had left and dropped it in her open palm.

"Put another one like it there, and you can have me in the bargain," said she. "M'crib's just down the alley, pretty." Her smile had returned.

"Please," said I, "I am in a great hurry."

"Oh, you young bucks is always in a rush, particular

under the covers. But if that's the way of it, then listen close, and I'll put you on Bow Street, for I may be a whore but I ain't no thief.''

She was as good as her word and described a route different from the one I had begun, yet presented it in such specific detail that I had no difficulty following it to my destination. I realized she had got the better of me and felt a bumpkin for my ignorance of this vast metropolis to which I had come. I determined to apply myself to my surroundings; and indeed I did so in the months and years that followed, so that today I may boast that few natives of this place know it as well as I.

Once I had Covent Garden in sight, I had no problem in putting my feet on Bow Street and directing them to Number 4. Yet when I entered, I realized the difficulty of my situation. For while I wished to communicate my discovery to Sir John, I could not directly do so, for there he sat at the bench, discharging his official duties. His court was in session. He would not receive it kindly if I was to attempt an interruption: that much was out of the question. And so I took a place near to the door where I might make my exit and hasten through the yard to his chambers at the earliest opportunity.

Sir John sat through two small matters: another action on personal debt and a dispute between merchants on a question of contract. I waited impatiently through them and was gratified at last when, after a brief discussion sotto voce with Mr. Marsden, Sir John declared a brief recess. As he got up and hurried off to the rear of the room, I jumped to my feet, squeezed impolitely through the door between two drabs who had come for the show, and then made my way by circular means to the yard. I arrived just in time to glimpse Sir John entering the privy.

I wanted his attention. Thinking no more of it than that, I went to the door of the privy and knocked quite rudely, calling his name.

''What is it?'' he called from inside. ''Who is there?''

"It is me, Jeremy Proctor."

"Go away, boy. I have a call of nature."

"But I have something important to tell."

"Well, tell it later. I am otherwise engaged." He spoke quite gruff.

At that I shrank back, of a sudden rightfully shamed at my audacity. I took a place some several paces away and stood quite meek awaiting him. At last he reappeared, buttoning his breeches.

He must have sensed me near, for he turned in my direction and said, "Good God, boy, can a man not have a piss without interruption?"

"I do most sincerely beg your pardon, Sir John," said I, "but I had a matter that could not wait."

"Jeremy, there are very few things in this world that cannot wait, and I have just attended to one of them. Now what is this matter that you deem so urgent?"

"I found it," said I.

"Found what?" said he.

"Why, sir, the secret exit from the library. Ebenezer and I together discovered a false wall behind the bookcases."

"Ah, well," said he, "good." He did not seem mightily impressed.

So I persisted: "It was at the end of a tunnel, and the entrance of it was that very same spot I found beyond the privet hedge. Remember, Sir John? You thought it would prove to be no more than the coal hole or—"

"Yes, I recall." He had started back to the building. I hopped to catch him up. "So you proved me wrong. Good boy."

"But," said I, faltering, "but is this not of great importance?"

He stopped then and, with a hand to his chin, seemed to ponder a moment before speaking. "No," said he at last, "it is of relative importance, Jeremy. All logic dictated that such a clandestine egress be there. The deed could not have been carried through without it. Furthermore, the history of the family as Stuart Papists strongly suggested that some entry of the sort would have been provided to smuggle priests in and out of the house in the last century; that is why I kept badgering that pinchfart butler for the house plan. What is now the library may once have done for a chapel. May still do, for it has not escaped my notice that Lady Goodhope now practices that faith quite diligently, albeit in secret—beads, prayers, fasting, et cetera. My inquiries reveal that she was pulled out of a convent in Belgium by her father to make the marriage—quite against her will, though that's neither here nor there. With all this, you see, Jeremy, the existence of the tunnel and false wall was not simply a matter for conjecture. We had become certain of it, had we not?''

I could not but give assent. ''Yes, sir,'' said I.

''Well, with such certainty, all that remained was discovery. I assigned that task to you, and you have carried it out with admirable dispatch. I congratulate you. But you do see, don't you, that discovery, in this case, was in the nature of a confirmation and not an astonishment?''

''As you say, Sir John.''

''Good. Then you understand. But I have a question for you. You referred to your discovery as a secret exit. It was, I take it, also a secret entrance? That is to say, the door, or false wall, could be made to move from either side, could it not?''

I paused only to make certain in my own mind of the recessed trigger on Ebenezer's side, then gave powerful assurances that the machinery to move the wall could be made to operate from the tunnel or from within the library.

''Thank you,'' said he. ''That may be an important point. Now, much as I welcomed your news and have enjoyed our discussion, I must now return to the bench.''

Then he turned from me and made a straight path to the door, a way he had no doubt rehearsed many times before. Yet there he paused, turned back to me, and said: ''Jeremy, you will recall that I sent word directing Charles Clairmont,

that newly arrived half-brother of the late lord, to report for
an interview at five in my chambers?''

''Indeed, Sir John, and I believe Potter carried the message to him personally.''

''Not surprising,'' said he. ''Well, I should like you to
be present during that talk. Bring a broom and whatnot for
cleaning the room. That should explain your presence and
put him at his ease. For that matter, my chambers, such as
they are, could use a good sweeping, since I will in no wise
allow Mrs. Gredge inside. You'll see to it?''

I saw to it; though it was no easy matter coaxing a broom
and a feather duster from Mrs. Gredge. She seemed deeply
offended that I, not she, had been chosen to give Sir John's
private lair its first ''touch'' (as she called it) in ''who
knows how long.'' I chose to say nothing to her of his clear
intent to have me there for other purposes. This was partly
because I knew not what those purposes were; and partly,
as well, because I believe I was just beginning to learn the
uses of discretion, one of the most difficult lessons for children (and most adults) to learn.

During the time that elapsed between my conversation
with Sir John in the yard and the five o'clock meeting at
which I was to be present, Lady Fielding awoke but once.
Though there was no outcry beyond a call for Mrs. Gredge,
I took it that the poor woman was again in pain, for upon
leaving the room up the stairs, Mrs. Gredge hastened to
prepare another dose of the potion that Mr. Donnelly had
prescribed. She was in the midst of heating the poppy seeds
down into a pulp when I noted the time and, thinking it
proper, asked her permission to leave.

''If you must,'' said Mrs. Gredge. ''I've my hands full
here, as you can see.''

''Sir John did want me there a bit before five,'' said I.
''He was most particular.''

''He has his ways,'' said she, ''though I vow I often do

not understand them. Go then, and see you make a good job of it!''

I promised and descended the stairs, broom and duster in hand. As it proved, I preceded Charles Clairmont by only a minute or two. Sir John had barely the opportunity to tell me just what it was he wished me to notice with regard to the visitor before he was upon us.

There were three sharp knocks on the door. Sir John called out an invitation to enter and into the room sidled a slightly misshapen man of indeterminate age. Was he humpbacked, or merely stooped? I could not rightly tell. I thought it best not to study him direct but kept to the broom work I had begun with that knock upon the door.

The visitor presented himself as Charles Clairmont to Sir John. He was thanked for his prompt attendance and invited to take a chair.

"Pay no mind to the boy," said Sir John. "This place needs a good sweeping."

"He is industrious," observed Mr. Clairmont.

"He had best be," said Sir John. "Caught for petty theft, he was. We've given him the chance to pay his debt with work about the court."

That stung a bit, for therein lay a kernel of truth. I looked hard at Sir John and saw a smile of mischief on his face.

"Ah," said Mr. Clairmont, "forced labor. We make good use of it whence I come."

"And where might that be, sir?"

"From the Caribbean colonies. My place of business and plantation are on the island of Jamaica, though I have interests in those of the Antilles not closed to us by the Spanish."

"Well, then, I see you are a man of parts."

"Of enterprise, rather. All that I have, I have achieved by my own person."

There was something about Mr. Clairmont's voice that grated upon the ears. It was nasal in tone and tenor in range. Yet there was something more: a disagreeable sharpness to it, a mode of barking out his replies.

"Enterprise, is it?" echoed Sir John. "Well, admirable, indeed admirable. But tell me, Mr. Clairmont, when did you arrive in London?"

"Last evening," said he, "on the tide."

"By ship?"

"Of course," he snapped, "on the *Island Princess*. It would be a wet trip by coach."

"Pray, be not so tetchy, Mr. Clairmont. Until this morning, I knew not of your existence. I am merely trying to establish certain facts about you and your presence in this city."

"Forgive me," said he, "I am still upset by the news of Lord Goodhope's death. But yes, we arrived at approximately seven, or half past, thereabouts. I disembarked quite soon thereafter. You may confirm this with the master of the vessel, Captain Cawdor."

"I shall," said Sir John firmly. "Could you give me some notion of the purpose of your visit here?"

"A matter of business."

"Details, sir. Could you be more specific?"

"I should prefer not to be. But this much I will say: I have received an attractive offer for some of my holdings; received it, that is, by ship's mail. Such matters must absolutely be handled tête-à-tête, you understand. There would be contractual matters to be negotiated. I must also ensure that the offer is authentic; that the prospective buyer truly has the funds available to make the purchase. Such matters I prefer not to leave in the hands of agents or solicitors."

"And the name of the prospective buyer?"

"That I must withhold. After the purchase has been consummated, or the offer left to lie, I should be happy to report it. At this point, however, matters are far too delicate. You understand, I'm sure."

"Agreed," said Sir John, after a moment's hesitation.

"You mentioned the news of Lord Goodhope's death. How did you receive it?"

"From a friend."

"Would that friend have been Potter, Lord Goodhope's butler?"

"Ha!" He barked at that, most derisive. "I have no friends of the servant class, Sir John."

"Who then?"

"From Mr. John Bilbo. Through much of the voyage, mal de mer had confined me to my cabin. It is an unpleasantness that prevents me from returning very often. Feeling solid land beneath me restored me so that I felt able for a night on the town. After establishing myself at my lodgings, I supped and found my way to Bilbo's gaming house. I must have arrived well after ten o'clock, near eleven, or perhaps even after that—I'd had a bit to drink by then, you see. I'd been at the table a good half hour and was winning—a proper run of luck it was. Then Mr. Bilbo came by and whispered his condolences in my ear. With that, my luck changed most immediate. I took my winnings, what was left of them, and then departed from the table. I sought out Mr. Bilbo, and he told me all that he knew of the matter."

"And what was that?"

"In sum, that Richard was a suicide. That shocked me, of course, for he seemed to have everything a man might need or want. I said as much to Mr. Bilbo."

"And what said he to you?"

"He owned that he, too, was shocked, though not completely surprised. He mentioned financial difficulties, a considerable gaming debt to himself, and rumors he had heard of difficulties at court, though he was not precise about any of this. He promised to tell me when he learned more. He said he would ask about."

"And you returned there this morning?"

"I did, yes, hoping to learn more, but also to puzzle with him over the advert of Lord Goodhope's death that appeared today in the newspaper. Death by 'misadventure' seemed singularly vague.''

"That," said Sir John, "I will grant you." Through all this the magistrate had sat erect, giving full attention to his visitor. Yet at this point he turned suddenly toward me. "Boy," said he, "I wish to hear that broom scraping the floor. Why has it grown so silent from your corner?"

Immediately, I became busy again. In truth, I had left off sweeping, so interested was I in the character of Mr. Clairmont and the tale he told. "Sorry, m'lord," said I to him. "I'll get it cleaner than it's ever been in here. You'll see, m'lord."

"See that you do," said Sir John in his most severe manner.

"Perhaps a bit of birch on his arse?" suggested Mr. Clairmont.

"I do not hold with whipping or flogging of those so young."

"It gets results."

"No doubt, though not always the ones intended. But now, sir, do tell me, what was your relation to Lord Goodhope?"

"Why, we were brothers, after a fashion."

"Half-brothers?"

"Just so. My mother was my father's whore."

Mr. Clairmont said it thus, almost casually. Though Sir John seemed to flinch at that expression of his visitor's bastard birth, he said nothing; he simply sat, hands together now on his desk, and waited for a continuation.

Which came as follows: "In point of fact we are quite near the same age. He was my senior by but a few weeks. There is, of course, no question of my claim to the title, nor any part of the fortune, no matter how diminished. His son, William, will inherit both upon his majority. Let him, say I, for I have need of neither. I am king in my part of the world."

Through all this I had done as Sir John bade me and kept

my broom moving. Indeed the floor was dirty. I had put together three piles of dust, dirt, and crumbs, but had strayed so far from the two at the desk that a question was asked which I missed. The answer, however, delivered in Mr. Clairmont's loud nasal, came through to me most clear.

"Oh," said he, "there are a few others around London, no doubt. My father was quite prolific. One, I know, has gone to the Carolina colonies—not transported but an emigrant. I was the only one who had contact with Richard, however. It pleased my father to put us together as playmates whenever Richard was with him in London. I often got my brother in trouble, though he never minded much. He had no difficulty finding trouble on his own."

"You were boys together then?"

"Off and on," said he, "but only in London."

"You knew the house well?"

"I suppose I did at one time."

"Were you aware of the tunnel? The passage into the library?"

I looked up from my sweeping, yet kept the broom in motion. For my own reasons, of course, I was much interested in how Mr. Clairmont would answer. The response on his face surprised me: he smiled. And Mr. Clairmont was quite an unsmiling man.

"Ah yes," said he, as if recalling golden days of yore, "the tunnel. Once we had found it, which wasn't so difficult, Richard and I played there often. We got one of the servant girls down there once. God, didn't we make her scream! She was quite at our mercy." Something like a laugh escaped him then.

"Did you, as an adult, remain in touch with him?" asked Sir John.

"Oh yes, for a time we were fairly close. We had the same bad habits, you see. But then I left for Jamaica over ten years ago. We exchanged letters for a while, but not often. We were, quite literally, in two different worlds." He paused, a kind of hesitation, then went on: "Then there

was one rather unfortunate incident, for which I must claim
the fault. He wrote me that with great trepidation he was
to be wedded to a convent girl. I took that for an invitation
to the ceremonies and I thought he would need support for
such an ordeal, so I, in spite of great difficulty, left on short
notice to be there. I remember that one as a particularly
nasty voyage, September storms and all that. In any case,
I arrived in Liverpool, made it to the place in Lancashire
where the family had its holdings, and let him know I was
there for the wedding. By that time, our father had passed
on, to hell no doubt, and Richard was now Lord Goodhope.
He came to me at my inn the day before the wedding and
made it plain that I was *not* invited. He explained to me
that the bride and her family made a great show of piety
of the Papist sort and that it would be very difficult to
explain my presence to them. I asked why he need be worried about that, and he made it quite plain that he needed
their money. I, having made the voyage, was greatly annoyed and fell to drinking. Drunk, I determined to attend
the wedding, whether invited or not. Somehow, I got past
the gate in my hired coach, and once past the gate, I got
through the door. Reeling about was I, finally having drunk
even more than my own generous limit. In my search for
an appropriate place to vomit, I chose the bride's gown.
And that, I'm afraid, strained relations between Richard and
me for quite some time."

"But it did not end them?"

"Oh, no. He got their money, or a good bit of it. That
and an heir were his only reasons for marrying. Of course,
I did not come often to London, but when I did we would
meet, as long as Lady Goodhope was not about. The last
time I was here he had me to one of his impromptu evenings. Most amusing."

"When was that last time?"

"Oh, about a year ago, I should say." He paused and
sighed. "But you wish me to be more exact, I suppose, so

eleven months ago it was—the end of April and the beginning of May.''

"In spite of your past difficulties with Lady Goodhope,'' said Sir John, ''you wished to call upon her, when you heard of her husband's death?''

"Ah, that, yes, the opportunity to send word presented itself—in the person of that butler. What was his name?''

"Potter.''

"Indeed, Potter. He arrived just at the time Jack Bilbo and I were trying to figure the sense of that damnable word, 'misadventure.' I thought if I presented myself to her, all spit and polish, and managed the visit without vomiting upon her, I might learn just what she meant by that. I *assumed* she was the author of the advert. But it was not to be. I received a very harsh rejection from her. Old enmities die hard. To be just, I suppose I can't blame her.''

There was silence between them for a long moment. I chose that as my opportunity to grab up the feather duster and attack the shelf of a few books and many papers behind Sir John. It was indeed dusty, and I made the dust fly all about. Mr. Clairmont took to coughing and cursing. Sir John flailed the air with his hands.

"What are you up to now, boy?'' he demanded.

"Dusting,'' said I.

"Well, leave off it till we finish.''

I retired to one side, waited, and watched.

"You have been most forthcoming, Mr. Clairmont,'' said Sir John, ''and for that I am grateful to you. I have but one more question for you, and it is this: Did Lord Goodhope have enemies? People who might truly wish to see him dead?''

"Indeed, he certainly had enemies—enemies of every sort. None, I think, would have gone so far. Yet what you ask me suggests you think murder a possibility. Surely you can't suspect that!''

"Like you, Mr. Clairmont, I am simply trying to define that word 'misadventure.' ''

Sir John rose, extended his hand, found Charles Clairmont's, and shook it in gentlemanly fashion. And with a curt "Good day," Mr. Clairmont left him then, making from the room more quickly than he had entered it. In spite of his odd, sidling, thrusting walk, he was quite light on his feet.

Until he heard the sound of the door shut, Sir John remained standing. He waited a moment longer, then sank down in his chair. "Come, sit down, Jeremy," said he, "and let us discuss this fellow."

"Are you sure, Sir John?" I asked, all innocent. "Will this count against my sentence?"

"Such impudence!" said he, laughing. "Do forgive me for presenting you so. And *do* sit down."

I did, of course, as he bade me, taking the place Mr. Clairmont had left.

He removed his periwig, as he seemed to do at every opportunity, and leaned forward in a posture of eagerness. "Now," said he, "what did you make of him, in general, as if met on the street?"

"In general? Well, he was an ugly man, with such a stoop I thought him at first humpbacked. And he has also a rather strange walk. He seems to scuttle, a bit like a crab."

"Yes, and he has an ugly way of speech, has he not? How would you describe it?"

"He speaks sharp. Even when he talks soft, he seems to be talking loud."

"Exactly. He is a man used to giving orders—and having them obeyed. What was it he said? 'I am king in my part of the world.' He no doubt believes that. Pride goeth before a fall."

"What of the substance of his answers?" I asked.

"All quite reasonable," said he. "Even his reservation regarding the name of the prospective purchaser of his property was the sort that any man engaged in commerce would make. All that he said must be confirmed, of course.

We now must certainly visit Black Jack Bilbo, an entertaining blackguard, if nothing more. And of course I shall send one of the constables to talk to Captain Cawdor of the *Island Princess*. Our Mr. Clairmont has evidently proved himself an alibi at the time of Lord Goodhope's death, but we shall see about that.''

He pondered for a moment, his lips closed in a tight purse. Then he asked: ''What was his reaction when I brought up the fact of the tunnel and the passage into the library? He hesitated at that point. Did he seem surprised we knew of it?''

''No,'' said I, ''he smiled, like to himself, as though with a sudden fit of remembering.''

''That indeed would tally with what he responded. He seemed to take pleasure in recalling the screams of that servant girl. A nasty sort of man is Charles Clairmont; but then, so also was Lord Goodhope, it would seem. Now, one last point, Jeremy. You have given me a general assessment of his appearance. I would like you to give me something in more detail now: his face, his hands, his mode of dress, all of that which occurs to you.''

''I must take a moment to think,'' said I, and take a moment I did. I pictured him to myself and then began to sketch him out to Sir John, making for him as accurate a picture as I was able. I mentioned Mr. Clairmont's large, bent nose and his most usually downturned mouth. ''It gives him an attitude of displeasure,'' said I in sum. His complexion I described as neither dark nor fair but somewhat darkened by the sun, though his hair was dark, but about the same color as the man in the portrait; he wore no wig. His height was hard to fix because of his stoop, though I judged it to be only two or three inches above my own, perhaps five and a half feet, no more. He was dressed in black, except for a white, lace-front shirt and white hose.

Sir John listened to all this, neither interrupting nor commenting. Then, when I was done, he asked: ''Nothing more then? That's as you remember him?''

I thought further. "Perhaps one more thing: Mr. Clairmont's face seemed to glisten somewhat."

"Glisten?"

"Yes, well, glow or glisten. It caught the light."

"Perspiration, perhaps," mused Sir John. "It is a bit close in here. Or it could be a touch of fever: something from that warmer clime. Though now that I think upon it, his hands were quite dry. That impressed me. I thought him either a truthful man or a well-practiced liar."

And then he asked a question I thought passing strange: "They are half-brothers, Jeremy, or so it has been given to us. You saw the portrait hung in Lady Goodhope's sitting room. What would you say as to the resemblance, one to the other?"

"Lord Goodhope and Mr. Clairmont? Why, there may be a brotherly resemblance," said I, "though it is dim to the view. The picture was said to be a good likeness. If so, Lord Goodhope was a handsome man, while Mr. Clairmont is indeed not. They are of about the same natural complexion, though Clairmont may now be a bit darker and has a great beak of a nose. I would not, ordinarily, have taken them to be related."

"Ah well," said he, "it is often so with half-brothers. I little resembled mine, though my memory of his face grows dim."

He stood, signaling the end to this episode. As I, too, rose, he smiled slyly and said: "Jeremy, do finish with this room, will you? The shelves must be terribly dusty. Do what you can, and I'll consider your debt to the court discharged."

I was quite overcome by all I saw about me. Never but in my fantasy had I seen such a place, and the reality quite beggared my fantasy. I had been to theatricals in Lichfield with my mother: My father thought them trifling and would not attend. As a boy, I had been taken by those simple productions, most especially by the show of *A Midsummer*

Night's Dream given by a troupe of traveling players from London. Even my father came along to it, for it was Shakespeare, and he had the autodidact's respect for genius. For months afterward I pranced about as Puck and played the rude mechanicals with my younger brother. And then he and my mother died.

And now here was I in the very Temple of Shakespeare, the Drury Lane Theatre, wherein I was about to witness the show of *Macbeth,* with no less than David Garrick himself in the primary role. It was all, so to speak, in the line of duty. Sir John, having ascertained his wife's soporific condition from Mrs. Gredge, had declared that a visit to the theatre was in order. Little as I wished to discourage him from such an expedition, I was curious as to the reason (for Sir John always had his reasons). He explained that the evening's performance of *Macbeth* had been billed as the farewell of Miss Lucy Kilbourne, who would appear as Lady Macbeth. She was taking an early and unexpected retirement from the stage, and that had put a number of questions in his mind.

So here we sat in the gallery, the balcony above and the pit below, with such a congregation in attendance as I had never before imagined, much less seen. The boxes on either side were filled with the gentry. It would seem that every seat in the house was filled. Was Lucy Kilbourne such a favorite? Indeed she was, Sir John assured me. In less than twelve years' time she had risen from one of the general company to principal player, and then was elevated still higher by audience acclaim, so that of all the ladies of the theatre who played opposite Mr. Garrick, she was by far the most applauded.

The curtain rose. The play began. I was soon lost in a story that though now well known to me, I had then never seen acted, nor even read. It is indeed a dark story, perhaps Shakespeare's darkest, and that may be why there seems to be some prejudice against it among players. The prophecies of the witches thrilled me. The plots of Lord and Lady

Macbeth baffled me. Each new murder shocked me. I was quite exhausted by the time of the intermission, but was assured by Sir John that there was more to come.

"Would you mind," he asked, "if we got up and moved about a bit? I am on my backside all the day long and often feel the need to stretch."

And so we went with care through the crowd, as they milled about and conversed in separate groups in the hall outside the gallery. He was recognized and greeted by some, ignored by most, and stared at as a curiosity by a few who seemed to wonder what a blind man might be doing at the theatre.

"What of Mr. Garrick, Jeremy?"

"He—" I started. "Oh yes, he is Macbeth, is he not? In truth, Sir John, I had quite forgot they were actors on the stage. It all unfolds in a manner so real."

"His performance convinced you then?"

"Oh, indeed. He does not move much about the stage as I saw some do in Lichfield, shouting and throwing their arms about."

"There is no necessity," said Sir John. "He has the music of the poet's words. That is all he needs." Then he added: "And indeed all I need."

It was at that moment that I spied the familiar figure of one whom I would have wished us to avoid. In one dark corner, alone, leaning against the wall, was Mr. Charles Clairmont. He had seen us. He smiled his crooked smile and started in our direction. I let out an exclamation of surprise and consternation.

"What is it, boy?"

"Mr. Clairmont," said I. "He is coming to us."

"Well and good. Why not?"

"Will I not be an embarrassment to you, considering how you presented me to him earlier?"

"Leave that to me."

And in a moment Mr. Clairmont was upon us, having

scuttled through the crowd in a manner so quick it surprised me.

"Ah, Sir John, what good fortune to meet you again so soon! What brings you here tonight?"

"Shakespeare," said Sir John simply.

"Then you come often?"

"Often enough."

"And your young companion? If I remember aright, he was serving out a sentence when last I saw him."

"True," said Sir John, "true, but you will recall, Mr. Clairmont, that I told you I did not hold with whipping or flogging?"

"I do, yes."

"I believe in rewards, rather. He did a tolerably good job cleaning my chambers, or so I am told, and so I decided to reward him with a visit to the theatre."

Mr. Clairmont then gave me a look which I can only describe as skeptical. "Lucky lad," said he.

"But tell me," said Sir John, "what brings you here tonight?"

"Ah, well, here I am a visitor in a city I once called home. I rattle about, looking for amusement and thought I might find it here."

"*Macbeth* is not what I should term an amusing play."

"Perhaps not," said Mr. Clairmont, "but entertaining in the higher sense."

"Ah, no doubt. But this performance is to be the last, I understand, by Miss Lucy Kilbourne. Did that attract you?"

"I made note. Tickets were damnably difficult to obtain because of it. I'm not accustomed to the gallery."

"She was a friend of your late brother's. He was something in the nature of her patron."

"So I'm given to understand," said Mr. Clairmont. "That made me curious to see her, of course."

"Of course," agreed Sir John, "and what think you of her talent?"

"Very highly. Her Lady Macbeth is a properly ruthless bitch."

"She might not thank you for that description, yet it seems accurate enough. Strange, don't you think, that she should choose to retire from the stage with so much of her career before her?"

"Perhaps. Yet I know nothing of life behind the curtain. I am satisfied simply to be one of the audience."

"And amused?"

"Yes, amused and entertained." Mr. Clairmont looked about and noted what I myself had observed some moments before: "Ah, but I see that it is time to return to the theatre. The play is about to resume."

"Good evening then," said Sir John. "Who knows when our paths will cross again?"

His hand was offered, and it was taken and given a manly shake.

"Whenever that should come to pass, may it be a happy occasion. Well met," said Mr. Clairmont, "and a good evening to you!"

Then he parted from us, moving swiftly through the crowd, disappearing into it; as we, for our part, proceeded to a door at the opposite end and thence to our seats.

Once we had settled in, Sir John said to me: "An interesting farewell on his part, don't you think, Jeremy? 'May it be a happy occasion.' Hmm. Well, he has nothing to fear from me *if* he has told the truth."

The remainder of the show of *Macbeth* brought further excitation to me with the reappearance of the witches and with them their mistress, Hecate, and the incidence of more murder still. Yet embarrassed by my earlier confession to Sir John, I sought to keep firmly in mind that these were actors, and the story they told was, after all, just a story. Thus I gave particular attention to the performance of Lucy Kilbourne, since she had provided the occasion for our visit.

She was indeed a favorite of the audience. Earlier, I had

noted an intake of breath from the pit as Macbeth voiced
a certain faintness of heart, and Mistress Kilbourne as Lady
Macbeth scolded him thus: "We fail? But screw your courage to the sticking-place, and we'll not fail." A murmur
ensued as she outlined the plan of Duncan's murder. And
then, as the end drew near, and she wandered about the
stage in her fit of repentant madness, the entire audience
applauded her exit; it proved to be her last appearance.

There was a great thunder of approval as the last curtain
came down. The players made their reappearance and were
given their separate ovations, none greater than Mr. Garrick's or Mistress Kilbourne's. At a signal from Mr. Garrick, all left the stage save Mistress Kilbourne. Again,
applause rang out for her. She listened to it, smiled sweetly,
then ended it with a wave of her hand.

"My dear friends," she began. "This is a sad occasion,
but there is some joy in it, as well. For the sadness I feel
in going is lifted somewhat by the happiness I feel in the
affection you show me this night. What I wish to say to
you all is expressed in some lines that were penned by me
with the help of a friend. It is to my great sorrow that this
dear friend did not live to help me through this occasion,
yet—"

A sudden whisper of "Goodhope . . . Goodhope" went
through her audience, followed by a murmur of comment.

"And *yet*," said she, raising her voice above the noise
of the crowd, "if he were here, he would be as proud of
the consideration you have given me, and as grateful to you
for it, as I most certainly am. If I may—"

With that, she began her recitation, a smallish figure on
the stage, still dressed in antique Scots garb. Yet she commanded the attention of the audience as might the King
himself have done on the most solemn state occasion. There
was no word, no whisper, as all seemed to bend in concentration to grasp each word she delivered with gesture
and flourish:

To you my patrons, all my thanks be due,
As I with sorrow take my leave of you.
Let not your hearts be heavy, do not repine,
For I offer you to hands far abler than mine.
May you remember me as one who tried
To please, and will honor you whatso betide.
And may the stage, to please each virtuous mind,
Grow every day more pure and more refined;
Refined from grossness, not by foreign skill,
Weed out the poison, but be English still.
Merits you have to other realms unknown;
With all their boastings, Shakespeare is your own!

There was silence, and then a great roar of applause and shouting. She curtsied nice, slow, and deep and with gravity. The curtains closed, and though the applause continued, they did not reopen. Gradually the tumult subsided, and the audience began slowly to make for the doors. A number pushed past us, yet Sir John held fast to his seat.

"Should we be leaving?" I asked him.

"No, Jeremy, our work here has just begun. Let me know when the house has cleared."

Then he fell into silence, whether pondering the play or meditating on other matters, I could not rightly conjecture. Nevertheless, silent he sat, and something of the nature of his silence told me he wished not to be disturbed. And so I waited, as he had instructed, until the audience had quite vanished and then informed him that we were alone in the theatre.

He stood. "Point me toward the door," said he. "And then let us ask our way to Mr. Garrick."

Passed from usher to stage manager, we made our way backstage, where there was a great hurly-burly of moving and removing. Forest boughs from the final scene were gathered and carried away. Castle walls were hauled up and out. I then realized how cleverly I had been deceived during the last hours.

Led through all this and down some stairs, Sir John was asked whether Mr. Garrick expected him. "Shall I announce you, Sir John?"

"As you see fit," the magistrate replied. "I have an appointment."

"Then I shall leave you here at the door," said the stage manager, and disappeared back up the stairs. Down the hall stood a number of players, still dressed in motley plaid. They talked and joked amongst themselves.

Sir John rapped stoutly on the door with his stick.

"Come ahead," came a call from behind the door.

And with that we entered a small room crowded with bits and pieces of costume from the play. A small man, not much taller than myself, stood, giving close attention to the mirror before him as he wiped diligently at his face with an oiled cloth. It was difficult to believe this was David Garrick and harder still to think him Macbeth.

Spying us in the mirror, Mr. Garrick turned reluctantly from it and with a ready smile greeted us in friendly fashion. If he and Sir John were not friends, it was plain to me that they were at least well acquainted.

"I'd give you my hand," said Mr. Garrick, "but it's quite besmirched with face paint."

"You must look a proper Red Indian then, David. But here: Let me present to you my young friend, Jeremy Proctor."

Young friend? That was indeed an elevation from my former status as helper. The smile I offered Mr. Garrick was thus inspired. He held up his greasy hand for my inspection by way of apology, then honored me with a proper bow, which I returned.

"Like you," said Sir John, "Jeremy is a Lichfield native."

"Not quite true in my case," said Mr. Garrick, "though I certainly grew up there."

"You are much discussed in Lichfield," said I to him.

"Ah, well. I have family there still. No doubt they keep my name alive."

"Come now, David," said Sir John, "modesty is a suit that fits you ill."

"I try it on from time to time and find it pinches in the chest and shoulders," said Mr. Garrick, with a wink at me. "Tell me, though, Master Jeremy, does London please you?"

"Beyond my dreams," said I. "This evening here would be worth a thousand in Lichfield, or any other city in England."

"You do honor to the Drury Lane, and I thank you," said he most sincerely. Then: "I do hope, Sir John, that your seats were not too unsatisfactory."

"By no means. Mr. Wren designed an auditory marvel in this place. I heard perfectly. And we thank you for the tickets."

"My pleasure, truly. But you deserve a box, and I regret I could not provide it: All this damnable fuss with the farewell performance of her highness." Mr. Garrick hesitated, then with a look of frank curiosity, he added: "I'd no idea you were one of her enthusiasts."

"Of Mistress Kilbourne? In all truth, I am in no special way devoted to her, though I credit her with a good performance tonight."

"The woman can act. I'll give her that."

"No, my interest lies in her conduct offstage. She figures somewhat in an inquiry now under way."

"Ah-hah! I thought it! Might that be in the matter of Lord Goodhope's death?"

A slow smile spread across Sir John's ample features. "It might," said he.

"Murder has been bruited! Is this so?"

"The inquiry is under *way*, David. It is not yet concluded."

"But—"

"Please, let me ask a few questions of you."

"Of *me?*" Mr. Garrick seemed a bit taken aback at that. "But of course I shall be happy to respond to any query. I am at your service, Sir John."

"Very good. Could you tell me, for instance, just when Lucy Kilbourne informed you of her decision to leave your company? I understand it all came about quite suddenly."

"Well, it was certainly a surprise to me," said Mr. Garrick. "That must have been something between ten days and two weeks past. In fact, it constituted a breach of her contract with the theatre, but she had dreamed up this plan for a farewell performance and bought me off with that. I give her credit. She filled every seat in the house tonight. It was not me they came to see."

"So long then? Ten days to two weeks? I had supposed it an even shorter time, since the bills went up but a few days ago."

"You must understand, Sir John, that a production takes time to prepare. Indeed, we rushed this one through. She had wanted to do *The Merchant of Venice.* Quite out of the question, I'm afraid, since the scenery and costumes were stored from last season, though I admit she does a good Portia. The Scottish play, at least, was done by us at the beginning of this season, so it was not difficult to return it to the boards for this single performance."

"I see," said Sir John. "And what about that—how would one call it? An epilogue? An envoi?—which she declaimed after the performance? When was that set?"

"Well, she brought that in but five days ago, of that I am certain. It was set only three days ago, again of that I am certain, for I did a good deal of editing of it, for which you may understand, rewriting. In fact, I supplied the last six lines. Did you not think them superior to the rest?"

"Oh, undoubtedly."

"The bit about resisting the influence of the French, and us having Shakespeare and them having nothing at all? I thought that quite to the point. I insisted upon their inclu-

sion. How was it her version ended? Ah yes, if I may quote
from memory:

> *May you continue to give support to those*
> *Whose task it is to fill our empty rows.*

Empty rows indeed! We never have empty *rows*. And even
if we did, it would not fall to her to call attention to them.
Not from *my* stage, in any case!''

"Quite understandable, certainly," said Sir John. "Did
she claim sole authorship of her lines?"

"She did not. And she said from the stage, it was in the
nature of a collaboration with her 'friend,' Lord Goodhope
presumably. She was quite open about the affair.''

"And how has she behaved since the advertisement of
his death?''

"Like a proper widow! All solemn dignity. It's a role
she enjoys, Sir John, and she has even costumed herself in
black, most fashionably in black.''

"Had you ever seen the dress before?''

To that Mr. Garrick gave thought for a moment. "No.
No, I had not.''

"What did she give as her reason for leaving? Retirement at her age is surely rare.''

"Oh, she had a good ten years left in her, perhaps more:
Though I vow I'd preferred she spend them at Covent Garden. But no, early retirement among actresses is not so rare.
I can think of several instances, yet all involved fortunate
marriages. Lucy has been quite vague about her reasons
and her plans. If I did not know better, I would say she has
come into money. Well, we're well rid of her—she and her
affairs! If there is anything I have striven for in the course
of my career, Sir John, it has been to elevate the dignity of
the theatre. And once Kilbourne was established, she has
done her all to pull it down.''

"You mentioned 'affairs.' I take it then that Lord Goodhope had predecessors?''

"Oh, a number. Jack Bilbo before him, and before him an even more disreputable individual with a showy name, Balthazar Barbey."

"Ah yes, a dealer in stolen and plundered goods, though always from the Continent. What became of him?"

"He failed to return from his last trip to France, and that was near two years past."

"Well," said Sir John, tapping his stick to the floor, "she has a history, has she not? Nevertheless, I should like to speak with her; that is, if her dressing room is not filled with those wishing her well."

"No fear of that," said Mr. Garrick. "She is not popular with the company, and the gentry have avoided her, smelling scandal. If you leave by the stage door, and I'm afraid at this hour you must, you will no doubt find a mob from the pit assembled to wish her a final goodbye. But go to her, with my blessing: last door on your right, as far from mine as possible."

"Goodbye, then, David, and thank you for your time."

"My pleasure. And good fortune to you, Master Jeremy. Should you see my valet lurking about the hall and reasonably sober, tell him to come in, won't you?"

I promised to do so, though once we had exited, I saw no one. The long hall had cleared completely during our time with Mr. Garrick. We walked the length of it. Sir John proceeded silently, his stick elevated and out slightly, tapping to a slow rhythm on the floor as he went. Nevertheless, I stuck close by his side, ready to pull him back from the wall that marked the end of the hall. Yet there was no need. Once again he amazed me by stopping just short of the wall, my hand mere inches from his elbow.

He turned to his right. "Her door should be just here. Have I got it right?"

"Quite perfect, sir."

He knocked firmly on the door.

"Who's there?" squawked a voice beyond it. "I ain't ready yet." Though pitched a bit lower, it matched Mrs.

Gredge's for volume and unpleasantness. I thought perhaps we'd got the wrong door.

"Sir John Fielding, magistrate of the Bow Street Court, is come to make inquiries regarding the death of Lord Goodhope." I had heard this voice from him but once before, and that from the bench. The occasion that presented itself to mind was the appearance of Mr. Bailey's attacker, Dick Dillon. Sir John had dealt with him severely and in just such a voice.

Whoever was behind the door attended smartly to that voice, for the door flew open, and a woman of no little beauty stood revealed, wearing her shift with hoops and a petticoat below. In my life I had not seen a woman in such a state of undress, save for my mother.

"Why, Sir John," said she in the sweet tones of Lady Macbeth, "what an unexpected pleasure. Do come in." This was indeed Lucy Kilbourne!

Sir John stepped forward into her dressing room, which was even smaller than Mr. Garrick's; yet I held back, thinking it improper to visit a woman who was in such a state. Yet she, with a shrug and a wink, beckoned me forward. From that moment, a vague air of conspiracy was established between us. I followed Sir John inside and looked about for the squawking woman who had yelled through the door: She was nowhere to be seen. I could only conclude that she had been Mistress Kilbourne, speaking unawares. Yet which was the real and which the false?

"I have a few questions for you," said Sir John.

"And I shall be happy to answer them," said she most winningly.

She grabbed at her dress, black and severe yet as fashionable as Mr. Garrick had described, and she swiftly pulled it on.

"I hear the rustle of clothing," said he. "Are you properly dressed, Mistress Kilbourne?"

"Why, of course, Sir John. I was merely clearing a chair for you. Won't you sit down?"

"I prefer to stand, as will my young companion."

"As you wish then."

She gestured toward her back and turned it to me, indicating I was to close the series of hooks and eyes that rose up from her naked back from waist to neck. I knew not what to do. Surely Sir John would disapprove, yet this woman possessed a glamour I found quite bewitching. She threw a smile at me over her shoulder, and the next moment I found myself doing her wordless bidding.

"How long were you acquainted with Richard Good-hope?" he asked.

"For less than a year," said she. "John Bilbo introduced us. If you are asking, however, when I became his companion—for I make no secret of that—then the answer would be six months ago."

"You were previously companion to Bilbo?"

"To my shame, yes."

"Did he take it ill when you transferred your affections to Lord Goodhope?"

"Perhaps you might say so. Yet that is something only he can truly answer."

"Well taken," said Sir John. "What drew you to Lord Goodhope? You knew, of course, that he was married and the father of a son? Or perhaps you did not know at the beginning?" He thus offered her a plea, one which she declined to use.

"It was indeed the consequence of his marriage that drew me to him," she declared quite brazenly. "He was deeply unhappy in it. I did what I could to make him happier."

"And would you behave in such a way with every man unhappy in marriage? There are countless thousands of 'em in London alone."

"Make not light of me, I pray," said she.

"*Damn!*" said I.

I had got up in the row of hooks and eyes to the middle of her back. There her body offered considerable resistance.

Straining to put the hook into the eye, I had them together, or so I thought, and then suddenly the hook had jumped from its housing, and thus prompted my exclamation.

"Jeremy! What are you up to?"

I hesitated guiltily. "I bumped into a chair, Sir John."

His head was cocked in my direction. "Try to be more careful," said he. "Come and stand by my side. I should feel more certain of you here."

"As you will, Sir John," said I.

I did as he bade, of course, directing a shrug to Mistress Kilbourne. She, in response, gave me a fierce look of annoyance. Then she began struggling manfully, if that is quite the right word, to contain her ample bosom within the confines of her widow's weeds.

"Where were we?" asked Sir John. "Ah yes, you had asked me not to make light of you. I do not, Mistress Kilbourne. I only mean to suggest that others find themselves in that selfsame situation. What was it drove you to Richard Goodhope, in particular?"

She left off her heaving and struggling long enough to say: "It was his wit, his intelligence, his sensibility. In truth, I had never met a man like him, and now, with him gone, I am quite sure I shall never meet another." This speech she delivered in the sweetest, saddest tones ever heard, though the vexed expression on her face seemed to contradict them.

"You attended a number of informal parties at his residence, evenings he termed his 'impromptus.' "

"I did, yes."

"What happened there?"

"Nothing untoward, if that is the implication of your question. Certainly nothing of a scandalous nature. Ignorant tongues wag. Those who were actually present will confirm me in this."

At last she had got the recalcitrant hook in place. She exhaled deeply and, shifting her arms, reached over her shoulders to attack the rest.

"What is it, Mistress Kilbourne?" asked Sir John.

"What do you mean, Sir John?"

"You seemed to sigh. Was it some memory awakened in particular?"

"Lord Goodhope is always in my memory," said she.

"Do you believe him to be a suicide? That would confirm his unhappiness in marriage, perhaps, though it speaks little for your ministrations. He left no notes. Did he communicate anything to you of his intentions?"

"No, he did not," said she a bit sharply. "And as to what I may believe regarding his end, that really matters little. It is, after all, you who are conducting the inquiry, is it not?"

"It is, yes, and I wish to have you available to speak further in it."

"That may be difficult."

"Oh? Why so?"

"I'd planned to go off to Bath."

"Rushing the season a bit, aren't you?"

"I have a complaint of a digestive nature. I had hoped the waters there might . . ."

"I must insist that you delay your trip."

She sighed once more. "Well, if I must . . ."

"You must," said Sir John firmly. "I have but one more question for you."

"And what is that?"

"Who is your dressmaker?"

"My *what?*"

"I spoke plain enough."

"But what . . . ? All right, she is Mrs. Mary Deemey. Her shop and fitting room is on Chandos Street."

"Ah, good, not far from my court. That will be all, Mistress Kilbourne. You will no doubt be hearing from me again."

"That will be my pleasure, Sir John."

She seemed at last to have managed the last of the hooks, for she busied herself smoothing the front of her dress as

Sir John turned to go. I made quick to open the door for him, and he stepped quickly into the hall. Before closing the door behind us, I risked a last glance back at her. Our eyes met, and she gave me a bent smile.

Sir John was moving down the hall at a recklessly swift pace. I ran to catch him up.

"That was a waste of time," he declared. "Or perhaps not entirely."

"In truth, she had not much to say," said I.

"Saint Richard, martyr to a bad marriage! Indeed!" He broke off then, brooding silently for a moment as he stormed ahead. "I might have stayed longer and put the screws to her, but I sensed . . . Jeremy, I know not what passed between you two there, and I wish neither assurances nor an answer from you, but somehow I felt there was an alliance against me."

"But I—"

"Not a word! Now, where is this stage door we must exit?"

"At the top of the stairs, which stand—just *three paces ahead!*"

He stopped dead then. "Oh," said he, "thank you, Jeremy." He put out his stick then and proceeded at a more reasonable step through the remaining distance.

Once out in the alley next the theatre, it was as David Garrick had predicted. A considerable crowd awaited Lucy Kilbourne. Indeed, when I opened the stage door, a cheer broke forth in expectation of her imminent appearance, but it soon died when Sir John stepped forth, though not in unfriendly fashion. A few laughed at their error.

"It's the Beak of Bow Street," called out one, identifying him to the rest.

I had earlier heard Sir John referred to thus by the court gallery, and sometimes less considerately as "the Blind Beak." I knew not the import of the term, yet it seemed well intended, and the magistrate took no offense at it.

In this instance, as we two merged into the crowd, Sir

John turned in the direction of the man who had spoken. "Will Simpson, is that you?"

"It's me for fair, m'lord."

"Back from your holiday, are you?"

"Newgate ain't Bath!"

"Nor was it ever intended to be!"

There was general hilarity at this. Sir John himself joined in the laughter. Though somewhat raucous, it was a good-natured collection of cutpurses, pimps, and their bawds who awaited the heroine of this evening. However, as we were still caught in their midst, Mistress Lucy suddenly stepped forth through the portal, and with a roar the crowd surged forward, catching us quite unawares and forcing us back.

Sir John grabbed fast to my arm. "Jeremy, get us out of this, will you?"

"I . . . I'll try!"

And try I did, pushing and heaving ahead of him through the mass of humanity trapped in that tight little alleyway, until at last we were clear of them. Sir John took a moment to regain his composure, straightening his tricorn, which had been knocked akilter, and making sure of his periwig.

"Good boy," said he. "I feared for a moment we should be trampled underfoot."

"She's certainly a favorite of theirs," said I.

"Of course she is," said Sir John. "She was once one of them. They honor her for her ascent." He turned this way and that. "I smell a horse," said he. "Is there a hackney carriage about? See if one is free, will you?"

Indeed there was one waiting near the alley entrance. I ran to it and inquired of the driver. Just as he informed me that he had been paid to wait, my eye was caught by movement behind the window of the compartment. I got a glimpse of something: a face seen for the merest instant before it disappeared. I could not be certain from such a view, of course, yet I had the distinct impression that it was Mr. Charles Clairmont who waited within.

Chapter 8

*In which an offer is made and an unexpected
meeting takes place*

THE NEXT MORNING BEGAN WITH A VISIT BY MR. DON-
nelly to his patient. When I responded to his knock and
opened the door for him, Mrs. Gredge being otherwise engaged, I was surprised to find looming beside him the large
figure of Benjamin Bailey.

"Mr. Bailey, sir," said I to him, "are you well?"

"Well and fit," said he with a show of confidence, "and
ready for duty."

"He's nothing of the kind," put in Mr. Donnelly, "but
he insisted on coming along."

"I will but a word with Sir John. Let him decide."

And so the two tramped into the kitchen, while at the
same time Mrs. Gredge flew in, warning Mr. Bailey not to
muddy her clean floor, though it had not rained for days.
Mr. Donnelly, whom she rightly took to be a gentleman,
received no such caution. She made her usual offer of tea,
bread, and butter, which both declined, then ran off to ap-
prise Sir John of their arrival.

"What of Lady Fielding?" Mr. Donnelly asked of me.

"She has slept, sir, quite continually since your visit yester morning."

"That's to be desired, of course, yet I would not dose her too strong. And her pain?"

"You had best talk to Sir John or Mrs. Gredge of that."

"Of course," said he. "It's never wise to speculate idly."

Then came Sir John into the kitchen. "Ah, Mr. Donnelly, thank you for your visit. And I understand you have a companion?"

"It's me, it is, Benjamin Bailey," said he, making a loud, healthy sound with his voice.

"Yes, 'the night watchman,' as Mrs. Gredge informed me."

"She has her ways, don't she?" said Mr. Bailey.

"How is he, Mr. Donnelly?"

"Not as well as he claims to be, but his recovery proceeds impressively. The wound is knitting nicely, no sign of fever."

"I'm ready, Sir John!" declared Mr. Bailey.

"He's not, in my opinion," said Mr. Donnelly. "Yet I am not here to argue that but rather to see Lady Fielding. You give me permission?"

"Nay, my blessing, sir. She has had her best day and night in months. I am grateful to you for that. I'm sure she would say more, were she not at this moment asleep. Mrs. Gredge is with her. She has attended her faithfully. Go see them now, by all means."

"I shall," said he, and with a quick bow to Sir John, he went up the stairs to the bedroom.

With the departure of the surgeon, Sir John turned in the direction of Mr. Bailey. "So now, Captain Bailey, you claim to be fit, but your doctor says otherwise. How do we account for this discrepancy?"

"He ain't me, Sir John. He don't know how I feel."

"There is a certain sense to that, I allow, but in truth, it does seem a bit early, does it not? Two days?"

"Well . . . I can only say, sir, that one *more* day in the constant care of Mrs. Plunkett, and I may take a turn for the worse. The woman exhausts me, if you get my meaning, sir."

With which remark Sir John broke into a hearty laugh, the sense of which then eluded me. "Why, I believe I do," said Sir John to him. "Indeed I believe I do. Perhaps we might work out a compromise between us. Would you be willing to try?"

"Whatever you say, Sir John."

"Well then, what about this? What if you were to return to duty, but in a somewhat limited capacity?"

"That would depend, sir."

"Upon what?"

"How limited, and in what capacity?"

"Fair enough, Mr. Bailey. What I had in mind was a bit of day work I need done. A Mr. Charles Clairmont, who, it has developed, is the late Lord Goodhope's half-brother, claims to have arrived from Jamaica on the night before last on the *Island Princess* and have disembarked at approximately half past seven. I would have you seek out the vessel's master, a Captain Cawdor, and verify this. But more, hang about the dock a bit and find out all you can regarding the ship and its voyage. Will you do that for me?"

"Indeed I will, Sir John."

"Go dressed as any layabout, but carry with you your commission and badge of service to board the ship and convince the captain that you are in earnest and represent me in this. But as for the rest of it, I would say there was no need to reveal your purpose in this matter."

"Talk to them all innocent, like?"

"Exactly, Mr. Bailey. You may buy rum to loosen tongues, but do not allow yourself to be carried away. You will be reimbursed within reason. Take your time in this. Find out all you can. Say . . . oh, say you are thinking of shipping on and wish to know about the vessel and its captain before you commit yourself. At this point in the investigation of Lord Goodhope's death, such information may count as very important.''

"Then rest assured, Sir John, I'll do a good job for you.''

"Jeremy has been doing good work for me in this matter, but I think you'll agree that the task I have put before you is beyond him.''

"If the boy showed his face on the docks,'' said Mr. Bailey with a grin at me, "he'd be likely to wake up outbound for Capetown.''

"Indeed,'' said Sir John. "Furthermore, this morning he and I are off for Newgate.''

This astonishing revelation set me agog and put me in a peculiar state of anticipation until, half an hour later, we departed on our expedition. The anticipation I felt was peculiar in that it was mixed. I had a natural curiosity about the place. What boy in England, nourished clandestinely by the thrills provided by "The Newgate Calendar'' and other such pamphlet collections, would not be eager to see the dreaded gaol for himself? Yet I, having so nearly missed incarceration there myself, felt understandably uneasy about any such visit. Nevertheless, I kept my peace and said nothing, neither to Sir John nor to Mr. Bailey, regarding the planned journey.

In any case, there was much for me to do in the nature of kitchen work, both sweeping and washing up. Applying my energies diligently and thus calling no attention to myself, I was presently witness to a further dialogue, and that between Sir John and Mr. Donnelly. The surgeon returned from his examination of Lady Fielding after ten minutes had elapsed, or perhaps a little more. I had heard a murmur of conversation between him and Mrs. Gredge, though its content was quite indistinguishable to my listening ear. He came down the stairs and into the kitchen alone; his step was slow and his manner grave. Seeking out Sir John, who sat silent at the table, he accepted the cup of tea offered him and made his report.

"She's sleeping well," said the surgeon.

"And thank God for it," said Sir John.

"She's not likely to rouse until past noon. Mrs. Gredge will attend to her then. I had thought to reduce the dose of opium a bit, but I've decided against that. Her comfort at this time seems paramount." With that, Mr. Donnelly paused, then put forth a question: "Sir John, you said that Lady Fielding had been attended by a number of physicians, that there was agreement that a tumor was the cause of her complaint, yet none as to its location. Is that as I remember it?"

"In the beginning," said Sir John, "there was no such agreement. The first doctor said her difficulty was gallstones, the next kidney stones, yet when two others came together a month ago they agreed solemnly that her loss of weight indicated a tumor was the cause, then they fell to fighting over the where of it. One said it was on her womb, the other on her liver."

"Her *liver?*"

"Indeed, her liver. The two were at her mercilessly, poking and prodding, asking if this hurt, or that; and of course it all caused her pain. The poor woman burst into tears and begged only to be left alone. What angered me most, Mr. Donnelly, was that having done all they could to torment her, they assured me *in her presence* that there was nothing to be done for her. But hold! I say wrong. The champion of the liver was all for bleeding her so as to coax the befouled blood from her body; he thought thus to 'drain' the tumor. Yet considering her reduced condition, I thought it just as well that we not subject her to that. Furthermore, that notion had been offered as an afterthought, in a speculative manner. I preferred that he speculate over someone else."

"In my view," said the surgeon, "bleeding does no good and can often do harm. But let me say, Sir John, that I am

astonished that there should have been any doubt as to the
location of the tumor. It is there to be seen, a tumor on her
left ovary, a lump in her abdomen as big as a lemon. Nowhere near the liver.''

Sir John sighed. ''I was aware of it.''

''Yet I fear that I, too, must concur in their prognosis.''

''You see no hope for recovery, then?''

''None.''

''Ahhh!'' It escaped him like a quiet wail. ''My poor,
sweet girl! I had no real hope for her, yet I would have
welcomed any slight cause for optimism as a drowning man
grasps a spar. You understand.''

''Yes, I understand,'' said the surgeon, ''but it would be
wrong to give you, or her, false hope. Indeed, I think the
end is not far off. Her heart seems weaker and the beat
slightly irregular. She's grown quite weak.''

''How near would you say? Today? Tomorrow? I'll shut
down the court, find another to sit in my place.''

''No, not so near: a week perhaps; a month at the most.
That she rests so well should extend her life rather than
shorten it. This should give you time to prepare for what
will surely come. My advice to you, Sir John, is to make
those preparations and to continue with your work in all its
aspects. It will not do for you to sit and wait for the end.
Lady Fielding would not have it so.''

The magistrate pondered this and concluded his considerations with an emphatic nod. ''No doubt you're right,''
said he. ''And I must say that of all the matters I have
before me, this inquiry into the death of Lord Goodhope
vexes and worries me most. I am troubled by the suspicion
that if it is not concluded soon, it will not be successfully
concluded at all.''

''Let me assure you, Sir John, if there is anything I can
do . . .''

''Yes, I believe there is, Mr. Donnelly. It sticks in my
memory that Lord Goodhope's corpus has not been properly identified, at least not to my way of thinking. I recall

from my first conversation with Lady Goodhope that she declined to enter the library on the night of his death and view the remains close at hand, understandable under the circumstances. That onerous task was left to the footman, who had just joined the household, and the butler, whom I frankly do not trust. Then, with the corpus removed, first to your surgery and then to the embalmer, I've come to doubt that she has looked upon it at all. I take it the body has been returned from the embalmer?''

''It is to be returned this morning.''

''The face has been somewhat repaired?''

''We were assured that what could be done would be done.''

''Well and good,'' said Sir John. ''You seem to have considerable influence upon her. I would like you to use it to persuade her to look upon the corpus and make a proper identification. You may act as my witness in this. I shall accept your word, and hers, without question.''

''It may not be easy,'' said Mr. Donnelly.

''I realize that,'' said Sir John, ''for she is indeed a willful woman. But you may tell her for me that unless she makes such an identification, I will in no wise permit the burial of the corpus, whether in London or in Lancashire.''

''That is indeed severe!''

''It falls upon me, from time to time, to be severe.''

''As you say, Sir John.''

Mr. Donnelly pushed back from the table, rose, and made ready to leave.

''I am curious,'' said the magistrate. ''Have there been callers?''

''None to my knowledge.''

''Messages of sympathy and condolence?''

''Very few.''

''It does seem passing strange, does it not? To be cut in life is common enough and of no great moment in Lord Goodhope's society. Yet to be cut in death is to be cut deep indeed. I must find out about this, though I confess my contacts at court are nil.''

"I wish you good fortune in the enterprise; in the inquiry as a whole. Now, if you will permit me, I shall take my leave. I have another call to make before looking in on Lady Goodhope and doing your bidding in that difficult matter.''

Sir John rose and offered his hand, which Mr. Donnelly took firmly in his own. "May I ask," said he, "has Mr. Martinez been of some help in setting accounts in order?''

"He has been of *great* help. He has arranged a meeting at the office of Lord Goodhope's solicitor, Mr. Blythe, this very afternoon. The situation will be discussed in detail.''

"You will attend?''

"As Lady Goodhope's representative, yes.''

"Then let me not keep you, for you have a busy day ahead. Goodbye, Mr. Donnelly. You go with my deepest, sincerest thanks.''

We were no more than a minute alone when Sir John, still on his feet, addressed me as though to the room at large. "Jeremy," said he, "have you completed the tasks given you by Mrs. Gredge?''

"I have, sir.''

"Then get your hat and coat, boy, for I must now take you on a trip to an outer circle of hell.''

When I climbed down from the hackney at Snow Hill, I beheld a structure the like of which I had never before even imagined. I had seen large buildings in my travels about London during the past few days, and this one was certainly among the largest. Yet it was not merely its size that I found so arresting, but rather its entire aspect which I found profoundly forbidding.

As Sir John followed me down, surefooted as always, and settled with the hackney man, I took the opportunity to study the facade of the infamous Newgate Gaol. It stood some three or four levels high, though this, reader, was difficult for me to reckon due to the fact it had not many proper windows. Since it was destroyed during the riots of 1780 and thereafter rebuilt, it now has even fewer openings to the world outside. Built of gray stone, begrimed nearly to black, it was not without some manner of artistic decoration. Above its center arch was a grouping of emblematic figures, though what they emblemized I was never very sure. There in the middle of them, unmistakable because of the feline pet at his feet, stood a representation of the late Lord Mayor, Dick Whittington. Below that center arch was a barred gate wide enough to accommodate a carriage or a good-sized wagon. It was to that common entry that we proceeded.

"Have I aimed us aright?" asked Sir John.

"Straight as an arrow," said I.

His stick waving, slightly extended, he found the gate and rattled the bars sharply. A man appeared, so ill clothed and in need of shaving that I at first took him to be a prisoner; yet he was the gatekeeper.

"Well, look ye here, it's Sir John Fielding come to pay a visit," said he. He produced a ring of keys and jammed the largest of them home. "Bring us a guest for the keeping, did ye?"

With a shock, I realized that he referred to me. Was this to be my punishment for hooking up Lucy Kilbourne's bare back?

"By no means," said Sir John, relieving me greatly. "We are come to confer with one sent to you two days past: Dick Dillon by name."

"Well, we'll look him up on the list and have you with him quick-like. One thing about the Sheriff's Hotel, we always know where our guests is staying."

The gate was thrown open, and we entered. We were brought to the gate house where the list was produced and the name of Benjamin Bailey's attacker found. A warder was summoned as our guide. He, only slightly more presentable than the gatekeeper, led us across a considerable courtyard and into the gaol proper, joking all the way as he chided Sir John for failing to fulfill some supposed quota. "How can you be so remiss?" said he quite boldly. "Us poor fellows depend on such as you send us for our livelihoods!" Then he cackled loudly, as though he had made a great jest.

Sir John was not amused. "Though it may be so," said he, "I would that it were not."

The warder continued cackling and giggling as he led us into the darkness. Ah yes, dark it was, the only light apparent coming from a few candles stuck here and about, and a torch at the end of the corridor. Though cloudy without and no sign of sunshine, it took me many moments to adjust my view to the all-pervading murk inside. And once the scene was visible, I wished that it was not, for along one side behind iron bars was a great common chamber of inmates, male and female. A few rushed to look upon us. Others lay inert on pallets against the wall. But the most ignored us, continuing their talk and browsing about among themselves, inured to indifference by all that did not directly affect them. And poor wretches they all were, clamoring for attention, moaning their woes, and snarling and laughing in a way that made both seem the same.

Hands were thrust through the bars at us as their owners begged at us for coins. Money, as I was later instructed, was all that mattered in Newgate. One or two grabbed at my coat. I shrank back in fear, making my way in a creep along the wall. The candlelight flickering on the contorted faces lent an aspect not quite human to them. Sir John was recognized. His name was called, importuning and in simple greeting, and once with a curse. Yet he plunged on, acknowledging none, driven as I was by the desire to get past this incarcerated mob.

But the smell, dear God, the stink of it! Any barnyard I've been in has smelt better, for there is something about human ordure that is more offensive to the nose than that of any other animal. Nor was that all, for added to it was an effluvium of decay that made me wonder, upon reflection, if some of those sleeping along the wall might not be dead; and if dead, how long.

"What you got here," said the warder, once we were past, "is your common felons—them as is serving short terms or waiting trial on lesser charges. Some waits a long time, it seems." This seemed to be said for my instruction, for it was given me with a wink and a cackle. We had come to the spot where the torch burned. From it, a dark flight of stairs led to a level above. "The Master Felons Ward is up these stairs. They is all waiting trial on capital offenses. Your man Dillon is there."

With that, he pulled a candle from his coat pocket and lit it from the torch. Holding it aloft, he began his ascent and we behind him, I taking up the rear.

"There's not so many in this section," the warder called out, "and they're a quieter lot. Something to be quiet about, I'd hazard."

We emerged at the next level where it was not only quieter, but also a bit lighter. A torch burned; there were candles about, and there was also light streaming in from outside through two narrow windows placed together halfway down the corridor. This gave me a better view of those beyond the bars. There were perhaps a dozen there, among them two women who stood together in idle conversation. Two men sat against the wall, staring vacantly at some distant point. The rest were grouped together, sitting on the straw-scattered floor, drinking from cups, talking in low tones amongst themselves.

There had been but a single warder stationed on the floor below. The Master Felons Ward merited two. Our man went over to one of them and informed him of Sir John's mission. Dick Dillon's name was called out, twice and loudly. At last a man in the group, one with his back toward us, bestirred himself, pitched himself up to stand unsteadily on his feet, then staggered over in our direction.

A foolish smile of triumph spread over his slack features.

"Well," said he, "it's the bleak, I mean the beak, I mean the blind beak. Ain't this an honor to be visited here by the magistrate himself!"

"You're drunk," said Sir John.

"That's as concerns me and not you, ain't it? I had my turn before you, and once was enough. So if I chooses to imbibe myself a bit of gin from the Newgate taproom, it is my right to do so and no matter of yours."

"Perhaps I can make it my matter. Perhaps I can have your gin taken away."

"Not likely, not as long as I got money to pay."

"You could be relieved of that."

"Let them try."

With a bit of effort, Dillon pulled himself up to his full height, which was considerable, made two fists before him, and growled down deep in his throat as he looked from one warder to the next. And then he laughed.

"Warders?"

"Yes, Sir John?" said the two in chorus.

"Be gone. I would talk to the prisoner in private."

They looked at each other, frowning. One of them shrugged. The other, our guide, removed his tricorn and scratched his head.

"If we are to do that," said he, "I must ask you, Sir John, to step back a good arm's length from the bars, for I must remind you it was you put him here."

"No, warder," said Sir John, stepping back as requested, "he put himself here, but now we have matters to discuss, and they are not for general knowledge."

"As you say, Sir John." He seemed a bit reluctant.

But the two removed themselves some considerable distance away. Sir John then turned in my direction.

"Jeremy?"

"Yes, sir?"

"Have they gone? Can they hear?"

"I would say that if you talk in your present voice, they cannot hear."

"Now, you, too, must step back, for the advice that was given was well given."

I did as he directed, and having heard, he nodded. Dillon once more growled, and once more he laughed.

"You do well to laugh in your situation," said Sir John.

"I ain't such a bad sort."

"Perhaps not, without a cutlass in your hand. This was, after all, your first arrest."

"Damned if it weren't! And that little whoreson-bastard cheated at cards, or I'd not gone after him as I did. I did no murder on him, though he fair deserved it."

"So you consider yourself unjustly here?"

"Yes, in a manner of speakin', your magistrate, so I do."

"Even though you lied at the time of your arrest?"

Dillon took great offense at that. He stretched out far through the bars, grasping at air, arms flailing at the two of us. Yet we were both just beyond his reach. At last he relaxed and drew back his long, strong arms.

"Dick Dillon don't cheat at cards, and he don't lie," he declared. "Did I not give my rightful name? My place of abode?"

"True enough," said Sir John quite mild, "but in the arrest report you gave yourself as unemployed."

"And so I am! Or so I was."

"Oh? What was then your relationship with Lord Richard Goodhope?"

There was a pause, a silence from Dillon, when only a moment before the exchange between them had been most lively. When at last Dillon spoke up, he seemed to be choosing his words as carefully as his gin-addled brains allowed.

"I was his former footman," said he to Sir John. He added, with pride, "I did all the heavy hauling."

"That's as it may be," said Sir John, "but when were you last paid by him?"

After that question, Dillon seemed to withdraw somewhat inside himself. There was much to be learned from his face as he stood before us. He worked slowly from defense, to suspicion, to hostility. "Yes, your magistrate," said he, "I sees what you're about. And you'll not trap me. No, you'll not trap Dick Dillon."

Sir John persisted in his line of questioning: "You left his employ quite suddenly. What was the reason?"

"You are tryin' to get from me for gratis what I shall only sell dear," said Dillon. "We talked of this in your court. I wish transportation. I own I got information of interest to your magistrate. But I peach on no one, give no story to you or to anyone, unless it is I got a firm promise of transportation."

"Life on the plantations can be hard," said Sir John.

"I'll take my chances, so I will. And I prefer it to the other."

"As would any man," agreed Sir John. "But hear me through on this, Dick Dillon, for your very life may depend upon it. No magistrate can give absolute warrant that his recommendation will be followed, yet I have given my recommendations for leniency in the past, and they have never been ignored. I promise you faithfully, Dick Dillon, that I, John Fielding, magistrate of the Bow Street Court, will pass to Lord Mansfield, chief justice of the King's Bench, my recommendation for transportation, rather than hanging, if you, in turn, provide me with material information dealing with the death of Lord Goodhope. What say you to that?"

"What say I to that? I says, can you put it in writing?"

"There is no need. My word is my bond," said Sir John. "But something I must add to what I have already said, and it is this: Your information, whatever it may be, must be directly forthcoming, for the inquiry continues apace and may soon be concluded. I expect it to be. Should what you have to give come late, say, at the time of your trial before the King's Bench, then there will be no need for it, and no need for me to make any recommendation whatsoever. Is this clear to you?"

Dillon glowered at Sir John. "Clear," said he. "Yes, it's clear."

"I have but one question for you before we go further. Does this information you have to give directly involve you in the matter of murder? For if so, I must say in all fairness, I cannot help you. So you see? I play right with you. I lay before you the limits of my power. Now how say you?"

"I was not involved in no murder. I never committed no murder."

"I accept that," said Sir John. "You may then proceed."

An interminably long moment followed, in which Dillon fought with himself and who knew what adversary. Again, in his face the conflict was clear. But there was what I had not read before, something of fear: strange to see in a man so large and powerful. At the last moment he seemed about to yield, but at last he shook his head.

He then spoke: "Sir John, at this moment my wits is fogged with drink. Your offer is a fair one, I vow, but I must have time to think on it sober. Will you give me that?"

"What works on you so?" asked Sir John. "What have you to fear?"

Dillon looked about him, as though pondering the possibilities. "Dick Dillon fears naught," said he, his voice dropped to a whisper. "He only needs time to consider."

Sir John sighed abruptly. "I will give you time," said he, making no attempt to hide his annoyance, "but only the rest of this day and tonight. In the morning I shall send two constables to bring you to the Bow Street Court. We shall talk in my chambers. You had best come prepared to speak to the matter at hand. When you have given your testimony, whatever it may be, you will be transferred to the Fleet Prison."

Having thus had his say, he bellowed out loudly, *"Warder!* We are ready to return."

Dillon watched us go, saying nothing more, his eyes near as heavy-lidded as one asleep, yet watchful withal. Though he had pleaded drunkenness, he now seemed sober.

The warder who had brought us hence now led us back, pausing at the stairs to relight his candle. Descending, I took the position behind him and felt Sir John's strong hand on my shoulder. We two said nothing between us, but the warder was as talkative as ever.

"He's a hard case that'n. What's his name?" He paused a moment, but when no response was forthcoming, he continued. "Ah yes, Dillon, so it is, Dick Dillon. I remember it from the list whence you sought him out. He bullies the others inside something terrible, he does. He takes coin from the men and uses the women most shameful. It's his size allows him to do it. They're all against him inside."

At that point, I reflected that Dillon seemed to be drinking in a reasonably convivial manner with that group of men above. Or perhaps not. Perhaps it was just as the warder said.

"I don't suppose you got much out of that'n. Thinks he'll beat the hangman, he does. Just watch your step now, Sir John. We're coming to the end of the stairs."

Then, having reached the level floor, the warder stepped back and blew out the candle.

The clamor raised by the common felons was not near what it had been earlier. In any case, having been once afrighted by them, I was better prepared and kept a steady pace to the exit. But the smell was as bad as before. My attempts to breathe shallow benefited me not at all. It was not until we found ourselves in the open air of the courtyard that I was able to fill my lungs without befouling them.

The warder walked with us to the gate, making no further effort to engage us in conversation. "I'll just leave you here, Sir John. The gatekeeper approaches, and I see a hackney parked beyond," said he then.

"May I inquire as to your name?" asked Sir John.

"My name? Why . . ." He was somewhat flustered by the question. For a moment he seemed almost to have forgotten the answer. "Why . . . indeed, my name is Jack Wilson, and it was my pleasure to serve you, Sir John.''

''I thank you for your trouble, Mr. Wilson, and goodbye to you.'' Waiting until Wilson had departed some distance away, Sir John whispered to me, ''I do not like that fellow.''

His dislike was given reason by the gatekeeper.

Grimy and unkempt though he may have been, the gatekeeper was an obliging individual, and he greeted us most warmly, inquiring if our visit had been worthwhile.

''More or less,'' said Sir John, ''more or less.''

''Well, I hopes it comes right for you,'' said he, as he pushed that biggest key on his ring into the gate lock.

As he swung open the gate and we made to depart, Sir John stopped and turned in his direction as if having had a sudden thought.

''It occurs to me,'' said Sir John, ''that I might inquire after the warder who served as our guide. He was most helpful. What was his name? I should like to commend him to the Keeper of Newgate.''

''Him what showed you about? That was John Larkin was who it was.''

''Thank you, gatekeeper. Don't mention it to him, though. It may be some time before I get to the matter. And your name?''

''Josiah Blackwood, at your service!''

''Thank you, and good day!''

With that, sniffing out the smell of the horse, Sir John led the way to the hackney and the beginning of a long trip back to Bow Street. It passed, for the most part, in silence. Sir John, as was often his way, withdrew into himself. And though I had many questions regarding Newgate and the conduct of Dick Dillon, I withheld them, thinking it best to allow him time to ponder. One, however, burned within me, and as we drew near our destination and the end of my time alone with him, I fairly burst to ask it. Finally, with Covent Garden in sight, it came forth.

"Sir John," said I, of a sudden, "why did he give a false name?"

He, roused from deep thought, came almost reluctantly back to me. "What's that, boy? What is it you ask?"

"The warder," said I, "he gave his name as Wilson. The gatekeeper said his name was Larkin. The warder lied. Why did he do that?"

"Ah, yes, that," said he with a sigh. "Well, it cannot have been done with any good purpose in mind. That's sure certain. Our man Dillon seems to place great store by his strength. Pray God it suffices."

Though I was confused by his response, I questioned no further. Had he wanted to tell me more, said I to myself, he would have done so.

We alighted at Number 4 Bow Street and proceeded forthwith to Sir John's chambers, though I was barred admittance at the door. "Go find Mr. Marsden, if you will," said he, "and bring him to me. Then wait about, for I shall have a message for you to deliver."

Doing as he had directed, I found the court clerk sipping a dish of tea with Mr. Thomas Baker, the constable who had taken Mr. Bailey's place as acting captain of the Bow Street Runners. They were quite jolly together, no doubt laughing at some sally made by Mr. Marsden, who was quite a witty man. Neither, however, took it ill when I interrupted their merriment and passed on the message from Sir John.

"Do you know what the matter may be?" asked Mr. Marsden, as we proceeded to the magistrate's chambers.

"No sir," said I, "except that he asked me to stand by to deliver a message."

"Ah," said he, "then once again I play scribe to Solomon."

I, having then little or no knowledge of the Bible, missed his reference completely. Nevertheless, I can assure the reader that though some irony may have been intended with the remark, no sense of disrespect attached to it.

I waited outside the closed door for no long space of time until Mr. Marsden, having completed his job of work, emerged and bade me enter. Then he himself was called back by Sir John. Pausing by the open door to wait, I heard the ensuing conversation between them:

"Mr. Marsden," said Sir John, "do you recall that fellow Sayer who gave false witness against young Jeremy Proctor a few days past?"

"I do indeed, sir," said Mr. Marsden.

"As I recall, the court plundered his purse to bring the debt of that Caulfield woman to rights."

"That's as I recall it, too."

Sir John dug into his voluminous coat pocket and pulled out some coins. Selecting them carefully by touch, he separated a few from the rest and handed them to the clerk.

"That was inconsiderate. I wish you to return these three shillings to his purse and hold it for the morrow. I shall then be sending two constables to transport a prisoner from Newgate. Have them return the purse and money to Sayer. Mind, it is to go into his hands and not to be trusted to a warder. Having just returned from that place of horrors, I was reminded once again how desperately those inside need all resources they can assemble."

"It'll be done, Sir John."

"Good. Now send Jeremy to me."

Thus, with Mr. Marsden gone, I entered and found Sir John standing behind his desk. He offered me an envelope closed with his seal.

"Jeremy," said he, "I wish you to deliver this note to Mary Deemey at her shop in Chandos Street. There is sufficient space at the bottom of it for her to pen her answer. She is to do that. You are to wait for it and return it to me direct. Is this understood?"

"Very well," said I.

"If need be, you must impress upon her the seriousness of the inquiry. Tell her that this is a court matter and that neither prevarication nor delay will be tolerated. Quote me on that.''

I agreed to do so, and he then gave me explicit directions to Chandos Street, but said that once upon it I would have to find the dressmaker's shop by my own devices. "Look sharp, and you may see the shop sign," said he. "Ask if you must.''

As it happened, I had no need to ask anyone of anything, neither for amplification of Sir John's directions, nor for the exact location of Mary Deemey's place of business. Once I had entered the street, I saw a hanging sign close by with the Deemey name, and below it, an attempt at French: "Modes Elegantes." I crossed the street to it, dodging a wagon team and leaping the usual pile of horse dung. (In those days our London streets were not kept near as clean as they are today.) I made to knock on the door, then thinking better of it, marched boldly inside.

I was met there by a Frenchwoman, or at least one who spoke French to me. *"Bonjour, jeune homme,"* said she, moving from behind the counter. " 'Ow may I serve you?''

I thought her English much subordinate to her native tongue. And so, continuing bold, I loosed upon her a veritable flood of French—first, a most polite greeting learned from my father, then an inquiry into her health, as I was told by him the French prefer before beginning matters of business. I waited for her reply.

Yet all I got from her was a puzzled look and at last: *"Comment? En anglais, s'il vous plaît."*

At that I was much chagrined, thinking my accent so bad as to be incomprehensible. I had been given reason to suspect my father's was imperfect. On the evening we were visited by the gentleman from France, with whom my father had been in correspondence, their conversation had begun in French, but following similarly puzzled looks from our visitor, had continued the rest of the night in English.

And so, thus humbled, I sought to retrieve my pride through the official nature of my errand. I declared in a

loud voice, waving the document in question, that I had in
my hand an official communication from Sir John Fielding
of the Bow Street Court for Mrs. Mary Deemey.

"Let me 'ave eet," said the woman. "Ah will see she
gets eet."

I withheld the letter. "No," said I. "It is to be put in
her hands direct, and I am to wait for a reply."

The woman looked at me somewhat perplexed, then said
she in plain English: "Hand it over then, for Mary Deemey
is my name."

"But, but," said I, all a-stutter, "but you were French
just a moment ago."

"That's for those who give me custom, which you have
proved you are not one. So let's have the letter, my lad."

Still I held it back. "How do I know you are who you
say?"

"Because I declare it."

"Let someone identify you, for you've deceived me once
already."

In answer, she sighed a great sigh and called out loudly:
"Katy! Margaret! Beth!"

From behind a curtain at the rear of the shop came a
ragged reply from all three: "Yes, missus?"

"One of you come out here."

After a moment's delay, the head of a girl of sixteen or
seventeen thrust through the curtain. She looked at me curiously and then at the woman who had summoned her.
"Yes, ma'am?" said she.

"Who am I?"

"Who are you?" echoed the girl. "Uh ... Madame
Claudette?"

"No, you stupid girl, who am I in truth? You must identify me for this presumptuous boy."

The girl looked at me again. She seemed not so much
stupid as nearsighted and exhausted. She addressed me direct: "That is Mrs. Mary Deemey." Then to her employer:
"Will that be all, ma'am?"

"Quite. Back to work, Beth."

The head disappeared as I handed the letter to Mrs. Deemey with a bit of a flourish. She, taking it, showed no special awe for its seal, but ripped it open and began hurriedly to read its contents.

Just then, as my sight flowed over the etchings of fashionable female dress mounted about the place and took in the two gowns hung on headless models at either side of the counter, the curtains recently pierced by the seamstress were suddenly thrown asunder, and there stood Mistress Lucy Kilbourne, once again wearing no more than her shift. As near as I could tell, it was her favorite mode of dress.

"Ah," said she, "if it ain't my young gallant from the night before! We were not properly introduced by your master, though you proved most helpful to me. What is your name, young sir?"

I hesitated to tell her. Having once been seduced, I knew her power. Yet she seemed to know it, too, for she gave me a slow, languid smile which quite melted my resistance.

"Jeremy," said I. "Jeremy Proctor, ma'am."

"A pretty name, and politely presented, too."

She took a step toward me, extending her hand, as if to shake mine, or to lend hers for kissing: I had no notion of the proprieties. But then, giving me to think that she had for the first time noticed her state of undress, she withdrew her hand, stepped back, and demurely crossed her arms over her shoulders.

"You must forgive me," said she. "I had not minded my nakedness. Please do not think that this is my habit." Then she turned to the proprietress of the shop and said sweetly, "Mary, I wonder could you come and mark the fit of my new gown?"

Mrs. Deemey held up the letter from Sir John. "But I must—"

"*Now,* Mary."

With a sigh and a worried look at me, Mrs. Deemey nodded her assent. She hurried after Mistress Kilbourne,

through the curtains, and into the back of the shop. I noted
that she had carried with her Sir John's letter.

So there was I, left alone with only two well-clothed,
headless models to keep me company. The pictures about
the place had little to hold my interest, and so, without quite
intending to do so, I found myself edging toward the curtain
which Mrs. Deemey had shut upon her departure. The
closer I drew, the more I heard of whispering. The words
were not distinct, except perhaps for a few. I did hear
clearly the urgent voice of Lucy Kilbourne demanding to
know, "Who's payin' you, Mary?" which was answered
by a muttered grumble from Mrs. Deemey. There was much
more insistent whispering and hissing on the part of Mistress Kilbourne, and at last—silence.

With that I retired to my former position and feigned
interest in the fashion plates posted about the room. I had
not long to wait, for Mrs. Deemey soon appeared, waving
the letter at me. I could see that a few lines in reply had
been appended at the bottom. She made swift to hand it
over to me.

"You have what you came for," said she. "Now you
may go."

Yet I held on. "I was asked by Sir John Fielding to say
that this is a court matter and that no prevarication would
be tolerated," said I.

She gave me a sharp look. "Do you seek to fright me,
young man?"

"No, I merely quote Sir John. In truth, he said, 'No
prevarication *or delay* would be tolerated.' But you have
penned your reply so promptly . . ."

Her face was set. She nodded toward the door. "Be
gone," said she.

And so I left the shop of Mary Deemey, glad to be gone
and out of harm's way. I went at a run back to Number 4
Bow Street. But I found, upon my arrival, that the magistrate's court was in session. What to do with myself? I had
no wish to return to the living quarters above, which were

so heavy with Lady Fielding's silence and the sighs of Mrs. Gredge. And so I let myself in the side door, went past the strong room where two Runners sat with an equal number of prisoners in chains, and on to the bench outside Sir John's chambers.

There I determined to sit until the magistrate appeared, no matter how long the wait. I wished that I had by me one of that store of books from my attic room, of which I had read but two. But lacking that, I fell to considering the matter at hand; and that, of course, was the inquiry into the death of Lord Goodhope.

I made reference earlier to certain childish notes I had kept on the affair. Indeed I had kept a kind of diary, solely concerned with the progress of the inquiry. I have no trouble reading it today, for even at the age of thirteen I wrote a good, legible hand. Yet, for the most part, it testifies less to the progress of the inquiry than to my bewilderment at it. I had noted in it Mr. Bailey's precise description of the wound to Lord Goodhope's head. But below it, I find only this notation: "Clean hands!" Modesty must have overcome me, for it could well be argued that my ignorant observation of the condition of the nobleman's hands was my only contribution to the entire matter.

There were other notations, but most of them were in the form of questions: "Mr. Donnelly—poison?" and "A tunnel? That place in the mews?" This was followed later by an account of my discovery, with Ebenezer Tepper, of that clandestine egress into the library. And so on. So I had kept a general record on paper and a more specific one in my head. There were two questions not yet entered in my notes: The first had to do with our visit to Newgate that day. What information did Sir John seek from Dick Dillon that he valued so highly that he was willing to do what he indicated in his speech from the bench that he would not do?—to recommend leniency for one who had struck a potentially murderous blow at an officer of the law. And why had Dick Dillon not grasped at the offer Sir John had made him?

What had he to fear, or further to negotiate?

As for my second question, it had to do with the errand I had just undertaken for Sir John. And here, reader, I blush to confess that sitting on that bench outside the magistrate's chambers, I did unobserved what I would never have done before a witness. I took out the letter from Sir John to Mrs. Deemey from my pocket and, the seal having already been broken, read its contents. The letter dealt with questions of fact concerning that very same widow's dress I had helped Lucy Kilbourne into the night before: When had Mistress Kilbourne ordered it and been fitted for it? When had it been delivered? Across the bottom of the page Mrs. Deemey had scrawled: "Said dress ordered and delivered a year ago in the winter. I recall it well, for it was cut and sewed in a great rush due to her father's sudden death. Parts of it was still pinned and tacked when she attended his funeral." Her signature, barely legible as "M. Deemey," followed last of all.

I understood this a bit better than the questions pertaining to Dick Dillon. For after all, it was evident even to me that had Mistress Kilbourne ordered her modish weeds recently, though somewhat preceding the death of Lord Goodhope, this would have indicated prior knowledge on her part. Since murder was the verdict, this knowledge would surely have made her party to it. Mrs. Deemey's response, however, put such a theory in extreme doubt. Yet that response had been penned in the presence of Lucy Kilbourne—perhaps, with all that earnest whispering, dictated by her.

As she entered as a factor in my reasoning, she came also as a picture to my mind. How could a woman of such remarkable beauty be thus involved in matters so base? I dwelt on that picture a bit, remembering not only her face and the pert, mischievous set of her fine features, but also (I allow) her naked shoulders and the demure gesture with which she covered them. Ah, woman! What contradictions that sex provides! And what food for contemplation!

Occupied as I was with my fantasies, I did not at first

see Mr. Donnelly when he appeared. He had evidently walked the length of the hall without my notice and now stood before me, clearing his throat to claim my attention.

I jumped to my feet and sought to greet him properly: "Mr. Donnelly! Good day! Forgive me, for I had not . . ."

He gave a wave of his hand, dismissing my concern. "Dreaming in the daytime? We all do it from time to time. I fear we Irish are more dedicated to the practice than most."

"Can I be of some help, sir?"

"Yes, you can, Jeremy." He lifted a sealed document from the pocket of his coat. It was much like the one I had delivered to Mrs. Deemey, except thicker, of two or perhaps three pages. "What I have here," said he, "is a report on Lady Goodhope's view of the corpus. She has made a positive identification. I set forth this finding in her person, and she has signed it; I have witnessed it. This should certainly satisfy Sir John. In addition, I have included certain of my own final observations on the condition of the corpus as an addendum to my earlier report—all this in the interest of thoroughness." He offered the document to me, and I took it. "I entrust this to you for delivery direct into the hands of Sir John," said he with suitable seriousness.

"It will be done just so," said I.

"I'm sure it will be," said he. But then he lingered, perhaps reluctant to get on to his next destination, or so starved for companionship in this great city that he was willing, for a few minutes at least, to share company and conversation with a thirteen-year-old boy.

"It was," said he to me, "something of an ordeal for Lady Goodhope."

"Oh, indeed," said I. "The face, when I vewed it, was in fierce condition. But no doubt it was much improved by the embalmer's art."

"They did not do as much as they promised. They managed to get the eye closed, but the nose was still a shapeless mass, and the face was still a bit blackened from the discharge of powder. No, they could have done better; I'm sure of it. With my years as ship's surgeon, I have become inured to such sights. She—Lady Goodhope, that is—had never looked upon the like; then to be told—so to speak, actually I asked—that this Christmas pudding of a face is your husband's! Well, no wonder she was tearful!''

"I noticed," said I, "that she was shortsighted. Did that make for greater difficulty?"

"Very observant of you, Jeremy. Yes, it did make for hardship. Once I explained to her the necessity for the identification, she was quite diligent in her duty. She put her face quite close and studied as long as she was able."

"As long as she was able?"

"Yes." He sighed. "You see, he's beginning to stink a bit. No telling how he'll smell when they get him to Lancashire. In any case, not a pleasant experience for her."

"Indeed not."

"What do you think of her?"

"Sir?"

"What do you think of Lady Goodhope?"

It struck me then as a strange question to ask. As I write this today, it seems quite an outlandish question to put to a boy of my age, one who had so little experience of the world. I count it to that sense of isolation he seems to have felt there in the city. Had I not found a temporary home with Sir John, I would then probably also have felt it even more keenly than he.

Nevertheless, I fumbled for an answer: "Well, she . . . she seems a strong woman. She has borne up well under great difficulties. But Sir John . . ."

"Yes, what does he say?"

"He thinks her willful."

At that Mr. Donnelly laughed most heartily. "Yes," said he, still laughing, "that might be said. Indeed it might!" But then he calmed and added seriously: "At the same time, though, like many women of her rank—or so I have heard—she is quite helpless in practical matters. It is not because she is unable but because she is uninterested. What she is not interested in seems not to exist for her. At this meeting which I am attending in her stead, I shall be discussing her very future in pounds and pence with Mr. Martinez and the solicitor, Blythe. Yet she could not be bothered to attend. Or perhaps I misread her in this. It may be a kind of fear of looking badly that keeps her away.''

Thus musing, he paused a moment and pulled out his timepiece from his breeches, consulting it with a nod. ''Just as I thought,'' said he. ''It's time I left for the solicitor's office.'' He gave me a nod and a manly squeeze on the shoulder. ''It's been a pleasure talking to you, Jeremy. I look forward to our next occasion.''

He turned and headed quickly down the hall. He had a swift, important step. I knew from past experience that it was difficult to keep up with him when he was in full flight.

I reflected as I returned to my seat on the bench that in truth he had done most of the talking. Yet he had addressed me from first to last as he might a grown man. That was what pleased me so.

Some time later, Sir John appeared. He came leisurely down the long hall, at first in the company of Mr. Marsden, the clerk, then exchanging words with Mr. Baker of the Runners, and on at last to his chambers. He sensed my presence before I announced myself.

''Who is there?'' he called out.

''It is I, Jeremy.''

''Ah yes,'' said he, ''of course—Mrs. Deemey's answer. Come along inside, and you may read it to me.''

He tapped the door to his chambers, found the door handle after a brief fumble, and led me inside. Seating himself in the chair behind his desk, he leaned forward in anticipation.

''So,'' said he, ''tell me. What had Mrs. Deemey to say?''

''You wish me to read it aloud?'' said I.

''Of course.''

"Your letter to her, as well?"

"No, no, I know what I said in it."

And so I read her response, verbatim, just as I earlier quoted it, immediately noting the change in his face to disappointment, barely disguised.

"Ah, well," said he, "perhaps another avenue will take us where we wish to go."

"But, Sir John," said I, "I believe it would be wrong to put much faith in what she says here."

"Oh? Tell me why."

And so I did, sketching out for him the scene at the dressmaker's, and the intense whispering that followed. He listened to it all with keen interest.

"And you say that when she returned, she had her reply written?"

"Just so," said I.

"Did you give her my warning about prevarication or delay?"

"I did, sir, yet not until after she had delivered her reply. There was not time earlier."

"Ran off on you, did she?"

"Yes, when Mistress Kilbourne demanded it."

"A demand, you say, and not a request?"

I thought about that a moment. "I should say the demand was in her tone of voice."

His reply to that was a sort of grunt and then a sustained silence. He considered the matter and perhaps others as well, as I stood before him, waiting to be dismissed. It was then that I remembered the sealed documents that Mr. Donnelly had given me.

"Sir John," said I, breaking the silence, "I also have two documents given me by Mr. Donnelly to be delivered direct to your hand."

"Don't concern yourself with my hand, boy. Give them to my ear. Read them to me, please."

I broke the seal and proceeded to do so. There was, as Mr. Donnelly had described, a rather short and direct state-

ment which he had headed "Certificate of Identification."
I read it out so and had barely begun on the body of the
work, only a paragraph in length, when I was distracted by
a disturbance outside the door, a loud sound of voices in
quarrel.

"Madam, you may not enter!"

"I shall, by God, I shall!"

"You must make an appointment to see the magistrate."
That voice belonged unmistakably to Mr. Marsden, the
court clerk.

I had broken off my reading and then attempted to begin
again, but the disagreement continued; a demand that Mr.
Marsden step aside; a threat by him to call a constable. At
last Sir John waved me to silence.

"Jeremy," said he, "do see what that row is all about,
will you?"

I went to the door and opened it cautiously. At first I
saw nothing but Mr. Marsden's back as he sought to block
the doorway with his entire body. Then, over his shoulder,
the face of Mrs. Deemey, ruddy with agitation, popped into
view. She spied me.

"He know me! The boy knows me!" she bellowed
loudly. "He knows why I'm here."

I shut the door quickly.

"What is it, Jeremy?" asked Sir John. "Who is it?"

"It is that woman, the dressmaker, Mrs. Deemey."

"Ah, is it now, is it so? Well, open the door. Let her
in." A smile of anticipation spread across his face.

I flung the door open, and Sir John called to Mr. Marsden
that he was to let her pass. With a confused and unhappy
look cast over his shoulder at me, Mr. Marsden stepped
reluctantly aside, and Mary Deemey flew past us both into
the middle of the room.

Her skirts had barely settled when she began her address
to the magistrate: "Begging your pardon for this intrusion,
Sir John, sir, but I am Mary Deemey, and I have come to
make right my reply to your kind letter."

"Sit down, Mrs. Deemey, please."

"Thank you," said she, somewhat out of breath. "But first I must offer my apology to this young sir you sent to my establishment. I was rude to him, but it was only because I was upset at what I'd been made to do, as I shall explain."

"Jeremy, do you accept her apology?"

"Oh, I do—certainly."

"Well and good," said he. "Now, come here and put those documents from Mr. Donnelly on my desk, if you will."

I did as he directed.

"That will be all, Jeremy."

"But . . . Sir John, I thought I might—"

"That will be all. Thank you, and please close the door after you."

How shameful it seemed to be treated as a thirteen-year-old boy.

Chapter 9

In which a pirate makes his report

THAT EVENING, FOR THE FIRST TIME SINCE I HAD ARRIVED in his household, Sir John took his meal alone in the small dining room next the kitchen. Aside from the snack of late-night mutton we had shared but a few nights past, I had seen him eat nothing but his breakfast bread and butter. Still, his girth had not shrunk; he was portly as ever; and when sure of his ground, he moved with a step no younger man could match—save, perhaps, for Mr. Donnelly. Nor had his fasting slowed his brain, as will be seen.

Mrs. Gredge made of it an occasion, cooking up two good-sized chops of beef, which she served him with batter and dripping. She bustled back and forth, providing claret as it was called for, and then at meal's end bringing a bottle of port, which she thought might aid his digestion.

He seemed to seek solitude, and it had been so since his return from his talk with Mary Deemey. All he had told me of it was that I had put some fear into her. Since this was offered in the mode of congratulation, I took it with thanks and waited to hear more. In vain, as it had proved,

for nothing more regarding Mary Deemey was said that
evening. He voiced his wish to dine alone to Mrs. Gredge
and went immediately to the dining room. There he sat in
the dark, which was all the same to him, until Mrs. Gredge
brought in a candle to aid her in her serving. After that, I
caught glimpses of him from my station at the kitchen table
as Mrs. Gredge passed in and out, bearing one thing and
another.

All this was possible because Lady Fielding slept. I knew
not when Mrs. Gredge had administered the last dose of
Mr. Donnelly's potion, but it must have been a powerful
one, for there had not been a sound from the bedroom since
Sir John had arrived, nor indeed since I had, nearly an hour
before him. Each time I glimpsed him in the dining room
he seemed quite lost in thought. Whether the subject he
studied so was his wife's mortal illness, Lord Goodhope's
death, or some other matter, I could not then say, nor can
I now. I only know that he concentrated upon it powerfully
and wanted no interruption from me.

However, when it came, he welcomed the interruption of
Benjamin Bailey—though Mrs. Gredge did not. The captain of the Bow Street Runners came up the back stairs and
to the kitchen door, as was his habit. His tread fell heavy
upon the stairs, and so we heard him coming well before
his loud knock came upon the door. Mrs. Gredge cast a
suspicious glance at me, as though I was the one caused
the disturbance. But then she scampered to the door and
called through it, demanding to know who was there.

"'Tis I, Benjamin Bailey," came the voice from beyond, "and I'll thank you to open up."

Reluctantly, she did it, though just enough to reveal him.
He seemed much the worse for wear.

"I have a report for Sir John," he declared.

"He'll not hear it from you tonight," she squawked as
loudly as ever before. "You're drunk, so you are. Been
down on Gin Lane, I'll wager."

"Not a drop of gin have I had," said he.

"No?" Mrs. Gredge sounded most dubious, as indeed she might have been.

"No," said he. "Rum. I'd forgotten the taste of it, as well as its power."

Sir John appeared at the door to the dining room.

"Let him in," said he to Mrs. Gredge, "for be he drunk or sober, I'll hear his report."

"Thank you, Sir John," said Mr. Bailey. "There's them need some convincing, but I'm glad to see you ain't one."

He sought to make a dignified entrance but staggered so that the effect was not at all what he intended. Even so, as he passed me, he bobbed his head and said, "Master Jeremy."

With which I remembered my manners, jumped to my feet, and gave him a proper greeting.

"Let us go up above," said Sir John to him, "to my study, if you will, Mr. Bailey. I must ask you, though, to tread a bit lighter as you pass the door at the top of the stairs, for my wife sleeps behind it."

Mr. Bailey said nothing but put a finger to his lips in agreement, as if Sir John could see him so. Yet he planted his foot falsely on the second step and managed to fall loudly against the rest. Nevertheless, with Sir John leading, they made their way up and disappeared a moment later.

Mrs. Gredge looked at me severely. "I do not like that man Bailey," said she to me.

"But why not?" said I, quite bewildered. He seemed to me the most likable of men.

"Because he reminds me of my late husband," said she.

And at that we parted, she to the dining room to clear Sir John's table and straighten up, and I to washing up the pots, pans, and various utensils as had been used in the preparation of the meal. I had been appointed by Mrs. Gredge her kitchen slavey. My labors seemed to satisfy her: What I lacked in skill I made up with energy.

Therefore I gave no thought to the time spent by Mr. Bailey and Sir John together. I had plenty to occupy my hands; and as for my brain, I confess I had not much curiosity about Mr. Bailey's report. Except for the confirmation of the master of the *Island Princess* that Mr. Clairmont had left the ship at the time he had said, I had no idea of what sort of information was to be gained down at the docks, nor how it might fit in with the bits of the puzzle I knew.

And so, about half an hour later, when Mr. Bailey departed, I gave him a friendly goodbye but little more. Mrs. Gredge gave him not even that, for he was still a bit unsteady on his feet. Sir John remained above. There were slight sounds an hour or so later from the bedroom; the door to the room had been left ajar so that Lady Fielding might be heard. Immediately Mrs. Gredge jumped up from the kitchen table and started for the stairs, but then Sir John's footsteps sounded from above. The door creaked, and a minute or two later his voice sounded, calling for Mrs. Gredge to begin the preparation of Mr. Donnelly's potion. She sent me a despairing look, then went about her task.

I felt quite superfluous to the situation. Unable to sit reading in the face of such distress, I stood and hovered unhappily as Mrs. Gredge beat the poppy seeds down to a fine pulp. As she added the boiling water from the kettle, Sir John appeared, making his way down the stairs.

"Mrs. Gredge," said he, "give me the preparation, and I shall carry it to her."

She seemed to look a bit doubtful, but, giving the soporific potion a final stir, she brought it to him and put it firmly in his hands. Holding it carefully, he turned and started his ascent of the stairs. Yet at some point low on the flight, his foot stumbled, or perhaps slipped, and down he clattered full across the upper stairs. The teacup left his hands and shattered, and of course its contents were lost.

(Could it have been the same spot which caused Mr. Bailey to tumble not much more than an hour before? Perhaps there was a warped step, or a projecting nail. Yet Sir

John took all the blame upon himself.)

I rushed to his side to assist him to his feet. But he shook away from me and pushed himself upright.

"Oh, *damn!*" said he. "Damn my blindness, and damn my conceit that I may move about as other men do."

I stood, with Mrs. Gredge close by, wishing I could say something to comfort him, yet there was nothing that would not have seemed presumptuous or patronizing.

He paused, breathing deeply for a moment, then, regaining himself, turned toward us and said, "Mrs. Gredge, I take it that the dose was spilled?"

"Yes, Sir John, all of it."

"Then please prepare another and bring it up. I shall be with my wife."

And saying that, he departed us.

She bustled off to do as he had directed, while I fetched a rag to wipe up the spill, then gathered up the broken fragments of the cup. When I came to her again, she was near done with the job of it, yet she sobbed quietly, and tears ran down her wrinkled cheeks.

"Oh, Jeremy," said she, "I must ask you to convey this cup to the bedroom, for I cannot stop my weeping, and I fear it would have a bad effect on Lady Fielding if she saw me so."

"I shall do it, certainly."

Mrs. Gredge left a teaspoon in the cup and instructed me to give the potion a final stir before I passed it on. With that I took it all carefully within my two hands and moved carefully toward the stairs and even more carefully up them.

The door to the bedroom stood open. I stopped at it and looked inside. The scene was illuminated dimly by but a single candle, which stood on a bedside table. Sir John sat in a chair beside his wife, her hand in his own. She lay quite listless on the bed, near a corpus already, but he bent toward her murmuring quietly in her ear. I could not hear what he said to her, nor under the circumstances would it have been proper for me to have done so.

Moving into the room, again with the utmost care, I went to Sir John with the cup and felt Lady Fielding's dull gaze fall upon me.

"Is that you, Jeremy?" said he.

"It is. Mrs. Gredge asked me to bring this to you."

"Your young hands are steadiest. I'm afraid that mine now shake so that I would spill the cup once again."

"And I," came the whisper from the bed, "am too weak to hold it."

"You must administer the potion."

I did not welcome the occasion, yet I met it fairly. Sir John and I exchanged places, and I, remembering to stir the cup, lifted Lady Fielding carefully and brought it to her lips.

"Slowly," said she, "very slowly."

And thus she took it in the tiniest sips, so slowly that she, asking to rest, gave me the opportunity to stir the cup once again.

But at last it was done. She had taken it all. I moved from her bedside, and Sir John reached out awkwardly and grasped my arm in silent thanks. I turned and left the room.

He remained above with her for near an hour, long past the time, I'm sure, when she had dropped into deep, unconscious slumber. Mrs. Gredge and I heard him leave the room quietly, then proceed into his study. Immediately he had entered it, he began pacing fitfully, in no particular pattern. It was not a large room. Three long steps would have traversed it in one direction and three in another. He took them so, then made two and three, two and two, with a halt between, then back to three and three.

Mrs. Gredge had turned pious with death so near in the house. She sat with me at the table, holding before her, upside down, *The Book of Common Prayer*. Yet her eyes strayed upward as the pacing continued. When they met mine she shook her head and returned purposefully to her putative reading.

It continued thus for many minutes. At last the steps

ceased—or was it only a temporary halt, a little longer than the rest? I had become near exhausted by the mood of the house and quite ready to go to bed myself. And so I was surprised when Sir John descended the stairs, dressed in his coat, wearing his tricorn, and carrying his stick.

"I shall be going out, Mrs. Gredge."

"So late, sir? But as you say, of course."

"My wife should sleep till morning, should she not?"

"Till morning, yes sir. If she should wake, I'll be close by."

"Have no fear, I'll not be gone so long," said he. Then: "Jeremy?"

I jumped to my feet, near tipping my chair.

"Yes, Sir John?"

"I wish you to accompany me."

With that, all thoughts of sleep vanished. I ran as swiftly and silently as I could to my attic room and fetched my hat and coat. I was back in a trice, dressed for the street, ready for whatever adventure the night could provide.

We set off together in a hackney. I had not been out so late before on the streets of London, and I was surprised to see certain parts as crowded as if it be day. Men—and women, too, in near equal number—made congregation upon the street corners, roistering uncommonly loud for such an hour. Had these people no need for sleep? Did they not labor, as most do, in the daytime?

As I sat, staring out the window of the hackney, I was drawn away from these speculations by Sir John, who, deep in thought, began thumping on the floor of the compartment with his stick in a gesture I had come to recognize as a sign of perturbation.

"Ah, Jeremy," said he at last, "this matter of dying weighs powerfully upon me. If I may ask, boy, at what age was your father when he met his death at the hands of that shameful mob of hypocrites?"

"Just past forty, I believe. He made little of such anniversaries, so I am not certain."

"Forgive me for bringing up what must be painful to remember. My Kitty has not yet reached even that age. You may not count it so, but rude as was his death, it was nevertheless swift, and that in its own way may have been a blessing."

Remembering the occasion, my father's lifeless body laid out beneath the stocks, I saw little benefit to his death. Yet against that awful picture I placed another: that of Lady Fielding's drawn and wasted face—all eyes, it seemed, yet eyes that had lost their life's luster. She had been in such a state for weeks, according to Mrs. Gredge; my mother's death, though of natural cause, took but a few days. And so, I reflected, though I would not grant Sir John's claim outright, I had to allow the sense of it. But surely death, in all its manifestations, was odious and unfair to all involved.

I held my peace, and after a moment Sir John spoke up again.

"I fear," said he, "she is being made to suffer in my behalf."

To that I objected immediately: "*No,* sir! How could that be?"

"As a magistrate, I have upheld the letter of the law and bound many men over for trial, and a few women. Who knows how many innocents I helped on the way to the gallows?"

"But you condemned none. You sentenced no one. The trial is given before the High Court judge. That's as you told me. Is that not so?"

"Yes," said he, "and thank God for it, but I assisted. I did my part. Indeed, I did my part."

And then silence for a long stretch, until he spoke up again.

"Jeremy, you must promise me one thing."

"I will, Sir John, what is it?"

"That you will never attend a hanging day at Tyburn Hill."

Though I knew little of such and had got that only by reading, I swore as he asked.

"They make a show of it for the amusement of the mob," said he. "A man's death is between him and God and not a performance to be viewed by others. I think we should have more respect for death. That has been brought home to me in the past weeks. A man's death is a solemn thing, whatever the circumstances." And then, after a moment, he added, "And a woman's, as well."

I can tell you now, though I could not have then, that we came to a halt at a location in Mayfair that was not far from Tyburn Hill and was indeed on the way to it. Though I kept my promise to him, in later times I viewed the gallows oft on days when it was not in use.

As Sir John paid the driver, I descended from the hackney and gave my attention to the house before which we had stopped. It was very much like Lord Goodhope's residence, which was also not far from it, though not so grand, nor of such handsome appearance.

Making ready to enter, he pulled me back and bent a bit so that his face was close to mine.

"Jeremy," said he to me in a loud whisper, "though I have just now voiced scruples and regrets, that does not mean that I mean to shirk my duty. And that pertains in particular to this matter of Lord Goodhope. It is an ugly thing. It is murder. This place I have brought you to tonight is one to which I would ordinarily forbid you to go. In spite of how it may appear to your young eyes, no good is done in it. But we must find a man inside and talk to him. I wished you to be present so as to study his reactions as I question him. I can hear much in a voice, yet some signs elude me. Be watchful for them."

"Yes, Sir John."

"Well then," said he, "let's be in."

He led the way up three steps, tapping each with his stick, then used it to rap sharply on the door. Even before it opened I could hear sounds of raucous commotion be-

yond: high laughter and a sharp, excited chorus of exclamation. What place was this?

The door opened, and the space it revealed was filled
completely by the imposing figure of a man in butler's livery. His purpose, it seemed, was to block our way.

"What's your wish?" said he, rudely. "This is a private
club."

"That's as may be, but you must admit us, for I am the
magistrate of the Bow Street Court."

"Then as you say, I suppose I must." Reluctantly, the
man stepped back, pulling the door wide before us.

We stepped inside, and I viewed the interior. A carpet
dyed red led from the door down a hall which ended in a
grand staircase, which was also red-carpeted, and curved to
a level above which I could neither see nor imagine. The
walls visible to me were painted a yellow that glowed
nearly as bright as the red on the floor, even in candlelight.
There were open entrances, each across the hall, to what
must have been very large rooms, for the clamor I had
heard through the door now issued from them much mag-
nified now that the barrier was removed. This side of each
door was a sofa on which women sat—oh, ladies surely,
dressed most finely, yet alone and waiting in an attentive
attitude of service. They had turned and now stared in curiosity at Sir John and myself.

The butler, or doorman, or whatever his position, advanced us down the hall and gestured broadly as he
spoke, as if by rote: "Games of hazard is to be found in
either room. Your even-odd tables is on the left and the
chemin de fer, as well as other games of cards, is played
in the room on the right. Ladies is available to show you
about—" He looked at me skeptically. "Will you be re-
quirin' one or two?"

"None," said Sir John. "We are here on an official inquiry. I wish to speak at some length with your employer,
Mr. Bilbo. If you will get him, I will be obliged."

"I cannot leave my post," said he who had met us at

the door. "So I shall put you in the hands of one of our ladies." Then, surveying the selection, he chose one and called out: "Nancy!"

She was up on her feet and over to us in the very fraction of a moment, addressing Sir John boldly and quite ignoring me: "A right good evening to you, m'lord. What is your pleasure tonight? Though I daresay the even-odd wheel would suit you best, would it not? And you brought your young helper to place your wagers and pull in your winnings, while I'll just accompany you and stand close by for good luck, like. Ain't that as you'd have it, m'lord?"

Sir John said nothing, but he had removed his tricorn as we entered (as had I), and I could see his forehead wrinkle in concentration.

"Nancy, girl," said the doorman, "just take him to Black Jack. That's all as he requires." So saying, he turned and walked back to the door.

"Plummer," said Sir John. "Nancy Plummer."

She, who beneath her paint and rouge appeared to be no more than five years my senior, pulled back quite stunned. There was a great and enthusiastic roar from one of the rooms behind her. At last it died.

"You remember?" said she meekly.

"Ah yes, you appeared before me regarding a matter of a stolen timepiece."

"But that was more than two years past, and I'm speakin' ever so much more proper these days."

"Yes, and no doubt you look quite the lady, too. Does she, Jeremy?"

"Oh, yes sir," said I, "she does."

She blessed me with a quick smile.

"But no matter how well you speak, you speak in the same voice, my girl."

"Well, I count that a wonder," said she, "remembering me from such a time past by my voice alone." And then she added, "You was quite fair to me."

"There were, as I recall, no witnesses, nor was the article

found in your possession—simply the suspicions of the victim. The usual. But enough of that, Nancy. Take us to Mr. Bilbo, if you would.''

''Now, where would he be?'' said she, casting glances right and left. ''I do believe he was in the even-odd room the last I saw of him. Let me look.''

''We'll follow you,'' said Sir John firmly.

And though she looked dubious, she set off in advance of us, offering Sir John the opportunity to whisper to me: ''In this instance, I do give you permission to take my elbow. Guide me well. Let me bump into no one.''

So we set off together: I steering and he responding quite deftly. Bringing him about to the left, we entered the room where she had ducked in, and for a moment I lost her there, such a number of people there was and such a hubbub they made. All were, to my undiscriminating eyes, dressed as lords and ladies. And while indeed there may have been some lords present, they had surely left their rightful ladies at home. Most had gathered around the table at the far end of the room; the one nearer to us was hardly attended. Nancy, our guide, I spied at last mixing in with the larger group. Another roar went up from them, and a whinny of female laughter, near demented in nature, that rose above it and lingered after.

I moved Sir John toward the crowd. A few glanced our way, but paid us no mind as we circled about its edge. Far more interested were they in the play at the wheel, which even then spun again and came to rest.

Another roar; another whinny.

By this time, Nancy had separated from the midst of those bunched nearest the table a man of quite singular appearance. He was large: tall enough, but so thick in the chest, long in the arms, and short in the legs that there seemed something ape-like in his appearance. Adding to this impression was the beard he wore, black and thick, at a time when facial hair was as rarely seen as it is today. To see one of such animal nature dressed as fashionably as he most certainly was that evening seemed somehow ludicrous. Yet one did not laugh at Black Jack Bilbo.

He and Sir John greeted each other almost as old friends might.

"It's the beak," cackled Bilbo. "The Blind Beak's come to call!"

A few turned and showed brief interest as Bilbo grabbed Sir John's hand and pumped it strongly. But then the even-odd wheel began turning again and all eyes but ours went to it.

"John Bilbo, we must talk," said Sir John, with not much of the severity those words might suggest. There was, in any case, a smile upon his face, the sort of smile of forbearance that one might bestow upon a mischievous child.

As the crowd cried out again, Bilbo threw an irritated look at the table and moved us away.

"Aye," said he, "but not here, eh? We'll go above, if it's all the same to you. Nancy, back to your place, girl."

With that, he shepherded Sir John and me out of the room, farther down the hall, and up the stairs, while all the while he talked most winningly. First he asked my name, and when Sir John gave it to him, he shook my hand cordially and declared himself delighted to make my acquaintance. And when, after inquiring, he found the doorman had admitted us somewhat grudgingly, he begged Sir John's pardon quite humbly and said the fellow was new in his position and not a Londoner but a seaman from the American colonies; he would set him right on such matters in the future.

At this point, Sir John interjected a question about the din in the e-o room: "Was that usual?" he asked. "On my previous visits here, I've never known such a powerful noise from your patrons, and all of it from one table. Why such a to-do?"

By this time Mr. Bilbo had seen us to the upper floor. He took a moment to fetch out a set of keys and open a door to what proved to be a small bureau. Inside, a single candle burned. He lit a taper from it and set aglow an entire four-stick candelabrum on one side of his desk. The whole room came forth in light, revealing an oaken desk, behind which he sat down, and chairs for Sir John and myself, where we took our places. On the wall were several pictures of nautical and sporting nature.

"Ah yes, well, all that noise," said Mr. Bilbo, leaning elbows on the desk and thrusting his great dark head toward us. "You got it right, Sir John, it ain't the usual, but it's one of them sometimes happening sort of things that pains me greatly to hear—and even greater to see. A fellow was having a great run of luck at the second table. Now, in the regular course of business I take in far more from the fellows what come here. I know that, and they know that. It's the mathematics of the place, so to speak. But I also know that if the tables be run fair—and mine are, sir, you have my word on that!—from time to time the luck must turn against my establishment in favor of the player. That's also in the mathematics of it, and I accept it. Yet when it happens, those who would play then become spectators—and that drives me quite daft! They come over from the other table to watch. Those at his table decline to play against him as his run continues. Some of the less sporting may bet with him, riding double on his horse, so to speak. But most simply stand back and take it in, like some grand bit of theatre. That way, y'see, my establishment loses double. It loses to the lucky man, and it loses the business of those who would otherwise be playing, as they by rights should be. This fellow has even pulled them in from the card room, which I do not like to see at all."

Sir John nodded, having taken all this in, and at last said: "This is all most interesting. Not being a gambler by nature and never having considered such matters from your side, I confess I had always thought of Black Jack Bilbo's simply as a place where men went to be quit of their money in pleasant surroundings."

At that Mr. Bilbo laughed a great guffaw. He was about to respond when from below came another chorus, this one not a roar but distinctly a groan; the whinny did not whinny. His face was for a brief moment quite expressionless as his sharp ears caught this, and then it relaxed into a smile. And from him came a quiet but prolonged sigh of pleasure.

"Well," said Sir John with a smile of his own, "perhaps the mathematics, as you put it, have caught up with your lucky man. Who is he, by the by?"

"Ah, it's that man Clairmont from the colonies."

"Charles Clairmont? Goodhope's half-brother?"

"So he claims, and I've no reason to doubt him. The two were in here together about a year ago, and perhaps once before—together. And that butler they sent over from the house a day past indeed knew him."

"Would you say the two looked much alike?" asked Sir John.

"Not so as you might notice, yet a bit—*half*-brother, after all. Clairmont was a bit shorter."

"We're getting a bit ahead of where I wished to begin in this matter," said Sir John. "Mr. Clairmont was one of the matters I intended to discuss with you, however. Let us do it in an orderly fashion."

"Any way you want, Sir John."

"Well and good. Now, John Bilbo, tell me, this visit made here a year ago by Mr. Clairmont with his half-brother—that was not his first to your establishment?"

"Oh no. We carried him on the books as a member, even though he only came here when he was in London every year or so—or p'rhaps a bit longer than that between visits from—where was it?—Jamaica."

"Yes, Jamaica. And you say he *may* have been here one time previous in the company of his half-brother?"

For the first time since they had begun this interview, Mr. Bilbo showed slight signs of exasperation: "Yes, and it may have been more—two, three, four, choose your number. Though I'm in the gaming rooms every night—indeed, I doss down the hall on this floor—I go from table to table, talk to the fellows, play the host, some I sees and some I don't. And mind, I spend a bit of time up here in this little hidey-hole every night, as well. So what I'm saying to you, Sir John, is that they *may* have been in together at least one time previous—I think they were, but that was some time back—seven, eight years ago, when I first opened this little house of chance. There may have been other times than one after, for as I say I cannot be sure certain.''

At about that time another groan issued from below. And again Mr. Bilbo's great bearded face relaxed into a smile.

"Do pardon me for goin' on so," he said. "I just wanted you to understand that I can't be as exact as you might want me to be."

"I do understand, and I accept what you say, John Bilbo. But let us talk of this man Clairmont, specifically. Do you know him well?"

"No, as I say, he came in here infrequent, just in those periods he was in the city from—Jamaica, was it?"

"Jamaica. Not nearly as well as you knew, say, Lord Goodhope?"

"Oh, sure not. Lord Dickie was *very* frequent, he was. Much to his undoing toward the end."

"Could you tell me something about the first *recent* appearance of Mr. Clairmont?"

"You mean two nights past when he just arrived?"

"I do, yes."

"Well, he must have come in before the twelve o'clock hour, though not *much* before. Anyways, that's when I gave him proper notice. I spied him at the roulette table, the first table that night, and I called him over from the game—I don't like to do that, but it seemed the occasion warranted it—and I told him that I had heard that his brother was dead; that was what I said, though half-brother would have been more right, would it not? His natural first question was how did he die. And I told him suicide, for that was how it had been talked about on the street, at that time. Now, I understand, there's talk of murder. Is that so, Sir John?''

"Let me ask the questions.''

"Aye, that I will.''

"And how did he take the news you gave him?''

"Oh, very well, I thought. He retired and took a pair of brandies. I took the first with him, and we drank Lord Dickie's memory—and then Mr. Clairmont went back to the gaming table.''

"He did, did he?'' said Sir John.

"Aye,'' said Mr. Bilbo, "and he came around the very next morning, when I was bare awake, whilst I was drinking my morning tea, and him demanding to talk about that item in the *Public Advertiser*. He wanted to know why the cause of death was listed as . . . how was it?''

"Misadventure.''

"That was it—'misadventure,' which usually means by accident, or so I'm informed. He sat there where you're sitting, Sir John, and he wants to know which is correct— suicide or misadventure? As if I had purposely told him wrong. Well, I pointed out to him that death by suicide ain't the sort of thing you put in the paper for all to read, which I think should be plain to anyone. He sits there, thinking this over, and up the stairs comes this butler from the Goodhope house asking to look at the late lord's notes and a certain document in question. Well, half-brother or no, I was not going into such matters in front of Mr. Clairmont, and so I asked him very politely to leave. And just as politely he did, but not before he'd asked the butler to offer his condolences to Lady Goodhope and ask if he might call.''

"The butler knew him, you said.''

"Oh, indeed. He greeted Clairmont by name. There was something strange about Clairmont that morning, though.''

"And what was that, Mr. Bilbo?''

"He was wearing paint, like a woman.''

"Truly?" Sir John considered that for a moment. "Well," said he then, "they say it is the mode in Paris for men, as well as women. Perhaps he is bringing the mode to London."

I had concentrated upon Mr. Bilbo throughout his recital as Sir John had bade me do. And while he was a most fluent and convincing talker, I did notice a certain alteration in his manner when he began to talk directly of Mr. Clairmont, say, from the time he told of informing the half-brother of Lord Goodhope's death. With that, he began throwing glances in my direction, whereas before he had talked to Sir John and only to him. I could note no other change, certainly not the usual signs of unease, such as the commencement of perspiration: Mr. Bilbo had been perspiring profusely from the moment he joined us below. I took it to be his nature.

"This appearance by the butler, Potter," said Sir John, "it came in response to a letter you wrote her. When did you do that?"

"Early that morning before bed," said Mr. Bilbo. "I left it with my man to be delivered."

"And so it was. Lady Goodhope read its contents to me shortly after receiving it."

With that, Mr. Bilbo leaned back in his chair and folded his arms over his chest: the gesture of a man determined to stand his ground. "Now, look ye, Sir John, if you have come here to argue against Lord Goodhope's debt to me, then I must turn a deaf ear to you, for I have his notes, and I have the document on the house on St. James. I satisfied the butler on the matter of his signature. I'll show them all to you—or to the boy here—or in any court of law, and they will be judged genuine, for genuine is what they are. Truth to tell, I've settled for much less than half his actual debt to me, which was near fifty thousand pounds."

"So much? Truly?"

Mr. Bilbo bobbed his great, dark head emphatically. "Truly," said he.

"But you are willing to settle for the house alone?"

"I like the house."

"You must indeed. You've been inside?"

"Many times—or it might be proper to say a number of times, a good deal more often than once, anyways."

"As a guest?"

"By God, sir, of *course* as a guest. I ain't no burglar!"

"Then you were on good terms with Lord Goodhope."

There was a long moment's hesitation before the answer came; and when it came, it came slowly, each word chosen carefully, it seemed: "I was on good terms with him, yes, for quite some time, though lately not so much."

"What came between you?"

"What came between us? Why, his debt, of course. I am a patient man, but there comes a time when patience wears thin. When he won at my tables, he would happily take his winnings home. When he lost, he would just as happily sign another note. It began to work upon me right sore."

"You would have been well within your rights to forbid him entry here until he had made right his debt to you."

"That I threatened to do, finally, and to advertise his debt so that he would not be welcome at other establishments like this one. And thus I got him to sign the document in question. He was willing to settle on the terms I offered."

"And when was that?"

"Two weeks ago."

"Not long before his death, then."

"Not long, no. Put it about ten days, give or take. The document in question has a date upon it. I could haul it out, if you like."

"No need. But let us suppose, without saying yea or nay to the proposition, that your first information was correct—that Lord Goodhope was a suicide. Did he seem to you when he, in effect, signed over his London house to you, as if he was one who might indeed commit suicide? Was he despairing? Despondent?"

"Well, he wasn't happy."

"I shouldn't think so. But did it ever occur to you, Mr. Bilbo, that pressing him as you did may have put him in a state of desperation that led him to destroy himself?—That is, supposing he did, in fact, do so."

Mr. Bilbo withheld his answer for a moment, casting his eyes about, first at me, then at the candle flames, then back to Sir John.

"That has occurred to me, yes," said he. "And supposing what you now ask me to suppose, I would naturally be distressed. It in fact happened just as you described it with another gentleman who was considerably in my debt, though not so deep as Lord Goodhope. He hung himself, he did. And there could be no doubt that my earnest attempts at collection drove him to it, for he left a letter to that effect. That was near seven years ago."

"I recall the matter," said Sir John.

"I've no doubt you do. Truth to tell, it was bad for custom. The gentlemen stayed away. You might say out of respect for the deceased. Or you might say because they was scared off—seen their little pleasures take a serious turn. I was distressed by the gentleman's death, believe me I was, and I was distressed when the gents stayed away. But when they started coming back, I became less distressed, and about the time custom was back to what it had been, I had put it all behind me. But let me tell you, sir, had I known in advance it would turn out as it did, all of it, I would still have pursued collection, just as before, because a debt is a debt, and it must be paid."

Sir John himself was silent a brief time, then said he: "I hear that often in my court, though the sums involved are paltry compared to those which you have quoted."

"Sums don't matter," said Mr. Bilbo quite severely. "It's the principle. And the earls and viscounts and such seems to think the common rules ain't binding to them."

"You have caused Lady Goodhope considerable distress at a difficult time for her."

"That's unfortunate. She has until the end of the month.

But I declare, Sir John, I believe your supposition to be false.''

''Suicide, you mean?''

''It was what we began with. Lord Dickie was not the sort.''

''What would you offer as a supposition, then? I fear you were right in what you told Mr. Clairmont about the use of that word 'misadventure.' It was used to obscure facts rather than reveal them. It was not I who chose the term.''

''Murder, then,'' said Mr. Bilbo. ''Let us suppose murder. It seems more likely.''

''Why do you think that?''

''Because, as I said early on, it's his *murder* now being talked of on the street and not his suicide. To which I might add, Lord Dickie had many enemies.''

''What sort of enemies?''

''All sorts—Whigs, Tories, take your pick. And if you've asked about him, Sir John, then you must know that the late lord was one who did not care who he stepped on.''

''Would you not count yourself as one of his enemies?''

Mr. Bilbo jerked back as sharply as he might if Sir John had slapped him. He stared, quite in surprise, saying nothing, and then quite unexpectedly, he laughed several great, loud guffaws. Hearing him, one would have sworn he had suddenly turned quite jolly.

''Why do you laugh?'' asked Sir John.

''Because it strikes me as funny,'' said he, recovering somewhat. ''I told you about the debt, did I not? That was a settled matter, as it concerned me. I knew my Lord Dickie well. He would recover in some way, and after a bit of a sulk, he would be back at my tables, and before he knew it, he would be in debt to me again. I might next time have a go at that place of his in Lancashire. So I put it to you thus: Why should I kill the goose that lays the golden egg?''

"That, I allow, makes good sense, Mr. Bilbo, but were you not one on which Lord Goodhope trod?"

"How so?" he asked quite dubiously.

"I'm told that before Lucy Kilbourne attached herself so firmly to Lord Goodhope, she had attached herself to you— and just as firmly. By her own admission—or declaration, indeed—he had won her away from you. Now that, in many situations, would be judged right proper cause for murder. You must admit that, Mr. Bilbo. Jealousy is always a factor to be considered."

All through this speech by Sir John, Black Jack Bilbo could barely contain himself. He would not interrupt the magistrate in his inquiry, but by God and all else that was holy, he would have his say.

"Sir John," said he, at last bursting forth, "whatever else you may think of me, I believe you know me as a plainspoken man, and so now I speak to you plain. Just so. That woman was not stole from me. I gave her away. You cannot suppose the burden she put upon me—the constant flattery she required, the applause she demanded for her each performance at Drury Lane; oh, indeed, I attended them all, to the neglect of my establishment. She was like unto a spider the way she sucked me dry—gifts of clothes, gifts of baubles, gifts of . . . but it was never enough, was it?"

Mr. Bilbo was fair panting from the force of his own words. Sir John took note of this and waited an interval for the man to collect himself before putting to him another question.

"How long were you thus made victim by her?"

"A year—no, something less: ten months perhaps."

"And when did you 'give her away' to Lord Good-hope?"

"Six months past."

"Yet she says she was acquainted with the late lord for a year."

"Oh, she met him here, merely, one of scores of gentlemen I introduced her to in the course of her visits. And she met him more than once at the gaming tables. They had words, a bit of talk. He was frequently after us to be joining him at his evenings, his 'impromptus' he called them. I thought it not proper to go, though we accepted his invitation on a pair of occasions, no more surely.''

''Why did you think it not proper?''

''First, there was the matter of his debt. It was large and growing. It seemed wrong to play the friend to him in those circumstances. Second, I liked not what went on during those evenings. Most of it was silly and not to my taste—singing and dancing of no matter. And this was all part of Lord Goodhope's theatricals—childish stuff for dressing up and shouting out lines made up by the host and by the guests. There was two little girls brought up from the kitchen, no older than the boy here. It seemed wrong to include them in such, for it all had bawdy purposes and little more.''

''You show a tenderness of feeling I would not have suspected.''

''You doubt me?''

''No.''

''I allow that the late Lord Dickie had keen interest in dear Lucy. He flattered her so it was quite shameful, and to have a great actress from the stage play in his parlor was to him very heaven—or so he said. And she also had some interest in him, though I made sure she knew of his debt to me and its steady growth, and that cooled her ardor somewhat. The way it all ended, she had worn my patience so thin in the way I described that I determined to be rid of her. So what I did, the next time Lord Dickie made his entreaty we should join him for an 'impromptu,' I said to her, 'My dear, I cannot leave the establishment, so you go on with his Lordship and enjoy yourself.' And to him I said, 'I entrust her to your care.' I did this knowing full well what would happen, and indeed wanting it to happen. And of course, it happened. She never returned to me again, except in his company. Now, would you not say that in using such a stratagem I threw her away?''

Sir John sighed, whether from fatigue or in some response to the tale just told, I could not discern. Yet I was sure it was not from boredom. I, for one, was fascinated by this instance of how men and women conduct their affairs. It was a glimpse into a world I could but enter in my fantasies.

''One thing only disturbs me in what you have said, Mr. Bilbo,'' said he. ''And that is the question of why, knowing the extent of his debt to you, Lucy Kilbourne should choose an apparently impoverished nobleman.''

''Oh, not impoverished, I can tell you. His holdings in Lancashire was worth many times his debt here. But there was his person, too. He was a pretty fellow—I know I compared ill to him in that way—and witty, too, and I've little to offer there. But the important word of those you uttered was 'nobleman.' He had what I do not have, cannot have, and with all due respect to you, sir, would not want— namely, a title. Some women is greatly impressed by such.''

In response to that, Sir John simply nodded.

''Something I would say,'' said Mr. Bilbo, ''for it came to me as I was telling you about Lucy's first meetings with Lord Goodhope here in my establishment when she was still under my protection, so to speak. I am sure certain that one of those meetings, and it may well have been the first of them, was the last one in which he was in attendance with his brother, Charles Clairmont. I thought that worth adding, for she is with him just now down below.''

Sir John sat up sharply. ''*Now?* With *Clairmont?* Indeed as we speak here?''

Taken aback somewhat by such reaction, Mr. Bilbo fumbled in his response: ''Well . . . well, yes, what I mean is, she was. You heard that silly high laugh of hers, like unto a horse's neigh? That's as she laughs when she is not on the stage, low drab that she is. She was sitting beside Clairmont as he was robbing me to—"

"Jeremy, you did not see her?"

"N-no, Sir John," said I in apology, "nor Mr. Clairmont. The crowd about them was too much for me."

"Well and good," said Sir John to me, and then: "Mr. Bilbo, thank you for your time and your willing answers. Now, if you would but take us to this oddly matched pair."

With that, he stood and I with him. Bilbo, somewhat baffled, rose more slowly and blew out the candles he had lit upon our arrival. "This way," said he.

And he led us back down as we had come, speaking little, and that only in condemnation of Lucy Kilbourne, remarking upon her facility in moving from companion to companion without a break in stride—now from brother to brother.

Upon our arrival in the room we had left, I saw that all had altered to a state I took to be usual: The crowd had dissipated and was now evenly distributed between the two gaming tables. But looking about, I quickly determined that neither of the two we sought was to be found there. Mr. Bilbo, coming also to this conclusion, led us back into the hall and summoned the ever-helpful Nancy.

"My girl," said he to her, "have you seen Clairmont and that silly twat Lucy about? Or have they already absconded with my funds?"

Then, turning, she pointed to the door. "Just leaving," said she.

And so they were, the two of them, adjusting their coats and skirts, making ready to go with the help of the doorman.

"I'll hold them for you," said Mr. Bilbo, and went on swiftly ahead of us.

"Take me to them," said Sir John to me, "but let us proceed at a sedate pace and feign surprise at meeting them."

Thus we advanced down the long, red carpet to the point, at its end, where Mr. Bilbo now detained the two in talk.

I spied Lucy Kilbourne (at last fully clothed in her widow's weeds) glance our way, recognize us, then give a tug at Mr. Clairmont's sleeve. This I conveyed to Sir John.

"Good," said he, "now gesture toward them as if you had just informed me of their presence. And that done, we may pick up our pace a bit and catch them up."

Just so. And even in advance of our arrival Sir John had put upon his face a most pleasant smile. "Is it you two?" he called out. "Mr. Clairmont? Mistress Kilbourne? Why, how fortunate to run into you here!"

"And such a surprise," said Mistress Kilbourne.

"Yes," agreed Mr. Clairmont, in a manner most dry, "is it not?"

Sir John took a place close to them by the door, and I by his side. Mr. Bilbo, displaying keen interest, remained.

"So you two mourners found each other, did you?" said the magistrate, still in the most jovial humor. "Well, I think that admirable. Oh, quite, for after all, life is a gift to us all, and we must celebrate it. Look into your heart, Mistress Kilbourne, and I'm sure you'll agree that if the late Lord Goodhope were able to speak to you from the beyond, he would urge you not to mourn him in sadness, but in that mode of good spirits and wit which I'm told he possessed in such abundance."

"Why, Sir John," said Mistress Kilbourne, "that was the selfsame argument Charles used in coaxing me out this evening."

"Well thought and well argued!"

"It seemed appropriate to the occasion," said Mr. Clairmont.

"Indeed, but how came you two to be acquainted?"

"Lord Richard introduced us quite some time ago," said she. "I believe it was on your last trip to London, was it not, Charles?"

"It was, yes, and in this very place."

"Then it is quite fitting you should return. I trust the occasion was blessed by good fortune?"

"Charles won handsomely."

At that point Mr. Bilbo intruded himself into the proceedings: "Though not as handsomely as I first feared. His luck left him."

"But still," said Mr. Clairmont, "a tidy profit—not so, Lucy?"

"I note," said Sir John, "that you two salute each other by your Christian names. Thus acquaintanceship has ripened to friendship. It would not be untoward of me then to invite you both, together, to an affair I have planned for tomorrow night."

"Oh? What sort of affair?" asked Mistress Kilbourne.

(I wondered that myself!)

"Simply a meeting, nothing formal; it will give us all a chance to discuss the matter of Lord Goodhope's untimely demise. I'm afraid my little house would not be at all proper for the occasion—others will be coming—and so I've decided to hold this meeting at the Goodhope residence. As it will be held under my aegis, Lady Goodhope will offer no objection to your coming to the house. I give that as my pledge. You, Mr. Clairmont, will have the opportunity to convey to the widow the condolences which you might have expressed had she not barred you earlier. You, Mistress Kilbourne, will have the opportunity to say to her whatever you deem fitting—or, indeed, to say nothing at all, if you deem *that* fitting. I would, however, advise against parading in that black dress you have been wearing lately."

As each detail of this surprise meeting emerged, the smiles fixed on the faces of Mr. Clairmont and Mistress Kilbourne began to fade until, at the end, both were solemn-faced, each regarding the other with serious looks. Yet they recovered somewhat.

"Speaking for myself," said Mistress Kilbourne, "it may not be possible for me to attend. I have a previous engagement."

Mr. Clairmont cleared his throat. "Much as I should like

to speak to Lady Goodhope, I'm afraid I must meet with that prospective buyer whom I mentioned to you. This matter is, of course, of the utmost importance. It is why I am here in London.''

"Ah, commerce, yes,'' said Sir John, "it is of inarguable consequence, and no doubt your engagement, Mistress Kilbourne, is also of considerable importance, too. Yet I must ask you both to cancel those appointments, for attendance at this meeting tomorrow evening—at nine, by the by—is not optional but obligatory.''

Mistress Kilbourne: "But . . .''

"I know,'' said Sir John, "it must seem a terrible annoyance, but do save us the trouble and you the embarrassment of sending a constable after one or both of you.''

"As you say, Sir John,'' said Mistress Kilbourne. Then, nodding at the doorman, she made ready to go.

Mr. Clairmont simply nodded. The door swung open and both departed. The door shut after them.

"Well,'' said Mr. Bilbo, "that was most interestin'.''

"I'm glad you judge it so,'' said Sir John, "for I shall also be requiring your attendance.''

"But, Sir John, I have matters that—''

"I'll hear none of that, Mr. Bilbo. You will be there promptly at nine.''

A great sigh from Mr. Bilbo. "I'll be there, Sir John.''

"See that you are.''

A nod from Sir John, and the door came open again. We marched out together into the night. A light rain was falling. I was glad to see Mr. Clairmont helping Mistress Kilbourne up into a waiting hackney, and glad also that there was one behind it for us.

As it drew up, Sir John shouted out, "Number Four Bow Street,'' to the driver. We climbed inside, and I began my report to him. I told him all I had observed, from Mr. Bilbo's glances in my direction as he talked directly of Mr. Clairmont to his hot desire to answer back on the matter of jealousy with regard to Lucy Kilbourne.

"What thought you of Mr. Bilbo, in general, as a witness?"

"I thought him very interesting," said I. "What I mean is, he is a great talker, is he not? He seemed to be holding little back."

"Little, yes. I like him. Probably I should not, but I do. Do you know, Jeremy, it is rumored that he opened that gaming house of his with a fortune he earned in piracy."

"Piracy?" said I, amazed. "Truly?"

"That is the rumor. There are, however, no witnesses about to testify as to his former life." He sighed. "He is quite capable of killing Richard Goodhope or indeed anyone else upon provocation. Yet I thought he argued well against that notion, didn't you, Jeremy?"

"Yes, indeed." I hesitated, but gathering my courage, I said, "Sir John, I think I should tell you something."

"What is that, boy?"

I had been arguing with myself, scolding myself, since we left Mr. Bilbo's office. I realized that I had been at fault, and that I must confess this. Yet knowing it had to be done made it no easier. Perhaps it was the lateness of the hour and my fatigue, or perhaps the overwhelming chain of events that had brought me to that moment, but trembling, as I was, on the brink of revelation, I lost control. Reader, I wept.

"Jeremy, what is it? Here, take this." He pushed into my hand a kerchief he had fished from his pocket. "Use it, please."

I did as he urged, wiped my eyes and blew into it lustily.

"Good job," said he in praise. "You play the man so well that I forget you are still but a child."

"But I *want* to be a man!" And having said so, I proved myself a child by beginning again at that moment to snivel.

"You will be soon enough," said he. "Now blow again and tell me this awful thing that must be told."

Again I did so and began at last to address the matter at hand. I recalled him to the night before and our exit from

Drury Lane by the stage door, Lucy Kilbourne's entrance, and the surge of the crowd.

"Yes," said Sir John, "I remember it all very well; what of it, Jeremy?"

"Once we were clear of them, you sent me to engage the hackney that waited at the head of the alley, by the street."

"Yes?"

"Well, the driver said he was engaged, and indeed there was someone inside, a man. I had but a glimpse of him, yet it seemed to me that it could have been Mr. Clairmont, sir." I hesitated, but then plunged on: "But that was just it, Sir John, I wasn't *sure,* and in court you are always so particular that witnesses be sure of what they saw and heard. I knew that if he was there, he might indeed be waiting for Lucy Kilbourne, and I thought that strange. Because I was not certain, I said nothing to you of it. But tonight I saw that it was of great importance to you. I . . . I didn't understand that."

"But it proved of no matter, Jeremy, for we did find them together tonight and had our little talk with them—did we not?"

"Yes, sir."

"And as for the principle you observed in keeping silent, you were, of course, quite right about matters before the court: Witnesses cannot guess; they cannot voice suspicions; they cannot repeat what others have said as truth. But an inquiry is conducted according to different rules. In an inquiry, guesses, suspicions, and hearsay are all relevant, for they may lead us to direct evidence of one kind or another. And remember, Jeremy, what I told you earlier about details—nothing too small, nothing too insignificant to call to my attention."

"I'll remember."

"I know you will. You've a good mind, boy."

So delighted was I to hear that, and so caught up was I in the spirit of confession that I then laid before him my transgression in the dressing room of Mistress Kilbourne. I was much relieved when he expressed amusement at the tale told him so earnestly.

Though he forbore laughter, he made to comment merely: "Better you should be engaged in fastening her up than in unfastening her." And that was said with a smile, somewhat ironic.

Thus, shriven and penitent, we arrived at our destination, climbed down from the hackney, and made our way up the back stairs to the magistrate's living quarters. I had no idea of the hour, though I was quite sure I had never been so late awake, not even in the course of my flight to London. Yet half-asleep was what I was, truly, so fatigued suddenly by the emotional expense of those past minutes in the hackney.

Saying good night to Sir John, I made my way up to my room on the topmost floor and undressed in the dark. I sank into sleep near immediate. It seemed, however, that the last sound I heard before succumbing completely was the resumption of that pacing from the study two floors below.

Chapter 10

In which a deal of preparations are made

I KNOW NOT ALL OF WHAT TRANSPIRED DURING MR. DON-nelly's visit the next morning, for most of it took place behind closed doors. There was, first of all, his examination of Lady Fielding, which he undertook with Sir John and Mrs. Gredge present. The poppy seed tea was administered, and the two men emerged from the bedroom, talking in grave tones, the sense of which was incomprehensible to me as I worked below in the kitchen. Though I was pow-erfully curious, I had made up my mind not to eavesdrop. If something was said in my presence, or said loud enough that I might hear without taking special pains—then well and good; but I would not sneak about like some furtive butler with my ear pressed to the door or my eye at the keyhole. I knew full well that Sir John despised Potter of the Goodhope household for such practices.

From thence the surgeon and the magistrate adjourned to the study, where, as it later came clear, much more than the patient's condition was discussed. I should haz-ard that the two talked at some length over the document

of identification signed by Lady Goodhope and witnessed
by the surgeon. A more sensitive matter was the meeting
that I had heard but late the night before was planned at
the residence. Not only did Sir John require Mr. Donnelly's presence, he depended upon him to make Lady
Goodhope aware of the absolute necessity that the meeting be held there in the residence, specifically in the library, the location of the crime.

That this second matter was thus discussed I am indeed
certain, for after half of an hour the two men left the study
and descended the stairs to the kitchen where I scrubbed
and polished. Mrs. Gredge had by then returned from the
sickroom, and after a word with her, ascertaining that the
patient slept, the surgeon returned to the subject which had
then been but recently under discussion.

"She will not like it," said he to Sir John. "She will
rail against it."

"Indeed," said Sir John, "that is certain, and that is why
I send you as my emissary to impress upon her why it must
be so."

"I'll do what I can, of course."

"You must do more than you can, or more than you
imply by that. The meeting *must* take place, and it *must*
take place there in the library. A dozen chairs are to be set
out, or more to be on the safe side. But she is to expect
near that number at final count."

"And all this by nine o'clock in the evening?"

"Exactly so," said Sir John, then added: "And do not
forget the kitchen girl, Meg. Tell Lady Goodhope that she
is to be present, and in proper dress."

"Very good, Sir John. I shall do all I can—and more."

"I trust you to it."

The two had by then reached the door. Upon those last
words, they shook hands solemnly. Sir John fumbled
slightly for the door latch, found it, and threw it open to a
powerful clatter and clump on the stairs below. Who should
appear but Mr. Bailey and his second-in-command, Mr.

Baker, each of them heavily armed with a cutlass and a brace of pistols. Mr. Donnelly ducked past them with a muttered, "Until nine then," and with a nod to Mr. Bailey, disappeared through the door.

Mr. Bailey seemed quite agitated, as indeed did Mr. Baker. The two men called together for Sir John's attention, setting up a considerable clamor in the kitchen.

"Please, wait!" said he. "One at a time. Give me your report. Is the prisoner now with us, Mr. Bailey?"

"He is not, sir, though we tried our damnedest!"

"And the circumstances is passing strange," put in Mr. Baker.

"Tell me then. You left near two hours past."

Let me here interject, reader, that I in no wise was aware that the two constables had been sent to Newgate to fetch Dick Dillon, as the magistrate had promised him. Their departure would have taken place even before Mrs. Gredge had roused me from my sound slumber. Since I had slept little, I was left to suspect that Sir John had slept not at all.

"Aye, sir," said Benjamin Bailey, "two hours past. We gone direct to Snow Hill. The gatekeeper let us in, after we showed him the papers all sealed with the court seal which you gave us. But instead of sending us to the Master Felons Ward where you said the prisoner was to be found, he directed us instead to the chief warder. So, having no choice in the matter, really, we went to him."

"I'd not met the fellow before," put in Mr. Baker, "though Ben had. Quite the blackguard, in my opinion, Jonathan Wild reincarnated, Sir John."

"A like description," the magistrate agreed.

"Well, this one whom indeed I have had dealings with on past occasions," continued Mr. Bailey, "he fiddled and farted about, reading your document and then reading it again, and then telling us that what you requested was quite impossible."

"I did *not* request," said Sir John. "I *demanded.*"

"That's as I told him, sir."

"Then we asked why was it impossible," said Mr. Baker, "and he says it's because the prisoner is down in the hole. Solitary."

"And why was that?"

Mr. Bailey: "For punishment, says he. He's a very hard case. He injured a warder during the night most severely."

Mr. Baker: " 'Knifed him,' said he, 'carved him up like a Christmas goose.' "

Sir John: "Don't tell me! I hazard that the warder's name was John Larkin."

At that, Bailey and Baker looked at one another, each with raised eyebrows, halted for but a moment in their collaborative account.

"It was so!" exclaimed Mr. Baker.

"Indeed," said Mr. Bailey. "That's as we discovered when we asked to see the prisoner. Well, they took us off to some part of the place that was nothing to do with the gaol proper, but was a manner of sickroom for the warders. There they showed us this warder, Larkin."

Mr. Baker: " 'See what your man done to this poor fellow,' the chief warder says to us. 'How can we let such a vicious animal outside Newgate, for this is the safest prison in the realm. What would he do if he were to escape from some other? He would be like some wolf loosed upon the innocent lambs of London!' Sir John, ain't that the utterest piece of nonsense ever you heard? Innocent lambs indeed! Were he to show his face in Seven Dials again, he'd probably have his nose slit for putting to bother one of their company."

"And then," said Mr. Bailey, "when we made to question this fellow Larkin as to the particulars of the incident, he became very shifty. In truth, sir, he was not all that bad hurt. His hand was pierced through, and he had what I would judge to be a slight nick on his throat."

"Why do you judge it so?" asked Sir John. "That could have been intended as a mortal wound."

"Well, it was bound up, sure enough, so I could not be

sure, but there was no blood on the bandage, and this Larkin had no trouble talking.''

"What did he say?''

"Oh, well,'' said Mr. Baker, "he made himself quite the victim of his own kindness. He claimed that the prisoner, Dillon, had called to him for water and said he was in the throes of the ague. And when this man, this warder, Larkin, had entered, he was immediately set upon by Dillon and wounded many times by him with a dirk. Well, 'many times' was a considerable exaggeration, for his wounds was as Ben described, and the whole account had about it the nature of a fabrication. You know how it is, Sir John, when we arrest them on the street they all have a story, or sometimes the supposed victim of the crime has one, but the story they tell is not quite right in their manner of telling. And of course with this one there were some questions that arose immediately.''

"Such as,'' put in Mr. Bailey, "how came the prisoner to be in possession of the dirk.''

"What said he to that?'' asked Sir John.

"Said it must have been smuggled in to him. He knew not by who.''

"Another question,'' said Mr. Baker. "What was the prisoner's intention in attacking him so?''

"Aye,'' said Mr. Bailey, "they claimed escape was his intention. Yet they were hard put to explain why he never left the Master Felons Ward. Larkin just pushed him out into the corridor and waited for him to be rescued by the warders, who set upon him and disarmed the prisoner. They said they got to him before he could decide which way to run. That, again, I doubt somewhat because the telling of it seemed false. We tried to go round a bit with him on it, get him to repeat it, looking for details that might not match up, as you might. But the chief warder would have none of that. He brought us away from Larkin. So then, we asks to visit the Master Felons Ward so as to put questions to the warders and the inmates and view the scene. And he says to us, 'Who are you to doubt that fellow's story?' ''

Mr. Baker broke in: '' 'We are constables is who we are,' said I to him, 'and if we cannot see the prisoner, then we demand to see the Keeper of Newgate.' ''

"He laughed at us, he did. And he said, 'The Keeper of Newgate will not see such as you.' ''

"Well, he will see such as me," said the magistrate, whose countenance had grown increasing dark during the telling. "Jeremy!" he bellowed of a sudden, "fetch my coat and hat from the study."

I jumped to his command and ran for it up the stairs. As I helped Sir John into his coat, I hoped fiercely that I might be asked along, yet I was not surprised when no such invitation was extended.

"You still have my writ in your possession?"

"Aye, sir, it is here in my pocket," said Mr. Bailey.

"Then let us be off, all three of us, for I promise we shall return with the prisoner."

And so they made a hasty departure down the stairs, Mr. Baker leading the way, then Mr. Bailey, and Sir John last of all with his hand on Mr. Bailey's shoulder, as was his wont when descending.

I watched them in excitement but was brought suddenly to myself by Mrs. Gredge's harsh command: "Shut the door, Jeremy."

I did as she bade me and went direct to her to comment upon this new turn in a matter already too complicated for my understanding.

Yet she cut me short, quite surprising me with a comment which betrayed her ignorance of the affair. "All this fuss about a felon!" said she with a dismissive wave of her hand. "What matter can it be?"

I had somehow fixed it in my mind that she, a grown woman and considerable more, would have the same interest in such concerns of Sir John as I had. Yet when I sought to explain the significance of what we had heard to her, which is to say, Dillon's likely importance as a witness in

the Goodhope inquiry, then she brushed it aside, saying it
was all the same to her. And so, I was forced to add indifference to her ignorance. And in truth, I had, in the time
I had been there, not heard her ask a single question of her
master regarding what went on in the courtroom below,
much less about matters more private, such as the inquiry
into the death of Lord Goodhope. This last demonstrated
the extent of her isolation from the talk of the street, as
well, for, as I was to learn, no subject was at that moment
of keener interest to the purveyors of speculation and of
gossip as that which one of the pamphlets soon to appear
would call "The Horror in St. James Street." Say what I
might of her, Mrs. Gredge was quite separated from such
stuff of sensation, which was perhaps best for a magistrate's
housekeeper and cook.

It was a bit later on when, having completed my appointed tasks, she asked me if I might go below to Covent
Garden and do some buying for her. I agreed readily, realizing that she was entrusting me with what she considered
to be one of her most sacred duties.

"Did you sometimes go to the market and buy foodstuffs
for your father?" she asked me.

"Oh, often," said I, "when he was busy with his printing work."

"Can you buy meat? Potatoes? Greens?"

"All of that."

"Well and good. I'll try you out. What I fixed for Sir
John and us last night fair cleaned me out, and I am loath
to leave Lady Fielding alone in the house."

So we sat down together and prepared us a list, she doing
the telling and I the writing of it, for as I had come to
suspect and later confirmed, she was without letters. Then
she presented me with the large market basket, put some
money in my pocket, and sent me on my way.

Although I had passed through Covent Garden on separate occasions with Mr. Bailey and Sir John, I had not had
occasion to tour the place as I did that morning. Mrs.

Gredge put no limit of time on me, and so I made a leisurely journey through the stalls and the crowds round them, choosing a cabbage here, and potatoes, carrots, and turnips there—for she had in mind to make a stew that might last more nights than one. But what makes a good stew but good spices? Therefore, when I heard a maid's call, rising above the rest—

> Here's fine rosemary, sage, and thyme.
> Come buy my ground ivy.
> Here's fetherfew, gilliflowers, and rue.
> Come buy my knotted marjoram ho!

—I thought it a particular invitation to me. I hastened to her through the mob, and after a bit of pleasant bargaining, bought bay leaves and thyme. The maid who had sung her wares was not much my senior; she was good in commerce but took no advantage. She did, however, advertise her leeks to me, and since I decided they would go well in the stew, I took a bunch of them, as well. Since none of these were on the list Mrs. Gredge had made up with me, I bought them from my own dwindling store of coins and then had but two shillings left and a few pence, but I assured myself it was all in a good cause. It made me feel quite the man to do a bit of buying on my own.

Turning away from the spice merchant's stall, my purchases in my basket, I felt a gentle hand laid upon my arm, looked about, and found before me a face that was familiar, yet difficult to place. Who could this handsome woman be?

"Your name is Jeremy, is it not?" she asked.

"Indeed it is, ma'am. I believe we have met, though to my shame, I cannot say your name."

"Katherine Durham," said she. "Sir John Fielding introduced us but a few days past in the Haymarket."

"Oh yes," said I, "you must forgive me for not remembering. Since I've come to London, so much has happened.''

I recalled her at that moment aright. She it was whose son had been saved from the gallows and sent to sea.

''Indeed,'' she said, ''it is a most confusing place. I well remember when I first came here with my late husband from Plymouth—the constant tumult, the babble—but I grew accustomed. You will, too. As I recall, you're a young printer. Has Sir John found you a place?''

''Not as yet, ma'am, no. He's been terrible busy on an inquiry.''

''Ah, the Goodhope matter, of course. They talk of nothing else in the streets.''

''And then,'' said I, blurting more than I should, ''there is Lady Fielding, as well.''

''Oh? What is the trouble there?''

''I fear she is dying.''

Though I immediately realized it was wrong of me to have said so much of concerns personal to Sir John, the look of consternation and genuine sympathy that appeared upon her face assured me that at least I had not told them to the wrong person.

''I had no idea,'' said she. ''The poor, generous, good man—he is then truly beset, is he not? Well, young Jeremy, since I have heard nothing of it from the gossips and prattlers, I shall treat what you told me as a confidence. I'll not repeat it.''

''I'd be grateful,'' said I. ''In all truth, I shouldn't have mentioned it.''

''Not a word.'' Then, gesturing at our like baskets, she said: ''You buy for the household. You have their trust.''

''I hope I've done well. Only the meat remains to be bought.''

''Would you like some help with that?''

''Oh, indeed I would. I fear I might buy what's old or spoiled. My eye is not the best for meat.''

"Then come along," said she. "We shall do our buying together."

And off we went to that corner of the Garden where the butchers' stalls and the vendors of sausages and poultry were set and the early-season flies assembled in number. The hucksters sang their songs—

> *Mutton chops to marrow bones!*
> *Pork loins and flitches and meaty stewing bones!*

—and the buyers gathered. It seemed that those who bellowed the loudest drew the greatest number.

> *Buy a young chicken fat and plump,*
> *Or take two for a shilling?*
> *Come buy if you are willing!*

But Katherine Durham led me past the mob and on to a stall which, though doing a good trade, did not resort to cries and calls. We took a place to wait for service by one of two young lads who busied themselves behind the board, offering and selling, weighing and wrapping. But as we waited there, we two were spied by the proprietor of the stall, himself a proper butcher for he wore a bloody apron; he left his post at the rear of the stall and beckoned us to him.

"Ho there, Mrs. Durham," said he. (He was a big man with a big voice.) "And how be you this excellent morning?"

"Oh, very good, Mr. Tolliver, and I have brought to you this fine lad, whose name is Jeremy, and he is come here to the Garden to buy for the household of Sir John Fielding."

He smiled a great wide smile at me, giving me the opportunity to puff a bit. "Well," said he, "Sir John, is it? We all wish to stay on the right side of him. What would you be needing today, Master Jeremy?"

"Stew meat," said I, consulting my list, "off the bone."

"Well, come over here, both of you, and have a look. I think you'll find this to your likin'."

So saying, he led us to a great pot at the far end of the board, which was covered over with a cloth. Unlike the meat put out at neighboring stalls, his was thus covered until showed and sold. Mr. Tolliver pulled off the cloth that we might view the contents.

"Mutton?" asked Mrs. Durham.

"Indeed, mutton it is, and very young mutton at that— near lamb, it is."

I looked at it with my unpracticed eye. It was filled with meat of a relatively light hue cut in good-sized chunks. Nearly all, it seemed, had morsels of fat appended. I commented on this, asking if this was usual.

"It's as you would want it, young sir," said Mr. Tolliver. "The fat gives body to the stew. The cook will know to skim it off the top as it simmers."

I looked over at Mrs. Durham, and she gave me a wise nod of agreement.

"Well and good," said I. "I'll take a pound."

"And I but half that," said she.

"All's right for both of you," said he, as he doled out our separate quantities. "Will that be all, then?"

Mrs. Durham indicated so and paid up. I asked for three joints of beef.

"Three, no less?"

"Sir John likes his beef."

"As any good Englishman would!" said he. "But I must go back and carve those from the side in the stall. It will be but a blink."

He left us then to attend to the matter, and Katherine Durham extended her hand to me, taking her leave. I clasped her hand eagerly and expressed my thanks, exclaiming at my good luck in meeting her thus by chance.

"It has been my great pleasure," said she quite graciously. "Now, Jeremy, it would be wrong of me to ask

you to give to Sir John my sympathy with regard to Lady
Fielding, because as you said, it is a personal matter and
was probably better left untold. But nevertheless he does
have my deepest sympathy. Simply tell him that you met
Katherine Durham. She sends her sincerest greetings and
hopes that he may one morning find time to visit at Number
Three Berry Lane. Can you remember that address? It is
the floor above with a separate entrance.''

"I can remember it, yes, and I will tell him.''

"Goodbye then, and good fortune to you.''

I stood, watching after her as she made her way through
the multitude, for I was quite taken by her beauty and gentle manner. Then, sensing the butcher nearby, I turned and
found him holding the big, raw slabs of meat out for my
inspection. I decided they would look better cooked than
they did at that moment. But I nodded my satisfaction, and
he wrapped them.

As he took my money, he glanced off in the direction in
which Mrs. Durham had disappeared. "A fine woman,''
said he—and only that.

Before I gained entrance to Number 4 Bow Street, a coach
pulled up at the door, and four men descended. Sir John
led the way; the prisoner was third between the two constables. Even at some distance I could tell that Dick Dillon
was much the worse for his ordeal. He walked slowly,
though without leg irons, and his head was bowed. I held
back, not wishing to impede them on their way, but also to
better observe them. Stopping briefly at the door that led
to the rear, Sir John turned and instructed the others in some
manner. I had not noticed before, though I saw it in him
afterward, that on certain occasions he took on something
of a military air—giving brief commands and curt directions. Most of his hours he spent as a judge, with proper
judicial demeanor, yet there were times when it suited him
best to play commander to his constables.

They entered, Sir John last of all, and I hastened to the

door to get another look. Inside, I caught the heavy tread of the party far down the hall; near running the length of it, I spied the four disappear into the magistrate's chambers. How I should have liked to accompany them! But of course I could not intrude, no matter how keen my wish to hear Dillon's testimony. And so, with a sigh of resignation, I turned away and climbed the stairs to the kitchen, basket in hand.

Mrs. Gredge was much pleased by my purchases, doubly so when she heard that I had bought the unlisted spices and leeks from my own small store of cash. And though she made no offer to reimburse me, she gave me time to myself that I might spend as I pleased. I went up to my attic room, suddenly weary, and though I took down a book to read, I soon found the lines of type swimming before my eyes. The lack of sleep I had suffered the night before won out over my resolve, and before I knew it I had fallen into a deep slumber.

Mrs. Gredge woke me a bit more gently than was her usual. She instructed me that I was wanted down in Sir John's chambers. I needed little more than that to bring me to a keen state of alertness. I had been abed near two hours.

I pulled on my shoes and made for the ground floor at once. I was surprised, on the way to my destination, to see Dick Dillon in the strong room eating hungrily of bread and cheese. But I had no call to linger and gape, so I went straight to the magistrate's door and banged on it loudly. Just as loudly I called my name, and Sir John bade me enter.

"Ah, Jeremy," said he as I approached, "I have two most important errands for you to run."

"Whatever you like, sir, it will be done."

"Good boy." He took two letters from his desk, each with the Bow Street seal, and offered them to me. "You have here separate letters to be delivered directly to the hands of those whose names appear on the outer face—and only to their hands. Is that understood?"

"Yes, sir," said I, taking them, "completely."

"There is a deal of distance between the two addresses and it makes no matter to which you go first. Find Mr. Bailey, Mr. Baker, or Mr. Marsden, and get directions from them. One of them should help."

"Is there an hour by which I should return?"

"Well, by dark, certainly. But it should not take so long, even if they ask you to wait for a reply. One or both may do that. In any case, you and I must have time to dine before going off to the Goodhope residence."

I could not but smile broadly at that. "Then I'm to accompany you?"

"Oh, yes. You shall have a part to play. But on your way now."

I bade him goodbye then and left to search out one of the three he had named. As it happened, I was fortunate to find Mr. Marsden, for he, the court clerk, not only gave me clear instructions to each destination, but also wrote them down for me.

Therefore, making haste into the city through a good many streets I had never walked before, I consulted my written instructions but once. I came quickly enough to Lloyd's Coffee House, a place where Mr. Marsden had told me much business was done besides that of coffee drinking.

It was well marked and well lit (for it had many windows). As I entered, I encountered a great hubbub in the house. There were tables all around, at which one or sometimes two men sat, conversing loudly with those at tables nearby. Yet their attention was divided, for many seemed to return again and again to a large slate at one corner of the place upon which a fellow in an apron made entries and notations. Some shouted at him. Others seemed to ignore him completely. While all the while other fellows in aprons passed among them, distributing pots and collecting cups.

I tapped one of these servers politely on the arm as he passed by and asked him to identify Mr. Alfred Humber,

as read the name on the envelope which I held. He directed
me to a gentleman of a settled look, corpulent, and somewhat senior to the rest. He sat in the midst of the throng
with a young man not much older than myself at his side.
As I approached, he appeared to be dozing, and I wondered
should I wake him. Yet upon my arrival at his table his
eyes snapped open of a sudden, like those of a cat. And
though he made not a move with his body, fingers still
folded over his bulging belly, he fixed me with a close look.

"What is it, boy?" said he, not rudely but indulgently.

"If you are Mr. Alfred Humber," said I, "I have a letter
for you from Sir John Fielding, magistrate of the Bow
Street Court."

"I am your man, so you may give it me."

At last he bestirred himself, put forth his hand for the
letter, and found a pair of spectacles in his waistcoat pocket
with which to read it. He tore the seal with indifference
and put the letter before him for study.

Having done so, he frowned at me. "He wants not only
the owners, but also the plan of its last voyage and its
next?"

"Sorry, sir, I know not the contents of the letter."

"I see, of course." He turned to the young fellow at his
side, who had quite openly read the letter over his shoulder,
and handed it over to him. "George, my lad," said he to
him, "take this about—oh, first to Timmons and then to
Craik. One of the two has this account, I'm sure. Have them
write the information on the bottom of the page."

Without a word, the assistant (if that was indeed his position) was off to the far corner of the large room.

"Would you like a cup?" Mr. Humber asked me. "Sit
down here."

"A cup, sir?"

"A cup of coffee."

He signaled to one of the servers, who brought cups and
a fresh pot, poured the black-brown brew, and was away
the next moment.

"I've never had it before," said I. "Will it make me drunk?"

"Oh no. The contrary is true. It will revive you, if you need reviving, as I do. And if you do not, it will for a short space give you strength you had no idea you possessed."

"A magic potion?" said I.

"An elixir," said he.

I tasted it and found it warm though not hot, slightly bitter though not unpleasant to the taste. And so I drank deep of it, liking it better with each draught.

"Thank you, Mr. Humber. It suits me well."

"I warn you, though, boy. Drink it careful, for it could become a habit. The dear Lord knows it has become so with me."

Just then Mr. Humber's George returned from his ramble about the room, tossing down the letter on the table, and seating himself once again.

"Craik's it was, sir," said he. " 'E's askin' what it's all about."

"That's for Sir John to tell, and I know him well enough to say he will not tell till he is ready."

Mr. Humber picked up the letter and glanced at the information appended to the bottom of it. He passed it on to me.

"There you are," said he. "Give my best to him."

I jumped to my feet and drank to the bottom of the cup.

"Thank you, Mr. Humber, and thank you for bringing coffee to my acquaintance."

"Mind it doesn't become a habit."

With a wave, I left him and departed the coffeehouse. Then, consulting Mr. Marsden's directions and traversing the city, I made for the East India Company in Leadenhall Street. It stood, a mighty edifice, hard by the houses of government. There was no difficulty in locating the place, but once inside and passed on at the entrance, I found it to be a perfect maze of stairs and corridors. Through opened doors I glimpsed great halls of clerks laboring at their separate desks with quill and ink. Where could I find the man I sought?

At last, climbing to yet another floor, asking one met along the way, I came to the door I sought—that of Sir Percival Peeper, who I have since learned was then a proprietor of that great enterprise. I knocked, and the door was opened by a man in usher's livery. He seemed quite unimpressed by my person.

"Yes, boy, what is it?" This in the tone of one permanently exasperated.

"I have a letter for Sir Percival Peeper."

"Give it me. I shall deliver it."

"I cannot. It is from Sir John Fielding, magistrate of the Bow Street Court. He instructed me to put it direct into his hands."

"Sir John Fielding, you say?"

"That is correct, sir."

"Wait here."

He shut the door in my face. I waited there in the corridor for a good space of time, growing increasingly annoyed that my long search for the proper door should end with me held outside it. Yet I was determined to carry out Sir John's instructions to the letter. I would wait here all day, if need be, rather than deliver the missive into the hands of that fellow. I was assuring myself I would welcome the opportunity to tell him that when suddenly the door opened, and he stood before me once more.

"This way," said he.

I stepped inside a room all dark wood and leather. The deep colors, the lack of daylight gave a sense of oppressiveness to the anteroom which seemed to fit my guide's demeanor. He led me through it and down a short, narrow corridor to another door. He rapped lightly upon it and, at a word from inside, threw it open and admitted me. A small, wizened man not much larger than a child sat there behind a large desk, frowning out at me. I was aware that the usher stood waiting as I marched up the carpet to the desk. Here, at least, the curtains had been parted and there was light enough to see.

I was quite certain he was the man I had come to see, of course, yet I chose to ask in a manner most bold: "Are you Sir Percival Peeper?"

"Of course I am."

"Then this is for you, sir."

I placed the letter on his desk. He looked at it and touched it impatiently with his fingers, waiting for me to turn and go.

"I believe an answer of some sort is desired," said I.

"Oh . . . all right."

With that, he tore it open roughly and read swiftly through its contents.

"Will there be an answer, sir?"

"Yes, yes, of course there will, but it will not be immediate. What Sir John asks for must be searched out from our files. Go, boy, and tell him that."

Although it might seem an impertinence, I felt that something should be said. "I believe an answer is needed by nine for a meeting at the Goodhope residence."

"So it says here. He will have it by then. If need be, I'll have it brought to him there. You may tell him that, too." He fluttered his hand at me, making it clear he wished me to leave. As I started to turn to go, he called after me. "But hold, boy, who are you to tell me what is and is not needed and by when?"

My face burned in embarrassment. Perhaps I had been a bit too brazen. "I beg your pardon, sir," said I. "I meant no harm."

"Do you think perhaps that you yourself are the law?"

"No, sir, but I am the law's messenger."

He laughed a dry little laugh and beckoned me forward to him. "A good answer," said he, as he went fishing into his pocket. He pulled out a shilling and offered it to me. "Such an answer deserves a shilling."

I hesitated to take it, thinking Sir John might not approve. But then, fearing even more that Sir Percival Peeper might be affronted by my refusal, I ducked my head in the semblance of a bow and took the shilling.

"Thank you, sir," said I.

"You may go," said he.

I was moved out swiftly by the man in livery and left in the hall without a word. Finding my way out offered no difficulty. And once on the street I felt most peculiarly elated. Perhaps it was the matter of the shilling—not the coin itself, but the reward. I felt as if I had passed a test of some sort, that I had acquitted myself well before a man of importance.

Or perhaps it was merely the coffee I had drunk by the generosity of Mr. Humber. He had promised me it would give strength I knew not I possessed, and that might also mean the strength to give good answers.

In any case, full of coffee, full of hope, I set off on a run through the dusk to Bow Street, thinking I could hardly wait for that nine o'clock hour to come.

Chapter 11

In which all is made clear

THE CHAIRS WERE SET OUT IN A CRESCENT-MOON ARrangement in the Goodhope library—twenty of them in two rows of ten. There would never be so many there, I told myself, remembering Sir John's request to be passed on to Lady Goodhope by Mr. Donnelly. Yet by the end of the evening many had been occupied, if only temporarily. To put it plain, there was to be a good deal of coming and going.

The chairs, then empty, faced and half-circled the desk at which a corpus had sat but a few nights past. I wondered at the necessity which dictated that this singular meeting be held in this particular room. When Sir John and I had made our entrance to the house a few minutes before, Lady Goodhope had met us at the door and protested loudly, and in unladylike fashion, against the meeting, against its location, and against her attendance at it, which Sir John required. He, urging her into the sitting room in which they had previously conversed on a number of occasions, sought to allay her fears. But entering, he called me to him and ordered me down the hall to the library to make certain the room had been prepared according to his wishes.

Except for the superabundance of chairs, all seemed to be in order. A fire blazed in the fireplace, making the room almost uncomfortably warm. All around the room, candles were lit. Two standing candelabra had been brought in from some other place to supplement the rest. The effect was to bring the library to a condition quite like that in which I had seen it previously in daylight. The burning candles seemed also to add to the warmth of the room.

I was standing at the desk, taking what I thought to be a last look about, when I was hailed from behind by name. Turning, I saw Mr. Donnelly advancing toward me from the door. He seemed not quite jolly, but in high spirits due to the occasion. His face was flushed. He moved with his familiar quick step.

"Well," said he, "what think you of this important evening?"

"I know not what to think," said I in all truth.

"Then . . . Sir John has given you no hint of what's to come?"

"None, sir. He asked only that I make sure the room was in order."

He looked about him. "It seems to be, does it not?"

"Only but there are a few too many chairs."

"He could not object to that, surely. It would seem the servants emptied the dining room."

I thought for something to say. I was quite bursting to tell someone of the letters I had delivered—of my first taste of coffee and the shilling I had earned with a sober answer—yet I feared that such would seem to Mr. Donnelly mere boyish prattle. And so I offered merely what came to mind: "Sir John is in the sitting room off the front hall with Lady Goodhope."

"Ah, yes," said he. "I perceived as much. I heard their voices, quite contentious, the moment I was admitted. I thought to wander about a bit until the two had settled their differences. Was that cowardly of me?''

Again, I wondered at the question and decided Mr. Donnelly had simply given voice to his private thoughts. But I was quick to answer: "Oh no, sir. The matter is, after all, between the two of them."

"Indeed! Precisely what I told myself. But perhaps I had best go and see have they made some progress in their negotiations." He turned with a sigh and took a step or two toward the door. Then: "Ah, Jeremy, but one question: I was surprised to be let in by Benjamin Bailey, my dear cousin's friend and boarder."

"He came with us here."

"All decked out he was with cutlass and pistols. Has that spying butler been sent on his way?"

"Not to my knowledge, sir."

"Well," said Mr. Donnelly, giving a shake of his head, "an armed constable at the door. That portends a most interesting evening, does it not?" Then, with a wave of his hand he was gone from the room.

For the first time since my entry into the room that evening, I ventured behind the desk and found it most uncomfortably warm there from the blaze. The fireplace itself, but three paces back, offered a surprise. There was a kettle on the crane I had not at first noticed. Turned back from the fire though it was, it still gave off a wisp of steam. I went to it, bent down, and gave it a heft. I found it well filled with water.

Then, hearing a sudden, startled "Oh!" behind me, I jumped up, kettle in hand, and found a serving girl bearing a tea service on a tray. She was smallish, fitted in black, with good color in her cheeks. It took me a moment to realize that this was none other than the kitchen girl Meg.

"Begging your pardon," said she. "I had not realized anybody was here."

She spoke!

Quickly she went to the cabinets at one side of the desk and placed her burden down atop one of them. With a swift little curtsy, she began to back away.

I watched her dumbly, still holding to the kettle. Yet before she turned and disappeared completely, I managed at last to say, ''Don't go.''

She stood then, eyes downcast, a tense little smile upon her pretty face.

''Sir John said you were to take part tonight. Is that as you wish?''

''Oh, yes,'' said she. ''I'm to serve tea merely.''

''Tea? Oh,'' said I, raising the kettle foolishly, ''tea, of course.''

We both laughed at that, no doubt longer than the situation warranted. I replaced the kettle on the crane, then I turned back to her.

''He seems a good man, your Sir John,'' said Mistress Meg. ''Have you known him long?''

''Not long, no. But I feel that in a way I know him well.'' Perhaps more should be said. I decided to tell her what I would not have told others: ''I came before him in his court, falsely accused of theft. But he saw through the perjury of my accusers and sent them away with a warning.''

''Then he *is* a good man.''

''Wise and fair.''

''Do you live now in his household?''

''Yes,'' said I, then added regretfully, ''though perhaps not for long. I have a trade. He is attempting to place me in it.''

''And what is your trade?'' she asked brightly.

''Printing. I learned it from my father.''

''Oh? And where is he?''

''No longer alive,'' said I, leaving it at that, offering no details.

She was silent for a moment. Then, with a grave nod, she said: ''Nor is my mother. My father I never knew.''

''Orphans,'' said I.

''Indeed,'' said she. ''Well . . .''

And again she began to back away.

"Until later, Mistress Meg," said I, in the manner of a goodbye.

"Until later, Master Jeremy."

It was but minutes after the hour of nine when an assembly composed of a number of those to whom Sir John had earlier spoken was brought together in the library. They were, you may be assured, a rather uncomfortable group. At one end of the crescent sat Charles Clairmont and Lucy Kilbourne, and at the other Lady Goodhope and Mr. Donnelly. Lady Goodhope threw daggers and dirks from her eyes at the couple at the other side of the room. Between them Mr. Black Jack Bilbo had situated himself. In the second row of chairs, to my surprise, sat Mr. Alfred Humber and a man whom I had never before seen.

All this I had surveyed upon our entrance. Sir John allowed me, on this occasion, to take him by the elbow and guide him around the two rows to the desk. There he took his place in the fatal chair. Once he had settled, I retired to a point some paces away and to his right. Mistress Meg stood nearby, and we exchanged covert glances. We were both too near the blazing fire for comfort. But if Sir John could stand such warmth at his back, I knew that I could do so, too.

Mr. Bailey had left his post at the street door, relieved there by Constable Cowley, and come into the library just behind us. He remained some distance to the rear of the chairs, about halfway to the door to the hall, which he had closed behind him. There were others still arriving as we three had made our march down the hall; they, however, would not be granted immediate admittance to the library; each, in his turn, would make his entrance. Sir John had decreed it so.

He cleared his throat and thrust his head forward in such a way that he seemed to be peering out at those before him. It was as if he, regarding them thus, were the schoolmaster;

and they, whether petulant or patient, bored or expectant, were his pupils.

"I have called you all here," said Sir John, "that we might discuss in some detail the violent death which took place here some nights ago. Most of you here by now hold some connection to it. It is my duty this evening to sort out those connections and to make some final sense of what at first appeared to be a senseless act.

"Suicide was what it first appeared to be."

At this point, Sir John signaled to Benjamin Bailey, a mere snap of his fingers, and Mr. Bailey turned about and proceeded on the tips of his toes to the door to the hall.

As meanwhile, Sir John continued his discourse: "Lady Goodhope argued vehemently against this conclusion from her knowledge of her husband and his character. Other factors may also have played a part in her certainty."

It was just then that Mr. Bailey threw open the door in one swift motion. From my vantage I saw the butler, Potter, immediately revealed. He was caught in a bending posture, listening at the keyhole. He straightened to his full height, which was considerably less than Mr. Bailey's, and attempted to make the best of a bad situation.

"I . . . I was wondering . . ." said he, flustered, "if there were something I might . . ."

"Ah, Potter," said Sir John, "come in, come in. You are just in good time. Yes, indeed there is something you might do for us. Come in and tell us—briefly, please—of your entry into the library and the condition of the body that you found in this chair I now occupy. Come ahead, man. Don't be shy. Address this little group."

As the butler moved forward so that those staring at him might not have to turn to see, Sir John added, by way of introduction: "For those of you who do not know him, and were not this evening admitted by him, Potter serves as butler to this household. He heard a shot from the library. With the help of a footman, he broke through the door, which was locked from the inside, and was then the first on the scene to view the remains.''

Potter, standing to one side, did as he was bade, confirming what had been said, and in short order describing the condition of the body. He concluded by telling that he had sent the footman off to the Bow Street Court to report the lamentable occurrence.

''Exactly,'' said Sir John, ''and we were here within an hour of the awful event.''

''May I go now, sir?'' asked Potter, still in the throes of embarrassment.

''No, you may not,'' responded Sir John. ''I must ask you to take a seat with the rest and listen to what transpires in these discussions. I think you will find it of interest.''

Meekly, and without further argument, Potter did as he was told to do.

''The constable who accompanied me to these premises is here with us now,'' continued Sir John. ''May I ask Mr. Benjamin Bailey to step forward and give a more precise description of the wound?''

That Mr. Bailey did, giving a quick, professional summary—the sort of report he was accustomed to making in court. When he had concluded, Sir John gave a nod of satisfaction, and Mr. Bailey retired to his former place.

''But in our company that night there was another—the young man who stands behind me and to my right. He noticed an important detail which he related to me. Jeremy Proctor, will you now tell it to them here?''

I was briefer than brief, telling only that I had noted the clean hands of the dead man, and making it a point to add that even at the time I told it to Sir John I had no idea of the significance of this fact.

''But,'' said Sir John, ''anyone who has experience with firearms knows the significance of it. Gunpowder dirties the hand of him who pulls the trigger. We looked upon the unwashed body and ascertained that Master Proctor's impression was indeed correct: The hands were clean. A less important, though significant, detail also emerged: that Lord

Goodhope was left-handed. And the wound described by Mr. Bailey was not consistent with that which might have been self-inflicted by a left-handed man. And so we had a suicide behind a locked door that was not a suicide, but a murder. But where had the murderer got to? How had he escaped?

"Nor was this the end to our puzzlement. For because of the surprise we had been given, I thought it wise that the body be given an examination by a medical doctor, and I asked Mr. Gabriel Donnelly, fully qualified as such by the University of Vienna and a former ship's surgeon in the Royal Navy, to perform that service. Will you stand, Mr. Donnelly, and summarize your report?"

Whether from inbred Irish loquaciousness, or his desire to impress Lady Goodhope, Mr. Donnelly's summary was anything but brief. It was also done in medical language, replete with Latin, which his audience scarce could understand. Yet the weight of it he made clear at the end: "It was certain that the victim had taken in a very severe amount of a caustic poison, something in the nature of an acid. The chemist to whom I submitted the sample from the victim's stomach was unable to identify it because of the quantity of blood and bile mixed therein, but judging from the damage done to the internal organs, it was *very* powerful indeed."

Sir John put a question to him: "Would you say, Mr. Donnelly, that the poison, as administered, was the cause of death?"

"I have altered my thinking somewhat on that account," said he. "As I indicated in my supplementary report to you, it could certainly have been so. It would have caused a long and painful death and would, in any case, have rendered the victim helpless. It *could* be, however, that the ultimate, technical cause of death was the gunshot wound, though Lord Goodhope would have died nevertheless."

"Thank you, Mr. Donnelly. The completeness and accuracy of your report is much appreciated."

Mr. Donnelly took his seat, and Sir John returned his attention to his class of scholars. None now seemed bored nor put-upon; their attention was full on their teacher. Ah, but there was an exception right near at hand: Mr. Clairmont, who sat, hands on stick, uncomfortably warm as we all were, yet with an ironic smile fixed upon his face, his eyes traversing the room in what seemed to me a most contemptuous manner. I wondered at him.

Sir John, resuming: "No end of surprises. First we have a suicide that proves to be a murder by gunshot. Then, not gunshot but poison seemed to be the cause of death. Now, we have a victim who may well have been twice murdered. And to further surprise me, I learned of the arrival of Lord Goodhope's half-brother, Mr. Charles Clairmont, in London from his plantation in Jamaica. I confess that without deeper knowledge my attention went to him as the possible malefactor, for it was known that on at least one occasion there was acrimony between them—and still exists between him and Lady Goodhope. But an interview with Mr. Clairmont, which he kindly granted me, put me aright on his location at the time of his half-brother's death. On this and a number of other matters pertaining to their relationship."

Then, turning in Mr. Clairmont's general direction, for he had somehow sorted out the placement of his listeners, Sir John asked, with a winning smile, "Mr. Clairmont, would you please tell those assembled the content of our conversation, as it pertains to the time of your arrival in London?"

Charles Clairmont remained seated and sighed as those deeply distressed. "I should prefer not to," said he.

"Oh? And why is that?"

"Because all this seems no more than a show, an extemporized play put on for the benefit of I know not who. I would not be here myself had I not been forced to by some vague threat. Richard died, perhaps was murdered. That is unfortunate. Yet as you well know, it does not concern me directly as one upon whom suspicions would fall. Many had reasons for wishing him dead. I was not one.''

All this was said in a nasal tone of complaint. Sir John listened attentively, his hand to his chin, giving full weight to the objections put forward by Mr. Clairmont. He heard him through to the end, gave some pause, and then spoke thus: ''I regret that the shape of this inquiry displeases you, Mr. Clairmont. An inquiry is what it is. It has not the gravity of a court proceeding. That is why I am asking each to speak his piece informally. If you would prefer, a court proceeding will be arranged—a formal inquest—and that tomorrow morning at the Bow Street Court. But surely you would not wish to cause such inconvenience to those who have assembled here, the issuing of summonses, et cetera. You yourself would receive one, of course.''

Again, Mr. Clairmont sighed. ''So it is a question of either speaking now or in court tomorrow?''

''That is the size of it, yes.''

''Then I suppose I must yield.''

Yet he yielded only grudgingly and not fully, for of all statements made thus far, his was certainly the shortest. In little more than a pair of sentences, he explained that at the time of his half-brother's death, he was at sea, probably rounding Cornwall, for he had not arrived in London until a full day later, twenty-four hours past the event. In the telling of this, he remained seated.

''That will do,'' said Sir John with a shrug. ''For confirmation of this,'' he continued, ''I ask Mr. Bailey to summon Captain Cawdor of the *Island Princess*. And while he is about it, let Mr. John Bilbo stand and give forth on his meeting with Mr. Clairmont on the evening of his arrival here in London.''

''At my place of business?''

''Indeed,'' said Sir John, ''just as you told me.''

And he did so, rising to his full height, looking neither right nor left at those around him but rather straight at the magistrate.

When he had finished, Sir John put to him a few questions.

"Since Mr. Clairmont did not cover this in his report, perhaps you could give us your opinion how he responded to your news of his half-brother's death."

"Oh, he was much concerned, sir."

"Did he shed tears?"

"Well, no. Nothing so much as that. Yet I do recall him saying, 'Poor Dickie, he had so much to live for' and 'Why would he do such a thing?' As I said, I gave it, as I'd heard it then, that it was death by suicide."

"And as to your earlier meetings with Mr. Clairmont, one or more took place when he was in the company of Lord Goodhope, were they not?"

"Yes, sir."

"And how were the two of them together?"

"Very friendly, sir. Two gentlemen out for an evening of pleasure."

"Thank you, Mr. Bilbo. And your own relationship with Lord Goodhope?"

"It was very good, sir, considering he owed me a considerable quantity of money."

"And with regard to Mistress Kilbourne?"

"There was nothing between us there, sir. I gave her away."

Before Sir John could respond, Lucy Kilbourne shot to her feet, all indignation and vengeance, and asked—nay, demanded—"May I speak to that?"

"No," said Sir John, "you may not. You will have your chance, Mistress Lucy, sooner than you know."

Slowly and uncertainly, she resumed her place.

During the course of all this, Mr. Bailey had reentered the room in company with a florid-faced, though quite grave individual, fully dressed in maritime uniform. He was not tall, but he walked so straight and stiff that he seemed so. This gentleman preceded Mr. Bailey and walked with his hat and a book of some sort tucked beneath his arm.

Moving with a sharp, loud step, he came as far as the second row of chairs, and there he stopped, giving his full attention to Sir John as he waited to be recognized. It was a most impressive entrance.

"You are Captain Cawdor?" asked Sir John.

"I am, sir—Josiah Cawdor, captain of the trading ship *Island Princess.*"

"Very good of you to come, Captain. I trust you brought your ship's log, as you were instructed to do?"

"I did, sir. Yes, I did."

"Before you open it up, just to reassure others present here, perhaps you could identify for us the man who was your passenger from Jamaica to London. Is he here in this company?"

Captain Cawdor had no need to look left or right. He answered directly: "Yes, sir, he is. The individual in question is Mr. Charles Clairmont. He was the ship's only passenger, and we saw a good bit of each other in the course of the voyage." Then, hesitating but an instant, he added: "He was also known to me before."

"For how long a period would that be?"

"Oh, a matter of years, I should say."

"Would you say, then, that he was your friend?"

"I could not say that, no sir. We met infrequent. It was usually matters of business."

"Yet he had previously made the voyage to London with you on the *Island Princess.*"

Captain Cawdor seemed slightly surprised that Sir John should know this. "True, but there were other passengers aboard on those occasions. Why, I recall that on one trip across we—"

"Forgive me for interrupting you, Captain, but there is no need to go into detail. Let us leave it simply that Mr. Clairmont is something more than an acquaintance, though not a friend."

"Yes, sir."

Sir John turned about him so that his head was inclined

in my direction. I thought for a moment he would then give the signal he had arranged between us. But instead he addressed my young companion from the kitchen thusly: "Mistress, would you prepare some tea?" Then to the company at large: "In the burden of his complaint Mr. Clairmont was correct. This is a tedious business. Perhaps we could all benefit by a dish of tea to stimulate our attention."

Meg went about her chore most efficiently, swinging the filled kettle over the fire, busying herself with the distribution of cups and saucers. Though hot tea seemed not the best drink in these close circumstances, it was hot tea they would have. I surveyed the group. Lady Goodhope appeared to be rather anxious as to Meg's handling of her china. Mr. Humber, though appearing indolent and casual as before at Lloyd's, had turned to give Captain Cawdor his continued and complete attention. The gentleman who was then unknown to me had also taken an interest in the captain. Nearest me, Mr. Clairmont seemed to behave in a somewhat strange manner. He perspired, as indeed I did, and with his kerchief he dabbed most carefully at his face, then afterward examined it, unseen by all but me. I noted, too, that in this room's stronger light his glistening face now fairly shone.

Sir John resumed: "But perhaps, Captain, you might read from, or perhaps interpret, your ship's log for us so that we might know the exact location of the *Island Princess* on the evening of Lord Goodhope's death."

"That would be the day before we docked?"

"It would, yes."

And so Captain Cawdor read a bit and interpreted more, saving us from a confusion of numbers, degrees, and knots, and locating the vessel's position just off the South Dorset coast in the early evening in question.

"Not off Cornwall then?"

"No sir, we'd rounded Land's End some time before and had a good wind behind us, as I recorded in the log. In fact we arrived early and was made to anchor in the roads near half a day. It's always so coming into London. The port's far too crowded.''

"Thank you, Captain. If you will but wait a moment where you stand, I should like Mr. Alfred Humber, presiding officer of Lloyd's, to give us the plan of the *Island Princess*'s voyage.''

That Mr. Humber did, after a bit of throat clearing and looking about. He read from notes on the very letter I had borne to him from Sir John, then carried back to its author: Kingston to Charleston to Bristol to London was the route he described. In truth, he seemed a bit sluggish. He would no doubt welcome that dish of tea, even more a cup of coffee.

"Now, what about those intermediate dockings in Charleston and Bristol?" Sir John asked of the captain.

"We carried a half-cargo of cotton—Charleston to Bristol. Our home cargo of coffee went to London.''

"How long did you remain in Bristol?''

"Just long enough to get it off. Well, there was a bit of a wait the first day. Call it a three-day job that should have been done in two.''

By this time, Meg had the tea nearly ready. She had filled the large, bell-shaped teapot from the kettle and was now waiting as the tea steeped.

"Did Mr. Clairmont leave the *Island Princess* during the time you spent in Bristol?" Sir John asked the captain.

"Indeed he did. He was quite happy to get his feet on land again. Mr. Clairmont would be the first to admit he has no sea legs.''

Meg had evidently decided the tea was ready to pour, though it had steeped bare a minute, for she took pot in one hand, cup and saucer in the other. Whoever received that first cup would find it weak in taste and quite hot to the tongue.

"And did Mr. Clairmont return to the *Island Princess* and then make the remainder of the voyage with you to

London?'' asked Sir John, as if trying merely to ascertain a specific detail.

"That's been *established!*'' cried Mr. Clairmont in a great fit of wrath. And as he did, he banged his stick on the floor, punctuating his anger. Lucy Kilbourne, beside him, jumped in her chair, so frighted was she by his display. She leapt again when he demanded to know: "What is the *meaning* of this?''

Meg moved toward him, intending to serve him first and ignoring Lady Goodhope's contrary signals.

"Well, indeed, sir,'' blustered Captain Cawdor, "of course he did. I would not embark without my passenger! He was feeling poorly, seasick he was. I visited him in his cabin twice on the way to London.''

Mr. Clairmont was twisted back in his chair, giving close attention to the captain, who stood behind the second row of chairs, more or less in the middle. He was thus exposed when Meg, bending over him and holding the cup off to one side, poured hot tea from the teapot direct into his lap! (Because of the drama and the shouting, her action went unobserved by all but me; I realized at once she could not have done it but purposefully.)

He jumped up to his full height, no longer bent, and howled mightily in pain as he clutched his crotch.

"Meg, you little bitch!'' cried he, in a voice much different from the one that had issued from him but a few moments before. "Jesus! Oh, sweet Christ!''

Mistress Kilbourne was up and dabbing to little purpose at the wetted part with her kerchief.

"Leave it, Lucy, that makes it pain all the more!'' He whimpered. He growled.

But then, unexpectedly and unthinkably, Meg began to laugh. She retreated, dancing back as he shot a hand out to slap her, leaving him pawing in the air, swaying to keep his balance.

"You will regret this, girl, I promise!'' He did not move in pursuit.

Every word he uttered declared him to be one other than he appeared to be. Where Charles Clairmont had previously spoken in a nasal, rasping manner, he now bellowed forth in a deep, strong tone that must indeed have been heard throughout the house.

So different did he now speak that Lady Goodhope rose from her chair and peered across the room at him as keenly as her myopic eyes permitted. "Richard," cried she, "is it you?"

"Yes, I believe it is," said Sir John. "I know that voice myself, having heard it once in debate in the House of Lords, and I can only surmise that it is Lord Goodhope returned from the dead. How good of him! I sensed his presence here, yet I would not have presumed to call him out. Now there is no need. He has identified himself to us."

"Why? What do you mean?" cried the other, assuming nasal speech once more and shrinking to his former posture. "What game do you play?"

"It is you who play a game, Lord Goodhope. Give it up! Pull off that false nose and wipe the paint from your face, for your imposture is ended." Sir John waited only briefly, then he called out, "Captain Cawdor, would you now care to alter what you have just told us?"

The captain stood, no longer quite so erect, but from Sir John to the one who had lately changed his voice not once, but twice. "Well . . ." said he, "I . . ."

"Oh, sit down, sit down. Perhaps we shall come back to you again. And if you are still standing, Lord Goodhope, resume your place, too, for having identified the true victim of the crime, we must now seek out its perpetrator."

"But who?" called out Lady Goodhope. "Who is the victim? I do not understand."

"Charles Clairmont," said Sir John. "It was his body that was carted off for burial in Lancashire."

"It can't be! How could that be?"

"That will be revealed. Mr. Bailey, are we ready to proceed?"

"Not quite, sir."

The constable had taken a place directly behind Clairmont/Goodhope, who had remained on his feet to that moment. But Mr. Bailey, placing his hands firmly on his shoulders, forced him down into his chair. There was no resistance, and for the moment no objection.

"Ready, are we?" asked Sir John of no one in particular. Receiving neither confirmation nor objection in the moment's pause, he declared, "Then let us begin."

He called another witness in from the sitting room, where the remainder were waiting. This time he used Mr. Donnelly as his messenger, for Benjamin Bailey did not move from his new post behind the impostor. Though by his name—Isaac Whelan—I did not know him, I recognized him immediately as a seaman when he appeared in the library. He was clean and cleanly dressed, yet his clothes were worn; though not tall, he walked with the rolling bigman's gait that seems common to all of his calling. He looked around the room, spied Captain Cawdor and his hostile glare, then chose a place to stand some distance away from him. He exchanged a nod with Mr. Bailey, and I took him to be one of the constable's drinking companions of the day before.

Identifying himself by name, Isaac Whelan gave his occupation as common seaman.

"Are you in the crew of the *Island Princess?*"

"I have been, sir, though I doubt, when I finish what I have to say here, that I shall again be welcome aboard." He was a well-spoken man for one who made his life on ships. After a moment's hesitation, he added, "In truth, it was my intention to leave the ship here in London, in any case."

"To jump ship, as it might be?"

"That is correct, sir."

"And give up your pay? To break your contract? That is a punishable offense in Marine Court."

"That's as may be, sir."

"Is Captain Cawdor such a hard master?"

"Not to his crew, no, but having made the full voyage once, I determined never to make it again."

"Be more explicit, man."

"Well, sir," said Whelan, "we are intended to proceed with trading goods to the Ivory Coast of Africa, and there to pick up black cargo for sale in Jamaica and the Antilles."

Sir John frowned. "Black cargo?"

"Human beings, sir, of black hue. They are chained in the hold and not allowed above decks until the long voyage is done. Fed poorly, they are. There is sickness among them. Many die, both men and women. It is an inhuman commerce, sir, and I will no longer have part in it."

The magistrate was silent for a moment. "I see. It is, however, legal commerce as long as it be conducted away from these shores. Do you object on religious grounds? Are you of some Low Church persuasion?"

"I object on the grounds that human beings is human beings, and they deserve to be treated better than livestock. No sir, cattle and pigs would be treated better."

"Well," said Sir John, "I have allowed this digression because it is of interest to me. It may also have some slight bearing upon the matter at hand. But let us return to it, Mr. Whelan, as it regards Mr. Charles Clairmont, the passenger on the *Island Princess.*"

"Very good, sir. I was on duty at the gangplank the night we docked at Bristol, when a man arrived and said he had an urgent message for Mr. Clairmont. I sent for the captain, and the two of them had a conversation in secret. Captain Cawdor then escorted him to the passenger's cabin. Some little while later, Mr. Clairmont with this messenger fellow appeared at the gangplank, ready to disembark. I asked him, would he be with us to London, and he told me it was no affair of mine. I asked him this because the big fellow with him was carrying a clothes case belonging to Mr. Clairmont, which was not near all his baggage. The big fellow then gave me a kind of threatening look as he departed."

"And that was the last you saw of Mr. Clairmont during the rest of the voyage?"

"In a manner of speaking, it was. I saw no trace of him from Bristol to London. To my knowledge neither did any of the rest of my shipmates. It was given out that he was seasick and had confined himself to his cabin, which would ordinarily have been accepted, for he had spent much of the previous route flat on his back, moaning his fate behind his door. Yet though we listened at his cabin door, we heard nothing. Yet though food was left for him, it was not eaten, nor was water drunk.

"Upon our arrival in London, there was then a strange end to this matter. I was not on duty, but neither was I off the ship. I saw what I saw from the ship's rail. Less than an hour after we had docked, a man and woman appeared on the wharf. They was all bundled up so their faces could hardly be seen. I saw Captain Cawdor meet them and bring them up the plank. And near an hour after that, I saw the woman leave with a man who appeared to be Mr. Clairmont. I saw them only from a distance, but the man had Mr. Clairmont's strange walk and was dressed as he dressed. But those who saw him up close was sure it was him. Those who heard him speak swore so."

"Do you see that man in this group tonight?"

"I see the man who left the ship. I would near swear he was Charles Clairmont."

"You would *near* swear," said Sir John, echoing him. "What is your reservation?"

"Well, facts is facts, and the fact is I never saw the man who came on board with the woman leave the ship. Nor did any of my mates. We talked about it much between us, because Mr. Clairmont was not no ordinary passenger."

"Please tell us what you mean by that."

"It was generally known on shipboard that he was the vessel's owner."

"Mr. Humber," called out Sir John, "is that correct?"

Alfred Humber pushed himself wearily to his feet, and

once again consulting the letter in his hand, he said, "The owner of the *Island Princess* is listed as The Island Company." Then he looked around him, shrugged, and returned to his seat.

"And Charles Clairmont," said Sir John, "has presented himself to me as the principal of The Island Company." Then, to Mr. Whelan: "Thank you, sir, you have been most helpful. You will be detained as a witness, so there will be no need to give up your wages and go into hiding. But be available. There is but one more matter, then you may go."

And having so said, Sir John rapped a good hard knock on the surface of the desk where he sat.

That was my signal. I leapt to my task. Having previously marked the place well, I lifted out five books from the shelves next the fireplace, exposing the trigger of the machine. I gave it a stout push, stepped back, and the entire case of books began moving slowly forward. There was sudden interest from all around. As one, they seemed to hold their breath and stare at the widening gap in the wall.

At last Dick Dillon was exposed, head and shoulders. He climbed up the ladder on which I knew him to be perched and entered the room, followed closely by Constable Baker, bearing one of two pistols in his hand.

There was a murmur of whispering among many, though not between Clairmont/Goodhope and Lucy Kilbourne. A look of great gravity passed between them, nothing more.

"Mr. Whelan," spoke out Sir John, "was this the man who came with a message for Mr. Clairmont in Bristol?"

"It was, sir. I spoke to him personal. I'd know him anywheres."

"Then you are dismissed with my thanks."

With a curt nod, Isaac Whelan turned sharply and left the library with the same rolling gait he had entered it.

Sir John gestured off to his right. "Here you see an attendant mystery explained—and that is how the slayer managed his exit from the locus of the crime so quickly and cleanly. There is a tunnel leading from the mews at the rear to the entrance just opened here. It was found, after diligent search, by Master Proctor, aided by Ebenezer Tepper of the household staff. Lady Goodhope, did you know of this tunnel?"

"No," she said with firm certainty, "I did not."

"And you, Potter, did you know of it?"

The butler looked left and right, clearly at a loss as to what he might say. At last, he managed uncertainly and in a low tone: "I . . . I heard it discussed, merely."

"Speak up, man!"

"I merely heard it discussed," said Potter, forcing it somewhat.

"By whom and in what regard?"

"By Lord Goodhope, once, in the way of childhood memories."

"Yet you gave us no help in this regard. I believe you are lying, Potter, but I will not delay this inquiry further to squeeze the whole truth from you. It will out soon enough. But now I give the floor to this man before you—Dick Dillon, an accused felon awaiting trial, formerly footman to the Goodhope household. Give us the story, Dick Dillon."

And he did, nor a more grim tale did I ever hear.

Dillon had left the Goodhope residence secretly at night, knowing full well that he was to take part in a sinister plot (though he swore in passing that he did not know when he began that murder was its end). He traveled to Bristol on the orders of Lord Goodhope, bearing a letter from his master to Charles Clairmont to be delivered to him aboard the *Island Princess*. He claimed not to know the contents of the letter, but said that, having read it, Mr. Clairmont was ready and eager to make the trip to London in the coach and horses Lord Goodhope had empowered him to hire for a swift journey to London. They made it in good time, and per Lord Goodhope's instructions, Dillon delivered him to the residence of Lucy Kilbourne.

"He was right glad to see her," said Dillon, "and the two of them flitted and flirted about in the way of ladies and gents. She offered him spirits to drink, and he drank most deep of them. Dick Dillon, he had none, for it was his instructions to wait and stay sober until his lordship appeared. That he did in a few hours' time, and though I was not privy to their conversation, I got the drift of it enough to know there was a great sale of property involved, and that him who was to be the buyer was to be brought direct there to Lucy Kilbourne's in an hour or two. The buyer was threatening to leave London to survey a plantation in the colony of Georgia. Promising to return, Lord Goodhope left, telling me to remain.

"Then Mr. Clairmont and Mistress Kilbourne continued their dalliance, and of a sudden, she said to him, 'Oh, Charles, we have but a little time to do what nature impels us.' And she takes him by the hand and leads him into her bedchamber, taking a bottle along with her. Though the door was shut, there was sounds from behind it, but soon those sounds seemed cries of misery, rather than pleasure, and they was quite loud. Just then Mistress Kilbourne opened the door and appeared to me quite near naked, and she said to me, 'Dick Dillon, come here. You must do something.' And I entered her bedchamber and saw Mr. Clairmont, himself quite naked, was in the most extreme form of agony, and him complaining of it in extreme tones. I looked upon him and said to her, 'What can I do?' 'You must silence him,' said she, 'for I have poisoned him, and he will move the neighbors to call a constable.' And I, thinking only to quieten him, asked her for a piece of cloth. She supplied a piece of her undergarments, and I wadded it up and thrust it into his mouth. Thus gagged, he could attempt to cry out but would not be heard.

"As she dressed and made herself presentable for the street, his attempts to cry out grew weaker, and he no longer thrashed about so on the bed. He was quiet enough as we dressed him in the clothes Lord Goodhope had provided. As I hauled him down to the Bristol coach, which we had kept waiting, he was quite dead upon his feet. I had to lift him bodily inside. Mistress Kilbourne said to the driver, 'You must take our friend to the doctor, for he has been seized deathly ill.' I rode up at the top aside the driver and directed him into the mews behind the big house on St. James. Mistress Kilbourne rode inside. Once in the mews, I hauled out Mr. Clairmont, or what was left of him, and we dismissed the coach back to Bristol, and we got no argument, for the coachman had been well paid.

"Then had I the great difficulty of moving Charles Clairmont through the tunnel, which was known to me through Lord Goodhope. I dropped him down the hole, climbed down the ladder, and carried him pickaback to the ladder leading into the house. That required the greatest effort of all, for Mr. Clairmont would not be pushed and he could not be pulled. He was a terrible burden. I could do naught but proceed pickaback up the ladder, holding tight to his arms with one hand and tight to the rungs with the other. In this way, I reached the top and dropped the body upon the floor where I stand now.''

All eyes went to that spot—all but Sir John's, of course; he, rather, raised his hand to halt Dillon's recitation and put to him a question:

"Where, in all this time, was Mistress Kilbourne? Did she follow you through the tunnel and into the library?''

"She did not, sir. She remained in the mews. I could have used even such help as she could provide.''

"Proceed then.''

"Well, sir, we, meaning Lord Goodhope and myself, we put Mr. Clairmont upon the chair where you now sit. He slumped and sagged a bit, which didn't matter much, but for the shot to be fired proper, it presented a problem.''

"Yes,'' said Sir John, "tell us about the shot.''

"Well, there was two separate purposes to it. The first

was, clear enough, to make it look like suicide, for here was this person sitting at the desk who was dressed in the exact same cut and color of clothing that Lord Goodhope at that moment wore, had the same color hair, and but for his stoop Mr. Clairmont might have been about the same height. But the features of the face was different, there was no arguing that. So that was the second purpose of the shot: to destroy the features of Mr. Clairmont's face, his nose in particular, so that the difference would not be noted.

''To deliver such a shot required careful aim, for there could be no second try. But Mr. Clairmont's head kept flopping down on his chest in a way that made a good shot near impossible. So Lord Goodhope says to me, 'Dick, you must hold him steady so that I can get a proper shot off.' Says I to him, 'How can I do that?' And he replies, 'Stand an arm's length away and hold his head with your hand, and I will put the shot true.' And so Dick Dillon did as he said, and Lord Goodhope took careful aim, steadying his hand on the desk, and delivered the shot. It was all he could have hoped for, because there was little to be seen of what was once the face of Charles Clairmont, what with the blood, and the powder, and the great hole made by the ball right by his nose. But he damned near took my hand along with it. It wasn't but a minute or two, but they were banging on the door trying to break it down. We hastened to leave, but so interested was Lord Goodhope in the job he'd done, he almost walked off with the pistol. I minded him of this, and he dropped it down by the dead man's feet. We was out of there then, and that great slow door, which was part of the bookshelves, closing behind us. He stayed behind on the ladder a bit to listen through the wall, then he climbed down, sure that his plan had worked, and we made our leave through the tunnel.''

He paused then, and there was a kind of universal sigh which went through those assembled. I looked upon Meg, hoping to catch her eye, yet she was staring hard upon that man whom she had some minutes before unmasked as Lord Goodhope. And the look she gave him was one of coldest vengeance. Her hate was something difficult for a boy of my years and experience then to understand. I could not feel as she felt even for the ignorant men and rude boys who caused my father's death. That look of hers did frighten me some.

For his part, the pretender himself kept his eyes cast down to the floor—not in sorrow, and even less in shame. He seemed, rather, to be gathering himself within, perhaps, thought I, he was even then planning a defense for his indefensible act.

"Was that night the last you saw of Lord Goodhope?" asked Sir John of Dick Dillon.

"No, the last till now, if I may correct you, sir. That's him, sitting close by." He pointed his finger at him. "He's done up quite well as Mr. Clairmont, he is. He's good, but he ain't perfect. I spent more than a day with the real man, and he don't fool Dick Dillon."

At that, the man now twice recognized as Lord Goodhope leapt from his chair and covered the twelve feet that separated him from Dillon in but two or three long steps. And as he did, the stick in his hand did, as if by magic, become a short rapier. With it, he stabbed his accuser deep in the chest. I went at him, but Meg reached him first, digging and clawing at his face. I grabbed him at the waist and held on tight, but Mr. Bailey ended it with a blow from his club. Yet it stunned him merely, and keeping his feet, he staggered away from the three of us, no longer armed, but in the direction of that gaping entrance to the tunnel.

"What is happening?" Sir John was shouting it over the tumult. "What is *happening?*"

Only Constable Baker stood between him and it. He held his pistol leveled square at him.

"You would not dare," said Lord Goodhope to the constable.

Then said Mr. Baker to Sir John, "He thinks I would not shoot a lord."

"Shoot away, Mr. Baker. You have my permission."

Mr. Bailey also had his pistol cocked and pointed. Lord Goodhope looked from one to the other and stopped where he stood. His face was scratched and streaked where Meg had dug her nails and pulled off paint and skin. Glancing at her now, I saw her heave and tremble so that I thought her about to go at him again. In the course of her attack, she had pulled from his face the bit of actor's putty that formed the hooked nose that had been Charles Clairmont's. Lord Goodhope was finally and completely revealed to one and all as the man he was.

Mr. Donnelly had hastened to the wounded man, now on the floor, and ministered to him as best he could. Yet it was quite useless, for the small sword which even now protruded from his chest had dealt him a mortal wound.

"I fear," said the surgeon, "that Dillon is dead. He has been run through the heart."

Sir John, who had a moment before been given a brief report on these dire happenings by Mr. Bailey, took Mr. Donnelly's news with an expression of deep anger.

"Had you thought, Lord Goodhope," said he, "that you might slay the witness against you and be free of the charge? All here witnessed your act of murder, just as all of us heard the victim's testimony and will not forget it. For all of that, I also have it sworn and signed by him in a statement at the Bow Street Court. No, indeed, you are not so easily out of your troubles. They are, I assure you, just beginning. Take him away, constables!"

As they moved to follow his order, he held up a hand to stay them. "But wait," said he. "We have not heard from her who may indeed be the slayer of Charles Clairmont. Mistress Kilbourne, I promised you your say. You may have it now."

She jumped to her feet. "They are *all* lies which that man told! How can you have believed him?"

"I believed him in the exact details he gave, and now in the fact that he has been slain for them. His death gives great weight to his testimony. If all he told were lies, then we have not the time to hear you refute them one by one. You shall have your chance to do that tomorrow in court."

To constables Bailey and Baker: "Take her away, too, and while you are about it, bring with you Captain Cawdor for his false witness. Put them all in the strong room, and let them spend the night, each blaming the other. As for Potter, we shall bide our time with him."

Exeunt Goodhope, Kilbourne, and Cawdor in the custody of the two constables.

Sir John took his seat again only after the footman, Henry, had been summoned from below and had, with Potter, borne the corpus of Dick Dillon from the room. In the meantime, those still seated in attendance conversed in tones of amazement amongst themselves at the events which had transpired in the past minutes. At one point, Lady Goodhope seemed quite near fainting, yet Mr. Donnelly saw her through this crisis. Sir John calmly waited to the end of it all.

"There is one last point to be addressed tonight," said he. "We first managed to fix the identity of the victim, and then that of the murderers, and perhaps most important of all, *how* the deed was done, for few murderous plans could match it in complexity and ingenuity. What remains to be answered is *why* it had been so conceived and why so cunningly executed.

"It could not be mere malevolence which inspired it. Lord Goodhope was, by report, on good terms with his half-brother since childhood. And while by no measure a good man, he was not so evil as to simply pick one known to him at random and destroy him as an exercise in sin. Such would be an act akin to madness, and Lord Goodhope is, most assuredly, a rational man. There was a rational purpose behind all this, and to help us understand it, I call upon Mr. Roger Redding of the East India Company.''

He, of course, was the single member of the assembly hitherto unknown to me. A tall man as he stood, fair of complexion and features, he appeared to be not much over twenty, yet was every inch the gentleman-to-be. He had most certainly been sent as an emissary, and the sheaf of papers he held in his hand would no doubt provide the information Sir John had sought in the request I had delivered. Sir Percival had kept his word.

"Yes, thank you, Sir John," said Mr. Redding to begin. "My part in all this may prove somewhat anticlimactic, yet as you suggest, it is essential to our understanding of this entire monstrous affair. The search through our files, which I undertook on behalf of Sir Percival Peeper, has yielded information directly pertinent to the matter at hand, information which I shall now summarize. To wit . . .''

And here, Mr. Redding made direct reference to the papers in his hand: "The Island Company was formed under a charter issued by the East India Company in 1758. Because of that, its papers of organization were held in fair copy by us. What is important is this: While thought to be the sole enterprise of Charles Clairmont, it was in truth a partnership between him and his half-brother, Lord Goodhope. Both put up equal amounts in capital to fund the company. Both were to share equally in its profits. Yet in all wise Mr. Clairmont was to act as its sole proprietor, administering the enterprise day to day, though major decisions regarding the sales of its parts or major expenditures in new areas had to be agreed upon by *both* partners. If I may interject here, it is my supposition that Lord Goodhope wanted it so because he had no wish that it be known that he was engaging in commerce, even at a remove. Such arrangements are more common than you might suppose.

"Now, our general knowledge of The Island Company is that it was a most successful enterprise which, under Mr. Clairmont's administration, yielded good profits regularly.

It continued to grow, acquiring properties in the Antilles and coaster vessels to serve them, until approximately three years ago—still profitable yet no longer growing. Sir Percival noted to me, as we discussed this matter, that it was about at this time that rumors began to be heard regarding Lord Goodhope's financial difficulties. These rumors persisted and grew. He saw not how this pertained, however, unless the first report of suicide be true. Now, however, though I apologize to Lady Goodhope for adding to her now quite overwhelming burden of embarrassment, those rumors seem quite pertinent. The revelation that Mr. Clairmont was the victim and not Lord Goodhope leads one to speculations that I shall leave to Sir John to make.''

And so saying, Mr. Redding seated himself and looked most hopefully at Sir John.

''Very well summarized,'' said the magistrate. ''I shall not at this point do much in the way of speculating. The details will out in time. However, Mr. Redding most helpfully emphasized the chief consideration, and that is that according to the papers of organization, *both* partners had to agree on matters of acquisitions and sales. While profits continued, they became latterly for Lord Goodhope but drops of water to a man who needed gallons to slake his thirst. If he had amassed a considerable debt to Mr. Bilbo over a period of years, I doubt not that he owed money to other, lesser gaming houses in this city. An inquiry I made to the proprietors at Bath yielded the information that a single visit made there of a week at the end of the season in the company of Lucy Kilbourne put him in debt to the gaming establishment there for no less than ten thousand pounds. Eventually we will know the extent of his debt. It is sure to be an astonishment. With all this, he must have asked, then demanded, that Charles Clairmont sell off properties. Mr. Clairmont must have continually refused. The result you saw before you tonight.''

Sir John then slapped the surface of the desk where he

sat and rose to his full height, which seemed to me a little greater than when he took his seat at nine o'clock.

"This meeting is concluded," said he. "Though it has come to the hoped-for conclusion, I regret the pain it has caused Lady Goodhope. I offer to you, my lady, all help I can give within the bounds of my official office."

He felt for his stick, found it, then took his hat and planted it upon his head. "Jeremy," he said quietly, "take me out of here."

Yet that was not so swiftly accomplished. Messrs. Bilbo, Humber, and Redding gathered round him, detaining us, showering congratulations upon Sir John, praising his acuity and boldness. I looked for Meg, but she was nowhere to be seen, having disappeared to her place below the stairs. I longed to discuss these events with her, even as they were now being discussed by those surrounding me. I might never have that opportunity. Indeed I might never see her again.

Lady Goodhope was not immediately in my view. I caught sight of her, however, slipping out the library door in the company of Mr. Donnelly. It was certainly the last I would ever see of her.

At last Sir John begged away from the group, complaining of exhaustion. We left the three, who were still conversing amongst themselves. We were down the long hall and nearly to the door when a timorous female voice was raised, and Mrs. Mary Deemey stepped out of the shadows.

"Sir John, I take it you'll not be needing me tonight?"

"Who is that? Oh, but my God, it's Mrs. Deemey, is it not?"

"It is. I was not called."

"My regrets. Mistress Kilbourne was so incriminated by testimony that we had no need to call you. Nor will you be needed tomorrow when she will be bound over for trial. There will come a time soon, however, when what you told me will be of the utmost importance."

"I see," said she. "Well, I said I would help in any way I could."

"So you have, and so you will. I shall ask Constable Cowley to see you home. You are no doubt as eager to be to your home as I am to mine at this moment."

Chapter 12

In which matters are concluded and a place is found
for me in the printing trade

MARY DEEMEY SAVED LUCY KILBOURNE'S LIFE. SHE WAS
called to testify in the latter's trial, which was held at Old
Bailey before no less than William Murray, Earl of Mansfield, Lord Chief Justice of the King's Bench. Such was
the grave urgency associated with this case, the most infamous of its era.

In her testimony, Mrs. Deemey made clear that, as Sir
John had suspected, Mistress Kilbourne had ordered up her
widow's weeds a bare two weeks before the arrival of Mr.
Clairmont in London and the execution of the murder plan.
And she went on to say that Mistress Kilbourne had ordered
up a goodly number of new gowns to be delivered before
her departure "to a place that had no proper dressmakers."
Among these, said Mrs. Deemey, were "two right fine ones
for her confinement." It was thus out, and to make it all
the more clear, she added: "Mistress Kilbourne is with
child, m'lord."

Of course the sworn statement taken from the late Dick
Dillon, read in open court, was so damning that there was

no verdict that could be returned but guilty, but the jury recommended leniency in sentencing, "taking in consideration her condition." Indeed, the Lord Chief Justice himself was bound by custom, and in lieu of condemning her to hang, as he made clear he would have preferred to do, he sentenced her to transportation and a life of hard labor.

Though there was a bit of back and forth with the Maritime Court, Captain Cawdor was tried in the King's Court in the same proceedings as Lucy Kilbourne. The jury believed his earnest protestations that, while he had cooperated in the plan on the promise of a continued share in The Island Company's profits—he had it in a letter from Lord Goodhope—he had never suspected that the end of the plan was murder. Yet he had cooperated, and the end of the plan proved to be murder, and so he was sentenced to transportation and ten years' hard labor.

Their fates were sealed by their separate destinations. Lucy Kilbourne was sent off to the colony of Georgia and sold into servitude at a very high price to a bachelor master. He made her his pet and eventually, when trouble came between King George and the North American colonies, he made her his wife. She became a very firebrand for separation, a local heroine in the struggle. And for all I know, she lives there still in her declining years, her past behind her, an eminent dame by their standards. I am assured, by the by, that although her husband is deceased, he lived a long life and died of natural causes.

Captain Josiah Cawdor was not so lucky. Although his sentence was lighter, he was sent to serve it back to Jamaica. There he was purchased by one to whom he had once given offense and sent out to work in the fields with the black slaves. Among them, as it happened, were some who had made passage with him on the *Island Princess*. He did not last but a month in their company, as I understand.

As for Potter, he disappeared the night of the revelations and was not heard from again. It came to be known that he was indeed privy to the plan—and its end—and so he must have felt it incumbent upon him to leave England. Perhaps he, too, made for the colonies.

A strange sort of trial it was in which the principal plotter and chief defendant was absent from the court. The Lord Chief Justice remarked upon this a number of times in the course of the case before him. Yet while his companions in mischief stood before the bar of justice, Lord Goodhope waited in Newgate in accommodations far more luxurious than I could ever have imagined were available there. He waited, and he waited, for Lord Goodhope had requested a trial by his peers—nothing, more or less, than the law allowed. Yet in his case, of course, that meant a trial before the House of Lords. That august body of nobles was, understandably, quite reluctant to try one of their own. And so they delayed, and Lord Goodhope waited.

But I anticipate somewhat. Let me, rather, describe a conversation with Sir John some nights after that night of revelations in the Goodhope library. There were many questions I wished to ask, of course, but there were events of a pressing nature which occupied Sir John, and so I bided my time. There were, first of all, the legal proceedings involving the three defendants which occupied most of a day. With them locked away—Lord Goodhope in Newgate, and his partners in crime installed in the Fleet Prison—he seemed to withdraw a bit, performing his duties in a routine manner, giving his attention to Lady Fielding as she required it, and resting himself as best he could. The last days had taken a great toll upon him.

Mr. Donnelly continued to make his morning visits and did all he could to ease Lady Fielding's last days. It was quite evident she could not last longer. And so at some point the house took on the hushed air of a deathwatch. Mrs. Gredge moved exceeding quiet through the place and saved her squawking and screeching for a later day. I did all the work I was bidden to do and more, wishing only to keep busy. And Sir John simply waited.

The nights seemed most especially long. Unable to sleep, I sat up with him in the kitchen on an evening a week past that one described in the last chapter. As we sipped dishes of tea from a pot brewed for us by Mrs. Gredge, we discussed one thing and another, and at last Sir John said to me: "You must have questions regarding the Lord Goodhope matter."

"I do, yes sir."

"Now is a good time to ask them, Jeremy."

I had so many. Where was I to begin? But so then, simply, "When did you first suspect that the corpus in the library was not that of Lord Goodhope?"

"Ah yes, that. Well, my first suspicion was only a suspicion, for it was given to me only as such. That poor child Meg, may the good Lord protect her, began to talk to me in the garden, and she told me a number of interesting things. First and foremost at the time was that she had a feeling that the body she and the other girl had washed was not that of her master. There was a darkness to the face and hands of the kind caused by repeated exposure to the sun and a certain anatomical difference about which she was not specific. I did not press her on the point.

"Then, further, she told me a little of Lord Goodhope's impromptus and his love of theatricals. It seemed that her master fancied himself an actor and possessed a talent for mimicry. One of his favorite turns, it seemed, was to parody his half-brother, Mr. Clairmont—his voice, his odd walk; those who knew the man said he had him down to the life. This meant little to me at the time, for if you will recall, I had only that day heard of the half-brother's existence. But when I talked with him later, you yourself remarked upon his glistening skin.

"He was wearing theatrical makeup, applied, no doubt, by his paramour Lucy Kilbourne. She may have convinced him that this charade would be possible with her aid in the arts of the stage. Yet he immediately grew overconfident.

The putty applied to his nose and the paint which darkened his skin were sufficient to deceive a few seamen after dark on the *Island Princess*. And tried upon Mr. Bilbo in candlelight later that night at the gaming club, they worked again. Yet he grew so bold that he tried his disguise in daylight the next day. And do you recall Mr. Bilbo's comment to us?''

I did remember then: ''He said Mr. Clairmont was wearing paint, like a woman.''

''Exactly. I put this together with your earlier remark on the shine of his skin and drew a tentative conclusion. Had he been given permission on the morning of his visit to Mr. Bilbo to pay his respects to Lady Goodhope, she would surely have recognized him, myopic though she be. It was for this reason that on the night all were assembled in the library, I made it as warm and light in there as was possible. I thought if the nose be wax, I might melt it, or the paint might be sweated off him. David Garrick has since informed me that the stuff has more sticking power than I had supposed.''

''But oh, how he did shine in the lights of that room!'' said I. ''And he seemed much worried by his sweating. I recall he dabbed carefully at his face with his kerchief, then examined it afterward.''

''I was sure enough that Mr. Clairmont was Lord Goodhope in disguise that I arranged that little mishap with young Meg. She was only too happy to play her part in it. It was perhaps a bit crude to play such a prank, but it worked surpassing well.''

''And then Dick Dillon's statement made it all most certain.''

''Yes, Dillon—an unfortunate fellow altogether. I doubt I could have saved him from the gallows after he defended himself so well against that attack upon his life—for that was what it was, of course, that supposed attempt to escape in the middle of the night. Had he taken my offer when it was first made, he would have had a far better chance. I told him as much in my chambers. Yet he was so angered at Lord Goodhope—for he knew who had bribed the guard to make the attack—that he would make his statement against him in spite of all. It is perhaps best that Dillon died as he did. I have made a move to have that warder discharged—Wilson, Larkin, whatever his name. I doubt much will come of it, however. What goes on in Newgate is closed to us outside.''

"And so Lord Goodhope awaits his trial before the House of Lords. Is that a usual thing?''

"Very rare, none such in my memory.''

Quite early the morning after our talk, Lady Fielding died. According to Mrs. Gredge, who was present with Sir John, she passed most quietly: "One moment she was with us. There was a hitch in her breathing, like, then the rattle, and she was gone. She said nothing. She was in that state between waking and sleeping. It was a blessing so, after these many months.''

Mr. Donnelly came shortly after the event on his regular call, viewed the remains, and made official what was manifest. Sir John then went to his study where he remained the better part of the morning. He called me to him once as he sat in that darkened room, and in a bleak voice asked me to fetch Mr. Marsden so that he might make arrangements for the funeral. "I cannot,'' said he. "I am not able. He will have errands for you to run, messages to deliver. I trust the two of you will act in my stead.''

And thus it was a busy day for me, and I welcomed it so. Surprising one and all, Sir John convened his court that day and sat through a brief session. Though I was not present, I afterward heard it discussed that he exceeded himself for leniency. He bound none for trial, sent none to Newgate, and settled disputes so evenly that he found no arguments from the parties thereto. Word of his bereavement had traveled swiftly.

The funeral service for Lady Fielding was held at St.

Paul's, just across the way. I remember little of it, and what was said by the priest. Yet I do remember the great crowd of people that was there. Sitting beside Mrs. Gredge in the pews at the front of the church—careful to go up as she went up, down as she went down, and sit only when she did—I had not noticed the number until I happened to turn halfway through the service. I seemed to me then that all of Covent Garden was there. At the conclusion, the casket was taken up by six of the Bow Street Runners, done into their best, and we filed along at the rear: Sir John behind the casket and I beside him, lest he make a false step, as he had asked; and Mrs. Gredge following us. I recognized a number from court along the way—Moll Caulfield, the street vendor, and Peg Button, whom he had charged to sin no more. And there were others whom I had not, for one reason or another, expected to see: Black Jack Bilbo, the former pirate; Meg from the Goodhope residence (this was truly my last glimpse of her) and at her side, Mr. Donnelly; Mrs. Deemey, the dressmaker; and Katherine Durham, who had so kindly assisted me in buying meat out in the Garden. But there were scores more—well over a hundred, I should say; perhaps nearer to twice that number.

At graveside, however, there were only a few. Besides we three from the house, there were the pallbearers, of course, under Mr. Bailey's command, Mr. Marsden, and the priest. Lady Fielding's people lived so distant in Hull that none of them, of course, were present; perhaps they had only just got word of her death.

As the casket was lowered, and I gazed down into that deep cleft and heard the words ''hope of resurrection'' from the priest, I played the boy again and wept with Mrs. Gredge. I wept perhaps not so much for Lady Fielding, whom I could not have claimed to know well, as for my mother and father and little brother; for the life I had lost and the uncertainty of the one that lay ahead. Sir John had no tears. I believe he lost the power to shed them with his blindness. He stood simply solemn and somber, his face a mask of dignity under that black ribbon mask which covered his eyes.

It was all soon done. And as we walked together to the coach outside the graveyard, a light rain began.

"How fitting," said Sir John, "heaven's tears." Yet he said it, let me be clear, in a tone laden with irony.

Time passed. The end of the month came. Lady Goodhope lost her London residence to Black Jack Bilbo. He was more than generous in extending her time for her departure. One month stretched into the second as packing proceeded. Dray wagons came and went, bound for Lancashire. At last what hurried her along was the impending trial of Lord Goodhope. The House of Lords had finally found a place for it, the last on its list before adjournment. As all London primed for the excitement such a trial would provide, she wanted only to be quit of the city.

Her situation at that time, as presented to her by Mr. Martinez, was not nearly so grave as it might have been. Though her husband's debts, all together, totaled nearly £100,000, inclusive of the debt to Mr. Bilbo, she nevertheless had the holdings of The Island Company to fall back upon. Since Mr. Clairmont had died intestate and without heirs, in the likelihood of her husband's death the entire enterprise would pass on to her son. She, as guardian, would be free to sell it off in its entirety or piecemeal. Her creditors were kept at bay by this probability. Leniency or a pardon would throw all this into confusion once again. And so she awaited the outcome of the trial with peculiar interest, though she waited at a remove of over a hundred miles.

Her final departure took place toward the middle of June. My interest in it rested in the fact that she took Mistress Meg with her to the Lancashire estate, though, as Mr. Donnelly told us, "She was not at all sure how the girl would get on with her French-speaking female staff." Sir John seemed satisfied by the news. "At least," said he, "she will be out of London."

Now, with the trial impending, Lord Goodhope no longer simply languished in Newgate but made ready his defense. I wondered what defense he could prepare, since he was to be tried not only for the murder of Charles Clairmont, but for that of Dick Dillon, as well. While the statement of Dick Dillon, alone, read aloud in court, had been sufficient to convict Lucy Kilbourne, Dillon's murder had taken place before a half dozen or more witnesses, any one of which was available to testify as to what he had seen. Nevertheless, Lord Goodhope met with his barrister daily, according to Sir John, and planned his defense.

There were not many gallery seats available to these proceedings, yet Sir John was assured of one daily. He was no mere spectator but an interested party. The first day of the trial was by far the most interesting, he informed me. It began with all the pomp and circumstance one might expect from such a procedure. There was a reading of a Proclamation of Silence by the Sergeant-at-Arms. "And then," said Sir John, "followed a good deal of hocus-pocus before the throne of the Lord Chancellor, much God save the King from the Sergeant-at-Arms, a reading of the certiorari, and a calling of the roll of all the justices present. All this, mark you, before any attention to my indictment. At last they settled down to the work of it, and the trial began. That part, of course, was all too familiar to me."

The proceedings lasted but three days. On the evening of the second day, Sir John, having spent the morning at the House of Lords and the afternoon conducting his own court, invited me out with him to dinner at the Cheshire Cheese. I went willingly enough with him, though not without some foreboding of ill, for this was quite like the earlier excursion which ended in Sir John's summons to the Goodhope residence. While there was no reason to expect such a conclusion to this evening, I well recalled that the earlier excursion had been undertaken to find a place for me in the printing trade. It seemed likely, though I put no question of it to Sir John in the course of our walk there, that some similar purpose had brought us out together again.

And so it proved to be. An appointment had been made, unbeknownst to me. While I felt grateful to sit at the same table with so eminent a personage as Dictionary Johnson, and quite honored to shake his hand when introduced, I was nonetheless quite apprehensive as the two men talked, for I feared where such talk would lead. Why could I not simply stay with Sir John and Mrs. Gredge? Had I not made myself useful? What did I lack beyond years and stature?

It was a blessing, at least, that James Boswell was absent. Sir John politely inquired after him, mentioning the long conversation he had had with him some weeks before.

"Ah yes," said Dr. Johnson, "he is returned to Edinburgh. He came down to London only to puff his book on Corsica."

"Is it a good book?" asked Sir John.

Dr. Johnson considered that a trifle longer than the question warranted. At last he said: "It is not a bad book, though not half so good as he thinks it to be."

"Should I have it read to me?"

"Do you intend ever to go to Corsica?"

"Never," said Sir John quite frankly.

"Then there is no need."

Though both, I'm sure, would have disagreed, they were in some ways alike. Dr. Johnson was the elder of the two men and the more set in his manner, yet both spoke with certainty and neither would brook argument in his field. (I have heard that Boswell gave it in his *Life* of Johnson that the "Great Cham" intended a career in the law but was prevented from it by poverty.) Sir John was blind, but Samuel Johnson seemed near to be, so scarred and misshapen were his eyes by scrofula. Both men were corpulent, though Dr. Johnson was huge, and each had arrived at his physical state by consuming great quantities of meat. So it was that night at the Cheshire Cheese. Each worked upon a slab of

beef that would have generously fed two, Sir John washing
it down with beer and Dr. Johnson with claret. I, with my
smaller chop, could not keep up with them and made no
effort to try. When they had finished, I was still eating.
They ended their labors, belched mightily in appreciation,
and resumed their conversation.

"I recall, sir," said Dr. Johnson, "that our last meeting
was aborted when you were called away suddenly. That
was the beginning of the Goodhope affair, was it not?"

"It was, yes indeed. I was called away from here by my
chief constable to inquire into the suicide of Lord Goodhope."

"And that suicide proved to be the murder of his half-
brother."

"Just so."

"You have visited the trial. Has he a chance?"

"None that I can see," said Sir John. "His entire defense
seems to be based upon his own weakness. He has laid the
blame for it entirely on Lucy Kilbourne, who as you must
know has already been convicted. It would seem that he
has taken literary inspiration from *Macbeth*. Hers was the
plot, he claims, and he but her tool in its execution. He has
made much of the fact that Mr. Clairmont was first poisoned by her, but the surgeon who performed the autopsy
was finally uncertain as to whether the poison given by
Kilbourne or the shot fired by Goodhope was the certain
cause of death. Both share in it equally."

"To cower, so to speak, behind a woman's skirts would
not seem to be a pose befitting a nobleman," said Dr. Johnson.

"Certainly not, and that is how it shall be viewed. But
do not neglect, as some have, that Lord Goodhope is on
trial for two murders. The second, of his former footman,
was committed before many witnesses. The boy here, Jeremy, saw it plain. He grabbed onto Goodhope to pull him
away, though it was after the fatal thrust was made."

"Did he? A brave lad."

I colored somewhat under Dr. Johnson's scrutiny. In truth, I had not known that Sir John was aware of the part Meg and I had played in the struggle. Mr. Bailey must have told him.

"Mr. Alfred Humber of Lloyd's was called as the most eminent of those who witnessed the act," said Sir John. "He gave a clear and unassailable account of it. Perhaps Lord Goodhope assumes that because the footman was a servant and had taken part in the plot, his murder will be forgiven."

"If all were known," said Dr. Johnson, "some of his peers may have been comparably guilty. Perhaps that was his stratagem in pleading his case before the House of Lords."

"Yet from their temper," said Sir John, "if that is his assumption, it is a dangerous one. They seem far more likely to view him as their scapegoat."

"He taking their sins with him to the scaffold—an interesting notion."

"But, Dr. Johnson," said Sir John, "I have a favor to ask of you . . ."

Then followed what I had feared, for Sir John began to eulogize me not only as a brave lad, but also well educated and well spoken. I quite blushed with embarrassment at his praise. He explained that I had a trade taught me by my father, now deceased. "That trade is printing," said he. "He can set type and is capable in all the attendant matters. Since he has made this beginning, I should like to see him continue. You know most, if not all, the booksellers, publishers, and printers of this city. I thought perhaps a word from you might see him on his way with one of them."

"If he is all that you say—and I am sure that he is, sir—no doubt a place can be found for him. And I should be happy to assist in it. Give me but a few days to ask about, and I shall arrange an appointment with the most suitable." Then, leaning toward me, he looked at me as close as his scrofulous eyes would allow. "Will you make a good apprentice, young man?"

"I shall try, sir," said I, and somehow managed a smile.

That night, when we had returned to the living quarters above Number 4 Bow Street, I said my good night to Sir John and prepared to make my way to my attic room. It came to me, as I took up the candle to light my way, that there might not be many more such journeys for me to the top of the stairs. Yet determined not to dwell on this unhappy matter, I put my mind to other things and my foot to the first step. It was then I was called back by Sir John.

"Stay, Jeremy," said he. "I think we should have a word together."

I returned to the kitchen, and with me came the candle, which brought light to the dark wherein he stood.

"I sense you are disappointed."

"Sir?" said I, not wishing to own up to feelings that at that moment I had most keen.

"Or perhaps it is that in my view you have a right to feel so," he continued. "Think not for a moment that I do not value your qualities, nor appreciate how well they were put to use in this Goodhope matter."

"Then *why*..." I began strongly yet did not conclude, for I had sworn to myself to give him no reason to think I doubted his wisdom in this or any other matter.

He waited, then satisfied that I would say no more, he addressed me thus: "Yes, why. That is a reasonable question." He paused, plainly looking for the precise words, before continuing. "In my vanity, Jeremy, it would be very easy to ask you to stay in this house, to run my errands, to fetch and carry for me. You would like that, I think. But I fear it would be wrong."

"Wrong!" said I, momentarily forgetting my resolve.

He held up his hand. "For two reasons, Jeremy. First of all, there is yourself. Consider your situation. You are young, a bit more than a boy yet not quite a young man, and you are an orphan. Usually one in your situation would have little reason to hope for his future, particularly here in London. But you are remarkably keen witted and well educated for one of your years. More to the point, you have been trained in a useful and important trade. Though you will begin as an apprentice, your natural talents and earlier training will far exceed that of your fellows. You will shine. At this moment in your life, you will need such recognition. Your employer, whoever he may be, will move you along swiftly. You will be a journeyman well before your majority, and a master in no time after that. You will have a fine future. Why, no doubt you will be welcomed as a partner or have started your own enterprise while your old friend is still tied to the bench here at Bow Street, listening to the woeful tales of humanity as they pass before him."

He ended with a hopeful smile and a nod. He seemed earnest in his wish to convince me.

"You refer to yourself here at Bow Street?" I had never before considered the possibility that he might wish to move onward. He was so complete in what he did.

"I do, yes."

"You said there was a second reason, sir?"

He sighed deeply. "Yes, Jeremy," said he, "and that second reason is my own condition. I fear that owing to my good wife's death, and the long dying that preceded it, I am in no state to give you what you want and deserve from me. I can scarce give myself what I require."

He stood silent for a moment, lost in his thoughts, as I was in mine. Finally: "You have been a good lad, Jeremy. I will continue to seek after your welfare, never fear. But it is time for you to make your own way in the world."

Emotion struggled with reason in my breast, but at last reason won. Sir John had spoken true.

"I understand, sir. I accept your judgment in this," said I, then added, ". . . gratefully. None but you was ever so generous on my behalf."

He extended his hand to me. "Then let us be friends."
"For all eternity," said I, grasping his hand firmly.

The verdict came down as guilty on both counts of murder.
Lord Goodhope would be executed as was customary and
binding by law for criminal members of the nobility: His
head would be separated from his body by the executioner's
axe. There would be no appeal. His only hope was the
clemency of the King.

This possibility was the subject of brief discussion when
Mr. Gabriel Donnelly came by one morning only two days
later to bid goodbye to Sir John and Mrs. Gredge, who had
served him as a nurse for Lady Fielding, and to me, as
well. He explained that he was moving his surgery to Lancashire, "where there are many more of my faith. I've been
told that I would prosper there."

"And have ample opportunity to press your suit, I trust,"
said Sir John, with a knowing smile. "Well, good luck to
you in it and in all things, Mr. Donnelly. It was good fortune that brought us together. I'm sure you will find occasion to return to London in the future. I would not want
us to be too long separated."

"Yes," agreed Mr. Donnelly, "good fortune for me, as
well—but decidedly bad for Lord Goodhope. They say he
languishes in Newgate, praying for the King's pardon. He
was once a favorite of the King."

Sir John laughed a bitter laugh. "But no more," said Sir
John. "No, he'll get no pardon. I recall telling you, Mr.
Donnelly, as I told Jeremy here, that Lord Goodhope had
a certain talent for mimicry, that he had oft portrayed Mr.
Clairmont to the amusement of his guests."

"I recall that, yes," said Mr. Donnelly.

"Well, I heard from the same source that on a few occasions he had also mimicked the King, done him as a
raving lunatic. Word must have got back to His Majesty,
and thus was Lord Goodhope banished completely from the
Royal Presence."

There were expressions of astonishment at that from both Mr. Donnelly and myself.

"Can you imagine it?" asked Sir John. "His Royal Highness King George the Third—a madman?"

On August first of that year, when all the gentry and nobles were in such places as Bath, Paris, and Venice, Lord Richard Goodhope, fourth Earl of Tibble, mounted the scaffold and surrendered his head to the executioner. None mourned him, least of all the King.

Yet by the time this came to pass, Sir John Fielding was deep into another demanding inquiry, this one into a crime of an even more shocking and sanguinary nature than the last. It may surprise you, reader, to learn that, notwithstanding the leave-taking described above, I myself took full part in the inquiry. Yet such are the turns of fortune. What may seem to be decided is often left open to chance. That which may seem at hazard is sometimes more certain than we could ever know. Such I have learned, and I am near as old as I write this as Sir John was when he lived it.

In which I but narrowly escaped an end by murder

In my research for materials pertinent to the murders in
Grub Street, which was indeed one of Sir John Fielding's
most infamous inquiries, I came upon the preceding document which I had kept near thirty years as a reminder of
just how this grisly matter began. Though but a broadsheet
written and printed in haste the day following for quick
sale throughout Westminster, it gives a fair and accurate
account of how the great crime was apprehended by those
who were first upon the premises. The writer, whom I later
had opportunity to meet, was not one of those present, yet
he talked at some length with three of them, including
young Constable Cowley, who was somewhat in disgrace
at the time. The information thus garnered, though colored
and flavored to the taste of buyers in the street, was quite
useful to the inquiry of Sir John Fielding, magistrate of the
Bow Street Court. He did, nevertheless, take it ill that such
information was made public so soon after the event.

Yet none of this was known to me when first I became
acquainted with the Grub Street matter. I was deep in a

sleep which I had believed would be my last in the household of Sir John Fielding when I was roused from it, shaken near awake by his housekeeper, Mrs. Gredge.

"Jeremy," said she to me, "you must rise and dress yourself quick, for Sir John wishes you to accompany him on a journey of great urgency."

"Oh, I will," said I, quite groggy with sleep, "indeed I will."

"I'll have none of that," said she. "I must see you out of your bed and in your clothes ere I leave. Boys of your age give promises in sleep they never mean to keep." She held the candle quite near my face and let its light torture my eyes open. "Awake, now!" she commanded, "and out of bed!"

"But I am not dressed," I objected modestly.

"Indeed you are not, and I mean to see you change that."

And so, having no other choice in the matter, I threw back the blankets, and did as I was bade. In truth, I wore my second-best shirt against the night chill, and so was not near as naked as I pretended to be. Mrs. Gredge threw to me my stockings and breeches, and I struggled into them, though still near half asleep. Holding her candle high, she pointed out my coat, hung on the back of my attic room's single chair, and my shoes tucked beneath. Silent and sullen, I pulled them on and stood ready at last.

She nodded, satisfied. "Come along so," said she, "and don't forget your hat."

Down the stairs then, feeling my way in the dark, for she flew before me, taking with her the scant light offered by the candle she carried. Yet once in the kitchen, I found light aplenty, as if it be lit for early evening, and there, deep in talk, were Sir John Fielding and his chief constable, Benjamin Bailey, captain of the Bow Street Runners. They took no notice of me, so urgently did they discuss. Sir John was poised in such a way as to observe my coming, yet in his blindness he saw me not.

I took a place nearby and waited quietly. Of a sudden, I was full awake. My resentment toward Mrs. Gredge for the rude awakening she had given me was vanished, now replaced by a sense of anticipation and curiosity as to the matter at hand. If leave Sir John's household I must for a life in the printing trade, I had rather it be at such a time of excitement as this might prove to be. . . .

Yet now, as I waited, I sensed something of great moment in the air. Though I might not see this inquiry through to its end, I should at least be present at its beginning. Remembering that evening, but a short time past, when we first visited the residence of Lord Goodhope and the mystery of his death began to unfold, I took heart that this night might also be one such. Little did I know the shocking revelation and attendant horror that awaited me.

And so, at a respectful distance, I made to eavesdrop a bit, catching words, names, and phrases from the conversation that continued between Sir John and Mr. Bailey. I distinctly heard the name John Clayton passed from Mr. Bailey, followed a sentence or two later by "under lock and key."

Sir John took that in, nodded, and said, "I shall talk to him, certainly."

Mr. Bailey laughed loudly and declared, "You'll not get much out of that one!"

"That's as may be, but I must try. But be on your way, Mr. Bailey. So much has so far been done wrong, you must do what you can to put it aright."

"As you say, Sir John."

"Who is on duty downstairs?"

"Mr. Baker."

"Good. Off you go then."

And with a touch of his hand to his tricorn, Mr. Bailey disappeared through the open door and thundered down the stairs.

"Mrs. Gredge," Sir John called out, "did you wake Jeremy?"

She was no longer present, gone back to bed perhaps.

"I am here, Sir John," said I.

"Ah, I had no idea. Dressed, are you? Ready to go?"

"I am, yes."

"Then we must first make a visit to the strong room to talk to one in a most unfortunate state and then be off to visit the place of his arrest."

All that sounded quite reasonable, as stated, yet what a world of pain it hid. He must have wished not to frighten me.

"Shall I put out the candles, sir?"

"Yes," said he, "do that, but leave the longest burning for our return."

I did so, and together we descended the stairs—I preceding him, and he with his hand on my shoulder. Thus came we to the ground floor, where only a few steps away lay the strong room. There Mr. Baker stood, staring with great fascination at its contents. From the angle of our approach it was at first impossible to glimpse inside, yet even then, knowing nothing of the prisoner and the cause of his imprisonment, I was quite curious, knowing not what to expect.

I confess that when I laid eyes upon the man who would come to be known to us all as John Clayton, I was somewhat disappointed. Because of the lateness of the hour, Sir John's solemn demeanor, and Mr. Baker's keen interest, I had expected to discover a more impressive figure behind the bars. What I found, rather, was a large man dressed in a nightshirt, looking more forlorn than any I had ever before seen. He sat on a stool, his knees wide apart and his hands clasped so tight between them that they seemed together to make a single fist. His eyes were quite impossible to read, for they were shut tight. There seemed to be nothing remarkable about him at all, except the sense of desperation that his posture conveyed, and the fact that he was dressed for bed. But then I noticed that the hem of his nightshirt had been splashed with blood.

I looked to Sir John, wondering if I should tell him of that detail. Such, he had ever said, were often of the utmost importance. Yet he was off to one side now, listening close as Mr. Baker whispered in his ear.

Whatever was said, it was not much, for Sir John turned from him with a quick nod and called out to the prisoner: "You in there, identify yourself. What is your name?"

The only answer he got was a great, sad moan.

"Are you John Clayton? Is that who you are?"

At that, he who had been addressed shook his head vigorously and spoke for the first time and in a deep, heavy growl. "I am Petrus," said he. And as he did so, he seemed to take heart, opening his eyes and regarding his questioner for the first time, rising from the stool whereon he had sat, striding with apparent confidence to the bars that separated them.

"I think you are not," said Sir John. "No matter who you think you are, or say you are, I believe you are John Clayton."

"And who are you?" asked the prisoner.

"I am John Fielding, the magistrate before whom you must appear tomorrow. My advice to you, sir, is to organize yourself. Prepare to answer questions, because I have many to ask. Do you hear me?"

"I hear you."

"Do you understand?" Sir John put the question to him with great severity. His face was but inches from the prisoner's, separated only by the bars of the strong room. Had he sight, one would say he was staring into the man's eyes, which were both wild and vacant and most frightening to behold.

For a space of time they stood thus. At last, with no answer forthcoming, Sir John turned in my direction. "Let us be gone, Jeremy," said he. "I fear we'll find no hackney carriage at such an hour. No doubt we must make our journey by shank's mare."

As I then started to follow him to the corridor which led

to the Bow Street door, Mr. Baker pulled me aside and, with a finger to his lips commanding silence, shoved a small pistol into my coat pocket. Then, with a wink and a slap on the back, he sent me on my way.

"Jeremy?"

"Coming, Sir John."

Indeed, as he had foreseen, there was no hackney waiting at the entrance, though Mr. Bailey had promised to send one to us, should he encounter it as he went ahead. Nor did we catch a glimpse of one as we went at length through the near-deserted, though not altogether quiet, streets of the city.

The reason he wished me to accompany him was made plain quite immediate. "Lad," said he to me, "you've made many a trip to Grub Street the past week or two. Can you guide me there? I know not the way."

"I'm sure I can, sir."

"In the dark of night?"

I looked down the street, which was dimly lighted by lamps. A wind had risen and taken with it the fog which so often, then as now, lay over London. The night was clear. "This way, Sir John," said I, giving him but a touch on the elbow to start him in the right direction.

Thus we went: I, moving him left or right at a crossing of the streets, giving him a word of advice when the walkway dipped, or disappeared altogether; otherwise he made his way quite by himself with the aid of his stick. We moved swiftly so, though the journey was not without incident. . . .

And Grub Street was where we then arrived, Sir John and I, at a late hour, near three in the morning, on that night which was to alter the course of my life for all time to come.

As we turned up the way, I spied a small crowd by the dim light of the lamps. They had gathered before a building of some size near halfway down the street. That place, I realized, was quite familiar to me. It had been my destination on each of my previous trips to Grub Street. That building housed the store and shop of Ezekiel Crabb, bookseller and publisher, the master to whom I had been apprenticed; it was to be my home and workplace beginning eight o'clock in the morning of that very day. Had Sir John taken it upon himself to deliver me early? That made no sense. And why this group of curious onlookers?

"Is *this* our destination, sir?" I asked. I had to know.

"Yes," said Sir John, "Ezekiel Crabb's home and place of business. A most terrible crime has been committed there."